THE BURIED WORLD

被埋葬的世界

ALSO BY JEFF WHEELER

The Grave Kingdom Series

The Killing Fog

The Buried World

The Immortal Words (forthcoming)

The Harbinger Series

Storm Glass

Mirror Gate

Iron Garland

Prism Cloud

Broken Veil

The Kingfountain Series

The Poisoner's Enemy (prequel)

The Maid's War (prequel)

The Poisoner's Revenge (prequel)

The Queen's Poisoner

The Thief's Daughter

The King's Traitor

The Hollow Crown

The Silent Shield

The Forsaken Throne

The Legends of Muirwood Trilogy

The Wretched of Muirwood

The Blight of Muirwood

The Scourge of Muirwood

The Covenant of Muirwood Trilogy

The Lost Abbey (novella)

The Banished of Muirwood

The Ciphers of Muirwood

The Void of Muirwood

Whispers from Mirrowen Trilogy

Fireblood

Dryad-Born

Poisonwell

Landmoor Series

Landmoor

Silverkin

THE BURIED WORLD

被埋葬的世界

THE GRAVE KINGDOM SERIES

坟王国系列

JEFF WHEELER

This is a work of fiction. Names, characters, organizations, places, events, and incidents are either products of the author's imagination or are used fictitiously. Any resemblance to actual persons, living or dead, or actual events is purely coincidental.

Published by 47North, Seattle

www.apub.com

Amazon, the Amazon logo, and 47North are trademarks of Amazon.com, Inc., or its affiliates.

ISBN-13: 9781542015035
ISBN-10: 1542015030

Cover design by Shasti O'Leary Soudant

Printed in the United States of America

To Sierra

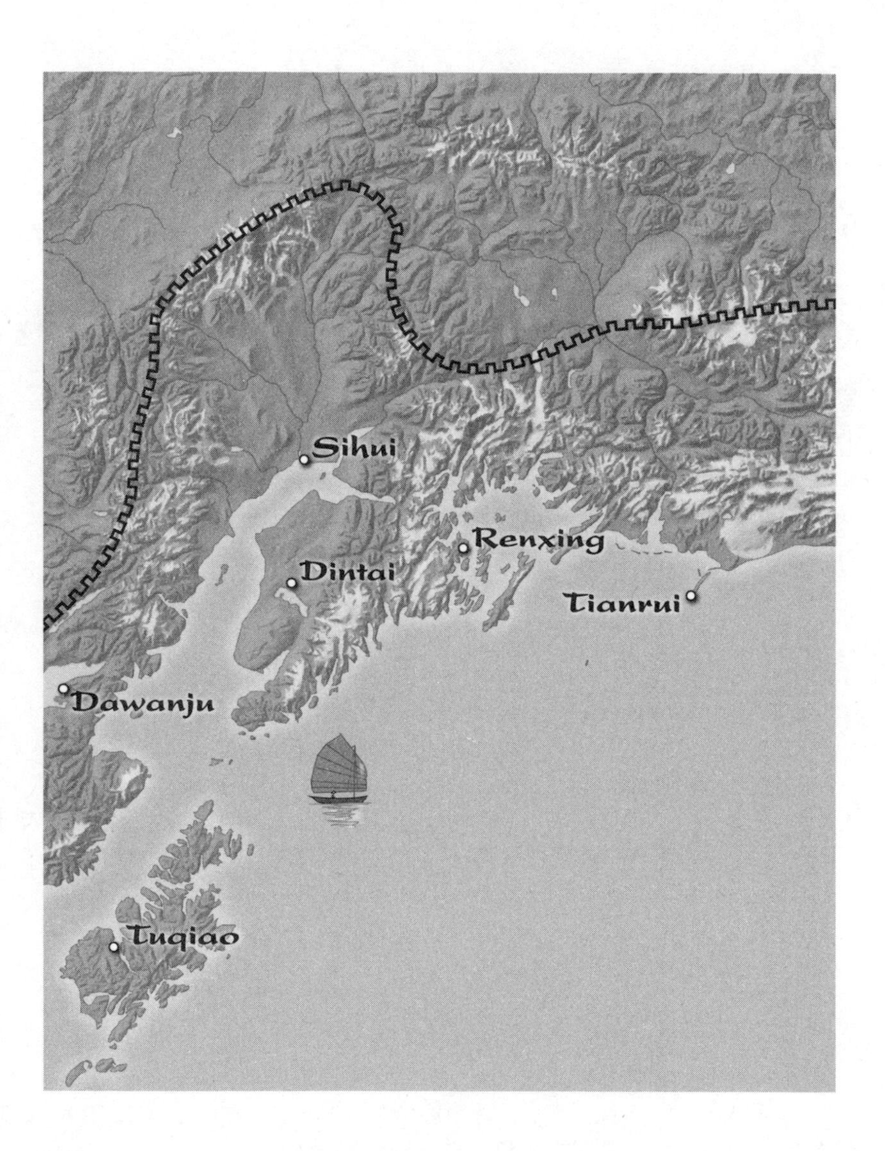
Sihui
Renxing
Dintai
Tianrui
Dawanju
Tuqiao

The Grave Kingdom
THE DEATH WALL
Bingmei's Quonsuun
Fusang
Kunmia's Quonsuun
Yiwu
Wangfujing
Shilipu
Yonfeng
Sajinau
Xidan

GLOSSARY

Baobei—宝贝—term of endearment for a beloved child

Dianxue—点穴—a long-rumored skill of rendering killing/paralyzing blows by touch

Dongxue—洞穴—series of caves where the Qiangdao had hidden

Ensign—舰旗—a band of trained warriors for hire

Jingcha—警察—the police force in Sajinau

Li—里—an approximate unit of measurement, less than a mile, used to estimate

Meiwood—檀香—rosewood, a hardwood used for magic and construction

Namibu Desert—纳米比沙漠—a coastal desert far to the south

Ni-ji-jing—逆戟鲸—killer whale

Qiangdao—强盗—roving bandits

Qiezei—窃贼—a thief, cat burglar, picklock, professional criminal

Quonsuun—寺庙—a temple, fighting school

Taidu—态度—one's attitude, demeanor, bearing

Taoqi—淘气—disobedient child

Tianshi—天使—angelic beings from the Grave Kingdom

Woliu—涡流—the vortex separating the Grave Kingdom from the mortal world

Xidan—西单—port town on trade route to Namibu Desert

Xixuegui—吸血鬼—the undead

被埋葬的世界

Sleep is the brother of Death.

—Dawanjir proverb

PROLOGUE

Dragon of Night

Sometimes when Bingmei fell asleep, she died. It was happening more and more, as if her ghost-self could be removed from her body as easily as a foot from a shoe. Only, she couldn't just return at will. No, her ghost-self would be forced on a journey, and she'd find herself leagues away, a thin invisible thread connecting her souls to her body. Until she returned, her body would lie still, unbreathing.

It was a terrifying feeling, knowing she might not wake up. If she was gone too long, she feared she would have no living body to come back to.

Someone always slept near her to shake her awake when it happened.

But this time, it seemed Mieshi had fallen asleep too.

Her ghost-self wandered down the shadow-draped corridor of the palace at Sajinau. The atmosphere had turned oppressive since the dark lord Echion had claimed the place as his own. The walls seemed to be closing in on her as she dreamwalked down the corridor, leaving no trace, no sound. Incense hung in the air, cloyingly sweet, but the stench of Echion overpowered it.

All her life, Bingmei had been cursed with the ability to smell emotions. Greed had a lemony smell. Dishonesty, a stench like rotting meat. In crowded places, like the trading hub inside a town, the stew of emotions quickly became overpowering, making her crave seclusion. But she'd never smelled anything worse than the terrible, pervasive scent of Echion. It was the smell of a million murders, of savagery masked in justice.

It was her fault the ancient ruler had risen from his tomb. She'd drawn the glyph that had initiated his release, compelled by forces she still didn't fully understand. According to Jidi Majia, the wise steward of King Shulian of Sajinau, she was the phoenix-chosen, the one person capable of destroying Echion for good. She didn't doubt him, but she had not chosen her role, and she didn't want any part of it. Not when the only way she could defeat Echion was by willingly sacrificing her own life.

A feeling tugged her toward a set of large doors leading to the audience hall. Prince Juexin's face surfaced in her memory. Sadness welled inside her. The prince was dead—she'd watched Echion kill him—and so was his once-mighty army. They'd been obliterated by the killing fog, a curse summoned by using ancient magic.

Only Echion could control the fog.

She felt herself tugged up and through the crack between the doors, entering the massive audience hall with its giant meiwood pillars. Moonlight poured in through the upper windows and silky curtains, drawing her attention to the room's altered appearance. The tasteful antiques had been replaced with huge casks of coins, coffers stuffed with jade and gold jewelry, and ornate statuary carved with lions, tortoises, and ravens.

A prickle of awareness shot down her back. The shadows looked . . . *alive*. As she watched, they began to twist and quiver, joining together, growing thicker.

She shuddered, trying to wake herself up, to escape the dreamwalk before her body remained dead forever. Her heart filled with dread as she felt an irresistible tug toward the light coming from one of the anterooms. She attempted to resist the impulse, but she kept moving toward the light.

The anteroom door was made of paper fixed to latticework. The smell of Echion was everywhere, and it horrified her. The shadows in the hall were pulling together faster, coalescing into a huge, beastly shape. Her fear multiplied when a pair of slitted yellow eyes opened.

It was Echion's shadow dragon.

As she reached the paper-thin door, she passed through it, and noticed that the paper rippled slightly as she did. She could almost feel it, which made a shivering sensation go through her.

Jidi Majia was working intensely at a desk. She'd not seen him since the fall of Sajinau, but his pale skin and white hair were unmistakable. Like her, he had the winter sickness, except her hair had turned a rusty amber—a transformation that marked her as the phoenix-chosen. Beneath the scent of Echion, she sensed the bite of sadness.

The steward wasn't seated at the desk—he stood over it. A large white paper lay before him, next to a collection of ancient scrolls. He had a paintbrush in his hand, glistening with an oily black substance. On the white sheet, he had drawn three rows of glyphs. As Bingmei watched him painstakingly finish another one, she saw the last stroke smudge. He gritted his teeth in frustration and crumpled the whole sheet, tossing it onto the floor, where she saw a mound of other similar failures. With a sigh, he mopped his sweaty brow on his sleeve and started again, poring over one of the ancient scrolls and retracing its sigils, stroke by stroke.

She felt the darkness gather behind the light of the oil lamps. She could hear the scratch of claws on the marble floor, the dragging of scales. The dragon was coming.

Jidi Majia, Bingmei whispered.

Nothing changed. He continued to pucker his brow and retrace the glyphs. What was this? Although she'd drawn the glyph that had awakened the dark lord, she hadn't been in control of herself. She'd never seen anyone else draw a glyph, or even try. It was best to be cautious when it came to the ancients' magic—no one knew what might summon the killing fog.

Echion had clearly brought back a lost art . . .

Or was Jidi Majia copying the scrolls in the dark of night because he'd stolen them?

Jidi Majia, the dragon is coming!

She reached her ghost hand out and tried to touch his arm, but her hand passed through him. He was oblivious to her presence. In short order, he had retraced several of the glyphs, his arm moving in a delicate fashion, pausing every so often to dip the brush again into the black oil.

Bingmei wanted to go—she saw yellow glowing eyes through the paper door—but she could not. Nor could she force herself to return to her body.

Jidi Majia!

The door slid open, and Echion stood beyond it. She had expected to see the snout and fangs of the dragon, but she sensed they were one and the same. Two essences fused together. He was both beautiful and terrible to look at. Tall and muscular, but graceful. His long pale hair was loose around his shoulders. He wore a black silk dressing gown embroidered with gold thread. His expression was always so kindly, gracious, and patient, all of which belied his true nature, his willingness to slaughter any who defied him. Sajinau had not been the only kingdom to fall in the time since his rebirth. And that was to speak nothing of the people he'd killed during his other reigns of terror.

Jidi Majia looked up, blinking in surprise. "Dread sovereign, I did not hear you approach."

"You do not sleep, Jidi Majia?"

Jidi set the brush down on a porcelain rest, the black tip away from the paper. "It requires great patience and practice to master the craft of writing," the old advisor said. "I must discipline my hands and my mind to do this. I wish I were younger. What a masterful invention, my lord, being able to relay messages across great distances without trusting the memory of faulty servants."

"Your tirelessness is impressive, Jidi Majia," said Echion. He entered the room, and Bingmei thought she heard the flutter of leathery wings. "Every general is being taught to read and write. Every officer as well. You do well by setting an example. Your service will be rewarded."

"Thank you, great one," replied the servant. His tone was humble, but she could smell his sorrow as well as the memory of pain inside him.

"Do you know why I am here?" Echion asked.

Jidi Majia's brow wrinkled. "I . . . I know you do not sleep, great one. You are tireless in your inventions that benefit the people."

"My laws are just; it is true. I impose order in the world. But that is not why I am here this night."

There was a burst of dread from Jidi Majia. Bingmei stood at his side, across the table from the overlord, who had not looked at her yet. But she knew he had the ability to see her ghost-self. Was he toying with her?

She wanted to fly away but could not.

"Have I displeased you, dread sovereign?" Jidi Majia whispered huskily.

"Only because you cannot see her, like I can," Echion answered, his eyes finally shifting to Bingmei's, a lurid smile twisting his mouth. "Come back to Sajinau, Bingmei. I *need* my queen." She could smell his impatience, his anger, his determination thrumming inside of him.

She stared at him, frozen in terror.

"Who?" Jidi Majia said, looking around in confusion. "Bingmei?"

"She's here," Echion said. "Come back to your cage, little bird," he said coaxingly, but she smelled death on his breath. Creeping around the desk, he surreptitiously lifted his hand and traced a glyph in the air.

Bingmei bolted. Echion's face twisted with hatred, and he pounced at her, trying to snatch at her with his now-glowing hand. She ran without looking back, but the dragon's claws closed around her tunic. She tried to scream as she was violently yanked through the audience hall, but no sound came out. When she looked up, a play of shadows revealed an enormous scaled snout and a pair of flaring yellow eyes—inhuman eyes filled with a reptilian menace that made her whole soul shrivel for fear of being devoured.

She heard a snapping noise, the clash of fangs, and then suddenly she was back in her body, being shaken vigorously, a voice begging in the distance.

"Bingmei, please! Please wake up! Please!"

It was Quion's voice.

And it was sick with worry.

"They've found us!"

CHAPTER ONE

Dongxue

The pricks of pain in Bingmei's palms and the soles of her feet were excruciating. Each time she died, it became harder and more painful to come back to her body. A small oil lamp sat nearby, exposing the deep night of the cave. She blinked, trying to banish the image of the dragon's snapping jaws and reorient herself.

They'd abandoned Kunmia's quonsuun in the summer because it was no longer safe to stay there. Kunmia was dead and had bequeathed the leadership of the ensign to Bingmei. At first, they'd gone west in the hopes of reaching one of the kingdoms that hadn't fallen. But Echion controlled the waters and the inland passages now. And he hunted for Bingmei relentlessly. Armed bands of Qiangdao chased them wherever they went. The thieves and murderers had been ushered out of their mountain lairs and made overlords.

The ensign had hunted for a safe place to spend the winter, and their search had ended here—a series of hidden caves they called the Dongxue, which ran beneath the faults of the mountains. The caves were cold, but not nearly as cold as the winter air outside. Water from mountain streams trickled through the twisting passages, some of which looked like the jaws of an ancient fish, with lumps of stone stretching from both the floor and ceiling. They'd taken up residence in an abandoned lair of a Qiangdao war band that had previously inhabited the mountain.

"She's awake," Mieshi said in relief. She was hunkered down near Bingmei, chafing one of Bingmei's fur-covered hands.

"What's happened?" Bingmei asked, still struggling to awareness.

Quion leaned closer, his smile evident. Behind him, his pet snow leopard yawned lazily. "Huqu was guarding the icefalls entrance when he heard noises coming up the trail. He had just enough time to escape deeper into the caves before the Qiangdao arrived. They have torches and gear."

Bingmei shook her head in confusion. "Why would they come here in the middle of winter?"

"Maybe winter is ending early again?" said Mieshi. "What are your orders, *Master*?"

The last word was said respectfully, but Bingmei caught a whiff of contempt. It smelled like the desiccated jujubes they'd found in storage in the caves, which hunger had finally forced them to eat. Not everyone in the ensign had taken to having such a young, inexperienced master.

She tried to stand, but dizziness washed over her. "Are they still at the icefalls?"

"No, they've entered the caves," Mieshi said. "Are we going to defend or run?"

"Where can we go in the middle of winter?" Bingmei said. "Move the young disciples and the servants into the deep tunnels. There are plenty of places to hide. Maybe these Qiangdao are a foraging party. Let's see what they're after."

"But how did they find us?" Quion asked.

Bingmei shook her head. "I don't know, Quion. Take the servants and the younger disciples and leave through the back exit. I don't want you part of the fighting if it comes to that." He was a fisherman by training, and although he could not be relied upon to fight, his survival skills had kept them all alive.

He nodded and then rose. "Here; keep the lamp. I know my way through the caves blindfolded."

He wasn't exaggerating. He'd spent weeks memorizing the trails in and out, learning to trust his hands and not his eyes. Dongxue held natural beauty, not the painted construction of Echion's palaces. The strange pillars of stone that decorated the caves had been formed over thousands of years by the steady dripping of water. It was a strange, ethereal sort of beauty. The woods outside teemed with life, but the only plant life that grew inside the caves was lichen. It speckled the strange stone sculptures only nature could fashion.

"Bring the warriors here," Bingmei said to Mieshi.

Mieshi nodded and then took the lamp and left, plunging Bingmei into darkness after she'd gone only a short distance. Bingmei grabbed the rune staff, which had been Kunmia's, and invoked its power. Wisps of green light danced on the meiwood.

She'd learned it could be used like this, for light, without summoning the killing fog. The power it used was too little, much like her meiwood cricket. With its dim light, she added to her fur clothes and then quickly ate some sour jujubes.

The tingling sensation from the lack of blood in her hands and feet subsided, but the vision of Jidi Majia and Echion still tormented her. She didn't know what to *do* with it. Why had the vision come to her? What did it mean?

She wondered what would have happened if Echion had caught her. Could he have harmed her spirit, or prevented her from returning to her body?

She rolled up her bed furs and there, hidden beneath them, lay the sheathed Phoenix Blade. In the green glow from the staff, it almost looked as if the phoenix carved in the hilt was flapping its wings. As she stared at it, she felt the urge to pick it up. To draw the blade and hunt down her foes.

She heard boots scuffing against the stone, and then Marenqo entered the chamber, eating from the huge leg joint of an elk.

"I was bringing this for you to eat," he said. "I promise. But then I realized you're so small, you probably weren't going to be able to finish it. And since you're also so nice, I knew you'd offer the rest to me. So . . . I thought I'd just start on it now. Thank you for being so generous."

She arched her eyebrow at him, watching him take another bite. Then another. He reached out as if to hand it to her, then took one more.

"Thank you, Marenqo," she said after she wrenched the bone from him, looking at him with exasperation.

She was hungry. They were all hungry.

Huqu came jogging up, winded, followed by Bao Damanhur, whose stump of an arm still made her wince. His sword was belted to his waist.

Bingmei lifted the staff, holding it up to give them light. "Where are the others?" she asked.

"Jiaohua has his men watching the Qiangdao," Huqu said. He was one of the warriors who'd been part of Damanhur's ensign before it had joined with hers.

Jiaohua had once been the head of King Shulian's Jingcha in Sajinau, responsible for fighting crime and keeping peace in the streets. The cunning man was their best source of information from the outside world. Sometimes he disguised himself as a beggar to seek news. Sometimes he intimidated someone for it with the threat of violence. He was always trying to stay one step ahead of everyone else. Of course he'd be right in the middle of the threat.

"Are we going to fight, Bingmei?" Damanhur asked, his voice serious.

Mieshi returned with three sister warriors just as the words were spoken.

"We need information first," Bingmei said. "I don't even know how many there are. Huqu?"

"They're still coming in," he answered. "It's probably up to a hundred by now."

She stared at him in disbelief. "A hundred?"

"It's hard to say," he answered. "Some of them have made camp by the icefalls. There's more light over there, but they've started sending search parties into the caves. Bands of ten or more."

"This isn't random, then," said Damanhur firmly. "We'll have to fight."

She knew he wanted to fight—he'd been aching for a fight ever since the battle that had cost him his arm.

"Are you even able to fight?" Mieshi asked. Bingmei could smell the worry in her, but she could sense Damanhur had misjudged her meaning. That happened a lot between the two of them. Bingmei hated that they argued so much, especially since most of their arguments could easily be resolved if they would only talk to each other.

"Of course I can!" he snapped. "I'm not helpless." And he wasn't. His wound was still healing, but Bingmei had watched him train with his nondominant arm. To her eye, he was just as strong and capable as he'd been before.

"That's not what I meant," Mieshi said.

"Enough bickering," Bingmei said, trying to mimic Kunmia's decisive tone. "I've sent the servants and the young to escape out the back. The icefalls isn't the only path out of Dongxue. We'll hide in the sentry row. The formations there will provide many places for us to conceal ourselves. It's a difficult climb to that spot. They'll be exhausted when they get there, and we'll attack from both sides of the trail. Then we can fall back and choose another place to attack from. If nothing else, we'll give the others time to evacuate. What do you think?"

"Sentry row is a good location," Marenqo said. "But we should leave now before their main group gets there first."

"Agreed. Let's go."

Bingmei lifted the Phoenix Blade strap over her head and felt it thump against her back. Gripping the rune staff, she led the way. Some of them held lamps, others clutched lanterns, but each of the lights could be shuttered if need be. When it was truly dark, Bingmei couldn't see her hand in front of her face, and all sense of distance faded. It really took *feeling* your way to travel in the dark. She set a quick pace. Drops of water splashed down on them intermittently. Before long, they reached one of the sections where they had to climb up boulders to reach the next level of the tunnels. Some of the trails were very steep, and the columns of stone from the floor connected with the ceiling.

In some portions of the cave, the ceiling came down so low that even Bingmei, who'd always been small for her age, needed to duck. It felt as if the mountain might collapse on them at any time.

When she reached the top of the rock, she smelled Jiaohua's strong odor, his rampant smell of trickery and dishonesty. Although his scent made it difficult for her to trust him, there was no denying those very qualities made him useful.

He tried to reach out and help her, but she bounded up the last bit on her own. She hated it when people tried to assist her in things she could do for herself.

"Where are they?" she asked him. His dirty face was outlined by shadows from the faint light exuding from the rune staff.

"Coming this way," he answered.

"How many?"

"Hard to say," he answered. "I hid some men closer to the icefalls to keep counting. Haven't heard from them. Hope they're still alive."

"We're going to hide here at the sentry—" Bingmei said.

"Of course you are," Jiaohua said, interrupting her. "Smart. I'm going to hide myself by the entrance to the sentry row. I'll see if I can identify the leader and capture him. Then we can question him."

"But if there are a hundred, you'll be cut off from the rest of us," she said.

He smirked and pursed his lips. "Worried about me, Bingmei? I didn't know you cared so much."

She knew he was goading her. "Just be careful."

"They're blundering around with torches. Don't look right at the flames, it will hurt your eyes after being in the dark so long."

"I know that, Jiaohua," she said.

"Just being sure." He stiffened. "I hear them. They're coming this way. Get into your hideouts."

"Do you think they brought a lot of food with them?" Marenqo whispered to Jiaohua. "If so, perhaps we should welcome them instead."

Jiaohua scowled at the jest—Marenqo had yet to get a smile out of him, but that didn't keep him from trying. He jerked his head and then slunk into the shadows, weaving behind the natural columns like a lurking spider. Bingmei silently commanded her people to take their positions, indicating with hand gestures who should go where. By the time she finished, she, too, could hear the voices echoing off the walls, the tromping footsteps of men who weren't bothering to conceal their movements.

Bingmei maneuvered past the various thick and thin columns. They were hunchbacked and crooked, nothing like the tall straight meiwood pillars that held up the quonsuuns and other buildings left by the ancients. Yet the stone had a rippled appearance that she found beautiful.

She picked out a spot behind a pillar of damp stone. With a thought, she revoked the power of the staff, and the runes went dark. Others settled in close to her, and those with lamps shuttered them.

"I've always been tempted to lick these rocks," Marenqo whispered from his perch next to her. "I don't know why that feeling keeps coming over me."

She leaned her back against the rippled edge of rock behind her. Light appeared in the distance, coming nearer, and soon she could see the outline of her arms and legs. Then her fur cloak and leggings. The caves were cold, although they didn't get much colder at night—the temperature stayed oddly consistent, given the lack of wind and sunlight. Turning her head, she saw Marenqo crouching, staring around the pillar he'd hidden behind.

"They're making a lot of noise," he whispered.

"So are you," she whispered back.

He ignored the jibe. "I'm just starting to pick out words." He knew many languages, a talent that had already proven useful in their travels. She held her finger to her lips for him to be quiet, and he obeyed, cocking his head to hear better.

The lights from the Qiangdao's torches made shadows writhe and dance on the broken edges of the tunnel walls. She crept back a pace, tucking herself more securely behind her pillar, when the light threatened to touch her knee. Pressing hard against the wall, she watched. And waited for the right moment to attack.

It was then the smell of the Qiangdao struck her, a noxious stench of murder and death. A few moments later, she saw the first of them. Dressed in layers of furs and thick boots, they carried torches and weapons. She heard their voices but didn't recognize the language they spoke. Patiently, she let the first arrivals pass without opposition. She wasn't ready to give the signal to attack. Better for the Qiangdao to believe they were safe.

A visceral feeling of hate filled her stomach as she watched them. A band of Qiangdao had murdered her grandfather, her parents. She'd had an opportunity to kill the leader of that band, Muxidi, but in the end she'd allowed him to live, a decision she still questioned. The Qiangdao were lawless marauders who preyed on the weak, and now they were ruling every village and town, eating food they didn't grow or cultivate. Getting drunk on drinks they hadn't made. The injustice stung her nose, making her despise them even more. But she wrestled down her hate. She would not let it control her. She would master it.

At least a dozen had already come up the rocky slope, and more were coming. If she waited too long, they'd be too many. She saw the worry in Marenqo's eyes, saw him waiting on her order to attack. She saw Mieshi looking at her too, a forceful look that said, *now . . . soon . . . now?*

Bingmei reached into her pocket for the meiwood cricket she'd gotten from her grandfather. She leaned forward, squatting low on her heels. This was another reason she'd chosen this spot for their attack—there was ample room for her to invoke the cricket's magic without crashing into the ceiling.

She nodded and then rubbed her thumb across the cricket, invoking its magic. The meiwood cricket sent a jolt of magic through her legs, and she sprang up from her hiding place, soaring into the midst of the Qiangdao trudging through the tunnels.

CHAPTER TWO

The Withering Touch

As soon as Bingmei landed, she swung the rune staff in a wide arc. The wood jolted against her hands as the staff connected with heads and bodies. Shouts of surprise were followed by cries of pain and alarm. Firelight from the Qiangdao's torches twisted and deformed the shadows against the walls of the cave.

Twirling the staff, she blocked someone who thrust at her with a blade, deflecting it, and then reversed the staff and jabbed him in the throat. She crossed her legs, sweeping the staff down then around, and struck another man in the face. Planting one foot, she flipped around and kicked another bandit in the gut, knocking him back into his fellows. With a quick glance back, she saw Mieshi do a dive roll, come up, and strike the heel of her hand into someone's jaw. Damanhur, one-armed, swung his sword in lethal circles, carving a path through his enemies with an almost bored look on his face.

She whipped the staff around and down, clubbing someone on the head, and then rushed forward to where new Qiangdao were clambering up the boulders to reach Bingmei's section of the cavern. The first one who did was met with a kick to the stomach, and he flailed his arms as he fell backward to his doom, his face grotesque with terror. She didn't care.

Someone grabbed her from behind, and she felt the cold bite of metal at her throat.

"I know who you are," the Qiangdao growled in her ear. "The master wants you alive!"

Dropping the meiwood staff, she gripped the wrist of the hand at her throat, then stomped backward on the man's foot. He grunted with pain, and she pulled the arm away, using it to flip him over her back. But he surprised her when he landed in a low crouch instead of falling onto his back—even more so when he swung his leg around to trip her.

Bingmei jumped to avoid the sweep and did a palm strike into his face, which he caught with his other hand before kicking her in the stomach.

The blow took her breath away and knocked her backward. She stared at him in surprise. This man was not a Qiangdao after all. He'd clearly been trained in one of the mountain temples, a quonsuun, in the ways of fighting. Although he was dressed in furs like the others, she thought she saw a flash of colorful silk beneath them. His eyes were dark and menacing as he lunged forward, the knife held protectively in front of his face. He did a series of jabs before dropping down to sweep her legs again.

More Qiangdao appeared at the top of the bluff, shouting as they joined the fight.

Bingmei retreated, and her adversary's leg struck the stone pillar formed by the natural processes within the cave. She ducked around the other side and attacked him again, only to notice one of the approaching Qiangdao had picked up her meiwood staff. Bingmei scowled and ran at him, launching into a flying kick that struck him in the side of his head, dropping him. She snatched the staff while it was still upright and then swung it around, catching the warrior's wrist with it as he swept the blade down at her.

"You *will* come with me!" he snarled at her.

She launched at him again, levering the staff behind her back before coming at his head. He dodged to one side and kicked her knee, the blow sending a spasm of pain down her leg. He then whipped his knuckles at her forehead, but she managed to yank away just in time.

She had the sinking feeling she was outmatched, even with the staff, but she tried to subdue her worry and focus on the fight. The Phoenix Blade called to her, whispering that she should use it to kill him, but she didn't have enough time to draw the weapon. He jumped high in the air, his boot aiming for her head. Bingmei dived forward and slammed him in the ribs with her staff. The Qiangdao were everywhere now, like an ant hive that had been disturbed.

He grabbed hold of the staff with one hand and yanked her toward him. Maybe she should release the staff. Maybe he was counting on her doing just that. Instead, Bingmei got closer and pushed with all her might, setting him off balance. She kicked the side of his leg, and he dropped down to one knee, his face twisting with pain. Then, pulling hard on the staff, she tried to lever him backward, but he let go, sending her reeling. Once she steadied herself, she reversed her grip and tried to crush his skull, but his reflexes saved him, and she hit the stone instead.

His foot swept out again and caught her, and she fell hard against the cavern floor. As lights exploded behind her eyes, she felt his knee crush her chest. He was on top of her. With one hand he grabbed her hair and pulled, and the wig she wore came off, the pins scraping against her scalp. He clutched the wig in his hand, his other fist still closed around the dagger handle.

Her red hair was exposed, and she was on her back, hardly able to breathe. He was staring at the wig, as if surprised to find it in his hand, when Mieshi's foot collided with his cheek. He fell backward off Bingmei, and she struggled to her feet, gasping for air.

When Mieshi lunged at the man with her staff, he dodged the blows and came at her with the dagger. Bingmei gripped her own staff and joined the fight, attacking him from behind. She landed two blows against his back before he adjusted his stance so he could see them both at once. His face flamed with anger.

Mieshi kept up the pressure with her staff, but he lunged too close, limiting the weapon's usefulness. She dropped it and switched to hand techniques, punches and flat-handed thrusts at his face. Seeing her opening, Bingmei hit him again on the back of his neck, which stunned him for just a moment.

Mieshi grabbed his wrist, torqued his arm, and the blade clattered onto the stone, ringing like bells. She hefted his arm, twisting it again to gain control of him, and Bingmei watched as he reached out with his other hand to touch her neck and cheek.

Mieshi's eyes widened with pain, and she crumpled to the ground, unable to move.

Bingmei looked on in disbelief. "Dianxue," she whispered in dread. The withering touch. It was a legendary fighting maneuver, one thought to be mythical. Not even Kunmia Suun had known its secret. Variations of the touch could paralyze, weaken, or even kill an opponent.

Echion must have brought this back as well.

The attacker turned, his face dark with anger, and Bingmei retreated from him. He lunged at her, trying to touch her, but she fled behind a column. When she came out the other side, she bowled over two Qiangdao whose backs were to her, shoving them forward with her staff. Her enemy followed her. She swung the end of the staff at his head, but he ducked the blow and continued to advance on her, feinting, shifting from stance to stance.

A quivering dart embedded in his neck. He flinched, his mouth twisting in pain, and pulled it out. His eyes clouded as he looked at the dart, and then he collapsed.

Relief made Bingmei's heart soar. She looked around for who had done it, but there was too much mayhem to tell. While she had been facing off with the more-skilled fighter, the Qiangdao had continued to make their way through the pass. Her ensign was badly outnumbered, but she joined the others, and they continued to fight, incapacitating the Qiangdao one by one.

After several long moments of fighting, the tide of the battle shifted, and the Qiangdao began to retreat down the bluff. Some of them were crawling to escape. She let them go.

After it was clear that her side had won, she let herself return to Mieshi. Her eyes were open, her breaths coming in shallow gasps. Bingmei could smell the sour scent of fear as she knelt beside her, feeling for the throb of a heartbeat at her throat. Her heart was racing.

"Can you speak?" Bingmei asked softly.

Mieshi stared at her, immobile but trembling. The one who'd attacked her lay nearby, eyes closed, breathing softly. She wanted to shake him awake and force him to cure Mieshi.

Bao Damanhur trudged up, breathing fast. He'd already sheathed his sword, and as he knelt, he stroked the side of Mieshi's face with the back of his hand.

"What happened?" he asked.

"She was struck by a dianxue attack," Bingmei said, trying to keep her voice calm.

Damanhur's face wrinkled with fury and despair. The sharp smells came off him in waves. "Will she live?"

Bingmei shook her head. "I don't know. He's the one who did it." She pointed to the enemy. "We need to get him to talk."

Huqu approached them. "Master," he said, bowing in respect to Bingmei. "They're fleeing. Should we go after them?"

"No," Bingmei said, shaking her head. "There are probably more down below, and if we go after them, we'll lose the advantage of the high ground. Guard the way up. Don't let anyone get past."

Jiaohua sauntered up next. He nudged the comatose man with his boot. He gave Bingmei a snide look. "You're welcome."

"You could have poisoned him *before* he hurt Mieshi," she said.

"I couldn't risk hitting you," he answered. He sniffed, looking down at her. "Dianxue. I saw it. I'll tie him up."

Jiaohua knelt by the body and turned it over so the man was resting on his stomach. Producing some leather straps, he made quick work of binding his wrists, then turned the body back over and sat it up. He withdrew a little wooden vial, unstoppered it, and held it up to the man's nose. The smell of acid made Bingmei gag.

The man shuddered and then twisted, trying to get away from the smell. His eyes fluttered open.

Jiaohua smiled at him with his rotten teeth and then punched him in the face. The man's head jerked back, and he winced but did not groan.

"The only reason you're still alive is because we have some questions to ask you," Jiaohua said with a wicked grin. "Do you understand us?"

"He understands," Bingmei said. She saw Marenqo walk up, his arms folded. She could smell his worry as he stood by her.

"What do you want from me?" the man said warily.

"Is the girl going to die? You used dianxue on her."

"She won't die if I stop the vibration," he said.

Bingmei stared at him fiercely, waiting to see if the smell of a lie came from him. It did not. He was telling the truth.

"Then stop it," Bingmei said angrily. Damanhur's eyes blazed with worry.

The man stared at her. "The phoenix-chosen."

"I said stop it," Bingmei said again.

"Why?" the man said. "You're going to kill me anyway. Why not take one of you with me?"

Mieshi was still alert, even though she couldn't speak, and Bingmei could smell her surge of panic. It made Bingmei furious.

"Do you want to live?" Bingmei asked.

"Do you think I'd trust you? Any of you?" the man said with contempt. "If I could, I would kill you all with dianxue. Except for you. The phoenix-chosen. My master, Echion, wishes me to bring you back to Fusang." His eyes flared with determination. "So kill me now. It doesn't matter. I, Liekou, will be a ruler in the Grave Kingdom."

"How many Qiangdao are out there?" Jiaohua asked.

"Enough," said the man with a sudden grin. "Enough to kill each of you five times over. We were expecting to be attacked. And we know about the other entrance to the caves. Several of our people are waiting on that side too."

Bingmei looked up at Marenqo. That was where she'd sent the younger ones and servants.

He nodded vigorously. "I'll stop them." He raced away.

The fallen man laughed. "Stop them? Don't you see? You're like rats in a cage. You're all going to *die* in here. We'll squeeze and squeeze until you run out of breath." His eyes glittered in the dim light. "And then you'll stop twitching too."

Bingmei looked at Mieshi, who had fallen perfectly still, her eyes still open. She'd stopped breathing.

CHAPTER THREE

Liekou

Damanhur's face contorted with anguish and fury. He unsheathed his blade, and Bingmei feared he would sever the man's head from his shoulders in one blow. She held up her hand to stave him off, glaring a warning for him to back down.

"You killed her?" Damanhur said breathlessly, his lips trembling.

"She will die very quickly unless I reverse it," said the man, meeting Damanhur's furious gaze without fear. "It's your choice, One Arm. I don't care."

"If we let you go free, will you reverse it?" Bingmei asked.

He turned his gaze to her. "You would trust my word?"

"I will know if you are lying to me," Bingmei answered. "If we set you free, will you save her?"

Jiaohua gave the man a nasty look, one that promised revenge. He inserted another needle into his blowgun. Bingmei's stomach coiled with dread as she watched Mieshi's still chest.

"I swear it," said Liekou. She smelled no trace of deception in him. "I suppose it will remain to be seen whether *you* can be trusted. Unbind me."

"Do it," Bingmei told Jiaohua.

His eyes darted at Liekou. "Her life is not worth his," he grumbled.

"It is to *me*," Damanhur said with venom.

Jiaohua stuffed his blowgun in his belt, within easy reach, then circled behind Liekou. Damanhur's sword was out, held low, the tip still pointed at their adversary. Bingmei was also prepared to fight, but she smelled no deception, no coiled violence.

When his bonds were loosened, Liekou rubbed his wrists, casting his gaze at each of them in turn, anticipating trickery. He crouched down by Mieshi, using one finger to trace a sigil from her cheek down to her neck. His body blocked what he had drawn, but Bingmei saw enough to know it was a glyph. Just like the one she had drawn to revive Echion. Just like the ones she'd seen in her vision of Jidi Majia. So, Echion was teaching glyphs to his followers.

A new danger was upon them.

Mieshi shuddered and gasped, bringing in a wheezing breath. She convulsed, and Liekou rose and backed away from her. Damanhur, his eyes bright with relief, set his blade down and knelt beside her as she looked around in confusion. Bingmei could smell the pain in her breath and knew that she was suffering from the same tingling loss of blood in her extremities Bingmei experienced after one of her living dreams.

Smirking, Liekou kicked out a foot, landing it just so on the hilt of Damanhur's blade. The weapon vaulted into the air, and he caught it by the hilt.

Bingmei swung her staff at him, but he blocked it deftly and retreated toward the edge of the cliff. Jiaohua whipped out the blowgun and raised it to his lips. With a puff of air, he sent a poisoned dart at their enemy's chest, but Liekou swiveled his shoulders and used the blade to knock it away.

"We will meet again, phoenix-chosen," he said to Bingmei as she tried to knock the blade away from him.

Damanhur was on his feet again, rushing forward to reclaim his stolen weapon. He snarled with rage, and Liekou gave him a mocking smile.

"Catch me, One Arm," he taunted. Then he jumped backward off the edge of the boulders down to the lower section of the tunnels. Damanhur looked as if he would chase him down, but Bingmei swung her staff around and blocked him.

"Don't," she warned.

"He has my sword!" said Damanhur angrily.

"I know. He's trying to get us to chase him. Think clearly, not with emotion. He brought back Mieshi. That's enough for now."

"I'll kill him," Damanhur vowed.

"Not yet."

Jiaohua strode up to them. "If what he said is true, we may be trapped between two forces."

Bingmei nodded in agreement. "Get your men and see if the young ones have been captured." She frowned, trying to steel herself against the worry blooming in her stomach. Trapped in a cave with no way out. "We may have to fight our way free."

被埋葬的世界

Thankfully, Marenqo had reached Quion's group before they attempted to leave through the other exit. The two groups had gathered in the high ground in the middle of the Dongxue caves, with guards at each side of the large cavern. It was clear Liekou had been correct in one respect—Qiangdao were coming in from both sides. Given their bold approach, they clearly thought their victory was a given. The queer reverberations of sound made it feel like their enemies were all around them.

She looked at the worried faces around her. Fighters. Servants. Children. They were looking to her for leadership, and she felt young and inexperienced. Quion squatted on his haunches, stroking the fur of his snow leopard. His eyes were fixed on Bingmei's face too, his faith in her disarming.

"What would you advise?" she asked the warriors. She looked at Jiaohua first. He was the most cunning of them all.

He rubbed his mouth, his eyes sly and devious. "They know we're here. What they'll likely do is summon their full strength and then attack from both sides." He brought his palms together with a resounding smack, as if he were squashing a bug. "We need to move to another place."

"What about the lower caves?" Quion suggested.

Jiaohua frowned. "It's a dead end. Nowhere to run."

"I know," Quion said. "But I've explored down there. There are many places to hide. We'll tuck ourselves away while Bingmei uses the meiwood cricket to lead them out of the caves. When they're chasing her, the rest of us will attack at the rear."

"Not a bad plan for a fisherman," said Damanhur with approval.

Mieshi smiled at him, nodding her head. She'd physically recovered from her brush with death, but Bingmei could smell her lingering fear.

Jiaohua frowned. "I thought the purpose was to keep her alive. If she's jumping around the tunnels in the dark, she's likely to kill herself on accident."

"You have no faith in me?" Bingmei asked him.

He grunted. "I don't have faith in anyone. I look at the worst that can happen. You getting captured—or killed—wouldn't be good for any of us."

"They're coming," called Huqu from his guard post. "I see a row of torches coming from the tunnel."

Bingmei scowled. "What about the other side?"

The other guard shook his head. "Not yet. They're only coming in from the frozen falls side."

Jiaohua nodded. "They can't communicate with each other. Maybe they're trying to push us out the other side. Like hunters herding prey."

"We need to hide," Bingmei said. "Let them herd air. I like Quion's plan. They'll chase me; I know they will. But don't attack them from behind. Slip out of the caves through the falls entrance and run. I'll follow you when I can."

"What if they're out there waiting for us?" Jiaohua said.

"The majority of them will follow me," Bingmei said. "Jiaohua, lead the servants and children to safety. Mieshi, you lead the warriors when I'm gone. Take them out in small numbers. Be as quiet as spiders."

Mieshi gave Bingmei a solemn nod, her cheeks flushed with pride.

"It's time for a chase," Bingmei said. She'd replaced the wig her enemy had yanked off, but she took it off again, stowing it in her pack. Her red hair would be a beacon to Echion's men.

Bingmei wasn't the oldest. She wasn't the strongest. She wasn't even the most clever.

But she was the one who had agreed to lead them. And just like Kunmia, she would take most of the risks herself.

被埋葬的世界

Bingmei knew the tunnels well enough to traverse them in the dark. But the light of the Qiangdao's torches helped illuminate her path—a boon offset by the awful stench that had invaded the underground caverns. She clambered down the boulders, keeping to the shadows, ignoring the occasional drops of water that rained down on her from overhead. At one point, she invoked the magic of the meiwood cricket to leap from one ridge of stone to the next, dropping low and listening for any exclamations of surprise.

Her heart beat nervously, but she was also thrilled by what she was doing. She invoked the cricket's magic again, hopping to the floor, and ventured around the rough ground littered with strange, grotesque statuary.

Her boot loosened a few rocks, which clattered against the wall. She winced, pressing herself against a stone pillar. A few men with torches came up to investigate, the glow from their torches all but announcing them, and she waited, gripping her staff. As soon as the first man poked his head around the rock, she swung the weapon around, catching him full in the face. He squinted in pain, his nose bleeding profusely, and she stepped around and thumped him in the chest with the end of the staff. The other two men gaped at her in surprise, one of them pointing at her in silent accusation. She quickly spun the staff and knocked both of them down. One of the men slid uncontrollably down the rocky expanse, plummeting down a ravine. Shouts of alarm sounded.

Let the chase begin.

Bingmei stooped and picked up one of the fallen torches, holding it high so her enemies could see her red hair. Then she plunged the torch into the rocks and sped the other way. The roar that filled the tunnel was deafening. She invoked the meiwood cricket and jumped up onto one of the stone statues. Then leaped to another. And another.

Confusion spread as the warriors tried to catch her in vain. Her pulse raced as she deftly bounded along the entire line of stone statues, using the magic of the cricket. A stone missile whistled past, just barely missing her.

Bingmei jumped down into the midst of a knot of Qiangdao. Her sudden appearance startled them, even more so when she slammed her staff into them. She gripped one end of the weapon and swung it around like a club. It knocked over three people before she backed up and swung it the other way. Four Qiangdao fell this time. Before they could recover, she used the cricket to bound over them, watching as the men collided with one another in their haste to follow her.

The torches, which had been going in a uniform direction before, were now scattered like fluff from a dandelion. She bounded over the main path, landing on a rock on the far side, and felt her boot slip. Just barely keeping her balance, she took a deep breath and invoked the cricket once more, springing to another boulder. Then another. She jumped behind a great stone and leaned back against it, trying to catch her breath again. The next chamber was getting closer. If she could get there, she might be able to vault ahead of the other Qiangdao, forcing them to backtrack and chase her. If she managed it, her ensign would be able to escape.

Feeling she'd paused long enough, she kept low and skirted around the boulders, trying to keep out of the light.

She heard someone charge her from behind. Bingmei thrust the staff behind her, making him howl in pain. She took off running again, only to collide with the body of a Qiangdao who suddenly lunged out from behind a boulder. He swung a chui at her head, but she ducked at the last moment, causing the iron ball to crash against the boulder. The man bellowed in pain and anger. She kicked him twice and invoked the cricket again when he fell. It sent her up and over the men who had begun to mass around her. When she landed, she ran with all the strength and speed she could muster.

Bingmei saw a shelf of rock higher up, almost like a trail, and used the cricket to bound up to it. At least she was out of reach, although the higher position left her exposed.

Then the unthinkable happened. Part of the ledge crumbled, and Bingmei started plummeting toward the ground. There was no time to invoke the cricket, and she winced in the expectation of pain. Falling from this height, she might break a limb or worse.

Except that didn't happen.

Warmth gushed down her spine, and when her feet touched the ground, it didn't hurt. She bounced off her toes, rising again in an effortless arc as the phoenix's feathery magic tingled inside her. This was the same magic that had helped her escape from Sajinau. Nothing she'd done had invoked it—at least, nothing she knew she'd done. But she didn't second-guess the power that sent her hurtling toward the next chamber.

Her heart sang with the magic as she looked down at the Qiangdao, who gazed at her in open astonishment.

In the next chamber, she saw another horde of men with torches, all struggling to get in through the mouth of the cavern. They shouted savagely at one another, pushing and shoving, as they tried to enter the maelstrom. Surprised shouts and bellows ripped through the air as she soared over their heads, her copper hair streaming behind her. Some pointed at her, others tried jumping to grab her. But she swooped past them to the end of the gang, where a few stragglers were relieving themselves against the stone pillars.

With precision, she flew to the entrance, where a frozen waterfall concealed the mouth of the cave. Dawn sunlight sparkled on the rocky wall. Her heart thrilled with joy, knowing Quion's plan was working. If she could maintain her phoenix magic, she'd be able to lead the whole army of Qiangdao away from the caves.

The tunnel began to tighten, and she swept lower down. Coming around the bend, she saw the huge wall of blue-gray ice of the frozen waterfall. A rocky bed of silt and stone hugged the narrow sloping wall of the cave, and melted water lapped against the frozen falls.

There was a man kneeling in the rock and silt, guarded by three men with swords, his hands bound behind his back.

He lifted his head as she swept toward him, and her heart lurched with recognition.

It was Rowen, the disgraced prince of Sajinau.

CHAPTER FOUR

Iron Rules

The last time she had seen Rowen, he had also been kneeling. Echion had forced him to submit to the emperor's justice at the palace of Sajinau. His brother, Juexin, had elected to die in his place. She'd heard no word of him since that day, although she'd often wondered what had become of him. Whether he was still alive. Now here he was, kneeling before the frozen falls, his haunted gaze meeting hers. She could smell his relief at seeing her.

Her presence was immediately obvious to his guards. One Qiangdao unsheathed his sword, but she flew straight for him and landed in the gravel, spraying rocks as she came to a halt. The rune staff whipped around, blocking his blade, and she charged forward, leaping up and kicking him in the face. When she landed, she struck the second guard, who was still fumbling to draw a dagger from his belt. The end of her staff clipped him on the cheekbone, sending him spinning to the ground.

The third man had also drawn his weapon, a saber, and he swung it down at her. She brought the staff up and caught the edge of the blade over her head. The saber bit into the meiwood, but it was a strong wood, one of the strongest that grew, and the damage was minimal. He backed away and then spun around, slicing the saber toward her legs this time. She intercepted the blow with the staff, planting a foot, and then kicked him hard in the neck. The pain jolted him, and she followed through with the staff again, dropping him onto the gravel with a blow to the head. She spun around again, feeling the tingling sensation that assured her the phoenix magic was still available to her. She could fly if she willed it so.

Once her three enemies were defeated, she hastened to Rowen, dropping down next to him and working at the knots.

"Bingmei," he said, shaking his head in disbelief. "Where are the others? You're not alone, are you?"

"Still in the caves," she answered, frowning at the knots that refused to yield. Without thinking, she set down the staff and drew the Phoenix Blade. As soon as it cleared the scabbard, she felt its power shoot down her arms. It was a relief, as if the sword were finally where it belonged. She inserted the sharp edge of the blade between the bonds and severed them effortlessly. The ropes crumpled down onto the gravel.

Rowen's wrists were red and chafed, but he paid them only cursory attention as he rose to his feet and turned to face her. He was much taller than her, and he wore the hide and furs of someone who'd been journeying during the winter months.

His hand reached out and toyed with one of her braids. She caught a whiff of something that reminded her of warm bread fresh from the ovens instead of the pomegranate smell of the past. He gazed at her, taking in her face, and she felt her cheeks grow hot. Men did not usually look at her this way.

"We have to get out," Rowen said. "One of them is very dangerous. He knows dianxue, and he—"

"I know," Bingmei interrupted. "We've already faced him. Where have you been all this time?"

She heard noise echoing off the walls. The Qiangdao were heading their way in a hurry. The plan was working, but they needed to escape.

“This way,” Rowen said, gripping her wrist. “I know of a place we can hide.”

“Where?” she asked.

“Just follow me. Come on. We don’t have much time.”

In the past he’d had a tendency for double-dealing, which gave someone a musty scent, but she couldn’t smell any deception on him now. She sheathed the Phoenix Blade and picked up her staff. Together, they jogged through the gravel until they reached the end of the frozen falls where the tunnel opened into the bright sky beyond. The light stabbed her eyes as she went out with him. Holding her hand up, she squinted, trying to see past the vivid blue of the sky. Snow covered the ground in every direction, but it had been trampled by dozens of feet.

“They won’t find our footsteps if we stay in this area,” he said, waving his arm toward the mess of crumpled snow. Their boots crunched in the debris, and she saw their breaths coming out in puffs. As they hurried along the path, she realized dozens of small snow caves had been dug into both sides of the trail.

“When did you arrive?” she asked him, her nose feeling the bite of the wind.

“Two days ago,” he answered. “We dug in here to wait for the rest of the Qiangdao to arrive. Both ends of the tunnel are being guarded.”

He led her from one snow cave to the next as if searching for something. Finally, he must have found the one he was searching for, because he motioned for her to go inside. She noticed an iron stake, branded with a dragon, driven into the snow near the door.

She looked at him in confusion.

“Trust me,” he said, gesturing again. She saw little cookfires still smoldering around the area, some even with small pots suspended above them on iron stakes.

No scent of deception muddied the air, so she did as he asked and ducked into the cave. The entry was so small she needed to crawl on her belly, which she did after scooting her staff in first. Once she was inside, Rowen crawled in after her.

The interior of the cave wasn't tall enough for Bingmei to stand in, although it was easily a span-and-a-half wide at its largest point. The inner wall was slick and solid and glowed with daylight. It was much warmer inside the snow cave than out in the open. Wide ridges were dug into the walls, large enough to serve as makeshift bed pallets, on which lay several fur blankets. She noticed a half-drunk cup of tea that had a flowery scent cut through with spiciness from several coils of cinnamon bark. There were other evidences of civilization in the close space, including a jade pendant carved into a lion, hanging from an iron nail driven into the snow.

Rowen popped through the entrance as she took off her pack and set it down on one of the ridges. He went to the other side.

"There are at least fifty of these caves," he said in a low voice. "We dug them as shelters when we arrived. The Qiangdao are very resourceful about surviving in the winters. I've learned a lot traveling with them."

"Why were you looking for this particular one?" she asked him.

"It belongs to Liekou," he answered. "The leader of this expedition. He's unlikely to come back without you, but if he does, you can bash him on the head with your staff." He cocked his head, then his expression went dark. "Shhh, I hear them coming."

He was right. Soon enough, the mountainside was full of Qiangdao searching for them. Working together by silent agreement, they stayed on opposite sides of the small crawl door so they wouldn't be seen unless someone came inside. Rough voices shouted, but the sound was muffled by the packed snow.

"Aren't we trapped here?" she whispered to him.

He gazed at her and offered a little shrug. "If we'd tried going down the mountain during the daylight, we wouldn't have made it far. If we go at night, it will be much easier to escape."

"I'm not leaving the others," she said, giving him a pointed look.

"Of course not. I didn't think you would. If I could have warned you and the others to flee, I would have. But I haven't been free myself until this moment." The sound of approaching steps put them both on alert, even more so when it stopped just outside their cave. Rowen paused, swallowing, and Bingmei gripped the staff hard.

Whoever it was started walking again, away from the cave, and they both sighed.

"Have you been in Sajinau up until now?" she asked him.

He shook his head. "No. I've been chasing you. Well, *pretending* to at any rate."

Her brows wrinkled.

"I can still sense the sword," he told her. "I can feel you whenever you train with it, Bingmei. I knew where you were. And Echion knows it. Despite all his powers, he cannot feel you through the blade. You're invisible to him, which is a good thing. But he is hunting you still. Every town, every village, every fishing boat will be looking for you now that the season is ending."

"Is it ending?" Bingmei asked. His words had sent a jolt of fear through her heart.

He nodded. "The snows are melting even earlier this year. He has power over the weather too, I think." He smiled at her. "If he captures you, his power will increase tenfold."

She stared at him in shock.

"Jidi Majia explained it to me before we left," he went on. "His power is only half of what it could be. If his queen is revived, he will have access to his full power. When we went to Fusang, you were supposed to resurrect them *both*." A smile flashed on his mouth and twinkled in his eyes. "You fled. That wasn't supposed to happen. Your power of smell saved your life, Bingmei. If you had resurrected Xisi, he would have killed you there at the Summer Palace."

"Xisi is his queen," Bingmei said thoughtfully. "I imagine she's very much like him."

Rowen nodded. "Jidi Majia said they are both dragons. They are the pair of dragons in all the effigies he's studied in his many journeys. Before we were captured. Before his fate."

"But he's still alive," Bingmei said, remembering her vision.

Rowen's brow crinkled with dread. "Yes, but he's a eunuch now. Any man who serves Echion in his palaces must be . . . castrated. Poor Jidi Majia. Everything is changing so quickly. I hardly know where to begin."

"Shhh," Bingmei warned, hearing other steps approach. Her stomach knotted in worry, but she waited by the entrance, gripping the staff. There wasn't enough space for a full swing, but she knew she could still summon enough force to crack a skull.

A shadow appeared by the entrance, and fear emanated from Rowen, sour and stressed.

A voice sounded a question from outside. It wasn't Liekou's voice, but she didn't recognize the dialect. They waited for several heart-tense moments, and then the person left.

Rowen sighed in relief. She reached out and touched his arm, giving him a reassuring nod.

His voice pitched even lower. "Echion has instituted a series of laws called the Iron Rules. He's teaching a language. It's like ours, only it has words written in black ink on paper. Each word is a symbol, a glyph. Positions of honor go to scholars now, people who are willing to learn to write the words. Echion assigns a leader to each town. It's not how I thought it would be." He winced, shaking his head, struggling for words. "I thought the Qiangdao would spread anarchy. Lawlessness. It's quite the opposite. The Iron Rules govern *everything*. Echion has these strange scrolls written on wooden slats. Each one is painstakingly carved. The laws are written on them, and the scholars have been studying them."

"What do they say?" Bingmei asked with curiosity.

"Which violations should result in death. Consequences for thievery. They are meticulously detailed. He has empowered judges to enforce his Iron Rules. The former kings and rulers have been deposed and executed. He's replaced them with military leaders mostly, in charge of defending. But judges enforce the rules on the populace. Every day, the scribes read the Iron Rules out loud in the village square. Let me give you an example. No one is allowed to carry weapons except the military officers and warriors assigned to them. If you are caught with a sword, the punishment is three years' imprisonment. No excuses. People have one chance to turn in their weapons of war, which are then melted down and turned into farming tools.

"Echion's disarmed the people so they cannot rise up in rebellion. Anyone who speaks ill of the Dragon of Night is sentenced to prison also."

Bingmei's eyes narrowed. "And where are these prisons?"

Rowen darted a look at her. "Those who have been rounded up already have been sent to the Death Wall to make repairs. Four years of service for many crimes, some even longer. If you refuse to work, you'll be put to death. Echion doesn't care."

Bingmei was grateful they had avoided the towns and villages for the most part. It would be dangerous for them to enter a village with their weapons.

"Every person is given a duty to perform," he continued. "That is part of the Iron Rules too. Most are assigned to grow or collect food, be they fishermen, hunters, farmers, or gatherers. Hunters are allowed weapons, but they have to hunt for the entire village, not just their family. The rules are very strict and control every aspect of life."

"Can someone choose to be a hunter?" Bingmei asked him.

He shook his head no. "Their positions are chosen for them by local judges. Each village or town has a certain number of roles to be filled.

Someone might not want to prepare food. It doesn't matter. If they are chosen for it, they must do it. If they refuse . . . the Death Wall."

Bingmei had a difficult time imagining what Wangfujing would be like under such oppressive rules. King Budai had never forced anyone to be a certain thing. Life in his kingdom had always been a little wild, a little lawless.

"What about the Qiangdao? Are they bound by the laws?"

Rowen nodded. "Yes. If they abuse someone without cause, they, too, are punished according to the Iron Rules. They have more freedoms and can carry weapons, but I heard the case of a villager who complained to a judge that a Qiangdao had abused his daughter. The offender was castrated. The Iron Rules are enforced systematically. My father could never have enforced such a strict code on his people, but Echion brooks no objections. The Iron Rules are the Iron Rules."

Bingmei felt a chill go down her back, and it wasn't because of the snow cave. "How far has his dominion spread?"

"As far west as Tianrui and Renxing," Rowen said. "His ships did not stop with the advent of winter. Out of the eleven kingdoms, there are only *four* that he hasn't yet conquered."

CHAPTER FIVE

Discovered

Bingmei and Rowen quieted as the mass of Qiangdao continued to filter back into the camp. It was impossible to hear what was going on outside, but they heard the unmistakable sounds of men marching, followed by shouts of command. They hunkered in the snow cave, waiting, watchful.

The shelter was warm, however, and their combined heat made it preferable to being outside. After a long time, the noise and confusion outside calmed down. The occasional muffled word reached them, but the frequency grew less and less. At last, it was still enough that they could risk talking again.

"Is Damanhur still alive?" Rowen asked, his brow wrinkling. "Did he make it out of Sajinau when you fled?"

"He did. But not whole. He lost his arm in the fight."

The furrow in Rowen's brow deepened. "That's . . . that's a blow. But he didn't quit, did he? That wouldn't be his way. He would train—"

"With his other arm," Bingmei interrupted. "You do know him well. He'll be pleased to see you, Rowen."

"Everything we thought we knew broke to pieces when Echion awoke. There is a lot I need to tell him."

Silence lingered for a moment, and then she felt compelled to say, "I was there when your brother was killed."

The moment had left a seismic impression on her, so what must it have done to Rowen?

He nodded slightly, staring at the small entry hole of the ice cave. Immediately, the interior filled with the sour smell of his guilt.

"I know," he answered, still not looking at her. She'd wondered about that. He had looked toward the place of her concealment, an iron grate at the base of the courtyard of Sajinau.

She waited for him to say more, but he didn't.

"How did you know I was there?" she asked him.

He glanced at her, his expression enigmatic. "I've already told you that I can sense you."

"But I didn't have the Phoenix Blade then," she said. "The man who murdered my parents had it. So how did you know I was there?"

He pursed his lips. "I'm not sure I can explain it." He cocked his head, looking at her with just one eye. "We're connected, you and me. Haven't you felt it as well?"

"I didn't know you were nearby," she told him. "It was a surprise finding you by the frozen waterfall."

"But I knew *you* were coming," he said. He turned his head and looked at her fully. "There is something between us, Bingmei. A bond. Maybe because of what happened to your parents, your friends, you don't let yourself feel. You shut yourself off from your emotions."

She smelled something then, something he was trying hard to keep hidden from her. She caught just a whiff of it, and it was a delicious smell. Her cheeks started to burn.

"Have you sensed it?" he said softly. "Has it happened to you too?"

She blinked in surprise. "What are you talking about?"

He sighed and shook his head, looking away. "I can't properly explain it, Bingmei, but there *is* something between us, some destiny that pulls and tugs at us like threads in a loom. Each day, I begin to see the pattern of the fabric more clearly. A story is being woven, and we are both in it."

She shifted forward, coming closer to him. "And what pattern do you see, Rowen? Tell me."

He shook his head, and this time, she smelled something else. Fear. "I cannot see the future. I'm blind to it. But I know how it feels. You *must* begin to open your heart, Bingmei. Before it's too late."

His words and scent both confounded her. What was preventing him from telling her everything he knew? Something told her the problem wasn't an inability to articulate his feelings.

Perhaps he dreaded telling her.

Or perhaps his hesitation to communicate his true feelings had merely taken a new form. Why couldn't he just say what he meant?

Annoyed by his lack of transparency, she said, "If you are asking me to accept the future of the prophecy, you're wasting your breath. I don't want to die. I won't go to the Death Wall. There has to be another way."

He gently reached up his hand and brushed strands of her strange red hair from her brow. No one had done that since her mother had died, and it felt surprisingly good. "I don't want you to die either," he said huskily. "This destiny chokes at me. At us. You are my protector, my ensign. How many times have you saved my life?"

She smiled at his words, because it had been *many* times already. Something inside her wriggled to get out, but she clamped down on it, refusing to let any fondness for him emerge. "I've lost count," she answered simply. "But I don't share . . . your feelings. I don't want to care about anyone in that way. It would betray who I am, what I've trained to be. I'm a warrior, Rowen. Not a princess."

To her surprise, he grinned. "There's no doubt about that. But you feel nothing for me? Not even enmity?"

"Is that what you want me to feel?"

He shook his head no. Quiet hung between them for another few moments, and Bingmei thought that perhaps he'd told her all he intended to share. When he spoke again, his voice was low, just above a whisper. "Damanhur and I used to be fascinated by the myths of Fusang. We sought out every rendition of the story we could and gathered them as if they were gold. I wanted to bring the Summer Palace back to its former glory. It sounds foolish now, but I thought *I* could bring all the kingdoms together against the Qiangdao. I thought I could rule the realms as Echion once did. I hate and fear Echion, yet I cannot help but be astounded by what he's accomplished. He is molding the world into his image. His cruelty frightens me, yet the people obey him because of it. I could never rule as he does, yet . . . I have to admit it's effective."

"Have you heard word from your father?" she asked. "Does anyone know where he is?"

Rowen shook his head with a despondent sigh. "Echion has sent servants to find him. He brooks no rivals." He gave her a solemn look. "I don't know where he is."

"I hope he's escaped to one of the remaining kingdoms," Bingmei said, reaching out and touching his hand.

He stared down at her fingers for a moment, then put his free hand on top of them. "Thank you," he whispered.

They waited in silence, resting and sharing a little food she had in her pack. It was a welcome, if temporary, respite from the conflict that had consumed the morning. Soon, the white walls of the snow cave began to turn a deeper blue and the daylight faded.

Still they waited, not trusting the lack of sound. Eventually, darkness fell, and they could hear wind moaning through the camp. There was no noise, no clattering of pots or voices. It seemed truly abandoned. They waited longer still, until Bingmei thought it was dark enough outside to conceal them. She pinned her braids higher on her head, noticing that Rowen watched her as she did so, although there was barely any light. His gaze troubled her but not as much as his suppressed feelings.

When she raised her hood to conceal herself, he hastened to say, "I'll go first."

She watched him crawl through the small opening. After his boots disappeared, she quickly followed. Night had fallen, but there was enough moonlight and starlight reflecting off the snow for them to see quite clearly.

As she'd suspected, the camp had been abandoned. Only the ruins of the fires remained, though nothing lingered but ashes. She smelled the air, trying to catch the scent of the Qiangdao.

Instead, she smelled fish.

She saw Quion and his snow leopard shortly afterward, searching the snow caves. The leopard caught their scent first and let out a little growl, making Quion look up hastily and draw one of his hunting knives to defend himself. She tromped through the snow and approached him.

"Bingmei," he said with relief. The snow leopard darted past her and circled Rowen, sniffing him and growling.

Rowen stood stiffly, eyeing the beast with trepidation. "What's this?" he said, but she could smell the fear roiling from him despite his calm voice. "A pet?"

Quion hugged her in relief. She patted his arm.

"Where are the others?" she asked him.

"Waiting at the falls," he said. "I came out to see if I could find any trace of you. After you flew away like a hawk, the Qiangdao went into a frenzy to chase after you. I think they're halfway down the mountain by now." He grinned at her. "You were hiding in one of the snow caves?"

"Yes. I think it's best if we try to get off the mountain after darkness falls. We're more used to moving in the dark than they are."

"Of course," he agreed. "Let's go back to the others."

Bingmei nodded and started to go with him, then stopped when she realized Rowen wasn't following them. He was looking worriedly at the leopard.

"Come on," Quion said, clucking his tongue. The snow leopard came to his side. The young fisherman eyed Rowen warily. "She doesn't trust you," he said, "which means I don't either."

被埋葬的世界

Everyone was surprised to see Rowen, and they were hungry for his news of the outside world. He shared everything he knew about Echion's Iron Rules. Sajinau had become one of the main palaces from which the ancient ruler oversaw his growing kingdom.

Jiaohua's face looked impassive, but Bingmei knew better. His training had given him a talent for hiding his thoughts. He could not hide his smell from her, however, and she sensed his growing concern and anger as the tale went on.

"Once the season ends, Echion will continue his conquest of the kingdoms." Rowen looked from face to face. "He is only using half of his true power right now. If he succeeds in awakening his queen, Xisi, then we have no hope at all."

"We only have one hope," Jiaohua said, giving Bingmei a look. "And she's not willing." If that hadn't mattered, she had no doubt he would have dragged her to the Death Wall months ago.

"We must keep Bingmei out of Echion's hands," Rowen said, ignoring the barbed comment. "Where were you planning to go after the snows melt? Did you intend to hide in these caves if you weren't discovered?"

Bingmei looked at him and then the others. "I was thinking Sihui," she said. "We can continue to follow the mountains until we get there. Unless anyone else has a recommendation?"

"The King of Sihui is Zhumu," Jiaohua said. "He's ambitious and resourceful. I think he would welcome us."

"Have you met him?" she asked.

Jiaohua shook his head. "But I have a few Jingcha in his court as spies. I could seek them out once we get there."

Bingmei nodded and looked to the others to see if anyone else had any input.

Mieshi hesitated, then shook her head.

"Please," Bingmei said, meeting her eyes. "What were you going to say?"

Mieshi frowned. "Kunmia didn't trust him," she said. "There was some run-in between them in the past, but I don't remember any of the details."

"If you remember them, let us know," Damanhur said. "I've never been as far west as Sihui. Won't we have to cross the glacier to get there? The one by Fusang?"

"I think the glacier ends before the Death Wall," said Marenqo, who looked unusually thoughtful. "And I would rather walk there than take a boat. No offense, Quion. I know you're a fisherman and you probably prefer boats, but with everyone looking for Bingmei right now, it would be best to stay in the hinterlands anyway. The Qiangdao aren't there anymore. The wall is guarded, but if we follow it at a distance, we will eventually get to Sihui. I think it's a good plan."

"I like the idea of going to Sihui," Bingmei said. "We can help them fortify their city so they're ready to defend themselves against Echion. We know what to expect. And Sihui may not be as vulnerable to a sea attack as the other kingdoms. So . . . are we agreed?"

They took a vote, and all were in favor of the decision. They finished their preparations for the long journey and left the caves, heading up the mountain in the moonlight, away from the trail the Qiangdao had taken. Climbing the mountain was rough work, especially through the deep drifts of snow, but they pushed on and managed to reach the peak before midnight. When the sun came up in the morning, they would be hidden on the other side, invisible to those hunting for them.

The other cave entrance was to the east, and so they followed the ridge of the mountain down, heading toward the unpopulated valley.

Since Bingmei had rested most of the day, she didn't feel the effects of fatigue until the sky began to brighten. The snow on the slope was surprisingly shallow for the time of year, and she could see there wasn't much at all in the valley below. It had already thawed, which meant Rowen was right. Summer was nearly upon them.

Some of the servants and young students complained of being tired, but they were quickly hushed by the others, who reminded them it was the safest traveling at night, at least until they were a greater distance from their enemies. Bingmei used the staff to guide her steps and set a steady pace down the mountainside, avoiding boulders on the trail.

The sun began to peek above the mountains to the east, and she could finally see the edifice of the Death Wall in the distance. She paused to gaze at it. The light stabbed her eyes, and so she shielded them with her hand and looked at the vast structure built so many years ago. They would have to be careful to avoid any guards Echion might have manning the walls.

Rowen came and stood by her, also looking in that direction. With him standing by her, she thought she felt the tug of the loom threads he had mentioned earlier. She felt a peculiar coaxing feeling in her chest—an entreaty. The Death Wall was *calling* to her. She shuddered and tamped the feeling down. No, she would not go there willingly. Not if it meant dying. There had to be another way.

She turned around to see the progress of the servants and younger students, who were still coming down the snowy slope.

Which was when she saw the smudge of black on the ridge. Someone was following their trail down. Even though he was just a smudge in the distance, she felt certain it was Liekou.

He'd found their trail.

被埋葬的世界

The lone sheep is in danger of the wolf.

—Dawanjir proverb

CHAPTER SIX

Xixuegui Falls

It was a game of hunter and hunted. Bingmei had thought they'd be safe once they reached the valley if they kept away from the shadow of the Death Wall, but the presence of the warrior stalking them could be felt in the air. For two days, nothing happened, but on the third day, one of the guards who had been assigned to watch over the sleeping camp was found dead. The other two guards quickly raised the alarm. His eyes were still open, his expression slack, as if he'd been struck by the killing fog. The lack of visible injury indicated he'd been killed by dianxue.

Three nights later, Liekou killed again.

The gap between the killings made Bingmei suspect that the warrior was trailing them alone. He was relentless, like a hungry wolf. So they moved into the plains, following the edge of the woods, and kept constant watch to see if he followed them. He never showed himself. Jiaohua set traps for him and grew angrier and angrier when they failed to trick or capture their nemesis. However, their enemy appeared to adhere to some kind of moral code. He never struck out at any of the children in the ensign, even if one wandered away from the group or lagged behind.

On the seventh day, their movement was finally noticed by the guards on the Death Wall, and a group of riders was dispatched. This forced Bingmei's ensign back into the wooded hills, where the landscape would make it more difficult for them to be found.

Bingmei's nerves were taut as she felt their enemies tail them. So far, they'd easily escaped their pursuers, but each time she saw one of the armored guards wearing the insignia of the Dragon of Night, she sensed the snapping jaws of the beast getting closer.

"If we don't get away from this place," she told Marenqo and Rowen, "they'll get ahead of us and enclose us." The three of them were hunkered down in a gap beneath a fallen tree, waiting for their most recent pursuer to show himself.

"They're hunting for twigs in a vast forest," Rowen said. "The odds are on our side."

"Still, they're too close. And there's a long way to go."

"I guess we could surrender," Marenqo said in an offhand way, but Bingmei knew he was joking before he smirked. "But maybe that's not such a good idea. I don't want to work at the palace. I would prefer to keep my body intact."

They heard the clomp of hooves farther down the slope, and Bingmei smelled the rider and the steed. She twisted around and looked through the small gap between the rocks and the fallen tree. A rider sat astride his mount, his back to them as he gazed into the wilderness. One hand was on the hilt of his sword in a defensive posture.

"He's alone," Rowen whispered.

"We don't know that," Marenqo warned. "There could be another close by."

"Let's wait it out," Bingmei said.

They looked on as the man maintained his position, watching and listening, turning his head in both directions. Bingmei knew she wasn't the only one who'd lost patience when she heard the shrill little whistle from Jiaohua's blowgun. The guard flinched from the sting and then toppled from his saddle a moment later. His horse grunted and started off, leaving its rider unconscious on the rocks.

Jiaohua slipped down into the crack with them. "Twelve more are coming," he whispered. "We'd better go before they arrive."

Bingmei nodded in agreement, and they clambered up out of the crag and followed the Jingcha leader into the woods. The rider lay still, unable to see them pass.

被埋葬的世界

In the days that had passed since leaving the caves, the air had grown increasingly warmer. Insects droned, and fowl began to fill the skies as they returned from their winter lairs, providing the ensign with another source of meat. But the warmer weather brought trouble too—as they pressed on, they discovered a swollen river blocking their way. It came from the mountains to the west, and it was ice cold, made of melted snow.

They followed it down the mountain a bit to where it plummeted into a series of falls. Mist rose from the gorge, but Mieshi caught sight of some huge crooked-back brown bears at the base of the falls, looking for fish. Bingmei joined her and stared down at them, crestfallen.

Jiaohua came up beside her, his scent acrid with bitterness and anger. He looked her in the eyes. "If we climb down there, we're all dead," he said. "We don't have the right weapons for fighting bears that large, and there are too many."

She nodded in agreement. "And the riders and Liekou are coming up from behind. We can't go back the way we came."

Damanhur approached. "Maybe we go higher up the mountain?"

"The river may be even harder to cross up there if the rocks are jagged," Jiaohua said. "We could be putting ourselves in an even worse position."

"Maybe it's time to turn and fight," Damanhur said grimly. "They've been chasing us for a long time. We can pick the ground to our advantage, force them to come to us."

"Or we can hide at the base of the falls. Maybe the bears will attack them instead," Marenqo offered.

"Too risky," Jiaohua said. "If the bears hear us first, and they *will*, we'll be dead."

Bingmei felt her insides squeeze with dread. They couldn't afford to be indecisive. The longer they waited, the sooner the riders would arrive, trapping them against the river. She gazed at the young ones who stood huddled together with frightened faces. They looked to her for leadership and protection. It was her responsibility to protect them from becoming slaves at the Death Wall.

Quion caught her attention then, mostly because he didn't smell panicked or worried like so many of the others. He stood at the edge of the river, gazing at the other side.

"What is it?" Jiaohua asked her.

She left him and approached Quion from behind.

"Quion?" she asked.

He turned to face her. "I have an idea," he said.

She grinned. She'd been hoping he would say that. "Tell me."

Some of the others congregated around him, and she smelled his discomfort. He didn't like being the center of so much attention.

"Well, what is it? Can you get us across the river, boy?" Jiaohua asked.

"I think so," he answered. "There are many trees on both sides. Sturdy ones by the looks of them. I have a lot of rope. We could tie off two lines, one to walk on and the other to hold on to. Two sets of ropes," he continued, using his hands and feet to mimic the actions. "We could have the young ones hold on to our backs. We could cross many at a time, I think."

"But how do we tie the ropes on the other side?" Marenqo asked.

"Bingmei can," said Quion with a shrug.

Oh. The meiwood cricket. She stared at the width of the river. It was not a short distance. She wondered if the magic would take her that far. One look at the young ones was enough to convince her.

"It's worth a try," Bingmei said.

"Can she leap that far?" Jiaohua asked.

Quion looked at him. "We'd tie a rope around her before she jumps. I'm not stupid."

Jiaohua gave him a snort, hands on hips, then looked back the way they'd come. "Let's get this crazy idea started. I'll have scouts watch for our pursuers."

Quion unslung his pack and began rummaging through it. He produced two long coils of rope. Freeing one of the ends, he motioned for Bingmei to come closer.

"I can tie the knots on this side to make the ropes very taut. But you'll need to tie them on the other side."

"I can't tie knots like you can," Bingmei said.

"This is a simple one. I'm going to teach you." He took her to one of the nearby cedar trees and brought the rope around it. "Like this. Around, under, back, and through." It formed a perfect knot. Then he undid it and demonstrated the technique again. "Around, under, back, and through." He tugged it tight, showing her how to test its strength.

She made a mess of it on the first try. He encouraged her to try again and showed her his method one more time. She blinked, trying to quell her fear that people would die if she did it wrong. Following his example, she tried again. And again. She got it right on the third try.

"Well done! Try it one more time."

She unloosed the knot and did as he asked. The knot held. He beamed at her. "We'll tie one of the ropes around your waist before you jump, and I'll secure it to one of the trees on this side. Once you've made it across, I'll throw a second one over to you."

She nodded quickly, warmed by his confidence in her. By that scent of plum sauce. He secured the other end of the rope to a thick tree while she took off her pack with the Phoenix Blade. She left the staff with Mieshi.

Quion prepared another coil and tied it off higher up on the tree. "We'll still hold on while you jump, but it's best to be safe."

Bingmei nodded. She looked at the others, feeling her nerves tighten, then shifted her focus to Jiaohua. "Any sign of pursuers?"

He shook his head no. Quion left the line loose enough that she could jump, and he and Marenqo both took hold of some of the slack. Bingmei blinked quickly, trying to banish her nerves, not liking that everyone was staring at her. That everyone was depending on her.

She took a few steps back from the edge of the river, then fished her hand into her pocket for the reassuring shape of the meiwood cricket.

Except she hoped she wouldn't need it. Her phoenix power, the one that had saved them at the caves, allowed her to fly. Sometimes. Crossing the river that way would be so much easier. She pictured herself floating on the breeze, soaring across the noisy river. Nothing happened. There was no prickling sensation down her spine. No swell of magic in her breast. She squeezed her eyes shut, trying to force the magic to come to her aid.

But it was a temperamental magic, and it did not come.

"You can do it," Quion said coaxingly.

She sighed in frustration. The magic came when *it* wanted to. Not when she needed it.

Opening her eyes, she stared at the other side of the river. She gritted her teeth and took a deep breath. Sizing up the distance again, she took another step backward. Then she rubbed the cricket in her pocket and ran toward the river, feeling the magic swell in her legs. Her confidence surged as she pumped her arms and pushed herself as hard as she could. She could do this. She could reach the other side. She *had* to.

She leaped off the edge and soared through the air, feeling the thrill of the magic as she vaulted over the river. The churning water was beneath her, seething and frothing as it buffeted the rocks. One of the crooked-back bears down below lifted its head to watch her. She was flying, soaring, giddy with the feeling. But a sickening sensation quickly replaced the excitement as she realized she wasn't going to make it to the other side.

Someone cried her name as she crashed into the frigid waters.

CHAPTER SEVEN

Grave Kingdom

Bingmei had just enough time to suck in a final breath before she was enveloped by the glacial water. The cold penetrated to her bones, and then she felt the impact of a river boulder against her knees. Reaching out, she grabbed at the rock, but the current yanked her away before she could get a hold. Her back smashed against another rock, whipping her around and tangling her in the rope. The noise of the falls was muted in her waterlogged ears, but she knew it was only a matter of moments before she'd fall to her death.

Pain knifed in her middle. The river was pummeling against her back, but the rope stopped it from carrying her away. Through the cold fogging her mind, she realized the pain was caused by the rope digging into her stomach. She lifted one leg and felt another boulder in front of her. Pushing against it with all her might, she managed to bring her head out of the water.

The river wasn't as deep as she'd first imagined, but if she went over the falls, there'd be no coming back. Water smashed against her. Turning her head, she saw Quion, Marenqo, and Jiaohua all pulling hard on the rope to keep her from going off the edge. Their faces contorted with the effort, but they were strong enough to hold her. As she watched,

Quion led the others in wrapping more of the rope around a tree to use up the slack.

Bingmei trembled with the cold. She was near the far bank, although the waters had swept her more toward the middle than she would have liked. Carefully, she turned herself around. The river continued crashing into her, but she could see boulders beneath the water. She reached for the first one and, with effort, pulled herself onto it. She gasped for breath, feeling every part of her body quivering. But she couldn't stop. She couldn't relent. She saw another boulder, close enough to step onto, and so she did. The bank was closer now.

She heard someone shouting to her, and the only word she could make out above the noise of the falls was "cricket." The terror of the moment had driven it completely from her mind. Balancing on the rock, she reached into her pocket, stroked the artifact, and then her legs shot her onto the far bank, where she landed amidst the rocks and saplings.

Her whole body was racked with shivers, but she couldn't change into warm clothes. Her pack was on the other side. She had to move quickly before she lost all sense of reason. Hastening to the tree Quion had pointed out to her, she worked at the knot around her waist. Her fingers were numb. Her hair dripped water into her eyes.

Why hadn't the magic saved her? She felt abandoned and a little resentful, but she couldn't think about that now. She needed to *hurry*.

After releasing the knot, she wrapped the rope around the tree near its roots. For a moment, she couldn't remember the knot Quion had taught her, but the words seemed to spring into her mind in his voice.

Around, under, back, and through.

She quickly tied the knot, and it looked like the one he had taught her. Looking up, she saw Quion adjusting his knot on the other end, ensuring the rope was taut between the two trees. He then took the other coil and flung it across the river to her. She quickly wrapped the rope around a thick, sturdy upper branch.

She failed at her first attempt to tie the knot. But her second effort held. Bingmei shivered from the cold. She knew she ought to keep moving, but fatigue overwhelmed her. Instead, she squatted down as she watched her friends scramble on the other side of the river, preparing to cross the makeshift rope bridge. Sleep was all she craved, but she kept her eyes open, watching as Mieshi grabbed Bingmei's pack and started across.

The lines sagged a bit, but Mieshi was nothing if not determined. She gripped the top rope and scuttled across.

Bingmei's lids grew heavier and heavier. The trilling of a bird sounded behind her, so peaceful and mild that she found herself smiling, her eyes drifting shut at last. Sleep, blissful sleep. The noise of the falls faded.

She dreamed.

Darkness engulfed her. Murmuring voices filled her ears. She felt as if she were walking deep in the Dongxue. The light increased gradually, and she discovered she was in a huge city, the buildings impossibly tall, and the sky above hazy with smoke. Smoke trailed through the streets as well, reminding her of Wangfujing when it had been under attack by the Qiangdao. People surrounded her, all of them walking together in the same direction, but despite their united sense of purpose, they looked confused and smelled . . . wrong. It was as if they were somehow incomplete. As if some essential part of them was missing.

They all followed each other past the towering gray buildings lined with shuttered windows. The shutters were intricately patterned, the windows in different sizes and widths, although all were too narrow to pass through. At the next crossing, an iron effigy of a black dragon loomed above the passageway, anchored on all four corners to the surrounding buildings. The sight sent a chill down her spine. Could Echion see his minions through it? Or was it merely a reminder to the denizens of the Grave Kingdom of his authority? At the intersection, people mingled and began asking one another if they'd seen this person or that. A couple of them turned around in complete circles, their faces twisted with confusion.

As Bingmei reached the crossing, a sweet, familiar smell reached her through the tart scent of anxiety. It was a smell she had hardly ever experienced since leaving her grandfather's quonsuun. A smell from her childhood. Warm porridge and cinnamon. It made her mouth water, and the crowd seemed to part ahead, revealing a woman.

Mother.

She looked different from how she had in life, but Bingmei recognized her in an instant. Her heart leaped in her bosom. She tried to run through the crowd, but the people pressed in around her, still hurrying forward, and blocked her mother from sight.

Bingmei felt desperate. The smell was so strong, so powerful, it nearly choked her with grief and longing. She pushed herself through the throng, trying to reach the source of the smell.

A little parting opened, and then she saw her mother standing before her, eyes gleaming with happiness.

"Baobei!" sighed Bingmei's mother, clutching her, stroking her hair.

"Mama?" Bingmei said, overwhelmed by the sensation of being held by her mother again after all this time.

The crowd subsumed them, and they had no choice but to continue walking, arms locked together, following the flow of the crowd.

"Where are we?" Bingmei said, trying to make sense of their strange surroundings.

"This is the Grave Kingdom," said her mother. They walked with urgency, like the others. The impulse to do so was impossible to deny.

"Have I died?" Bingmei asked with horror.

"No, baobei. Dearest. No. Not yet. But you'll be coming here soon. We all must come here."

"Where is Baba?"

"I don't know." Mother's smile dropped away. "I can't find him. There are so many people here. It's easy to get lost. But when you arrive,

I will come for you. Don't be afraid, Bingmei. We must all enter the Grave Kingdom eventually."

"But where are we going?" Bingmei asked. She tried to look at the others and saw it was a horde of women. They all had the same frantic look, as if they were searching for lost loved ones. She saw no side streets, just the one avenue lined with high walls, all the windows barred.

"Why am I here if I'm not yet dead?" Bingmei asked. She tried to stop walking, but the flow of the crowd continued to press against her. She wanted to hug her mother, to sob and linger, but she felt as if time were spilling out like a ruptured water bag.

"This happens *before* people die, baobei. I dreamed of the Grave Kingdom too. My mother came to warn me days before Baba and I found ourselves here. I was worried about what would happen to you, my child, but Mother told me someone else would take care of you."

"What?" Bingmei asked, her heart clenching with anticipation.

"Kunmia Suun is here," said her mother with a smile. "She became your mother for me."

"Can I see her? Where is she?" Bingmei asked, her heart swelling painfully.

"Not yet, baobei. Soon. You will see her soon."

Bingmei looked away for a second, trying to spot Kunmia in the crowd, and when she looked back, her mother was no longer at her side. She twisted around frantically, searching for her, but there was only the throng. The endless crowd of women searching, seeking, overwhelmed with despair.

"Mama!" Bingmei shouted, frantic and anxious.

She felt her throat tighten, and suddenly she couldn't breathe.

被埋葬的世界

"Drink, Bingmei," Mieshi urged, pressing the flask to her mouth. Bingmei coughed and spluttered. "Good, wake up!"

Light stabbed her eyes. The sun was directly overhead, indicating it was afternoon. She winced, blinking, and held her hand up.

"Drink some more," Mieshi said.

Bingmei gulped down the tepid liquid. The water tasted leathery, but it warmed her up from the inside. She noticed she was wearing a different set of clothes—her favorite red shirt and the dusky pants she liked to travel in. Her boots were leaning against a boulder, but the woolens on her feet were dry and warm. She lay in a strong patch of sunlight on a flat rock that felt warm to the touch. The warmth seeped into her clothes and her body. The roughness of the stone against her palm tickled her skin, bringing back the sensations of life.

It struck her that she didn't feel the stabbing pain she'd experienced each time she'd left her body in the past. Why? Had it been a normal dream, different from the waking visions she'd experienced? Or was it because the vision was of the Grave Kingdom itself?

"Where are the others?" Bingmei asked after swallowing more water.

"On the other side of those boulders," she said, waving a hand at them. "You can still hear the falls, can't you?"

Bingmei concentrated for a moment, listening, then nodded.

"I didn't think you'd want all the men seeing you unclothed while I changed you out of your wet things," Mieshi said with a smirk. "I know I wouldn't have."

"Thank you," Bingmei said, relieved but still perplexed. She reached for the other woman's arm. "Was I . . . dead?"

The words startled Mieshi. "No. You shivered the whole time. I never once thought we'd lost you."

Bingmei stared at her in surprise.

"What's wrong?" Mieshi asked.

Bingmei shook her head. She didn't understand it herself. Had she actually been to the Grave Kingdom, or was it just a strange dream?

Some of the younger girls, the students, approached the rock, peeking up at them. "She's awake!" one of them called out.

Marenqo joined them, kneeling on the warm stone. "Well done, Bingmei. You managed to scare not only us half to death, you also scared away the bears! With all the shouting we did, they ran off, leaving the salmon for Quion's spear. I'm going to ask him to catch some for supper after everyone has crossed over."

"Food?" Mieshi asked with disgust. "Again?"

"It's always a good day when you're alive for another meal, Mieshi," he replied. "I need to cross over again and help bring more children." He darted a glance at Mieshi. "Damanhur made it across."

"I wasn't worried," Mieshi said, but Bingmei smelled her relief. With one arm, the maneuver would have been more difficult for him.

"I'm glad you're safe," he said, touching Bingmei's shoulder. "And dressed. I'll be back soon."

Mieshi stood and reached down to help Bingmei to her feet. The motion sent a piercing wave of pain through her head that settled as a headache, but she fought it off and walked over to her sopping-wet clothes. Mieshi had slung them over a rock. The cricket was still nestled in the pocket. Bingmei transferred it to her new outfit. Her pack sat on another boulder, along with her staff and the Phoenix Blade, the gold hilt blinding in its brilliance. She studied the creature emblazoned on the hilt and pommel. Looking at it gave her a feeling of foreboding, amplified by the dream of the Grave Kingdom.

It had warmed her heart to see her mother again, to smell the sweet porridge scent of her love. But what strange words she'd spoken. What *ominous* words. Mother had presaged Bingmei's coming death. She'd made it sound like it would happen soon.

Bingmei smelled Rowen before she saw him. He circled around the boulder, his expression full of anxiety as he gazed at her. To her surprise, he took the last few steps at a run and pulled her into an embrace. The act of intimacy startled not only her but Mieshi too. The scent of fresh-baked bread mingled with the perplexity that was emanating from Mieshi.

"I'm all right," she said, pulling back.

"They're coming up the trail," Rowen said worriedly. "Jiaohua's spies just warned us. Not everyone has crossed yet."

Bingmei was already shaking her head. "I want everyone across. We leave no one to get captured."

He put his hand on her shoulder. "There might not be enough time! I think we need to cut the ropes so that *they* can't cross over."

Bingmei stepped around the large boulder, which blocked her view of the other shore. Quion still stood on the far bank with Jiaohua and a few others. There were two crossing over, walking cautiously on the swaying rope as they shuffled ahead, clutching the rope overhead, hand over hand. Marenqo waited near the tree for his turn to cross back.

"How much time do we have?" Bingmei asked.

"If more than two cross at once, the rope sags into the river," Rowen said. He shook his head. "I'm not being heartless, Bingmei. Just practical. What's the point in crossing the river if we leave the bridge intact?"

CHAPTER EIGHT

Into the Void

Bingmei frowned in frustration and shook her head no. "We don't leave them," she said. "Everyone gets to cross."

"Bingmei . . ." Rowen sighed.

She pointed her finger at him, silencing him with a Mieshi-like glare, and then stormed toward the edge of the falls. Looking across the river, she saw movement in the trees. Their enemies were too close. She seethed with impatience, watching as Quion lined up another two people to make the crossing. Of course he was still focused on others' safety. That was just like him, and while she found his selflessness endearing, it made her stomach churn with dread.

What would she do if he were captured?

She saw Rowen moving toward the tree, a hand on the hilt of his knife. She smelled his frustration. Would he sever the ropes on his own, defying her?

"Rowen," she said warningly.

Maybe he didn't hear her. Maybe he pretended not to.

She reached into her pocket and rubbed her thumb across the cricket, bounding over Rowen's head and landing by the tree anchoring the ropes. A man and a young girl had just reached the shore.

She put herself between the exiled prince and the knots she'd tied.

They met each other's gaze. "You know it's the right thing to do. We're out of time," he said in a low voice.

"I don't accept that," she said. "We can't abandon our friends."

"There is no more time!" he shot back at her.

And that was when Bingmei noticed the eagle perched in a tree on the other side of the river. It had a blazing orange beak, white plumage at its head, and dark brown feathers across the rest of its body. She noticed another. And another. Four massive eagles. One of them lifted itself up and spread its wings, the sight making her gasp. Its wingspan was wider than she was tall. The birds looked powerful and savage, almost otherworldly because of it.

Had the birds always been there? Had her party wandered beneath their nest tree without even noticing it?

The one with the spread wings launched itself from the tree. The other three followed suit.

"Bingmei, please listen to reason," Rowen said, trying to divert her attention back to him.

"Do you see them?" she asked, pointing.

He turned and noticed the massive birds rising from the tree. A few moments later, she saw the first few men approaching from the trail, armed with spears and swords. To Bingmei's astonishment, the first of the eagles let out a shriek and attacked her enemies. Their wings flapped furiously as they raked the armored men with their talons.

Cries of alarm came from them. Jiaohua, who was hiding behind a tree, poked his head around the thick trunk and sent a poisoned dart into their midst, stinging one of the men in the neck. In an instant, the man collapsed, unconscious.

The other members of the Jingcha were hustling across the ropes, each one supporting a younger person. Many of them were on the ropes at once, and the lower one sagged into the water, but they continued in spite of it. There were only a handful left. They could make it.

Bingmei stared as the eagles continued to swoop down, making cries as they attacked. Their enemies were driven back, trying in vain to shield their heads.

Watching the birds, she suddenly felt a presence in the woods, by the falls. She looked up, blinded by the sun, and thought she caught a glimpse of another eagle circling high overhead, although the plumage was too colorful, the body too large. Squinting, she tried to get a better look, but whatever she'd seen had slipped out of view.

Jiaohua sent off another dart, then another, before retreating to the shore. All the children had safely made it across. Only Jiaohua and Quion were left on the other side, and a couple of Jingcha were still on the ropes. Bingmei watched in horror as one of them lost his grip on the rope. The river caught hold of his legs. Powerless to help, she watched as the river yanked him from safety, and he went over the falls. A collective groan came from those who stood watching on the riverbank. The fall was fatal.

Quion untied the lower rope from the base of the tree and tossed it into the river. From his side, Marenqo began pulling it up. That just left the upper rope. Jiaohua motioned for Quion to grab it, but he shook his head no and began fidgeting with the knot. He produced another, shorter length of rope and quickly worked in a series of knots. Bingmei yelled at him to cross already, since no one was left on the ropes, but he didn't heed her. What was he doing with the knots? Why not just cross?

He finished whatever he was doing and motioned for Jiaohua to go first. It alarmed her even more when Quion lifted the snow leopard up onto his shoulders as if it were a mere housecat. He intended to carry the leopard across! His big heart would be the death of him.

Jiaohua grabbed the rope with both hands and swung his legs up onto it, starting to pull himself across. Quion watched to make sure the rope held, and the rest of them took in the spectacle from the opposite shore.

Bingmei saw Liekou emerge from the trees higher up the slope. Her breath caught in her chest as she watched him follow the river down to where Quion stood, bearing the strain of the mountain cat.

"Quion! Now!" Bingmei screamed.

He looked at her across the river, not seeing the threat coming his way. Jiaohua had made it partway across the river, and the rope was swinging with his weight. Bingmei gritted her teeth, watching as Liekou picked his way down the river stealthily. She shouted to Quion again, but she knew he couldn't hear her.

Quion grabbed the rope. He started to pull himself up, and she noticed he still held a piece of rope in his left hand, tied to the knots connecting the rope to the tree. Like Jiaohua, he slung his legs up on the rope, but she could see the fatigue in his expression, and the leopard yowled and dug its claws into his cloak to keep from falling into the river. He moved at a turtle's pace, his burdens weighing him down.

Liekou reached the edge of the other shore, and he gazed at his prey on the opposite bank. A dark look came across his face. Because of the river, she couldn't smell him, but she sensed his pulsing anger.

Jiaohua made it to their side, huffing for breath, but Quion wasn't even halfway across. He was struggling, his pace slow.

"I told him to go first," Jiaohua growled, his expression grim. She smelled the minty scent of fondness wafting off him.

"He knew he would go slower," said Rowen, his eyes fixed on the scene.

Liekou grabbed the rope. Bingmei feared he'd untie it or try to shake Quion loose, but instead he pulled himself up onto the rope. Rather than creep across it like Quion, he stood atop it, arms outstretched for balance, and began walking. His pace was much faster than Quion's.

It wouldn't take long to overrun him.

"Can you hit him with a dart?" Bingmei asked Jiaohua. He blinked in surprise, but he pulled out his blowgun and began searching for a dart.

Bingmei watched in suspense, her heart in her throat, as Liekou came up on Quion, who still struggled to make any progress.

And then Quion sprung his trap.

CHAPTER NINE

Escape

Gripping the rope with one hand and his legs, Quion yanked the other length of rope hard, which unraveled the knot at the other tree. Suddenly, they were both falling. But only Quion had a good grip on the rope.

Bingmei gasped in surprise as Quion and the snow leopard hit the water. The big cat snarled at the unexpected plunge and swam fast and hard for the shore as Quion pulled himself across the rest of the way, much faster and stronger now. Marenqo and some others pulled on their end of the rope to help hasten the process. The snow leopard scampered away as soon as it made it across, although Bingmei had no doubt it would return.

Liekou had fallen into the river, and the current dragged him toward the falls. But just like Bingmei, he found a boulder at the edge and caught himself with his feet. Bingmei stared at him, willing him to fall, to die, but the ensign master managed to pull himself up onto a boulder protruding from the waters. He was midway across the river, stranded at the edge of the deadly falls.

He faced them, sopping wet, his face nearly purple with rage.

Jiaohua raised the blowgun to his lips and shot a dart at him.

Liekou twisted, and the dart sailed past him. He glared at them, his eyes promising revenge.

With effort, they hauled Quion out of the river. He was still clutching the other rope, the one he'd used to destroy the knot, which meant they'd salvaged all three. Bingmei grinned when she saw him come up on their side of the bank, teeth chattering.

Jiaohua readied another dart, but Bingmei gripped his arm and shook her head. "Don't waste any more."

"I'd rather kill him now," Jiaohua said.

"I'd rather you not lose all the rest of your darts," she answered. "Come on. Let's get Quion into some dry clothes. We made it."

She shifted her attention to the other shore. The eagles she'd noticed were gone. Men climbed up on the other side and stared in disbelief at their leader, stranded on a boulder in the middle of the river.

Liekou didn't appear to be cold. His attention was fixed on her, the look on his face assuring her that he would still come after her.

She smiled at him, a crooked smile of victory. Then, gripping her staff, she walked away.

被埋葬的世界

That night, they camped in a canyon of broken boulders on the valley floor. She'd ordered a few Jingcha to remain behind to watch the progress of their pursuers. They'd caught up to the group near sunset, with some heartening news—although Liekou had been liberated after several hours of being marooned on that boulder, he hadn't even tried to lead his forces across the river. They'd abandoned the mountain, returning on the trail they'd taken up to the riverbank.

Since it would take some time for their pursuers to find them again, Bingmei had allowed some fires to be built at the base of the broken boulders, hidden from the guards patrolling the Death Wall by the canyon. With fire came warmth and cooked salmon, which Quion had caught and seasoned to perfection. Marenqo grunted with pleasure, licking his fingers as he enjoyed the meal. The snow leopard had eventually skulked out of the woods to join them. In apology, Quion had tossed a bit of raw fish her way.

For the first time in a while, Bingmei experienced the lulling sense of relief. She knew better than to think Liekou would stop hunting her. But he no longer had Rowen as a guide. It would take much longer for him to find evidence of their passage.

After everyone had eaten, she noticed Quion cleaning the pan near the cooking fire he'd used. The light of the flames danced off his face, revealing his deep concentration on the task at hand. She wandered up and squatted near him. He glanced at her, but then kept working.

"I forgot to thank you earlier," she said.

"I'm glad you're not tired of salmon yet."

"It's delicious, but that's not what I was thanking you for. Without you and your knots, we wouldn't have crossed the river. That trick at the end . . . that was pretty clever."

He smiled with pleasure at her compliment, but he didn't say anything. He only shrugged.

"What knot did you use?" she asked him.

"I didn't want to cut the rope if I could avoid it," he said. "So I used a different knot on my side of the shore—one that could slip free if tugged a certain way. I had a feeling I wouldn't make it across in time. Jiaohua and I would have been in trouble if those eagles hadn't come when they did." He glanced at her when he said it. "That was strange."

"It was indeed," she said. Eagles were powerful creatures. They usually hunted fish and rodents, not men. Why had they attacked their pursuers? And what of the other bird she'd seen, the larger one with the strange plumage? "It doesn't make sense."

"I'm not complaining," said Quion with a grin. "I thought maybe . . . you summoned them."

Bingmei shook her head. "I can't control the magic, Quion. I've tried, but it only comes when it wants to, like in the caves. When it goes, there's no way I can make it return. It's all very confusing."

He looked back down at the pan and kept scraping it. He always took care of his tools and his gear. Because of his meticulous ways, he didn't let others help him, but he didn't seem to mind the work.

He stopped scraping a moment, his eyes still downcast. "Maybe it hesitates because of you."

She fell quiet, staring at him.

He didn't look at her, but she could see he was serious. "Maybe it's because you haven't accepted that you were chosen by the phoenix."

It felt like a knot tightened inside her chest. Could it be that simple? If she embraced her destiny, would the magic come when she called for it? Part of her believed he might be right, that he'd seen down to the root of the issue. It didn't escape her that Rowen had told her much the same thing.

"I don't want to die," she whispered, glancing over her shoulder to make sure no one else was close enough to hear them.

He didn't respond to that, choosing silence instead as he continued to scour the iron skillet. But it was a companionable silence, not fraught with awkwardness.

"When I went into the river and got so cold," she said, edging closer to him, "I had a strange dream. Or a vision. I thought I'd died, like I have in the past, but Mieshi said I never stopped breathing."

"What did you see?" he asked.

The memory of it was still poignant.

"I dreamed I was in the Grave Kingdom. I saw my mother."

He stopped with the scraper, looking at her in surprise and wonder. She explained her dream to him, including as many details as she could remember. The endless walls lined with painted, barred windows. The smoke-filled sky overhead, the deep chasm of the street. And the mass of women, all seeking and hunting and worrying.

He listened patiently, taking it all in.

"She implied I was going to die soon," Bingmei concluded. "She told me that dreams of the Grave Kingdom come to prepare us for death, and she promised to try to meet me after it happens."

He stared at her for a long moment, lips pursed in thought. Finally, he said, "I'd give anything to see my mother again. I loved my father, but I miss my mother even more. She . . . she always cooked for me. I learned how to use all the spices from her." He let go of the scraper and gently touched the edge of the pan. "This was hers. That's why I couldn't leave my pack behind in Sajinau. I couldn't bear the thought of someone misusing all her things. It's how I stay close to her memory. She loved me, Bingmei." A wonderful scent surrounded him—the deep love and affection a son had for his mother. It was similar to the smell of a mother's love.

He looked into her eyes. "I'm glad you got to see her, Bingmei. What a gift. And a curse. I've always thought that I would never see my mother again." His eyes filled with tears. He gave her a little smile. "Our loved ones still remember us in the Grave Kingdom. Maybe they're even waiting for us. You've given me a little hope. Thank you."

His words made her heart ache and feel glad at the same time. He was right. Although the Grave Kingdom did not seem like a pleasant place, it was better than going into a void of nothing.

She wondered what buried world lay beyond their awareness.

Rising again, she walked away from the fire and hugged herself. Her head tipped up toward the sky, and she gazed at the stars, which had come into view in all their majesty. What were they really?

She lowered her gaze to find Rowen sitting in the shadows of a boulder, arms crossed atop his knees. It was his smell that had drawn her attention.

The smell of jealousy.

被埋葬的世界

Fortune does not come twice. Misfortune does not come alone.

—Dawanjir proverb

CHAPTER TEN

Sihui

They approached the kingdom of Sihui from the north. The season of the Dragon of Night had long since ended, and the air was muggy and full of ravenous insects. Thankfully, Marenqo, who'd traveled more than most of them, knew of an oil from local plants that kept the mosquitos at bay. But the bugs' sickly droning still filled the air, and the thick green canopy they passed under gave the world a greenish cast. Enormous hills covered in gingko trees became more abundant the farther south they went.

After they left the glaciers, flocks of blue herons passed overhead constantly, and it seemed to Bingmei that the birds were almost leading them to Sihui. They followed a wide river that forked through the upper valley and finally came to the first sign of civilization they'd witnessed since leaving the shadow of the Death Wall. In the distance, a stone bridge straddled the river, different in style from the wooden ones she'd seen in Wangfujing. The bridge was made of three stone arches, the largest of which straddled the river. The two smaller arches, one on each side, supported covered shelters with shrine-like pagodas. The roofs of the pagodas were steeply slanted, and they met at a high point in the middle with iron knobs on top. The river was wider at that spot, the water so smooth and slow that they could see the reflection of the arches and bridge in it, which had the appearance of a huge eye.

The air was thick with haze, but through the bridge's arched opening, she could make out buildings in the distance. She had not worn her wig while traveling through the wilds, but this view told her it was time to put it back on, and so she did.

"We've made it to Sihui," Marenqo said with relief, coming up next to her. They were all footsore and weary from the long journey, the indeterminable weeks spent crossing the hinterlands. Bingmei's pack dug into her shoulders, and she imagined the pleasure of sleeping in a bed instead of on the turf. Even though the oil mostly warded off the insects, they each sported scabs from where it had failed to protect them. She looked behind her at the straggling ensign and hoped that their presence in Sihui would be welcomed.

And she hoped the kingdom hadn't fallen.

Guards armed with longbows waited on both sides of the bridge, standing in the covered areas. Bingmei did not attempt to conceal their intention to cross. The trees had been cleared around the base of the bridge to a fair distance, so approaching under cover would have been impossible anyway.

Loud frogs croaked from the edge of the river. Her scalp felt itchy beneath the wig after being so long without it, but she ignored the discomfort and motioned for the ensign to halt as several horsemen rode forward to meet them.

"Are you ready to translate?" she asked Marenqo.

"I may not need to," he said. "Many of the nobles are fluent in other languages."

The horsemen approached, and Bingmei tried to catch their scent. She did not trust that these were not Qiangdao.

"Be prepared to flee back to the woods," she said, speaking loudly enough for the others to hear. They relied on her ability to smell friend from foe, which had saved them more than once.

The riders drew near, stopping close enough to talk but far enough away for safety. The lead horseman wore armor made of square patches of hardened leather, dotted with metal studs. Pieces of the leather had been sewn together to cover his chest, back, and shoulders. His lower arms were covered in thick cloth down to his wrists, and a thick scarf was wrapped around his neck. The lopsided cap on his head reminded her of the shape of a gourd.

The leader frowned at them, his look suspicious. He smelled of sweat and green onion, nothing rancid. It was nothing like the stench of the Qiangdao.

Bingmei nodded to Marenqo, who stepped forward a pace and offered some form of greeting, his palms up, hands spread apart.

The leader's eyebrows rose in surprise at being addressed in such a manner. He asked a few questions in a strange language, which Marenqo promptly answered in the same tongue. Then he backed his horse up a few steps and began conferring with the other soldiers.

"What did you tell him?" Bingmei asked Marenqo in a low tone.

"That we are an ensign from the east come to offer useful information to King Zhumu. I told him that we fought at Wangfujing and Sajinau and knew of the enemy coming to invade Sihui. I think it roused his interest. Don't you?"

"It seems so," Bingmei replied. She glanced back at the others, her hope beginning to grow.

After several moments, the leader returned and spoke to Marenqo in quick, curt language. He gestured to the river and pointed a few times.

Marenqo bowed respectfully and nodded. "He said that they will send word of our arrival to the palace. We must wait here by the edge of the river. If we are allowed to enter, then they will send boats up the river to bring us to the palace. Do we think this is acceptable?"

Bingmei looked at Rowen, and he nodded briefly. She didn't need his approval, but like Kunmia, she preferred not to make important decisions without counsel from her people.

"It's agreeable. See if they have any food they can spare."

"Are you sure about that?" Marenqo asked, his eyebrows lifting.

It seemed an odd question, especially for one so obsessed with food, but she just shrugged. "I'm sure even *you* are a little weary of fish by now."

"One can never have too much fish," Marenqo said. But he posed the question to the other man, who nodded in agreement. They mounted their horses and rode back to the bridge. Marenqo led the others to the river's edge, where they found a man-made stone embankment half hidden in the scrub. It was long enough for all of them to sit down, and the water was well beneath their feet.

"They asked us to wait here," he said.

Bingmei shrugged off her pack, easing the ache in her shoulders, and set the rune staff down near it.

"You've mentioned before that King Zhumu is shrewd." She glanced at Marenqo, then looked around the guards. "Have any of you met him before?"

Only Marenqo had traveled this far before, but he had never met the king in person, it turned out, only by reputation. No one could say what he looked like or anything other than a vague sense of his qualities. Jiaohua said that the Jingcha spies had reported he was cautious and cunning but not vengeful.

After they were settled, some sentries from the bridge approached them with a few baskets. Marenqo thanked them and took the baskets, and everyone sat in the long grass to eat the feast. Some of the bowls held noodles with little strips of meat. Others contained strange bits of meat that had a nice, smoky smell.

"What is that?"

"Tongue," Marenqo replied, grinning. "Or lung. Hard to tell. It's a delicacy here. They gave us the best parts. We must be honored guests."

There were also a few steamed buns, and Bingmei grabbed one of those first. Even though it wasn't warm, she bit into it and found the middle full of dark meat and dripping juices. Others reached as well, and they began devouring the food while Marenqo withdrew his knife to cut the tongue into smaller strips.

Bingmei started chewing the bite of bun, so grateful to be eating something different, when it felt like her mouth exploded in fire. Her tongue was burning. Had they doused the food in acid? Although she had thought she enjoyed spicy fare, this was much different from the scorpion sticks she enjoyed in Wangfujing.

Tears came to her eyes, and she looked up to see the others looked—and smelled—as aghast as she felt.

Bingmei reached for her water flask and started to gulp down some of the precious water, while Marenqo began howling with laughter.

"What's wrong?" he said, grinning. "You wanted some food. Enjoy!"

"You knew it would be this spicy?" Damanhur said in outrage. "And you didn't warn us? My tongue is going to blister!"

"Perhaps I should have mentioned that small detail," Marenqo said, still chuckling. "In Sihui, they have more refined palates. Or perhaps they've lost the ability to taste their food because it's so hot. Everything is spicy here. And I mean . . . everything."

Bingmei would not have been surprised if blisters truly did sprout in her mouth. While the water had soothed the worst of the burn, she revolted against the idea of eating more of the bun.

"Even the noodles?" she asked, staring at them hungrily.

"Even the noodles," Marenqo replied with a sigh. "But they are delicious. If you can stand it." He picked up a noodle and slurped it up.

She heard laughter coming from the bridge, and a quick glance confirmed the sentries were having fun watching their suffering.

"That's why you asked me why I wanted some of their food," Bingmei said, giving Marenqo a withering look.

He shrugged. "I haven't been this entertained in a long time. And yes, the same thing happened to me when I first came. No one told me either. But if you could see your faces!"

被埋葬的世界

Three boats came for them. They were made of bamboo, strapped together in thick flat bundles. A small pagoda was built atop each, supported by columns made of bamboo shafts. Three boatmen with long bamboo poles pushed the boats up the river. She saw a soldier wearing the uniform of Sajinau on one of them.

"Do you recognize him?" she asked Rowen, her stomach twisting with surprise. "I know I've seen him before."

"He was an officer for General Tzu," he said. His gaze was full of wonder . . . and she thought she smelled a new tinge of hope, like the sweet smell of honey. Like her, he must have assumed the general's men were all dead.

Bingmei pulled on her pack and lifted the staff as the boats eased their way up to the stone wharf.

The man smiled at them in recognition. "Bao Damanhur, Prince Rowen." His gaze shifted to her. "Bingmei. Welcome to Sihui."

"What is your name?" Bingmei asked him. "I know we've met."

"Pangxie," he responded, bowing. He looked at her. "You bear the staff of Kunmia Suun. I'd wondered what became of it."

"Is General Tzu here as well?" Rowen asked, and she could smell his eagerness.

"Yes," said Pangxie. "He sent me to greet you, to be sure you were not imposters. Greetings, Jiaohua. Many members of the Jingcha still serve us here. Come with us back to the palace. You are most welcome."

His words were truthful and earnest. Bingmei nodded at the others, and the sweet smell of relief filled the air.

Quion inspected the lashings of the ropes used to hold the bamboo shafts in place and nodded in appreciation. But then he turned to Bingmei and said, "Can I stay behind and camp out here by the woods? I don't think the leopard would do well in the city, and it probably isn't used to this kind of terrain. It may even wander off."

"Not likely," said Marenqo. "It follows you relentlessly because you keep feeding it."

"I don't know," Quion said, giving Bingmei a pleading look. "I need to ease it into the situation."

Bingmei understood his concern. The snow leopard was too savage to bring into Sihui, but it had been a good friend and helper to them all. It would feel wrong to abandon it now. "All right," she said. "But I will come check on you myself. Where will you camp?"

He smiled in relief and put his hands on his hips, looking at the edge of the woods. "Somewhere over there," he said, pointing.

"Very well. But you'll be missed, Quion."

He smiled in pleasure at her compliment. They waved goodbye to him, and the rest of the ensign boarded the boats to enter Sihui by river. Soon they'd pushed off and glided away, passing beneath the massive stone bridge.

Prince Rowen's feelings grew more and more peaceful as they approached the city. She felt the same way. Relief and hope had been in short supply. At last they would find out what was going on. And the fact that General Tzu was here, safe, indicated the news wasn't all bad.

Once they passed beneath the bridge, their view of the city opened, some of the mist clearing. The layout was similar to that of Wangfujing, with crowded buildings on both sides of the river, but the river itself was much broader. There were lily pads everywhere, lotus flowers growing on them, and peasants stood in the mud on the sheltered sides of the river, farming some strange kind of plants. They wore wide-brimmed hats, their pants hiked up to their knees as they worked.

Sihui was not as vast as Sajinau. She could see the fringe of trees surrounding it, the hills hemming it in. As the mist continued to clear, she saw another huge bridge under construction on the far side of the city. It appeared they were making the bridge even wider. Several boats were positioned beneath the arch, and ropes were fed up and down, supplying stone for the project. Hundreds of workers massed around it.

It didn't take her long to realize what they were doing. General Tzu was here in Sihui, so they knew how Echion's fleet had attacked Sajinau. They were building a wall within the river to make it impossible for his ships to pass through.

King Zhumu *was* shrewd.

The palace rose above a towering stone wall. It was situated in the midst of a market street, but she could see the huge stone gate protecting it. The bamboo boats parked at the river's edge by the front of the market.

When she exited the boat, the smell of people struck her nose.

She'd been away from humanity for so long, she had almost forgotten what it was like to smell a huge crowd of people. This was not a greedy city like Wangfujing. The people buying and selling by the wharf weren't out to rob each other, but they were immediately wary of the newcomers. She smelled it. Felt it. No one called to them, trying to persuade them to come and buy their wares.

Pangxie and the other soldiers who'd escorted them took them down the main street toward the palace.

As they came closer, her nerves grew taut. Echion could transform his appearance. Although she didn't understand how he did it, that ability had allowed him to depose King Budai in Wangfujing. What if Echion had already infiltrated Sihui?

Were they truly safe at last? Or was safety always just an illusion?

"Are you all right?" Rowen asked her.

She glanced at him and nodded as they followed Pangxie beneath the thick stone arch leading to the palace. The walls were very impressive, with carved blocks at the top, providing shelter for the warriors stationed atop them. Sihui was preparing for war.

General Tzu awaited them in the sunlit courtyard. His features were impassive—he looked neither concerned nor relieved. But Bingmei did not have to depend on appearances—she could sense his relief.

Jiaohua, who had also been part of Juexin's council, approached him first. "General, it is good to find you here."

"You've come a long distance, I can see," said the general. He glanced at Rowen, nodding at him. "Welcome, Your Highness. I did not know you were coming, or I would have sent you assistance. How did you escape Sajinau?"

"I was used by Echion in his hunt to find Bingmei," he answered. "She freed me."

General Tzu looked at her, his eyes still unconcerned. "Are you still opposed to the destiny that Jidi Majia foresaw for you?" he asked her.

"We came here to help King Zhumu fight Echion," she answered, dodging his question.

General Tzu studied her for a moment before nodding. "All help is needed. This is truly a fortunate moment. We're expecting to be attacked and have been preparing all winter to defend Sihui. But your arrival, Prince Rowen, is a double blessing. King Zhumu has only one child, a daughter. He had long considered your brother as a possible husband for her. Now that you are here, I see an opportunity to unite our kingdoms."

Rowen's face was impassive, neutral. But she smelled the sudden fear inside him, the resistance to any such scheme.

"Tell me more, General," he said, falling alongside him.

She had the strong suspicion that he would refuse. It distressed her to realize that she *wanted* him to refuse. The thought had no place in her life, and so she shoved it aside.

CHAPTER ELEVEN

The Eagle Palace

As the entourage crossed the courtyard, Jiaohua walked alongside General Tzu, his expression greedy for information.

"How many survivors from Sajinau are here?" he wheedled. "Pangxie said that some Jingcha came with you. Have you been contacted by the others who were already here?"

"There are several thousand refugees," the general answered curtly. "I haven't had time to keep track of all your underlings. Our people have been my greatest concern. Some fled to the other kingdoms. Before his execution, Prince Juexin commanded me to instigate a rebellion and defy Echion."

"I will help you do that," Jiaohua said eagerly.

"King Zhumu has his own security force," said General Tzu. "Your order was to protect Bingmei. That was what the prince charged you to do."

Jiaohua snorted. "But we are here now, Tzu. I can be of service in many ways."

Bingmei could smell his disappointment. He liked being within the circle of power, always, but the balance had shifted now that they'd arrived in Sihui.

"When can we see the king?" she asked, if only to remind the others that it was her ensign.

"Presently, of course," the general replied, nodding to her.

"Has there been any word from King Shulian?" she asked.

The general shook his head. "Rumor has it that he was captured, but we've lost all word from Sajinau because Echion controls the shipping routes to the east. Anyone who betrays information is sent to labor for years at the Death Wall. For all I know, he may still be in hiding. We do have one advantage. We took a prisoner with us from Sajinau. He's confined in the dungeon here at the palace, but his information has been accurate and useful."

"Who?" Jiaohua asked.

"He was a leader of Qiangdao and one of Echion's supporters at first. But he failed in his assignment and fled for fear of being executed."

"His name?" Bingmei asked, her stomach twisting in anticipation of his answer.

"Muxidi," General Tzu said.

The name struck her like a fist to her stomach, even though she'd tried to prepare herself for it. He was the man who had murdered her parents and her grandfather. She'd left him alive—and now he was here in Sihui.

"He's *here*?" Damanhur said in shock. He'd been trailing behind them, close enough to hear their conversation.

Muxidi had cut off Damanhur's arm in their last battle in Sajinau. The smell of revenge and fury became overpowering, like snapping cinders in a fire.

General Tzu stopped walking and turned to face Damanhur. She clearly wasn't the only one who'd noticed his rage. "He has provided valuable information, Bao Damanhur. We've learned much about Fusang and its defenses from him. If we are ever going to defeat Echion and his minions, we need to learn as much as we can about him and his Summer Palace." His eyes narrowed coldly. "Muxidi is guarded by loyal men. No one can see him without permission. I hope that is clear."

It was clear, but the knowledge that he was close made Bingmei queasy. She'd hoped to find some peace reaching Sihui. Instead, she felt more unsettled than ever.

"He won't do anything foolish," Rowen said, putting his hand on the general's shoulder and shooting Damanhur a warning look.

"I trust he will not," said General Tzu. He gave Damanhur a final glance before continuing toward the main entrance, which was flanked by armored warriors. "Now, you need to understand that making an alliance with Sihui, in my opinion, would be the wise course of action. We are refugees from around the rim. The influx has strained their food stores. Our people have labored not to be a burden, but we are still considered a lower caste among these people. If you were to agree to marry the princess, it could change the situation overnight."

"I can see that," Rowen said, his voice neutral. But she felt the roiling emotions inside him threatening to burst free. He dreaded the thought.

The guards opened the doors as they approached, and they entered a dimly lit corridor with aged stone walls. A design of birds was carved into the stone. At first Bingmei thought they were phoenixes, but the bald heads and hooked beaks and talons were very different from the carvings she'd seen on her sword and in other places. The corridor smelled faintly of cooking spices, which stirred her hunger—until she remembered the spicy bun she'd eaten by the shore.

This palace was much smaller than the one in Sajinau. They reached the inner sanctum more quickly than Bingmei had expected and approached the meiwood throne of King Zhumu. An elegant young woman stood by his side, hands clasped together. Her hair was held up by different jeweled pins and combs, and the multiple silk layers of her emerald-colored gown spoke of her status. Her eyes fixed immediately on Rowen.

This had to be the princess.

Her father, King Zhumu, had a short beard and mustache that had been fastidiously trimmed and a full head of dark hair with a few streaks of gray in it. He wore a topknot bound with a golden clamp, and a jeweled collar piece adorned his dark plum robes. His hair was elegantly combed, not a strand out of place, and he looked at them with wariness and a cunning intensity. Behind him, she saw a huge bald eagle tethered to a golden stand, its eyes shielded with a hood.

As they approached the throne, Bingmei breathed in deeply, trying to get a measure of the man. Thankfully, there was no deception in him. This was no imposter. That brought a feeling of relief, but the man's scrutiny was intense. He looked at each of their party in turn, taking their measure with his vigilant gaze, one hand clamping an armrest, the other grazing his beard.

An immaculately dressed servant approached them from near the foot of the throne. "Greetings!" he said in a booming voice, speaking their language fluently. "And welcome to the Eagle Palace, the court of King Zhumu, lord of Sihui! I am Kexin, His Majesty's advisor."

Bingmei and her ensign bowed in respect.

"Is it true that you have come to offer information?" Kexin continued. "Who leads this ensign? King Zhumu and his daughter, Cuifen, are prepared to take you into service."

Bingmei stepped forward, and she smelled their shock that someone so young should lead such an esteemed group of warriors. She smelled something else too, a vaguely familiar odor that she struggled to place.

"My name is Bingmei," she said, holding on to the rune staff. "My master was Kunmia Suun, who perished during the fall of Sajinau. My grandfather, Jiao, and my parents also ran an ensign in the eastern lands. My family was murdered by the Qiangdao. We need food and shelter, but we offer our services in return. Like General Tzu, we're determined to resist Echion's lust for dominion and power."

There was that smell again, growing stronger. She resisted the urge to look around the room. It wasn't coming from those assembled in front of her.

"Welcome, Bingmei," said King Zhumu. He looked at her closely. "She who is the chosen of the phoenix. I see some strands of your real hair, which has escaped the wig you use to disguise it. If you would, please remove the wig and prove your identity."

Bingmei hadn't been expecting that. His request alarmed her—and so did the eyes digging into her. Many servants and military officers had gathered in the small throne room.

Fearing it would displease the king if she refused, she held out her staff, and Mieshi stepped forward to take hold of it. Mieshi looked at the princess with a smirk of disdain that Bingmei instantly understood. These people were preparing for battle, yet they clearly spent hours each day on grooming and fashion.

She felt filthy standing before them. Her clothes were stained from the journey, and everyone in the ensign was desperately in need of bathing. The last thing she wanted to do was reveal her unusual appearance to them, but she felt she had no choice. The king had asked, and if she wished to stay, she must do as he asked. She reached up and pulled out the pins, one by one, then tugged off the wig.

King Zhumu leaned forward slightly, but the expression on his face was not one of disgust. "You are the one," he said. "General Tzu has told us about your visit to Sajinau. He shared the prophecy of Jidi Majia. You are welcome here, and I would be honored to accept you into my service. Your ensign is weary from travel and toil." He raised a hand and gestured. "We will prepare a great feast in your honor tonight. For now, you will receive fresh clothing and clean water to bathe in. We will also find a place for your ensign to stay. Daughter, please see that my words are fulfilled."

"As you command, my father," said Cuifen in a melodious voice that suddenly made Bingmei feel even more self-conscious about her appearance.

The smell she'd noticed earlier wafted toward her again, and this time she recognized it—the lemony smell of greed. She turned her head and saw King Budai lurking in the shadows wearing sumptuous robes. His girth had diminished, but she'd recognize his scent anywhere.

As soon as their eyes met, he abruptly walked away.

被埋葬的世界

Because the palace was so crowded, Princess Cuifen brought Bingmei, Mieshi, and the other women from the ensign to her own personal chambers. The men were escorted somewhere by the king's advisor. Other servants were preparing a bath for them. Unlike the tub Bingmei had used in Sajinau, this pool was built into a room attached to the princess's chambers. The steaming water had a slightly odorous smell that suggested the water came from a natural hot spring.

"Leave your clothes here on the stone bench," said Cuifen as they entered. The marble tiles were wet and squeaked as they walked. "My servants will wash them for you. We will provide silk garments for each of you, even the children. What you are wearing now will be quite uncomfortable here in Sihui." Gesturing to a wooden shelf lined with vases, she added, "Use these oils to rid yourselves of the fragrance of the water after you've bathed. We will provide some refreshments and cots so you may rest. I will return later."

"Thank you, Your Highness," Bingmei said. It felt strange bathing in the princess's personal space, but Cuifen gave no indication that she was offended or disgusted by their presence.

"I honor my revered father," she said, bowing to them. "Be at peace."

A slight filmy haze covered the water, illuminated with light from four small windows framed in the ceiling. The windows were covered in paper, but they provided some light in the dim interior. Steps led down into the pool. Bingmei squatted near them and scooped up some water in her hand. It was hot to the touch.

"You winced," said Mieshi. "Is it that hot?"

"I think they might want to boil us alive," Bingmei said teasingly. She straightened, shaking off the water droplets that hadn't slipped through her fingers yet. "Budai is here."

Mieshi looked startled. "Did you see him?"

"In the crowd," said Bingmei. "But I sensed him first. There's no mistaking his odor."

Mieshi's eyes narrowed in concern. "You banished him from the quonsuun. He won't have forgotten that insult."

"I also told him he owed me a debt," said Bingmei. She bit her lip. "I'm beginning to regret that decision."

"Do you think he's hoping to marry the princess?" Mieshi wondered.

Bingmei hadn't even thought of that. "That would . . . be revolting. He's older than her father."

"Since when has that ever stopped a man?" Mieshi said with a snort. "Rowen's coming is timely, then. Perhaps it was fate that we came when we did."

Bingmei felt her insides twisting again. Why did the thought of Rowen marrying anyone bother her so much? Was it stubbornness? The prince could marry whomever he wished. He had indicated he had feelings for her, but that wouldn't stop him from making a practical choice. She didn't wish to explain any of that to Mieshi.

She looked down at the steam, eager to shift the conversation off Rowen. "Are you getting in, Mieshi?"

"You first," said the other woman with a smug smile. "If you survive, then I will."

被埋葬的世界

After bathing in the near-scalding water, Bingmei dried herself and used some of the oil from the vessels to rub over her skin. It had a pleasant smell that reminded her of rare juniper. An array of garments had been laid out for them, and Bingmei selected the pair made of red silk fabric. It whispered against her skin as she put it on. The sleeves of the jacket were long and wide, different from any style she'd worn before.

After she'd dressed, she grabbed her pack and staff, which she'd refused to let out of her sight, and entered the princess's chambers. The oil felt cool on her skin, and the looseness of the jacket and pants helped reduce the discomfort of the humidity. She brushed out her hair, braided it, and coiled it above her head. When she pinned on the wig, she took care to make sure that every strand was covered.

Mieshi joined her shortly thereafter, wearing lavender-colored garments. The other woman smelled sharply of impatience, just like what Bingmei felt. The younger girls had not yet bathed, but it felt wrong to stand here, idle, when they should be preparing for battle. They needed to *do* something.

Bingmei and Mieshi sent the younger girls in to bathe, then collected their gear and left the room. They had not gone far before they encountered Pangxie, who was hurrying toward them down the corridor. He almost didn't recognize them because they were dressed in the clothing style of Sihui. Bingmei had to call out his name before he stopped. His anxious scent caught her nose as he came to a stop before them, panting.

"Ah! You're finished! This is good. General Tzu wishes to see you at once, Bingmei. The prince has refused to marry Cuifen. He says he's made an oath of service to you as part of your ensign. He said he will not violate his oath unless you command him to. King Zhumu is angry. He thinks this is some trick. You must come! This could ruin all we've worked to achieve."

CHAPTER TWELVE

The Prisoner

As Bingmei and Mieshi followed the warrior, conflicting thoughts swirled in Bingmei's mind. She had hoped—wrongly—that coming to Sihui would alleviate all their problems. That they would be able to follow rather than lead. Instead, it felt like their problems were stacking up like boards, the burden getting heavier and heavier.

"What is Rowen up to?" Mieshi wondered aloud as they walked quickly down the dimly lit corridor. She smelled of suspicion, which had a dampness to it, like grass after a storm.

"One thing about him is he's good at getting into trouble," Bingmei pointed out. Why had he put her in the middle of the fray? Was he hoping she would say no as an indication of her favor? Frustration pressed in on her. Although she *did* care for Rowen, it was obvious his affection for her was much stronger than hers for him, and she was not interested in pursuing a relationship. If only he would explain what he knew about the "bond" they shared, perhaps they could clear this up and put it behind them.

Mieshi's lips turned up into a smile. "What are you going to do?"

"I don't know yet," Bingmei said. "I often wonder how Kunmia solved problems. She was so wise."

"Her wisdom came from long experience," Mieshi said. "She learned who she could count on." She gave Bingmei a sidelong look. "You have an advantage there."

"One that I'm not about to divulge," she said, appreciating that Mieshi didn't blurt it out.

As they approached the throne room, they heard voices raised in anger. Bingmei braced herself for what was sure to be an assault on her senses.

The door opened, and her eyes immediately shot to General Tzu, Jiaohua, Rowen, and Damanhur, standing in a knot in front of the throne. They seemed to be surrounded by the courtiers of Sihui adorned in jewels and silk robes trimmed in fur. The king's advisor, Kexin, stood before Rowen in an adversarial posture, one hand on his hip, the other held at eye level, finger pointed in expressive demonstration. King Zhumu sat on his throne, watching the argument with keen interest. Princess Cuifen, she noticed, was not present.

The lemony scent of Budai was unmistakable now that she'd identified it. She began searching for him with her eyes, finally finding him leaning against a pillar at the side of the room.

"You are outsiders here," Kexin said, each word clipped with anger. "Do you not realize that if not for the graciousness of our compassionate king, you'd be struggling to survive in the wilds? We have provided your people with food and shelter at great cost. But we uphold the virtue of hospitality. Surely an alliance between Sajinau and Sihui would be of benefit."

"We are not saying that there *cannot* be one," said General Tzu placatingly. "Our people have labored to help fortify this city against Echion's fleet. We sleep in tents and barns and do not complain of how the merchants treat us. The prince and his ensign have only just arrived. They don't understand your society yet."

"But their arrival changes the nature of the situation," Kexin said. "The phoenix-chosen and the crown prince of Sajinau are both here.

This changes the very tide. Let us come to an agreement. We know not how long we have before Echion attacks us. His attacks are sudden and deadly. We'll do better if we're united."

The lemony smell grew stronger as Budai stepped away from the pillar and advanced to the front of the throne room. "And what have you against an alliance with Wangfujing if the prince is unwilling? My case should be equally strong. We are both the second sons of our fathers, but my father chose *me* as king of Wangfujing." She smelled his fiery determination, and she realized that he had been lobbying for this throughout the winter. Mieshi had been right. He wanted to marry the princess, the mere thought of which brought Bingmei another strong feeling of revulsion.

Kexin shot him an angry look. "An alliance with Sajinau is far more likely to bring glory and honor to Sihui. You trade in frogs and scorpions, Budai."

"I have collected far greater wealth than you know," said Budai, his eyes glinting. "In my treasury are meiwood weapons of every sort. I've collected them for years!"

Another man from Sihui, whom Bingmei didn't know, scoffed at that. "Which Echion has undoubtedly claimed for himself and his own warriors! You have nothing."

"I have magic still," said Budai. His hand reached into his pocket, and Bingmei wondered what it held. Did he have a relic like she did? "How do you think I survived the attack in Wangfujing? Not all my treasures were hidden in the palace. Don't mock me. I have performed great service for this kingdom."

"You have," said King Zhumu in a calm, patient voice. "And your suit of my daughter is not without merit."

The others hushed as the king rose from the throne. "I encouraged my servants to question you all, your motives, your intentions. You are all foreigners to Sihui and have no true allegiance. You reveal much by what you do *not* say." He turned his gaze on Bingmei, who still stood near the entrance. "Welcome, chosen one. Would you grant your consent for Prince Rowen to marry my daughter? Perhaps this argument has been for naught."

All eyes turned to her, the attention flaying her already raw nerves. She didn't want to argue as the others had been—she hated the feelings it produced. And yet, she couldn't give the king what he wanted. He confounded her, and the room was too much a morass of emotions and smells for her to get a good sense of him. The only thing she knew about him was that he wasn't riled in the least. His carefully combed hair and immaculate garb made him seem impressive, but who was the man behind the mask of calm?

She could not release the prince until she knew what the king wanted with him. Besides which, she didn't think it fair to force anyone into a marriage they found disagreeable . . . and there was that little voice inside her that didn't want Rowen to marry. At least not yet. But she pushed the feeling away again. They were here to help the city stand strong against Echion, and nothing could be allowed to distract her from her mission.

It was the only way she could make amends, somewhat, for what had happened in Sajinau.

"Gracious king," Bingmei said, bowing to him with respect. "We have only just arrived. I think it would be . . . premature to work on any arrangement so soon." An idea struck her mind. "We came here as your servants, not your equals. The might of Sajinau has fallen, as has the splendor of Wangfujing." She gave Budai a pointed look, showing him that she acknowledged him. "Let us serve you first. We will do all we can to help Sihui avoid the fate that we have suffered."

She heard a few murmured grumbles at her words, but King Zhumu lifted a finger and silenced them.

King Zhumu cocked his head to one side. "Wisely spoken, Bingmei," he said. "The matter will not be settled at present. I will hear no more on this subject for now."

Budai gritted his teeth, smoldering with anger, and gave Bingmei an accusatory look. But then he mastered himself and acknowledged the king with a respectful nod.

King Zhumu opened both palms upward. "Serve the feast."

At his command, one of the far doors was pulled open, and the smell of spices and cooked fish and rice and a variety of different sauces floated into the room, mixing with the smells of those who had been arguing so recently. In the commotion that followed, Rowen made it to her side, giving her a grateful look.

"Why did you not speak for yourself?" Bingmei asked him in a low voice. Mieshi arched her eyebrows at the prince. "Why not tell Zhumu no?"

"I told you before," he said, smelling once again like freshly baked bread. He gently touched her arm, his fingers pleasantly warm. "We are bound, you and I. What could I say without your permission? I've promised myself to you already." His look became more intense and so did the smell coming from him. "And besides, I don't want to marry her."

"If she marries Budai instead, he'll get his revenge on us," Bingmei said, trying to ignore the way the smell made her feel. Trying to pretend, both to herself and to him, that he didn't affect her at all.

"Possibly," Rowen answered, but he didn't sound particularly concerned. Damanhur gestured to him, and he pulled away with one final look over his shoulder. The two walked off together.

Mieshi gave Bingmei a curious look, one that seemed not only perplexed but also disturbed. She had noticed their interplay. "Is there more between you than I supposed?" she asked quietly.

Bingmei felt angered by what Rowen had said. She'd told him before that she didn't share his sentiments, yet he still acted as if she might. It was confusing, and so were her emotions. And now Mieshi had noticed. The discomfort of the position flamed her anger higher.

"Now is not the time to answer you." But the answer she withheld was *no.* There wasn't anything more between them, and there couldn't be.

They walked into the other room, both deep in thought. The feast had been arrayed on long tables assembled in the feasting hall. The air held an aroma of heavy spices, punctuated by the pleasant and shrill tones of musical instruments, which combined into a sweet assault on the senses. The tunes were haunting, without any specific melody, just a series of notes both high and low, the lead of the music switching between different kinds of reed flutes and an instrument that seemed to be made from small gourds.

They were guided to pillows on the floor, and the servants bustled around, bringing them steaming dishes of fish and fowl, black rice, and tubers soaked in sauce. As the meal was served, Bingmei prepared herself for the spiciness of the fare, but the dishes were still excessively hot. She reached for a cup of water, and it wasn't until she brought it to her lips that she discovered the water must have come directly from the hot spring—it was scalding.

She and her compatriots ate slowly, all save Marenqo, who was more used to the spicy food, and she watched in disbelief as he sampled each of the various dishes and spoke to his hosts in their language. The feast went on well into the night, with new dishes brought out at intervals, accompanied by fruits she'd never seen before, all displayed in an appealing manner. Even the fruits had spices put on them, but thankfully the spices were more savory than hot, and she enjoyed how they eased the burn in her mouth.

After the feast was finally over, Kexin approached her with King Zhumu's orders. Her ensign would sleep in the northwest courtyard of the palace. Cots and bedrolls had been assembled for them, and fresh water would be made available for them to drink and bathe in. In return, her ensign would be responsible for patrolling that quarter of the palace. She needed to ensure the walls had sentries at all times, day and night.

Bingmei thanked Kexin and asked Mieshi to make the assignments, instructing her to save the least favorable watch duties for Bingmei—Kunmia had always taken them when she was their leader. Mieshi left to make the arrangements, and it surprised no one in the ensign when Damanhur followed her.

Bingmei watched their hosts in their fancy clothes, and despite the borrowed clothing she wore, she felt a piercing awareness that she wasn't one of them.

She smelled Jiaohua before she felt him appear at her side.

"What is it?" she asked, staring at the crowded hall.

"Muxidi wants to see you," he said.

She could have denied the request, but something told her the confrontation was inevitable and they were supposed to meet again. And she was so very tired of fighting fate at every turn.

被埋葬的世界

The dungeon beneath the palace was dank and fetid, studded with the stone arches supporting the weight of the palace. Bracketed oil torches illuminated the darkness, but shadows writhed everywhere. It surprised her to see so many people down below, sleeping on cots. These weren't prisoners. It showed her how unprepared the city had been for the influx of refugees. She saw little children hunkering down close to their parents and could smell the fear coming from them. The fear of the dark, the unknown future, the enemy who might attack them again. She clenched her fists and shuddered as she passed through the huddled masses.

There's one way you could help, a traitorous voice whispered in her ear.

But she was a warrior. She couldn't just lie down and die for them. She'd rather fight.

Jiaohua and a Sihuian guard led her down the cramped corridor, past more cots and cells that contained sleeping prisoners. At the end of the hall, they arrived at a cell with only one captive. He was sitting on the floor, one knee up, his black silk outfit filthy. His gaze shifted up to meet hers. A scraggly beard covered his cheeks and mouth, and his hair was also unkempt and stringy, hanging in clumps across his face.

He looked terrible, beaten, but he smelled like a man sick with shame, regret, and the torture of self-recrimination. This was Muxidi, the once-fearsome Qiangdao leader. He was broken inside. There was no anger churning in him now. No ambition. It was all guttered out.

He stared at her. She stared back.

"I felt you coming," he said hoarsely. "I feared it was the beginning of madness, yet here you are."

Bingmei approached the bars, which were pitted and stained. The air had a sulfurous smell to it.

"You wanted to see me," she said, wondering what he would say. She had hoped to never see him again.

"Yes, I've wanted to see you," he said. "I've tortured myself day and night, wondering if it might happen. Yet here you are, and I find I cannot speak the words. I've wanted to speak them. Why is that? Why can I not say them now?"

"He's raving," Jiaohua muttered. "Say what you wished to say, or I'll take her away and never bring her back down in this muck hole. Say it, you coward! You told me. Now say it to *her*."

Muxidi's eyes became feverish. He looked up at her, and she felt a little whisper of hope before anguish choked it out. Clenching his fists, he beat his own head. "Say it! Just say it! How is it that some words can choke? I . . . am . . . sorry. There. There. It works now." He stopped beating himself with his fists and started banging his head back against the wall. "I am sorry. I am sorry!" he nearly shrieked.

Bingmei stared at him, aghast, her heart surging with violent and conflicting emotions. She wished she were anywhere but deep in this dank dungeon.

"I murdered . . . I did . . . I murdered your family. Your parents. They are both dead because of me. You saw me kill your grandfather . . . you saw it. And I didn't care. I would have killed you too had you not bounded away by some infernal bit of magic. I could have killed a child. I would have." His voice cracked. "Back then I was consumed by a sickness. By a need for revenge because of what your grandfather did."

Bingmei groaned. She couldn't help it. She gripped the bars. "If you speak ill of my grandfather, if you try to taint my memory of him . . ."

"I won't! I won't! I swear it on my two souls, one of which is already sold to the Dragon of Night. I won't. I won't." He started gasping, choking for breath.

Bingmei thought him the most piteous man she'd ever seen. Tears welled up in her eyes.

"It was all in my mind. He . . . he never did me wrong. Not truly. He sent me away from the quonsuun. Banished me because of my pride. My conceit. He had killed my grandfather in a competition by accident and took me in because of his guilt and to make amends. I used the leopard banner for my own purposes. To fight in competitions as my grandfather once did. All for the sake of glory, to prove I was better than him! How our minds savor the things they *want* to believe. The glory wasn't for him. It was for *me*. Master Jiao saw through my self-deception, and he rightly banished me from his quonsuun when I injured someone who had quit the fight." His lips twitched as he spoke the words. Then he hung his head low, and his greasy, unkempt hair covered his face. "But I believed at the time he had wronged me and my grandfather. And I wanted revenge. If I was unworthy to be part of it, then no one was worthy. I vowed in my heart I'd destroy it. And I did. Oh how I did," he groaned. He fell silent, his shoulders shuddering with sobs.

After an immense pause, he lifted his head. "You should have killed me. You were entitled to exact revenge on me. You chose not to. Why? How could you *not*?"

It felt like a hand had gripped her throat. Until this very moment, she'd doubted her decision to let him live. But now, taking in the depth of his suffering, she knew at the core of her being that Kunmia Suun had been right all along. Was this alone not evidence that revenge did not satisfy? That the dregs of its cup were the bitterest to drink?

She clenched the bars with her hands, pressing her forehead against them. She sorrowed for this man, for the ruin he'd made of his life. In her mind, the only reason he hadn't committed suicide was because he dreaded the Grave Kingdom.

The words came slowly to her, but they did come. "Because of what my master taught me. She warned that revenge would never heal, only harm. And I see in you that it is true."

He rushed to the bars in an act of utter wildness. She was so shocked by his sudden lunge that she pushed herself back as he slammed into the metal. Jiaohua kicked him through the bars, making him grunt in pain and sink to his knees.

"Forgive me," Muxidi pleaded, groaning, his eyes full of anguish.

"You dare ask her this?" Jiaohua said and then spat on him. He looked like he was about to do further violence, but Bingmei grabbed his arm and pulled him back.

"Back away," Bingmei warned. She'd struck him before. They both knew she could.

Jiaohua's frown was terrible. He shifted it to Muxidi, staring at him with daggers in his eyes. "You have no right to ask for it!"

"Forgive me," Muxidi pleaded, gasping, grunting.

Bingmei walked back to the bars. She heard the former Qiangdao sobbing. Her suffering at losing her parents, her beloved grandfather, had scarred her deeply. But this . . . this regret and despair were infinitely worse. Her wounds had eventually healed. His were still oozing.

She'd never smelled so much sorrow and regret. Nothing she did was likely to change it. There was simply too much.

She squatted by the bars, bringing their faces level with each other.

She reached through the bars and stroked his tangled hair. "I do forgive you," she said. She wasn't sure how much she meant it, but seeing someone in such agony moved her. If he'd been the least bit deceptive, she would have withheld her comfort.

His sobs stopped as he lifted his head, eyes full of disbelief. A little spark had kindled inside him. It smelled like candle wax.

"You . . . you do?" he whispered thickly.

She stroked his head again and rose, nodding once. Then she turned and walked away, thinking about the princess's bathing chamber.

Would any number of baths rid her of the memory of such smells?

But her heart felt a peculiar sense of lightness. As if a heavy stone she'd been carrying inside her had been left behind in the prison. She hadn't expected that.

Jiaohua grumbled as he walked next to her. "You didn't have to—"

"Just shut up, Jiaohua," she said.

CHAPTER THIRTEEN

Unassailable

Birdsong awoke Bingmei the next morning. There were different breeds in the western rim, and their sounds jarred her awake. Were they finches? It sounded so. She lay on a pallet on the floor of the courtyard they'd been assigned to defend. Although she'd gone to sleep sweating after performing her night duty, she felt pleasantly cool now. She lifted herself up on her arm, surveying the sleeping bodies scattered around the area. At least it wasn't the cave anymore. Or the thick forest.

Bingmei stood and walked through the courtyard, enjoying the subtle breeze against her red silk jacket and pants. The wide sleeves let in the morning air, almost cool enough to make her shiver. Breathing in deeply, she smelled the freshness of the air, savoring the lack of emotion since everyone else was still resting. She walked by a huddle of sleeping students. She felt remarkably light, as if a weight had been lifted from her heart. She felt more peaceful and solemn. More attuned to her body. Was she a different person today than she'd been the night before?

Gazing around the courtyard, she realized there was enough space for her to practice a form, so she went back to her pallet and retrieved the Phoenix Blade from its scabbard. After putting on her shoes, she walked to the far edge of the courtyard. Marenqo waved down to her from the wall where he squatted, hand gripping his staff.

Bingmei started with the salute position and then launched into the routine called dragon straight sword. As she performed the movements, she felt an inner peace settle within her, and she glided through the form. She'd practiced it so many times it felt like part of her now.

When she finished the form, her breath coming faster now from the exercise, a strange feeling came over her. She set down the Phoenix Blade and started on a hand form next. Her body was invigorated, her mind alert, but a strange feeling bloomed in her heart. It felt as if she'd done this before, here in the courtyard in Sihui. She hadn't, of course, but the sense of nostalgia was overpowering.

The feeling swelled as Bingmei started a new form. She dropped into low stances, swinging her legs around in circles that would trip opponents. Her body wove and ducked, her arms coming around like sweeping wings. Her fists were closed, but she noticed that her pointer finger was bent so that the knuckle protruded, her thumb pressed into the crease. She'd never done this movement before, but power thrummed through her, and she sensed that striking someone with that knuckle would be incredibly painful for them. She leaped and turned midair, landing gracefully, then dropped again, sweeping low. It was a complicated form, and it felt every bit as much a part of her as dragon straight sword did. Only she'd never done it before. It felt as if it had been hiding inside her.

At the end of the form, she smelled Mieshi's curiosity. When she turned, the other woman was coming toward her, her brow wrinkled. She gave off a hint of admiration.

"What form was that?" she asked.

Bingmei straightened after her final salute, a sense of belonging in her heart. She shook her head as Mieshi reached her. "I don't know."

"I've seen all the forms taught in the school," Mieshi said. "I've mastered most of them, but I've not seen that one before. It looked like you were a . . . bird."

"It's called five birds," Bingmei suddenly said, the compulsion to speak startling her.

"Would you teach it to me?" Mieshi asked.

Bingmei nodded and started teaching Mieshi the form. It was the first time she had taught Mieshi anything.

被埋葬的世界

General Tzu took Bingmei and Jiaohua on a tour of Sihui's defenses before midday, while the heat was still manageable. They walked down the main street, passing through the merchants' stalls, and he showed them the heavily guarded bulwarks. There was a wide bay leading to Sihui, which would be easy for Echion's fleet of enormous ships to pass through, but the river itself was a different matter. Defenses had been constructed to block the river, which she'd seen the previous day, but she hadn't grasped the magnitude of the endeavor. People labored day and night to construct walls of stone and dirt and timber to protect the city.

General Tzu had not been idle during the season of the Dragon of Night.

"We learned at Sajinau," the general said, "that stone docks lay beneath the waters, giving the ships a place to land. After searching the banks here, we've found the same docks beneath the water here. We have used them as a foundation for our walls."

"Echion won't have a solid place to land," said Jiaohua, nodding in approval.

"No, he'll be forced to disembark farther away from the city and march on Sihui. To counter this, we have troops hidden in the woods that will attack and retreat. We want him to pay for every li that he tries to claim."

"We're better prepared this time," said Jiaohua with a smirk.

General Tzu shook his head no. "Hardly. We're still quite vulnerable. We have escape routes set up should we need to abandon the city and food stores set up in outposts farther away."

"What if Echion strikes from behind?" Bingmei asked him. "The way we came." They had to move aside to dodge a cart carrying stones to a group of workers.

"To address that risk, we have scouts in the woods," General Tzu said. "Your ensign is the only group that has come from that direction since the season began. And you were spotted long before you reached the guards on the bridge. Echion won't be able to hide an army from us. If they come that way, we'll see them days in advance."

"So you're prepared either way," said Jiaohua. He was silent for a moment, as if considering the situation, then made an urgent gesture. "But what about the killing fog? He used it to destroy the army at Sajinau!"

Although General Tzu's expression did not shift, Bingmei smelled the fiery scent of anger beneath his calm. He was still furious about his loss in Sajinau, but something else lay beneath it. Despite all the defenses he'd built, she could smell the unease within him. He didn't believe it would be enough.

"That is where Muxidi has been most helpful," replied General Tzu.

"How so?" Bingmei pressed.

They reached the first bridgework, and the general gestured for them to follow him up. She'd mostly heard the Sihuian dialect in the streets, but now that they were on the wall, amidst the laborers, she heard her own tongue. Bingmei could smell the fear of the people but also the hope General Tzu had given them. She caught a few whispers, and while she couldn't distinguish all the words, which were often mumbled or spoken low, she could breathe in the sentiment. Calmness, in the scent of dragon fruit, seemed to radiate from the people General Tzu passed.

They reached the top of the massive bridge straddling the wide river, arches extending into the water on either side to support it. The height of the new bridge had been calculated so it would allow for smaller junks to pass beneath, but not one of the massive ships Echion had used at Sajinau. As they stood midriver, gazing down at the vast waterway, Bingmei saw other bridges in various stages of construction. But would it be enough? Could the bridges stop a huge ship that tried to crush its way through? Or could Echion bring some other magic to bear that would demolish these efforts?

"What about the fog?" Jiaohua prompted. "What did Muxidi tell you?"

General Tzu folded his arms, gazing down the river. He'd chosen a spot where there were no workers and they could speak in private. Roof shelters protected them from the burning sun. "He said the fog didn't affect the Qiangdao because Echion protected his armies with one of the Immortal Words."

Bingmei stared at him in interest.

The general pursed his lips. "Most of what we've learned has come through our spies. When Echion defeats a population, he establishes a series of laws."

"The Iron Rules," Jiaohua said.

The general nodded. "Indeed. They are written. He assigns the people a role to play in society. The smartest ones, usually the courtiers, are taught to read an ancient language. It is a series of sigils, or what Muxidi called glyphs. They represent different words, but they can also be combined to form new words. They're painted on slats of wood or bamboo and bound together so they can be folded."

Written words were powerful. Bingmei had first seen that in Fusang, but the lesson had been repeated again and again: Jidi Majia perfecting his ability to write. Liekou felling Mieshi by tracing a glyph on her. Rowen, too, had talked about the power of the glyphs.

"How does this protect a soldier?" Jiaohua asked in confusion.

"Muxidi said the officers are taught a particular glyph. The glyph is drawn on the back of the soldier in ink mixed with blood." He turned to face them, his lips firm. "As long as they have the glyph on their back," he said in a low voice, "the fog will not kill them."

Jiaohua's eyes blazed with eagerness. "What is it? What does it look like?" Everyone was afraid of the sleeping death caused by the fog.

General Tzu shook his head. "Echion changes the glyph frequently," he said. "He uses the fog to destroy his enemies and keep his own officers from rising against him. He knows the Immortal Words. We do not. My strategy, should Echion attack us, is to use some of the Jingcha to capture an enemy soldier. We see what glyph is on his back and then paint the same one on our soldiers. That way, the fog won't decimate us as it did our last army."

Bingmei was impressed by his wisdom.

"How do you know Muxidi wasn't lying, eh?" Jiaohua said. "What if he was giving you false hope?"

The general turned to Bingmei. "I was hoping you could confirm his words. I shared this information with Prince Rowen last night, and he told me that you have a gift, Bingmei. That you know when someone is lying. If you could confirm what Muxidi told us, then it would further strengthen my belief that we actually stand a chance to defend ourselves." He paused, looking back over the river. "If not, all of these walls have been built in vain."

"I will ask him," Bingmei said, "but after I speak to him, I would like to leave the city and check on Quion. He has a somewhat tame snow leopard and didn't want to risk bringing it into the city yesterday. He's camping on the outskirts."

"I know," the general said. "Our scouts found him by his cooking fire yesterday."

"Is he all right?" Bingmei pressed.

"We knew he was part of your ensign, so we left him alone. It doesn't matter to me if he stays out there. At least he's not adding to the overcrowding. I've ordered rations to be sent to him each day."

"Thank you, General," Bingmei said. She paused, then added, "My priority is to help defend Sihui against Echion. Wherever he attacks, I want to know so that my ensign can help."

"If he attacks, we'll all be needed to defend. There's no doubt of that. But you are still an important factor in this whether you intend to help or no. I just ask that you do not go anywhere alone. Jiaohua, you must always be sure she has a bodyguard."

Bingmei bristled. "I don't *need* a bodyguard, General."

He turned to face her, his lips firm and impassive. "I wonder something, Bingmei," he said. "I wonder how many will have to die before you accept your fate. Jidi Majia told me that the sacrifice must be willing. If it were otherwise, believe me that you'd already be bound in a cart heading to the Death Wall. No matter what I do to defend Sihui, I fear I will lose. The art of war teaches me, my dear, to rely not on the possibility the enemy will *not* come, but on ensuring we are ready to receive him. We can't ensure he will not attack, but we can do what we must to make our position unassailable." He sighed. "I think he's made Fusang unassailable. I wish I could do the same for Sihui."

As he spoke, she remembered the sacrifice Prince Juexin had made for his people. It made part of her stomach shrivel to think what would happen in Sihui if they lost. She couldn't bear to have the guilt of even more souls on her shoulders.

被埋葬的世界

By the time they'd finished inspecting the defenses with General Tzu and returned, it was the hottest time of the day, and sweat dripped down Bingmei's neck and cooled against her body beneath the silk. The food they'd stopped to eat was too spicy for her, making her stomach ache to be filled with something that didn't burn.

The emotions she held back burned enough.

She checked on the ensign, and after finding all was well, went with Jiaohua back down to the dungeon. The shade of the fortress made it cooler within than without, but she suspected the hot spring was beneath the palace itself because the air felt almost too wet to breathe.

After passing the dispossessed families again, they found Muxidi pacing within his cell. As soon as he saw her, he rushed to the bars, gripping them tightly, his eyes almost feverish.

"What is it? Is he coming?" he gasped with dread. The sharp scent of worry wafted off him.

"Do you know something?" Bingmei asked him with suspicion.

He grunted, looking away. "I am bound to the Phoenix Blade, not to him," said Muxidi.

"Talk sense, man," complained Jiaohua.

"Even if I spoke it, would you understand it?" said Muxidi with a taunting edge.

Jiaohua took a menacing step forward, but Bingmei interposed herself. "Do you know he's coming?" she asked him again.

He gazed at her, agitated still. "Now that you're here, yes, I do think he's coming. But I cannot see into his mind."

"Can he see into yours?" Bingmei asked.

"I don't know. He knows things he shouldn't. Maybe these palaces he built are his eyes, his ears. Who can say? But he's fixed on finding you, Bingmei. He *must* find you, for you are the only one who can bring back Xisi, his queen."

Bingmei took a step closer. He smelled of sweat and the taint of his murders, but it was a softer smell today. Muxidi started to pace again.

"Why?" Bingmei asked.

"He cannot achieve his full power without her. You remember the marble slab in Fusang. You saw it, just as I did. There are *two* dragons.

The male and the female. Both are needed to achieve his conquest. You were supposed to awaken them both when you came to Fusang. Yet . . . you ran away. You sensed, somehow, his true nature." He paused, eyeing her. "No matter what he does to threaten you, do *not* let her rise from the dead. He will become twice as powerful."

Bingmei had no intention of making the same mistake twice. "Thank you for the warning. Will you speak truthfully if I ask you something?"

"I will not lie to you, Bingmei," he said, his voice growing more humble. "Whatever task you assign me, I will do it. Whatever penalty I must pay. You have a claim on me. I will submit to any revenge you impose."

"I only ask that you be truthful," she said, coming closer. His hands were filthy, as were his face and his unkempt hair. "You told General Tzu that Echion paints a sigil on the back of his warriors. A sigil done in ink and blood."

"Echion doesn't do it," he said wryly. "He trains his officers, and *we* marked our men." He chuckled softly. "Oh how he'll torture me now. He'll punish me in the Grave Kingdom too. Yes, it's true. A blood mark. A sign to the killing fog that we are not to be harmed. By the blood, we are saved."

"Whose blood?" Bingmei asked.

Muxidi frowned. "It doesn't matter to Echion. Blood is blood to him. And he can change the glyph whenever he wishes. No one is safe from his treachery. Not even his own army."

CHAPTER FOURTEEN

Broken-Hearted

Water sloshed against the side of the bamboo raft. The man directing it extended his pole, catching the edge of the stone wharf to slow their momentum. Insects buzzed in Bingmei's ears, but the lotion they'd been given in the palace was keeping them away. The afternoon sun blazed down, but thankfully the shade from the raft's roof helped.

Looking back, she saw the arched bridge with the soldiers on it. They, too, were taking shelter from the sun. Jiaohua nodded for her to get off the boat, impatience coming off him in sour waves. He had insisted on coming with her to visit Quion. Not because he cared for the young fisherman, or because he was overly worried about her, but because he wanted to win his way back into General Tzu's good graces.

Whether he wanted to be there or not, Jiaohua did his job effectively and looked for threats where there weren't any. But she didn't go anywhere without the Phoenix Blade strapped to her back and her staff in hand. She knew how to defend herself, but the general's words had made an impression on her.

She rose from the woven-reed bench and walked to the edge of the raft as their boatman tied it off at the makeshift pier. He would await their return to bring them back to Sihui.

Bingmei and Jiaohua entered the long grass, the sun beating down on them. While it was not yet the peak of summer, it felt like it. Sweat oozed from her pores, but the light silk clothing helped keep her cool. The grass hissed as they walked through it, the heavy tops swaying as they passed. She grazed her palms across the tips as they ventured closer to the woods. Before they reached the edge, she smelled Quion, and then he appeared from the trees, a gentle smile on his face in greeting.

"He would never make it in the Jingcha," said her companion gruffly.

"And you wouldn't make it far as a fisherman," she replied, waving to Quion. "Stay here. I don't want you listening to our conversation."

He grunted. "I'm supposed to stand out here in the heat? Are you trying to cook me like an egg?"

"You could jump into the river," she suggested.

He hissed in contempt and turned around. "Have your little tryst, then. I don't care."

He was only trying to rile her, which meant she'd succeeded in riling him first.

"Quion is my friend, Jiaohua. Not everyone is as seedy as you imagine them to be."

"Most are," he countered over his shoulder.

She continued walking through the grass to meet Quion. The snow leopard crouched next to him, its tail swishing in the foliage.

"It hasn't left you yet?" Bingmei said.

"I don't think she wants to leave," he said with a sigh. He shielded his eyes from the sun as he looked up. "There's plenty of game for her, but she keeps coming back to my camp to stay with me. Come into the woods. It's cooler beneath the trees. I like your new clothes."

He walked her back to the shelter of the trees. He gave off the same satisfied smell as when he'd cooked an especially enjoyable fish dinner. There were no intruding smells, not even that of Jiaohua. They were totally alone.

Inside the trees, she found his makeshift camp. He had a fire ring made of stones, a blanket tied up at an angle for shelter, and a broken log he'd brought over for a seat.

"Please, sit," he said, waving at it, and then dropped down beside her once she was settled.

"You have more space here than we do at the palace," she said, bumping his shoulder.

"Is it crowded?"

"Very much. We've been given a courtyard in the corner of the stronghold. That is our position to guard against intruders. King Zhumu and General Tzu are busy strengthening the defenses, preparing for Echion's fleet to come through. They've barricaded the river so that those large ships can't pass. At least, we hope they can't."

"What is King Zhumu like?" Quion asked with genuine interest. "Is he like King Budai?"

"They are very different. And speaking of Budai, he is here in Sihui. This is where he sought shelter after he left the quonsuun."

"He didn't leave in a good mood," Quion said. "Is he still very angry?"

"Quite. Zhumu has a daughter named Cuifen—his only child by the looks of it. Budai has been trying to woo her, but Zhumu would rather strike an alliance with Rowen. Rowen isn't interested. It's all a mess."

"That's . . . that's . . ." Then he shook his head, at a loss for words.

"Nothing's been settled, and for the moment we are welcome here. General Tzu said the city is full of refugees from Sajinau. They are treated unequally. But then, if the situation were reversed, would Sajinau have treated the survivors very well?"

"Probably not," said Quion.

"Have you eaten well? Are you hungry?" she asked.

He shook his head. "They bring rations every day, but it's hard to eat their food. I've found bog bilberries all over these woods. The river is warmer here. The fish are fat and lazy. You can almost grab them. There's plenty to eat, and the mosquitoes aren't too much."

The snow leopard, which had been prowling around them, came up in front of Quion and then dropped onto its haunches so that he could scratch its neck, which he did. Bingmei shook her head. The beast would never leave now.

She tried to reach out and stroke it but heard a little purring growl from the back of its throat.

"Hush," said Quion, shrugging in apology. "I'm sorry."

"I think it remembers me stabbing it," she said. "Of course, it was trying to kill you at the time."

"It was just hungry, I think," said Quion. "Do you want some of the berries?"

"Yes!" said Bingmei.

Quion gave the leopard a little shove and then walked over to his pots, some of which were suspended from the branches by twine. One of them sat on a large rock, and he pulled off the lid, revealing an assortment of wild berries. He brought it back to the log and sat down, holding it between them.

Some of the berries were very tart, but the sweetness in others offered a balance.

"How is the food at the palace?" he asked. "Spicy?"

"This is much better," she said with a sigh. The food was better, it was true, but she also valued Quion's companionship. Friendship was something she'd always seen in other people, like the bond between Mieshi and Zhuyi before Zhuyi had died. Bingmei and Mieshi had become closer, but they would never reach that same depth of feeling. Something crucial stood between them: Bingmei could smell Mieshi's aversion for her pale skin and red hair, and they both knew it.

"Are you all right?" Quion asked her.

Maybe the look on her face had revealed too much. She tried to smile, but there was a prick of pain in her heart. The pain of never quite being accepted. Well, except by Quion and Kunmia.

And Rowen.

"Can I tell you something?" Bingmei asked.

"Of course. Anything," he said, his brow narrowing with concern.

"Remember that dream I had? The one I told you about?"

"The one about your mother and the Grave Kingdom?"

She reached for his hand and squeezed it. "I'm afraid, Quion. I'm afraid of dying. It's the end. There's no coming back. Isn't it? I mean, Echion has found a way to keep coming back. How is that possible? If I hadn't seen it with my own eyes, I wouldn't have believed it. But here . . . there . . . it doesn't matter. He rules both worlds. In my vision, I could feel him watching us. A huge metal dragon loomed over the street. People were fearful, lost. They seemed . . . incomplete." She bit her lip. She was constantly trying to prove herself with the others. Although she didn't understand why, she felt she could be herself with Quion. She could be vulnerable.

He stared down at their entwined hands. A new smell came from him, something warm and sweet, like a raisin cake.

"I'm afraid for you too," he said simply. "I don't want you to die."

She leaned against him, resting her head on his shoulder, and stared at the gray ashes of the dead fire he'd built. In the end, all became ash and dust.

What was the point of all this struggle when it would end the same way regardless?

被埋葬的世界

They spent the better part of the afternoon talking. Bingmei revealed her burdens—her fears about the future as well as her determination to evade her fate—and felt better for having done so. She even gave him a kiss on the cheek and told him she hoped the leopard would wander off so he could join them. He grinned and said he wasn't in a rush to join the crowded city. Or to lose his new friend. When she left, she found Jiaohua dicing with the guards and the river guide on the bridge. In the few hours he'd spent with them, he'd already picked up some of their language and was joking and teasing with them as she approached. The sun sank lower, turning the sky a vibrant orange.

They took the raft downriver to the city, which was once again hazy because of the humid air. When she arrived at the courtyard, she immediately smelled tension in the air. Everyone was doing their duty, but the smell hung over them like a dark cloud.

"What happened, Marenqo?" she said, pulling him aside.

"Mieshi and Damanhur had a falling out," he replied quietly. "It was rather loud and quite unseemly. He left in a huff. Mieshi started crying, if you can believe it. She's calmer now, but you missed quite a storm."

That explained the ill feelings. And because there were so many witnesses, everyone else had been infected by the ugliness between them.

Bingmei sighed. "Did Kunmia often deal with things like this?" she wondered aloud.

"Never. Everyone was always on their best behavior with her. I think it's a sign of your bad leadership."

"Marenqo," she sighed, giving him a sharp look.

He smirked. "Yes. Quite often. Thankfully, I never have any problems."

"Except for being hungry all the time."

"True. That is a problem. I miss the cuisine from our part of the world. But there's something to be appreciated about a good meal under any circumstances." He looked beyond her. "Ah, another storm is coming your way."

She smelled Rowen's roiling emotions before she turned to look at him. His cheeks were flushed, his eyes penetrating. He smelled of *jealousy*.

"Can I speak with you, Bingmei?" He shot a glance at Marenqo, then added, "Alone?"

Marenqo quirked his brow, shrugging. "I'm just a potted tree. Ignore me."

"Is there a place you know that is private?" she asked Rowen.

"Yes. Will you come with me?"

Bingmei nodded, already feeling the relief of the afternoon fading. They entered the palace, which was crowded with servants and officers bustling around.

"I heard about Damanhur and Mieshi," she said as they walked down the corridor. She didn't want to address his feelings and sought to change the topic. "Did you see them argue?"

"No," he answered. "But they've fought before and will mend the rift eventually. What I would speak of concerns us."

"How so?"

"I'd rather speak in a private place," he said.

"This might not be private," she said, waving a hand at the crowded corridor, "but hardly anyone can understand what we're saying."

"It's not that," he stammered, trying to subdue his feelings, which were churning violently within him.

"What, then?" Perhaps she was being unfair, but if he insisted on talking to her in such a manner, she would prefer for him to be direct.

"I don't think I can stay here much longer," he said in a low, tight voice.

That surprised her. She'd expected him to express his jealousy.

"We just got here, Rowen," she said. "And where else could we go that is safer? If we're going to take a stand against Echion, why not here? Tzu's defenses might be sufficient. This is our best chance."

A servant shoved his way between them. Bingmei sensed his contempt—they weren't from Sihui, and so he considered himself above them. Rowen glared at the man, but he motioned for her to continue walking.

"Where are we going?" she pressed.

"Anywhere but here," he said.

She stopped, and he kept going a few paces before turning back to look at her.

"I've been gone all afternoon," she said. "I need to help smooth over the ill feelings in the ensign. Can we not talk later? Please?"

His lips pressed tightly together. He looked down, breathing out roughly, and said, "And what about *my* ill feelings?"

"What do you have to say?" she said, smelling the bite of jealousy again.

"You know all of our hearts. You already know," he said, coming closer. Someone nearly collided with him but veered away in time.

She looked him in the eye. "I know, but why shouldn't you say it? I can tell you're jealous but not why."

"You truly don't know?" His voice and his grunt betrayed his disbelief.

It struck her that she'd smelled jealousy on him once before, after she'd spoken to Quion by the fire. She looked at him incredulously. "You're jealous . . . of Quion?"

As soon as she said it, the smell grew a thousand times worse. His emotions flared inside him.

Her own feelings began to churn, anger and self-protection and resentment. "He's my friend, Rowen. My *friend*."

"I know," he said, his voice nearly biting in its intensity. "But you will not let *me* get that close to you." He took a small step toward her as he said it.

"How can I?" she replied. "He doesn't make any demands on me. Doesn't try to compel my affection. He offers friendship. Your feelings come with other expectations."

"You've never given them a chance. You've spent your whole life dealing with other peoples' emotions, but you bar your own. What I truly feel would frighten you," he whispered, "if I let it show a little more."

"Oh?" she asked, raising an eyebrow. "Prove it."

His emotions flared again, but he shuttered his expression, and the scent seemed to drift away on the wind. His forbearance was maddening. He was proving her point, but she didn't say so. "You have no idea, do you? No idea at all what it means to be one of the phoenix's chosen."

"You're talking in riddles again," she answered. "But I know one thing for certain: I'm the phoenix-chosen, not you."

"I know who you are. And I can't understand how that's so." He turned and walked away without her, leaving her in the crowded corridor even more perplexed than when she'd entered it with him.

CHAPTER FIFTEEN

Darkness Comes

Wounded feelings prevailed in the ensign, and not even Marenqo's humor could lift the darkening mood. Bingmei tried to offer a sense of calm, but she was unable to shift the tide, even after two days. Mieshi and Damanhur had not spoken to each other since the outburst, which Bingmei came to learn was about more than the words that had been spoken. Damanhur's injury had damaged more than his flesh, and as much as he loved Mieshi, there was some kind of tangled knot in their relationship. She made sure that they were not assigned guard duty together, but that did little to help.

The conflict between the couple had also worsened Mieshi's grief for Zhuyi. The scent of her suffering was as familiar as the smell of the spicy cooking that occurred day and night in Sihui.

Rowen had kept his distance from Bingmei since their confrontation in the hall, although he seemed to be getting along well with King Zhumu. He was called upon to discuss matters with the king while Bingmei, as leader of the ensign, was not. That rankled her, but she chose not to make an issue of it. General Tzu walked the defenses daily to inspect the progress, and sometimes he would invite her along to discuss the latest news.

On the third day following their arrival, he reported that ships had been sighted at anchor in Renxing, Echion's westernmost stronghold. Which of the western kingdoms he'd strike next was still up in the air, but the news of a fleet had been brought by no less than five fishermen.

"Where do you think Echion will attack next?" Bingmei asked. "Do you believe he'll strike here?"

The general pursed his lips, his eyes gazing down the hazy river. "Tuqiao is the most vulnerable to a sea attack," he said. "The island can be surrounded on all sides, and while there is a rib of mountains in the middle of it, those can be crossed as well. King Zhumu has received offers of aid from other kings should we be attacked—in return for his promise to come to their aid should they prove to be the target. Sihui does not have a strong merchant fleet. We'd be at a disadvantage if we have to go to their assistance."

Bingmei nodded in agreement. "But we can learn much from a battle."

"Indeed," he answered. "All the kingdoms he's conquered so far have been through trickery and cunning. Those are the weapons we must use against him. I advised King Zhumu that if another kingdom gets attacked, we can learn much if we try to aid them. I support it."

"We should. Why do you keep bringing me on these walks, General?" Bingmei asked.

He gave her a sidelong look. "Kunmia Suun entrusted you with her staff, and you also hold the Phoenix Blade. When Echion's forces strike us, we can anticipate them attacking with meiwood weapons. I've also heard that you are quite . . . nimble. That you have a magic that enables you to fly."

Yes, he did know a lot about her. The question was: Who had told him?

"I have a magic that I got from my grandfather. It's a little cricket made of meiwood, and yes, it enables me to leap distances. But the magic of flight is not something I can control. It comes and goes as it pleases. I can't command it."

Still leading the way, he climbed up the arch bridge that was done, the one that overlooked the other bridges downriver.

"It would be helpful if you did learn how to control it," he said.

"I agree," she answered. "But I can't rely on it."

"A pity," said the general. He folded his arms as he gazed toward the defenses. "After all the bridges are done, we will start building walls along the river's edges. There and there." He pointed with two fingers. "Every day we aren't attacked gives us more time to ready our defenses. This is time we didn't have before. If we can last through the Dragon of Dawn, then the weather will once again become our ally."

A familiar prickle went down Bingmei's spine. She stiffened.

The dragon was close; she knew it.

"General," she said urgently, touching his arm. She stared at the crowds of people thronging the streets, her eyes searching for anything out of place.

"What is it?" he asked.

Gooseflesh danced down her arms despite the oppressive heat.

"He's coming," she whispered, still searching the crowd. There was no smell yet, nothing else to alert her.

"Who?"

"Echion." She planted her palms on the edge of the railing and leaned forward. She took a deep, long breath of the swampy air, but there was nothing out of place.

General Tzu raised his hand to shield his eyes from the sun and stared downriver. "If any ships were coming, we'd be told of it in advance. I have spies all along the shore."

"I promise you, General. He is coming in person. I *feel* it." Her voice trembled as she spoke.

"Behind us? Where?" he said, turning around, looking back toward the far bridge where Quion was still encamped.

Bingmei raised her hand to her eyes, trying to block out the sun so she could better see.

A shadow fell over them.

Which was when she realized that the danger was coming from the one place they hadn't considered: above.

"Jump!" she shouted to General Tzu. She heard the leathery rustling of wings and a reptilian hissing as something enormous blotted out the sun and swooped down toward them. Looking up, she saw the hulking beast, the dragon made of shadows looming above them, its gaping maw lined with razor teeth. One of its claws was reaching, reaching . . .

Bingmei dug her hand into her pocket and stroked the meiwood cricket, the magic filling her legs just before the dragon's claws caught her. She heard General Tzu splash into the water at the same instant her own feet landed in a crouch on the cobblestone street.

Screams of terror erupted from the citizens of Sihui. Bingmei paused, one palm touching the warm stone, the other gripping the rune staff. She felt the urgent need to do something. To help. And yet, she remembered what Muxidi had said—if Echion captured her, he would force her to awaken the other dragon.

She couldn't let that happen.

The dragon let out an ear-splitting shriek that made her very soul tremble. Roused to action, she lunged through the crowd. They were all facing the bridge she'd just left behind, many of them cowering in terror.

The wings sounded like the sails of a fisherman's boat. She looked over her shoulder, saw it crouching atop the bridgework, the muscled torso hunched over, the huge wings fanning out. Its fiery eyes searched the crowd, and trails of smoke came from its reptilian nostrils.

In this moment, nothing about the dragon was smoky or ineffable—it was a colossus, the danger real and terrifying. Still, the stone arch held.

Bingmei's heart hammered violently behind her ribs as she bolted back toward the palace, her feet pounding the cobblestones. Those who weren't petrified with fear were now running with her.

Soldiers holding spears ran against the crowds, shouting for everyone to move out of the way. They were brave souls, but the dank, terrible smell of their fear permeated every gulp of air she took as she ran.

She looked back and saw the dragon open its maw. It spewed out a plume of black smoke, swiveling its head as it did so. The smoke didn't dispel, rather it grew thicker once it met the air.

Did this creature breathe out the killing fog? Were they all about to die?

Bingmei tried to outrun the black fog, but it quickly engulfed her. It didn't smell like anything, but once it struck, she couldn't even see a hand in front of her face. It was like being in the darkest cave in the depths of the Dongxue.

被埋葬的世界

Bingmei staggered in the darkness, trying to feel her way back to the palace. She'd been bumped into multiple times. No one could see anything, and the air was filled with sobs of fright and the pained cries of those who'd stumbled and fallen. The darkness was absolute. They'd all become blind.

Only through her gift of smell had Bingmei made it this far, for she knew when someone was before her or about to collide with her from behind. She walked with her staff held out, sweeping the air in front of her to avoid stumbling into inanimate objects.

She hoped she'd reach the end of the unnatural darkness, that she'd be able to see again. But it didn't seem to end. Finally, a familiar scent reached her—the food stands she'd passed after leaving the palace with General Tzu.

She kept going, the crowd becoming thicker and more panicked as she went. People sobbed in despair. Some cried to Zhumu to save them. The sheer terror in the air was almost as bad as the darkness. Her heart cringed with worry. They had not expected this. Nothing had prepared them for the dragon's coming.

Bingmei tried to summon the power of the rune staff. It was capable of dispelling magic, but it used magic to do so—enough that it could summon the killing fog. Still, she felt she had no other choice.

She felt the power of the staff as she invoked it, but nothing happened. It was powerless against the darkness.

Bingmei released her command, and the power drained from the staff again.

She bumped into several carts as she walked, hearing fruits thump to the stone ground. The caretakers had already fled. Carefully, she continued up the street, trying to judge how far she was from the gates. A few more steps, and she heard soldiers barking orders. Another few steps, and she reached the gates, her fingers closing around the metal. Other citizens were next to her, clamoring to be let in.

"No one may enter!" said a gruff voice ahead of her.

"I am Bingmei, servant to King Zhumu. Let me pass."

There was a pause, and then the man muttered, "Hurry. We can't let the others in. Come inside quickly!"

When the gate groaned open, Bingmei heard a stampede of steps as others tried to crowd their way into the palace. She was wrenched inside—one hand on her arm, the other behind her neck—and the gate was slammed shut behind her. The citizens continued to clamor, to shout and plead, speaking a language she didn't understand.

"You are Bingmei?" said the soldier holding her arm.

"Yes," she answered.

"Where is General Tzu?"

"He's in the river. Echion's come. Bring me to the king."

"I will."

She could smell his worry and fear, but he was a soldier and knew how to follow orders. They went together, walking along the path, and every so often he called out in the language of Sihui. She smelled others gathered there, heard the clank of weapons. But what could they do? What could they fight?

In the dark, they were just as likely to attack friends as they were enemies.

Although she'd learned to navigate the caves in the dark, she was still new to Sihui. The journey in utter blackness had her totally turned around, but she felt the change in the stone as they entered the palace, and all the natural smells were replaced by fear. It was so heavy and oppressive it made her eyes water.

Eventually, after dodging several servants, they reached the throne room.

"I have Bingmei," said the soldier.

"Where are you?" shouted King Zhumu in confusion. "Bingmei?"

"I'm here," she said.

"What is this darkness?" demanded the king. "Not even the sun can penetrate it."

"It comes from the Dragon of Night himself," she answered. She tried to smell who else was present, but raw fear pervaded everything. "Echion has come. He landed in his dragon form on the bridge, and this darkness came out of its jaws."

"Father?" Princess Cuifen said, her voice trembling.

"Then we evacuate the city," Zhumu said. "I will not allow my daughter to be taken as one of his thousand concubines! Go, Daughter. You will flee."

"But how will we escape? We cannot see!" she said.

The helplessness of the situation pressed in on Bingmei. "General Tzu was with me when the dragon attacked. He jumped into the river."

"He will live or die, then," said Zhumu. "We cannot help him. Bingmei, please take my daughter away from Sihui. I order your ensign to escort her to Dawanju. You must leave at once. Perhaps the entire world is smothered in darkness. But you have survived in the wilds. If anyone can help her, you can."

"Father, no!" Cuifen pleaded.

"Obey me, Daughter. I will not forsake my people. But you must survive. I will not have you become victim to Echion's cruelty."

"Great king," said Budai in a sniveling voice. "Command her to bring *me* as well."

Now that she heard his voice, she detected the lemony bite of his greed. *Of course* Budai was only interested in his own welfare. She didn't doubt he'd sell one of his souls to Echion if the price were high enough.

"He would not survive the journey," Bingmei said.

"It is not your privilege to command here," snarled Budai. "I beg you, my lord!"

"No," said Zhumu. "You will face the same fate I do. You said a relic protected you from your fate in Wangfujing. I've seen your meiwood turtle. Give it to my daughter."

"It is mine!" Budai shouted angrily.

"Take it from him," ordered the king.

Bingmei shook loose the guard who'd guided her here, then followed Budai's lemony scent. She grabbed his hand, torqued it quickly, and he was soon on his knees, writhing in pain.

"I swear I'll be revenged on you, Bingmei," he seethed.

Ignoring the threat, Bingmei set down her staff and quickly searched the former king. She checked his pocket first but found the turtle hanging around his neck on a braided silk rope. She pulled it off and then shoved him away from her.

"You'll regret this," he said dangerously.

She picked up her staff. "I don't think so," she replied. "Your Majesty, I will do as you command."

"As will I, Father," said Cuifen. "But I would rather stay and face the same fate as my people."

"You are my heir and must survive," said the king. Bingmei could smell his despair, his growing sadness.

"Come, Princess," she said. She reached for the girl's arm and, after fumbling a bit, found it. "Lead me to your room. You need clothes suitable for a journey. And wear this for protection." She put Budai's pendant around her neck.

"I will guide us there," the princess said, taking her hand.

Together they left the throne room, and Bingmei struggled against the constant feeling that she was about to walk into a wall. Once they were in the corridor, she caught scent of Rowen following behind them.

"Are you coming too?" she asked.

"Who?" Cuifen said.

"Of course I am," he answered. "I can find you in the dark, Bingmei."

Because of the Phoenix Blade. They walked a ways and then reached the princess's chambers. The sulfurous smell of the bathing chamber wafted toward her as she opened the door.

"We must be prepared to enter the mountains," Bingmei said. "Silks will not do. You will need something heavier, something warmer." And so would she. Although the clothes she'd worn on the journey to Sihui were in bad condition, she'd prefer to wear them than the wispy silks.

"I know," said Cuifen. "I'm not a simpleton. Let me find something." She began to rummage in the dark. "There," she said after a moment. "I can wear these. Let me change."

There was no need of a changing screen now. Bingmei folded her arms, listening as the princess began to disrobe.

"Rowen," Bingmei said. "Go to the courtyard. Tell them we are coming and that I will be choosing a few members of the ensign to go with us on this journey."

"Who will you choose?" he asked.

"You will find out with the others. Now go and prepare them."

"Very well," he said. He went back to the door and twisted the handle. As soon as he opened it, a new smell wafted into the room.

Bingmei stiffened.

That smell of confidence and determination belonged to Liekou, the man who had hunted her through the mountains.

And he was coming toward them down the corridor.

CHAPTER SIXTEEN

Fate's Vengeance

"Shut the door!" Bingmei cried out.

"What? Why?" asked Rowen.

"Liekou. Now, shut it!"

She heard the door close and then the latch being jiggled. She smelled growing panic. "How can I lock it?" Rowen said in a panic.

"I'll help you," Cuifen said. She started across the room and then stumbled into something and fell.

The door latch rattled again, and then there was the grunting of two men working against each other. Rowen tried to hold the door closed, but Liekou was just as determined to enter.

How had he found the room in this awful darkness?

Cuifen gasped as she struggled to rise again, her smell sharp and fearful. The door crashed open, and Bingmei heard Rowen's body slam into the wall. Liekou had entered the room, his smell clawing at her nose.

Bingmei gripped the rune staff and took small steps toward him. "Princess, get back!" she ordered. She sent the end of the staff straight out, trying to catch Liekou's body without hitting the princess. She missed and pulled the staff back.

Rowen tried to join the fight—she could hear him shuffling forward, smell his determination—but the sound of fist striking skin and bone could be heard. Liekou's victorious smell told her Rowen was the injured party. Bingmei took another step forward and banged into a piece of furniture blocking her way. The edge of the wood bit into her thigh. She managed to catch herself and went around the small table.

She swung the staff and felt it connect, but it was Cuifen who cried out in surprise and pain. Bingmei cursed herself for the blindness. She smelled Liekou approaching her from the other direction and reversed the staff. She struck him solidly, feeling the wood crash into him.

The next moment, a foot kicked her in the stomach. She fell backward, toppling into the table, which fell with her. The rune staff was yanked out of her hand. Bingmei rolled to one side and heard the staff collide with the table as Liekou struck at her with her own weapon. She rolled again and then flipped onto her feet.

The total absence of light made this fight very uneven. Because it was increasingly obvious that Liekou *could* see. He wasn't stumbling in the dark. His smell came closer as he rushed her, and she jumped forward in a flying kick, trying to strike him. She missed. He reached for her, touching her through the silk jacket she wore.

If he touched her long enough to draw a sigil on her, the fight would be over before it had truly begun.

She blocked his hand and spun around, kicking out to push him back. But her blow landed nowhere. She turned and ran, but only made it a few steps before she collided with a couch and knocked it over.

She felt his fingers touch the back of her silk jacket. Clenching her hand into a fist, she tried to hammer-strike him in the neck, but his fingers were already tracing a symbol against her back.

No!

Immediately her muscles seized up, although the instant paralysis did not affect her mind. She felt everything inside her shrivel, as if her muscles had been starved for weeks. She had no choice but to stand there, helpless, while he traced another symbol on her ribs.

Her legs crumpled. She felt as weak as a tadpole. Before she hit the ground, Liekou grabbed her around the waist and hauled her up onto his shoulder. She tried to speak, to shout for help, but her mouth was just as paralyzed as her limbs. She couldn't utter a sound.

"Bingmei! Bingmei!" Cuifen cried out. "What's happening? Where are you?"

Rowen's groans of pain rang with desperation. He was struggling to get up. To help. She could smell his agony, his despair, his dread. She longed to reach out to him, but she was limp against Liekou's shoulder. He held her legs to balance her weight as he walked out of the princess's chambers and into the corridor.

Where was Jiaohua? She needed someone cunning like him, someone who could sense trouble and be counted upon to act. *Please, Jiaohua, find us!*

Liekou walked at a determined pace. She could hear and smell the frightened servants who came down the hall. Were they responding to the ruckus from the room?

"Princess? Princess? Are you all right?"

Bingmei felt her innards tie into knots. The weakness she felt was worse than a fever sickness.

Liekou slipped along the edge of the corridor wall, bypassing the servants rushing the other way.

Desperate to escape him—to escape *Echion*—Bingmei tried to invoke the magic of flight. She bent all her will into it, but nothing happened. Just as before, she couldn't coax the magic, and even though she was in terrible danger, it forsook her.

Someone help me! she thought with desolation.

But there was no one to hear her silent cry.

被埋葬的世界

Before long, they were in the streets of Sihui. She felt no outside breeze, but she could smell the people, hear their whimpers and cries. She could even understand one family, who must have been refugees from Sajinau.

"I've tried lighting a fire, but it won't burn!" a woman shouted in a panic. "There is no light!"

"It's the Dragon of Night," a man replied. "He'll devour us all in this darkness! I heard the dragon landed on the bridge in the middle of town. We're all going to die."

"Can't we escape? Can't we flee with our little baobei?"

"Flee where? We cannot see! I don't know which way is which anymore. Just stay close to me. I'll protect you both as long as I can."

The mothering smell, sweet and nourishing as cinnamon porridge, wafted from them. The father's smell was sour with worry, yet it had a strong undercurrent of determination. Grass. Not even the worry and fear could overpower his vow to protect his wife and child. And then she and Liekou were gone, walking away from the scene.

Bingmei wished she could struggle. She would have bitten, kicked, twisted, or wrenched her way to freedom. But Liekou hadn't needed to tie her up. Her body was the bond.

Liekou walked for a distance and then stepped over something. He did not speak to her, not that she could answer. Carrying her on his shoulder seemed inconsequential to him, although at one point he paused to shift her to his other shoulder.

Crying and whimpering filled the air. She smelled the populace as they shivered with dread.

Beneath the smell of fear, she smelled water, and soon she heard it lapping against the stone walls being constructed. Liekou wove around bodies too frightened to move. Their smells came and went. Everyone was terrified.

She soon caught the scent of Echion, that hideous stench of a man who'd murdered uncountable numbers. They were going directly toward it.

No, not him! Not him! Bingmei thought in despair.

She remembered the vision she'd had of her mother and realized it was about to come to pass. She would die, and then one of her souls would be trapped in the Grave Kingdom forever. Well, if she had to die, it would be better if she did so before Echion made her revive his queen. She willed her spirit to shed her mortal body as it had done before. But she didn't know how to forsake her body any more than she knew how to fly.

Guilt pressed in on her as Liekou marched her closer to her nemesis. She'd escaped the dragon's clutches so many times before, she'd hoped that she could avoid her fate through cunning and skill. Now that her dreaded capture was about to be realized, she wished she'd tried to fulfill the vision of Jidi Majia. It pressed on her mind like a dozen sharp daggers.

Why had she been so selfish?

Liekou shifted her body again, and then they were climbing one of the arched bridges. She could smell the fishy waters below, but that was inconsequential compared to the stench of Echion. Each step brought them closer together.

Please, I'll do anything! Bingmei thought in a silent scream. *I'll do it! I swear I'll do it if you free me!*

Liekou slowed and then stopped. The terrible odor was choking her, but she couldn't vomit. Not even her stomach would obey her.

"You found her," said Echion with a hint of malice in his tone.

"I did, grand one," said Liekou. "She was at the palace."

"And she brings me the Phoenix Blade on her back. This is a great moment. You are a valued servant, Liekou. You will get all that I promised you. And more."

"It is my honor to serve you, grand one," said Liekou submissively.

"Bingmei," said Echion with a throb of exultation in his tone. "I know you cannot speak, but you can hear me."

She felt fingers pry beneath the wig, followed by pricks of pain as he wrenched it away. This was no dragon she was facing. The fingers felt like a man's.

"Ah, the stain of your hair brings back memories. How many times have we met like this? Do you remember any of those other lives? For thousands of years we've thwarted one another. The phoenix and the dragon."

His hand caressed the scabbard of the Phoenix Blade on her back. The touch of his hand would have made her shrink in revulsion, but she could not move. "It always comes back to you, but it won't help you now. This is the moment of my victory. But I will not savor it here in this benighted kingdom. Come to my court at Fusang, Liekou. You will be present when I honor my queen."

"I will come with all haste, grand one," said Liekou. "Should I bring the girl with me?"

"I will bring the ice rose," said Echion. "Go back to the palace and fetch Zhumu's daughter."

"I will obey," said Liekou. "Will the darkness last long enough for me to accomplish what you've asked of me?"

"Long enough?" said Echion. "It will reign for three days before it vanishes like a dream. That is when my army will arrive to subdue Sihui." There was a snort, a laugh she supposed, then he said, "I put the symbol of the eagle in this place in my last life. But even an eagle is blind in darkness."

There was another snort, this one more reptilian, and a ripple of scales. A foul stench filled the air, and Liekou set Bingmei down on the arch bridge. She smelled him back away, and she heard the creaking sinews of the dragon as it came closer.

She felt a huge clawed hand grasp her helpless body and lift her effortlessly. And then the dragon let out a call, a primal cry of triumph and glee that was so loud she feared her ears were bleeding. Screams filled the air.

The beast snarled with pleasure.

Echion was proud of himself for causing such mayhem.

The guilt ripped into both of her souls. She was going back to Fusang as a prisoner. Back to the glacier, if it was still even there. Back to the magical city that had survived for thousands of years.

How could she have let this happen? Why hadn't she tried to stop it?

And the knowledge of her own failure made the anguish that much worse.

被埋葬的世界

Respect out of fear is never genuine. Reverence out of respect is never false.

—Dawanjir proverb

CHAPTER SEVENTEEN

Fusang's Rebirth

She'd imagined the dragon would need to flap its wings to gain momentum, but no, some ineffable force moved the beast, as if it were a leaf blowing on an invisible river—its wings merely acted as guides to swerve and alter course.

Once the dragon lifted her far enough above Sihui, she could see again. A great blot of inky darkness surrounded the whole city. Beyond it, she saw mountaintops. Seeing the world from beyond the domain of eagles filled her with wonder and dread. But the stench of the beast carrying her made her dizzy.

In the distance, she saw the impossibly long Death Wall, a strand of graying stone built in and over mountain ridges. A vast, untamed forest lay beyond it. Even from this height, she saw no signs of civilization, just lakes and rivers and huge stretches of veined mountains extending as far as the eye could see.

The dragon that carried her said nothing, but she felt the wisps of smoke that seemed to ooze from beneath its scales. Breathing in the fumes made her chest ache. It felt as if they'd flown for a very long time when suddenly the dragon banked and went lower. Her stomach came into her throat.

The beast flew down into a huge canyon, angling carefully to avoid the sudden expanse of trees and rocky ridges. She saw bears ambling along the river, searching for their next meal. Huge bull moose lifted their heads and then fled for their lives as the dragon floated past. Then the great beast let out a piercing shriek that sent all the animals beneath it scattering in confusion and panic. A clicking, chuckling noise came from the beast's long throat. It was pleased by the terror it caused.

The canyon wormed its way through the heart of the mountains, and soon they were rising again, following the broken spine of rocks that jutted into the sky above them. They soared into the air, higher and higher, following the ridge until Bingmei saw a solitary mountain ahead. Sheathed in glacial snow, it rose above the rest. The dragon's wings angled, and the push of the wind in her face grew stronger as the dragon ascended the mountain. Up they soared, up until it was so cold that not even trees could grow. Bingmei felt her lungs aching for air, but they went higher still. She shivered relentlessly, feeling her chest begging for relief. She tried to cry out to the dragon, but her body was still incapacitated, and the beast seemed intent on reaching the pinnacle.

Bingmei felt a sense of frantic energy growing within her. She was suffocating, unable to breathe. She'd die before they ever reached Fusang.

The dragon alighted on the top of the mountain, its huge clawed feet crunching into the snow, causing avalanches to fall on each side. She felt frost on her eyebrows and eyelashes.

The dragon Echion set her down. The smoke coalesced around it and suddenly the dragon was a man again, his pale hair stroked by a breeze. The scales had shifted into ancient armor, elaborately crafted with little embellishments on the edges and across the pieces. Lifting his finger, Echion drew a sigil in the air. The image hung in the air, sparking with fire, and heat emanated from it. He drew another symbol, one with a different set of lines and angles, and suddenly she could breathe again. He then touched her back, tracing a symbol on her, and the dianxue paralysis ended. Free to move at last, she hunkered down near the twin symbols, emblems of his power and command. Warmth. Air. Such simple things. Yet a mortal would quickly die if deprived of them.

She gazed up at Echion, smelling his rank scent as she stood, his eyes focused on the sprawling scene below them.

"This whole world is my dominion," he said, although he did not look at her as he spoke. "Every city. Every town. The mountains, including this one, are mine. Every river and stream. Each tree and each blade of grass. All of it belongs to me." He gave her a sharp look. "*Only* to me. That I allow you ants to dwell here is a sign of my benevolence. If my laws are followed, I protect those beneath me. Disobey, and I bring ruin. I brought you here to show you your insignificance. If you tried to flee, you'd perish almost instantly. You are powerless against my strength."

He reeked of murder and ruthless depravity. But she could smell the lie just as strongly. He was *lying* to her. Why? It struck her that he didn't know she could sense his dishonesty. Could she somehow use that to her advantage, or was all lost?

"What will you do with me?" Bingmei asked through clenched teeth. She was still cold, but the heat from the burning sigil was working through the thin silk robe. The cold wouldn't claim her this night.

"I will use you as I always have, Phoenix. Our little game. You will bring back Xisi, the queen of my empire. Only with her can my full powers be restored. Then I will continue my quest."

She stared at him, unsure of what he meant. Was he motivated by something other than murder and death? "What do you seek?"

"Permanence," he said, folding his arms across his armored chest. She saw the strange ring on his hand, like a spider that had enclosed its legs around his finger.

She stared at him in confusion.

"Every civilization I have founded has ultimately ended in death. Some have lasted a thousand years. Some perished after only three generations. Each one has eventually plunged toward chaos, self-destruction.

I take what I have learned from each failed society and apply those lessons to the next incarnation. I seek to create a society that will never fail. One that will be permanent. One that will achieve perfect order." He smirked. "The ants are always killing themselves. I seek to prevent it."

"But you killed thousands at Sajinau," Bingmei said, gaping in disbelief.

"I don't need to justify myself to you or to anyone, Bingmei," he said. "I have shown mercy before. Always there is rebellion. I have learned that order can more easily be achieved through cruelty. Cut the dead branch, and the tree will continue to grow. Just do not cut the roots. The widows mourn . . . for a season. Then all life begins anew. Their *grandchildren* will remember me as their great liberator, the source of their prosperity. I control the stories that are told, Bingmei. Don't you see? It doesn't matter what they think now, only what they *will* think."

His ruthlessness made her mind stagger. This man had ruled and conquered for thousands of years. He had countless ages of wisdom and knowledge to call upon.

The only hope of defeating him had been her.

And she'd fled from her fate. From the peak of the mountain, she could see the Death Wall far below. But she could not escape. It was too late for her to do what she should have done months ago.

Anguish crushed her souls.

被埋葬的世界

They arrived in Fusang after the end of the day. She'd watched the sun set over the mountains, and then the sky had become swollen with stars. In less than a single day, they had crossed so much distance. No wonder Echion had beat them to Wangfujing after she'd awakened him. They had nothing that could move as quickly as his dragon form could fly.

He swooped down from the sky and then transformed back into a man just as they reached the inner courtyard of the palace. It felt like stepping out of a fog. One moment they were in the air, and the next they were walking along the courtyard, his hand no longer gripping her arm. Her legs were weak, and she was devastatingly hungry.

No traces of the great glacier remained within the Summer Palace. It was open to the sky overhead, although the eerie light glowing from the sigils carved into the meiwood poles drowned out the stars. The place had changed as surely as the man before her. It was reborn.

The soldiers standing guard on the palace walls wore black robes and armor etched with golden symbols. She recognized the huge marble slab in the middle of the twin staircases, sculpted with a depiction of the twin dragons.

Noticing her perusal of the carving, he asked, "Shall I tell you how we moved that stone into place?" His tone was smug. "Or can you guess?"

"I have no idea," Bingmei answered humbly.

He paused and gestured toward it. "It was moved during the winter. A path of water was spread across the ground, and when it froze, animal servants dragged the stone across the ice." He gazed up at the palace before them. "I have rebuilt this palace many times over the centuries. This time, it will endure forever. Come."

He started again toward the steps to the right of the slab. A red velvet carpet had been thrown down to cover them. That had not been there before, but it was similar to one she'd seen in Sajinau.

He walked up the center of the steps, and she walked alongside him. As they climbed, she saw servants assembling at the top of the steps to welcome their sovereign. Their courtly attire matched that of Echion.

He seemed eager to boast of his prowess and power, which emboldened her to ask a question.

"Were there servants here when you and the queen were entombed? I didn't see any remains."

If he was bothered by her question, he didn't show his displeasure. "They were here," he said, "beneath the floors of the palace. After they were all sealed in, along with the soldiers of my army, they drank poison and died. They were only too willing to serve me next in the Grave Kingdom. That is where I go while I await the next season of my rule. It will all make sense to you . . . soon enough," he added with a dark chuckle.

Had they all willingly perished? The thought chilled Bingmei's heart, as did his mention of the Grave Kingdom. Was this what her mother had foreseen?

When they reached the top of the steps, the fawning servants bowed in deep reverence, prostrating themselves on the floor, heads touching the stone by his feet.

"I have brought the phoenix with me," said Echion. "See that she is bathed, dressed, and given something to eat. When the sun rises over the mountains, she will awaken my queen, Xisi."

The servants rose, nodding and bowing in deference. They looked like they were from different kingdoms, but they all wore the same clothing, and their hair was arranged in elaborate styles. They smelled uneasy but eager to please Echion. Fear made them loyal.

Bingmei clenched her hands into fists. "I will not bring her back," she said to Echion, giving him a bold look. Even as she said it, she couldn't help but remember that she'd summoned him back to life in a manner that wasn't entirely within her control.

She smelled a whiff of annoyance, there and then gone.

"You will, Bingmei," he said, not even looking at her. "Trust me. You will do exactly as I say. I advise you not to try to escape. You are in the heart of my kingdom now, and every person here is loyal to me."

Bingmei glared at him, feeling both frightened and rebellious.

Her head swiveled around as a familiar smell came toward her through the crowd. It was the smell of sadness. She searched through the servants until she saw the pale man coming closer. It was Jidi Majia, whom she'd last seen in a vision months before.

"Ah, Jidi Majia," said Echion in a pleased tone. "You came."

"As you ordered, grand one," said Jidi Majia. He caught sight of Bingmei, but his expression didn't change. If anything, the sadness within him grew even deeper. His heart was breaking.

He knelt before Echion and touched his forehead to the floor in another act of ultimate submission. The sight flooded Bingmei with more guilt.

"Have my concubines attend to her needs," Echion said. "She will not be staying with us for very long."

CHAPTER EIGHTEEN

Deceiver

Before Bingmei was escorted away, the Phoenix Blade was taken from her by Echion himself. Her despair had intensified at the sight of it cradled in his hands. She was still drawn to the blade, and her longing for it increased.

"Be sure she has no other treasures with her," Echion said and then made a dismissing gesture with his free hand.

Servants marched her down a long hall and out of the palace itself. They passed under a roofed walkway that allowed her to look down at the courtyard beneath them. The calamity that had befallen her weighed on her like boulders, and she had the urge to fling herself to her death. But she held her head high and walked forward with determination.

As they moved along, she noticed a man trailing after the party, one who kept to the shadows. She glanced back at him and saw his martial bearing. Was he a member of Echion's ensign?

They arrived at their destination—one of the outer buildings along the courtyard wall. The compound of Fusang was impossibly big. Night had fallen, but it was not dark. Eerie light still emanated from the sigils carved into the meiwood pillars—a smokeless, scentless light that illuminated the room and the pathway.

Once inside, she found two women preparing for her arrival. She recognized one of them by sight immediately. It was Eomen, Rowen's sister, although her scent had changed. She smelled like bruised fruit spoiling in a basket. Her beauty was still intact, but her spirit had been crushed, her heart full of despair.

"The dragon has asked for her to be cleaned and garbed appropriately for court," said one of the servants who'd escorted her. "She may rest if she desires."

The two women bowed instead of speaking in response. The servants left, although the man who had been trailing them remained behind, pacing languidly by the door. Bingmei glanced around the room, her eyes darting from the high windows, which were enclosed in latticework, to the sumptuous decorations. There were divans and couches, several beds, and beautiful cabinets inlaid with dragon designs.

"We will bathe you first," said Eomen dispassionately as she approached.

"Do you remember me, Eomen?" Bingmei asked.

There was a sharp onion smell, and Eomen pursed her lips. "Yes. Come this way."

What happened next was utterly humiliating. Bingmei was doted on as if she were a royal personage, her body sponged and cleaned while she was made to stand unclothed before the two women and, undoubtedly, the man guarding the only way out of the building. She'd tried to sneak her meiwood cricket out of her pocket, but it was snatched away from her and set on a table nearby. It felt as if the last part of her family had been ripped away from her. If that weren't disconcerting enough, she was buffeted by the emotions of the two women—revulsion from the woman she didn't know, who was sickened by the signs of her winter sickness, and Eomen's feelings of indignity. She, a princess, was being made to bathe someone of a lower station. Eomen's self-identity had been shattered by her new situation, and the despair that wrung her heart was nearly unbearable to Bingmei. And the worst part of the experience was the certainty that the guard was enjoying every minute of the spectacle.

After the bathing, the application of powders, the trimming of nails, the plucking of eyebrows, and the smoothing of calluses with a pumice, Bingmei was adorned in the court robes of Fusang. The climate was farther north, and while the air was no longer frigid, it wasn't warm either. Still, the clothes felt weighty and cumbersome, from the silk skirts hemmed in velvet to the long-sleeved robe that was so wide at the wrists the ends nearly touched the floor. Made of red silk and trimmed in black velvet and silver fox fur, it bore the symbol of the phoenix.

But they weren't finished with her yet. After clothing her, both women sat her down on a stuffed bench and proceeded to style her hair. They tugged and yanked on the red strands, braiding them and pinning them in different ways that lifted her hair above her ears on each side, with long strands of hair running down her back.

When the ordeal was finally over, she was brought to stand before a sumptuous mirror that was as clear as looking into a glass lake. Bingmei didn't recognize her reflection. Her face was lathered in powders and tinged with rose at the cheeks. Her lips and eyes had been painted as well.

But despite the bizarre visage staring back at her, she could smell the odd scent of jealousy coming from the other two women, strong enough to be noticed beneath the reek of disdain and despair.

"I will tell the overservants she is done," said the concubine Bingmei didn't know.

"I will stay with her," said Eomen tonelessly.

The other concubine took the meiwood cricket and handed it to the guard before leaving. Bingmei had kept her eyes on it the whole time. It was gone now, likely never to be hers again. The loss made her mourn her grandfather's death all over again.

"Are you tired, Bingmei?" Eomen asked. "It may be a while before one of the eunuchs comes to inspect our work."

Bingmei was more mortified than weary.

"Will you talk with me?" she asked quietly. She glanced at the guardian by the door.

"Is there something you wanted to say?" Eomen asked with indifference.

"Rowen is alive."

There was spurt of emotion from Eomen, something pungent and sickly. "Oh," she said, turning way.

"You don't care?"

She turned back, her bottom lip trembling. "I thought he was dead. I'd *hoped* he was dead."

That was not the reaction Bingmei had expected. "He's your brother."

"It's more complicated than that, Bingmei. I was there, you see. I was there when he promised Echion he'd bring you back to Sajinau. If he failed . . . which he *did* . . . the dragon promised . . ." She swallowed, the smell of fear suddenly overpowering. "He said that he would kill me in a most savage manner. As it stands now, at least I'm a concubine. One who hasn't been summoned yet. He has so many already. Now, when he summons me, I know I'm going to die. So no, your news doesn't comfort me, although at least I know this misery will be over soon." She turned away again.

Bingmei's own feelings had sickened with the words. Rowen had promised to capture her? Had he truly intended to bring her back to Echion? Was this why he'd attempted to get her alone? Except . . . they had been alone together, in the ice cave, and she'd never smelled such an intention from him. But then again, he knew that she could divine someone's feelings. He knew her secrets.

"I'm sorry, Eomen," Bingmei said helplessly.

The princess turned, her eyes red-rimmed. Hate wafted off her, as acrid as burnt rice. "Sorry? My brother is dead because of you. And my other brother betrayed us because of you. My father is a *slave* because of you. If you had at least *tried* to act on your fate . . . it might all be very different right now. Instead of saving us, you . . . you ruined us. And all you say is sorry?"

Raw emotions struck Bingmei like so many fists, but emotions couldn't be fought or blocked. Her mind snagged on one point Eomen had made.

"Your . . . father?" Bingmei asked, feeling utterly miserable.

"Yes . . . he is *here*. He's a prisoner. I only found out when we came." She swallowed, her heart thick with anguish. "And they will make him watch my death. I know it. Echion has no sympathy, no compassion." She pressed her fingers to her forehead, looking as if she'd begin weeping. But she didn't. Maybe all her tears had already been wrung out. "If I could only die of grief," she whispered in a choking voice, "I would spare my father the anguish of witnessing my execution." She sighed, composed once more, although she seemed like a woman only half-alive. Her hope had been smothered. "Where is my brother now? Where did he flee to?"

Bingmei felt her own throat thicken. "We were caught in Sihui."

"Sihui," said Eomen with a mirthless chuckle. "Princess Cuifen will be joining us soon, I imagine. Every noble's daughter has been brought to join the ranks of the concubines. He'll destroy our lines within one generation." She sighed. "Such is the nightmare we wake to every day. Get some rest, Bingmei. You will need your strength."

被埋葬的世界

A hand lightly shook Bingmei's shoulder. She'd fallen asleep on one of the couches, her legs tucked up. She'd wanted to stay awake, but exhaustion had overruled her wish.

"He's coming," said Eomen. As Bingmei sat up, she noticed the other concubine from earlier had returned.

"Who?" Bingmei asked, about to wipe her eyes when Eomen seized her wrist and shook her head.

"You'll ruin our work. Stand up. They sent Jidi Majia for you."

Bingmei quickly rose from the couch, squeezing her eyes shut to try to banish the itching that had grown worse the moment she'd been told she couldn't relieve it.

The smell that came from beyond the open door was not one of sadness or grief. The reek of murder indicated it was Echion himself. She looked at the two concubines worriedly. Eomen and the other woman didn't smell of deception at all. They both stood in formal poses, hands clasped meekly before them.

Soon she heard the slapping of sandals approaching on the marble floor. Bingmei's insides twisted with worry and dread. The news she'd heard from Eomen had only intensified her guilt. Yes, she, too, wished she'd at least tried to accept her fate as the phoenix's chosen.

A memory struck her. Hadn't Echion called her the phoenix, not the phoenix-chosen? She'd been confused by that statement but too mind-sick to ponder it in light of her extreme circumstances.

Jidi Majia appeared in the doorway and entered the visiting chamber. He looked just as he had when she'd last seen him, dressed in the royal robes of his new office and station. But his smell was undeniably wrong. It was Echion standing before her in disguise. In fact, there was a hint of honey in the smell, a savoring of his deception.

He trudged into the room as if fatigued by a very long walk. "Dawn is coming soon, let us see the work you have done. If she is suitable to present to such a powerful man."

Bingmei wanted to recoil from his presence, but she guarded her reaction, not wanting to reveal that she recognized him.

As the imposter Jidi Majia arrived, he bowed his head slightly. "Greetings, Faguan, Eomen." To Eomen he offered a sad smile, a consoling touch on her arm, both of which were belied by his smell. "Your father is faring well, my dear. He is a patient man. His mind is going a little soft, but that's to be expected in his current role." Removing his hand, he finally turned to face Bingmei.

"Here you are," he said with a sad sigh.

Echion was almost giddy inside.

This, combined with the lies he'd told her the previous day, seemed to confirm that he didn't know about her gift. That he didn't understand that his identity and his moods were plain as glass to her.

He didn't *know*. A little spark of hope started inside her.

"I wish I had listened to your counsel, Jidi Majia," she said, playing along with the ruse.

He gave her an apologetic look. "Would it have changed the outcome? I very much doubt it. His power dwarfs our own, Bingmei. He's from another age, with wisdom we cannot match."

Not to mention arrogance, Bingmei thought to herself. He was practically preening before her. Why had he chosen this disguise? In all likelihood, he'd done it to gain her trust. To influence her thinking. She'd have to respond to him carefully. Did his disguise mean the real Jidi Majia was dead?

"We've underestimated him at every turn," Bingmei said, shaking her head, and she smelled his delighted reaction to her words. "Did you hear how he defeated Sihui?"

"Is it defeated?" came an innocent-sounding reply.

"He blanketed the city in darkness so thick that not even a torch could make light," Bingmei said. "We were stumbling into each other. Chaos and despair. I think he savors confusion."

Her choice of words brought a pang of disappointment in him.

"He's always shown a predilection for order . . . with me, anyway," came his humble reply, hand on his chest. "I've read the Iron Rules several times. Everything has its placc in socicty. It's really rather impressive."

She fought the urge to laugh in his face.

"Is it much different from what we had before?" she asked, trying to appear uncertain.

"Very much so. Crime has been extinguished in Sajinau. There's no need for the Jingcha anymore."

She wondered how Jiaohua would have reacted to that statement.

"Really?" Bingmei said.

"Yes. Trade is flourishing. The trickery and deceit of cowry shells is gone. Only imperial coins are used now. I have to say . . . life has *improved* since Echion's return. I fear I may have misinterpreted the danger we faced."

"But he destroyed the army of Sajinau," Bingmei said, unable to help herself.

The face of Jidi Majia looked at her with sympathy, but inside, Echion was enjoying himself. "He has not done that to the other kingdoms, Bingmei. Sajinau was an example to the others. They have all surrendered without such bloodshed. As will Sihui now that they've witnessed his power. His might. He is not without mercy. I've seen that myself."

The words spoken seemed so reasonable, so calm. But they were the bitterest of lies. Perhaps they were even lies he told himself.

"He's going to kill me, Jidi Majia," she said, shaking her head. Her voice shook on its own without any need for duplicity.

"When someone is useful to him, he can be quite forgiving. He didn't slay Prince Rowen. You are special in this world. The phoenix-chosen. If you use your power to assist him, you could be very important in the new empire. After all, it was you who revived him from the Grave Kingdom. He was willing to honor you before, but you showed yourself to be an enemy. Of course he's hunted you. But if you were to humble yourself . . ." He sighed. "I know that will be difficult for you. You've always been rather headstrong." He gave her a kindly smile, but she saw through it. His words were all lies. He would kill her because he knew she was the only one who could destroy him.

"Can you advise me, Jidi Majia?" she pleaded, biting her painted lip. The paste tasted peculiar.

"Would you hearken to my advice? You didn't before."

She had to be careful. One wrong step, and he'd know she hadn't been deceived.

"I think . . . I think I could listen to you," she stammered. "What should I do?"

He gave her a solemn look, as if weighing his words with careful deliberation.

"I think you should raise the Dragon Queen," he said seriously. "That is the only thing you can do, willingly, that will earn his trust. Then plead for forgiveness. I've served him for many moons now, Bingmei." He put his hand on her shoulder, as tenderly as a father would. She imagined she could feel the claws. "He is a benevolent ruler. I think he would pardon you. I really do."

And that was the biggest lie of all.

CHAPTER NINETEEN

Slaves of Fusang

After Echion left in his disguise as Jidi Majia, Bingmei could not even think about sleep. Nor would she be allowed to since they had just prepared her for her audience with Echion. Her insides clenched and twisted with dread as she worried about what would happen the next morning. After pacing in agitation, she decided she could bear the confinement no longer and walked to the doorway of the building. Her guardian, the man she believed was from Echion's ensign, stepped out of the shadows and barred her path.

"I want to walk," she told him.

"It makes no difference to me," he replied.

"Will you let me leave?"

"The palace?"

"No, this *room*," Bingmei said with impatience.

"You may. But there are many forbidden places within the grounds. The Hall of Unity is one such place."

Bingmei nodded. "Then guide me. I'm sure you aren't allowed to let me out of your sight."

"You are our honored guest," he said in a sly way, and she smelled the lie.

"Your prisoner," she countered. "Is there a garden we can see?"

"The concubines' garden is this way," he offered, one hand behind his back, the other sweeping in the direction of the garden.

Eomen and the other girl bowed and then followed her from the room. They were her underservants, it appeared, and they both clearly resented it.

Her guardian fell in behind them, staying out of reach should Bingmei decide to attack him. She was tempted, although her new clothing would make it difficult.

The sky still had a scattering of stars, but the horizon was starting to pale. She realized, with growing dread, that the day would be coming soon. If only she could grow wings and fly, escaping the confines of the palace. The last time she'd fled Fusang, she'd done so with the help of her strange power. She tried to summon it now, but it was as distant as it had been since that day in the caves, when it had saved her from capture. Was it eluding her because, as others had suggested, she had closed off her own feelings? Once again, she wondered if perhaps Rowen had a point.

They guided her through a bronze gate into the concubines' garden, where the flowers' pleasant fragrance filled the air. She walked along the small footpath that wound through the garden, taking note of the well-manicured trees that had been planted in straight rows, each limb purposefully devoid of excess growth. Small stone benches lined the carefully curated space, the legs carved into the shapes of various animals, and a night bird called out from somewhere within the greenery. The tranquility of the scene was at odds with the heaviness in her heart.

Above all, Bingmei was determined to survive. Her self-destructive thoughts from earlier had passed. Taking her life here, now, would do nothing to help the others. If she were to make such a sacrifice, and she still didn't know if she could bring herself to do it, it would have to be at the Death Wall.

No, she would fight Echion with her last breath.

She closed her eyes, shuddering. Kunmia Suun had failed to defeat him, and Bingmei was nothing compared to her old master. But fight him she would, rather than submit to such tyranny. If she could continue to deceive him, that might buy her some time.

The sky continued to brighten, the growing light revealing more details within the garden. Each sculpture was indescribably beautiful. How many craftsmen had been employed just for the concubines' garden?

Then she realized the truth of the matter. No craftsmen had been *employed*. Every bit of this garden—every slab of stone, every decorative ornament, every bush and tree—had been the work of slaves. Perhaps they had been chosen for their craftsmanship and skill, perhaps laboring in the palace was preferable to building the Death Wall. Even so, it was wrong.

She paused in her wandering, coming to a stone bench and staring at the subtle details. A strange sensation twisted in her stomach. Although she hadn't been here before, she felt an aching familiarity, the same sensation as when she'd perfectly executed the five-birds form. Looking up, she stared at a tree with grafted limbs. The work was seamless, so how had she known they were grafted?

A tickling sensation worked through her stomach. And then it struck her forcibly—the notion that she had sat on this very bench with a man beside her. Although she could not remember the man or see him in her mind, she felt an overpowering sense of rightness. She *had* been there before.

That other person wasn't her—and yet it was.

Had Bingmei been one of Echion's concubines in another life? Was that why this garden was so familiar to her? Was it Echion himself who had sat next to her on the bench?

Her skin crawled at the thought. Bingmei had a warrior's heart. She was the daughter of warrior parents and the granddaughter of the founder of an ensign. Being trapped within such walls, no matter how beautiful, awaiting the orders and pleasure of a ruler she despised, sickened her to the deepest parts of her two souls.

Slowly, with a trembling heart, Bingmei sat down on the stone bench. It was cold and a little wet with dew. Her hand dipped down to touch it, the sensation reminding her of that other time, the memory she could not quite touch. She'd sat here and drawn out a glyph.

She hesitated, afraid, then closed her eyes and let her fingers move, tracing the glyph that she knew but didn't know.

Almost.

It was an unspoken whisper in her mind. And then it felt as if a hand closed gently atop hers, guiding her finger into the correct pattern.

Whatever she had drawn with the dewdrops couldn't be seen, but she sensed it, nonetheless. She'd drawn two small squares, one slightly larger than the other. One had two markings within it. The other had two markings that slashed out of the square, connected with a stroke.

What had she drawn?

The answer came.

Xisi.

Her eyes opened wide. She'd drawn the name of the Dragon Queen. And she felt a burning sense of rightness that reviving Xisi was something she was *supposed* to do. It didn't make any sense. Why should she contribute to Echion's power?

"Can you write, Bingmei?" asked Eomen with curiosity.

Bingmei looked up and noticed the princess had been watching her closely, especially her hand.

"No," Bingmei answered honestly. "I've . . . I've seen it done." In a vision, but she deliberately didn't mention that part.

"It's something that has been brought back from the Grave Kingdom," said Eomen. "Those who are taught to write are given the greatest responsibility here. I thought maybe . . . they'd finally allowed a woman to try."

"It is a manly art," said their escort with a dismissive chuckle, his hands clasped behind his back. He stood with his profile facing them. He smelled of arrogance and self-satisfaction, which were both greasy smells. "Women may read, but they are forbidden to hold a brush and touch ink."

Bingmei wanted to punch him for his conceit.

"Why is that?" Eomen asked, although the question wasn't spoken in challenge.

"Because only men are taught the Immortal Words," he said. "Should a woman ever learn them, the entire world would be undone."

He smelled like he believed the words, but Bingmei knew that meant nothing. Truth was unequivocal—a belief, no matter how powerful, could not sway it.

被埋葬的世界

Dawn had come, bringing vivid light to the gardens as they walked toward the palace. Echion had sent servants to the garden to collect her. Faguan and Eomen inspected her hair and made sure to fix any smudges in the face paints. Her heart pounded worriedly as she followed the eunuchs. Her original escort followed them, his eyes on her back. Eomen and the other girl also trailed her.

As she crossed the grounds, the bright colors adorning the walkway struck her with wonder. Each pillar had been hand-painted—by slaves—and there were various sigils carved into the trunks of meiwood. They'd been glowing last night, just like they had when Echion had first awakened. As they walked, she saw stone creatures ambling through the courtyard below, enlivened by the magic that controlled Fusang.

A stone lion like that had killed Zhuyi.

After several long steps, she realized the servants were bringing her to the chamber where Xisi's sarcophagus lay. Her agitation was tempered by the memory of that strange moment on the bench. It had felt so right to trace Xisi's glyph. She still didn't understand it or what power had guided her hand. Was it the phoenix? Or was it Xisi herself who had done it?

As they walked along, she noticed warmth emanating from the stones beneath her feet—a warmth whose source was something more than the sun shining into the courtyard. The magic of this place was awe inspiring. She saw warriors patrolling the outer walls, some holding spears, some holding bows. Glyphs were carved into the walls too, and she remembered how some of those glyphs had blasted out lightning on her last visit to Fusang.

Very few knew the location of the Summer Palace, but even if King Zhumu and the other western kings knew of it, they'd never be able to breach the walls and the magic guarding it.

They crossed an arched path and then went down some steps she remembered mounting the night before. Through the wall, she saw the impressive palace rise before her again, and her anxiety heightened to a fever pitch.

They mounted the steps on the east side of the palace—a different path than she'd taken with Kunmia's ensign. Part of her screamed to turn around and flee, knocking down the warrior behind her. Yet that would be cowardly, and it still felt *right* to go there.

It felt right before too, a voice whispered to her, *until you awakened him.*

How was Echion manipulating her feelings like this?

And yet . . . something told her this was different. That the entity that wished for her to do this was not Echion at all.

When they reached the top of the steps, the eunuchs brought her to the side door and pulled it open. The door was several spans taller than her, as if giants lived inside. Echion awaited her, his murderous stench announcing him from afar. The servants held the door open but did not enter themselves. An equal number waited on each side of the door, and one of them gestured for Bingmei to go inside.

She hesitated.

"Go on," said the warrior behind her.

Eomen and the other girl split up, each joining one of the lines of eunuchs, heads bowed in a posture of submission to match that of the men.

Bingmei mustered her remaining crumbs of courage and marched inside the massive palace.

The upper windows were closed, the latticework blocking out much of the day's brilliance. The etchings on the walls were all overlaid in gold. Beautiful vases displayed fronds. She remembered seeing massive chests spread throughout the palace, but those had been cleared away. The two stone tombs of Echion and Xisi still lay in the center of the room. She sensed the Phoenix Blade hidden within the one she'd helped open before.

Echion was back to his true form, the real Jidi Majia beside him. The two were conversing. Bingmei was surprised to see the advisor from Sajinau. She'd wondered if Echion had already killed him. This meant that he could take the shape of a person who yet lived. That was useful to know.

"You may go," Echion told Jidi Majia.

Before he left, he gave Bingmei a pleading look, one that seemed to beg her not to do the ancient ruler's bidding. He exited out the door on the west side of the palace. As both doors thudded closed behind him, it struck Bingmei that she was once again alone in Echion's presence.

"I am curious, Bingmei," he said in a pleasant, conversational tone while standing next to the bier where he had lain. He smoothed his hand over the carved marble effigy of himself. "Why did you flee after you invoked the sigil? You were almost immediately afraid. Why?"

She swallowed, feeling her courage wilt in his presence. Her knees felt like water, but she forced herself to step forward. "We came expecting to find abandoned treasures. Not you."

"So you feared me? Why? I offered to reward you, Bingmei. All of you. It was you who made the first move against me."

"I was afraid," Bingmei said, her voice trembling. "You were more powerful than I could comprehend. I didn't understand how I brought you back. I don't know how to make the glyphs."

He chuckled and came around in front of the bier, facing her. He was pleased by her fear, by her lack of strength in his presence. She could smell the satisfaction.

"Some people do flee when fear overtakes them," he said. "It's understandable. But then there was Wangfujing. Budai's palace. You warned Budai against me." His jade eyes narrowed, his gaze penetrating. "How did you know I was there? It shouldn't have been possible."

Not wanting to relinquish the truth, she bowed her head humbly. "Perhaps the phoenix warned me?"

He tilted his head to one side. "Does the phoenix try to speak to you still? Liekou told me its power saved you in the caves. But it fails you now. It has abandoned you."

"Yes," Bingmei said, nodding. "I cannot control it."

"You cannot control it, because you do not understand it," he replied. "But how could you? I have destroyed its cult from the face of the earth."

The stench of his lie struck her like a blow.

"You are a girl with the winter sickness. A condition that is despised because of me. The phoenix grows more and more desperate each thousand years. It cannot win this contest any longer." He chuckled. "There used to be two seasons, Bingmei. The season of the Dragon of Night. And the season of the Phoenix of Dawn. It is no longer called that because I forbade it. Every emissary it has chosen has failed to usurp me. You are just another scrawny branch that popped out of the tree. A branch that I will snip away and discard. No, Bingmei, the phoenix may think it chose you, but it no longer has even the illusion of control. You were *chosen* . . . by me."

Again his lie made her eyes water.

"I am the one who brought you here with the Phoenix Blade. I am the one who taught your hands to draw the sigil."

More lies.

"And I will use you one last time to bring back my queen. I am ready to renew my powers, to open the Woliu, which separates the Grave Kingdom from the living world. With Xisi at my side"—Those words reeked of contempt and loathing. How he hated her!—"we will rule again and bring order and unity once more. You are *my* pawn, not the phoenix's."

Bingmei realized what he was attempting to do. He wanted to crush her sense of self—to make her prostrate herself at his feet, begging for forgiveness.

A thought struck her mind like a bell.

Before she could stop them, the words tumbled out of her mouth.

"If you are so powerful, grand one, why can you not draw the glyph yourself?"

CHAPTER TWENTY

Wrathful Emperor

She watched Echion's eyes narrow with anger at her words, her accusation of weakness. His haze of fury stank of sulfur as he marched toward her, his face contorting to a mask of outrage and sudden hatred. Her heart quailed at the onslaught of violent emotion.

Echion grabbed Bingmei by the throat with one hand, lifting her off her feet. His fingers were powerful, the long nails digging into her skin, and breathing became impossible. She grabbed his wrist with both hands, trying to pry herself free, but it wouldn't budge.

"You insignificant maggot!" he hissed at her, his lips curling back in a snarl. "You dare belittle my power? All that I have conquered and won by my wisdom and cunning?" She felt his fingers tighten around her throat. The savage fury of the man beat against her. In an act of pure self-preservation, she tried kicking him. It felt like kicking a marble pillar, and he did not even flinch. He only squeezed harder.

"You will obey me, taoqi, or I will punish you in ways you cannot imagine. I have thousands of years of experience in torture. You will be broken like so many shards of pottery."

Her throat felt bruised. She wriggled and struggled against his iron grip, unable to pry even a single finger loose. His strength was beyond that of mortal men. Her fear of imminent death eclipsed even the awful pain he was inflicting.

Staring into Echion's eyes, she saw the unlimited depth of his depravity and cruelty. There was blackness inside him, as thick and impenetrable as the darkness he had unleashed on the people of Sihui. All that lay beyond was the raging fire of his hatred, and he *hated* her.

That darkness inside him seemed to penetrate her soul. Her strength vanished, and her arms dropped, too weak to continue the struggle to free herself. She was nothing to him, not a life—just a worm as he'd said. The pinpricks of pain began to come up her arms and legs, the feeling of death she'd experienced many times.

Bingmei sloughed out of her body, as if it were a canvas bag that had burst a seam. Her spirit form lay at his feet. She shrank from him, even though she was incorporeal. She sensed the awful presence of the dragon that lived within the man, could hear its clucking, reptilian sound tear from his lips.

Echion threw her body to the floor, and she watched her own head strike the ground before lolling to one side, her eyes glassy, lips parted, a trickle of blood running from her nose.

"I'm not done with you yet," Echion snarled, and he reached down, not for her discarded body, but for her soul. His hand, trailing pungent black smoke, gripped her soul and lifted her as effortlessly as if she'd been a leaf. The tendrils of smoke crept up his arm, as if his very pores oozed it out. The smoke billowed out of his jade eyes as well. The dragon bound within him strained to come out and attack, and she feared he might sprout a snout with daggerlike teeth and devour her whole.

Echion took her insubstantial form and walked to one of the burning braziers. She couldn't feel the heat, but she saw the orange coals blazing inside. He bent down and stuck his other hand into the grille. The flames danced against his skin but did nothing to injure him. He brought out a living coal and then frowned as he squeezed it, pulverizing it in his hand. When he opened his palm, she saw black smoldering ash. The little flecks of livid fire winked out, one by one.

Then he walked back to where he'd tossed her body. He crouched down, a look of harsh determination on his countenance. He spat on her face. With his soot-stained hand, he then drew a sigil on her body's forehead with the ash. Next, he used his littlest finger to dab some of the blood from her mouth and then, using it as red ink, traced another glyph on her forehead. Finally, he murmured the words, "Shui, Xue, Po."

As soon as he uttered the words, she felt a charge of power. The meiwood pillars within the hall flared with life, their sigils blazing with sudden fire. To Bingmei, it felt as if her body quite literally *sucked* her soul back in. It wasn't a gradual easing but a snapping feeling, hooks wrenching her back to the mortal plane.

Her swollen eyes parted, and she saw Echion rise and stagger backward until he caught himself on the edge of the sarcophagus. He looked drained, weakened, and for a moment, he breathed unnaturally fast. The runes he'd drawn had weakened him. She could smell his worry, his sense of vulnerability. She stared at him through half-closed eyes, wishing she had the strength to rise and attack him. But her body felt crooked, weak, and darkness crowded in on her as surely as it had in Sihui.

被埋葬的世界

When Bingmei regained consciousness, she did not know how much time had passed. But she smelled a deep impenetrable sadness. She blinked, coming awake slowly, her eyes not quite able to focus. Someone was softly rubbing a damp cloth on her neck.

She tried to say his name—Jidi Majia—but her throat was so constricted it was impossible to do more than grunt.

"Don't speak, Bingmei," said his calming voice. "I'm grateful you are awake finally. I was afraid he'd killed you."

He had. Her arms and legs ached, but that was nothing compared to the pain in her throat and neck. Squinting, she attempted to focus on her surroundings. She was lying on a bed, covers drawn up to her chest. The constricting clothes Eomen had helped her into, the ones she'd worn to see Echion, had been replaced with a looser outfit. She lifted her arm and watched the flowing white silk robe slide down. The amount of light in the room showed it was still daytime.

"Rest, Bingmei," Jidi Majia said coaxingly.

She tried to clear her throat, and that was agony. It frightened her how much damage she'd endured.

"Some tea might be helpful," he suggested. He rose and went to a little table near the bed and poured some tea into a ceramic cup with peonies engraved around the rim. The flowers reminded her of Kunmia Suun, who'd always smelled of peonies, and her heart ached with the memory.

"Let me help you," he said. He put his hand behind her neck and lifted gently, assisting her to rise. When he pressed the cup of tea to her lips, she took a little sip, and it burned all the way down, making her wince. "I'm sorry," he said softly.

After she drank another few sips, she felt she might be able to whisper. She held on to his arm to steady herself and looked around the room, recognizing it as the chamber where Eomen and the other girl had bathed and dressed her. There was no sign of the ensign guardian. Had she been left unprotected? Her heart began to swell with hope.

"How long have I been here?" she managed to get out in a whisper.

"It's the second day since they carried you out of the Hall of Memory," Jidi Majia answered. He glanced back at the door and then gave her a reassuring smile. "We thought you were dead at first. You still have bruises on your throat. But Xisi hasn't returned, so you were successful."

"Where is the guard?"

"He wanders down the corridor sometimes. He must be bored by now." His gaze sharpened with warning. "The door is open, and there is no other way out of this room. He'll return any moment."

Bingmei nodded, trying to save her words. "You . . . came to see me . . . the night I arrived . . . but I know it wasn't you. Do you . . . remember?"

His face darkened, and she smelled his sadness deepen. "It felt like a nightmare," he said, looking away. "When I'm asleep, I have these dreams sometimes. Darkness smothers me, and I can't awaken. When I eventually do, much later, memories start to flit through my mind." He pressed his lips together. "I think those are the times . . . when Echion controls me. So I don't . . . I don't remember visiting you, Bingmei. I'm sorry if I did anything hurtful to you."

She tried to smile, as much as she could, and squeezed his arm. "You didn't. He tried to convince me to revive her willingly."

Jidi Majia shook his head. "And you refused?"

Bingmei felt a cough begin to rattle in her chest, and she instinctively tried to quell it, knowing it would be painful. But it erupted anyway, and the agony it caused nearly made her black out again. It took several long moments after the coughing subsided before she could accept another sip of tea. Tears danced in her eyes, not just from the pain, but from the feelings that welled up at the memory of her horrible confrontation with Echion.

"I did," she finally managed to say. "But I think I must do as he asks."

"No!" Jidi Majia said with desperation. "Bingmei, you mustn't. The Dragon of Night cannot regain his full powers without the queen. Their powers are inextricably linked. You are the only one who can revive her. So you must resist!"

Bingmei felt his deep worry and determination to persuade her. "I agree with your logic." She paused, wincing again, waiting for the pain to subside. "But something in my heart tells me that I should. The morning this happened"—she gestured to her neck—"I went for a walk in the concubines' garden." It was agony to speak, but she kept going. "I had an experience there, something that overcame me. My hand traced the name of Xisi. And it felt *right* to bring her back."

Jidi Majia looked even more panicked. "It is one of Echion's tricks!"

She squinted again and shook her head. "I don't think so. It didn't feel like it. I can't explain this." She licked her lips, tasting the residue of the tea. "It felt more like a premonition from the phoenix."

Jidi Majia stared at her in surprise.

"I can't explain it," she repeated.

"Bingmei. Please listen to me. Was it this same feeling that compelled you to awaken Echion? Were you not subverted then also?"

She sighed. "I don't know. I didn't know who he truly was until after he was revived. And I didn't know about the phoenix until I met you."

"He has the Phoenix Blade. I think he can use it to control your feelings."

"Then why did he kill me?" she said.

"He didn't kill you. He choked you close to death in a fit of rage."

Bingmei shook her head. "I was dead. I know what it's like, Jidi Majia. You remember when it happened to me at the palace of Sajinau." She smelled the ensign guard returning. They could only talk openly for another moment. "Were there marks on my forehead when they carried me out? Stains?"

"Yes, I saw some smudges."

"I heard him speak the words that brought me back to life. *Shui, Xue, Po.*"

He looked surprised. "I know those words. They are the old tongue."

"What do they mean?"

"They are the words for water, blood, and spirit."

"He's coming," Bingmei said, then lowered herself back down onto her pillow.

Jidi Majia turned and faced the doorway. "Who is?"

A few moments later, a shadow dimmed the room as a person stepped into the doorway, blocking out the light.

She heard the warrior ask, "Were you talking to someone, Jidi Majia? I heard your voice."

"I was talking to Bingmei, of course," he replied. "I was hoping some soothing words might help revive her."

"Go. I will watch over her now. Report to the Hall of Splendor. Liekou has arrived with the princess of Sihui. You will be needed, eunuch." He said the last word with a tone of disdain.

"As you command," said Jidi Majia. He rose from the bed, but not before squeezing her arm in sympathy.

Bingmei's thoughts had turned to Sihui and the people she'd left behind. What had become of Rowen? Had he been struck by a dianxue blow? Was he dying or already dead? What about Marenqo and Mieshi? Damanhur and Jiaohua? She'd been so caught up in her own nightmare, she hadn't paused to think about what had become of her companions. Her ensign.

Although she could not hear the guard's approach, she could smell it. She feigned sleep but worried whether she would be successful. A moment later, she felt him standing over the bed, staring down at her. His perusal made her skin crawl.

"You are wise not to awaken," he said softly in a mocking tone. She remained as still as she could. "The master is so angry with you. You pricked his thumb with your thorn, ice rose. You made him bleed. I wonder how?"

She smelled the ambition behind that question. The desire for power and authority. He was intrigued by what she'd done because he wanted to know how to weaken Echion too.

Yes, in Echion's world everyone had a place. But no one was content to stay in theirs.

CHAPTER TWENTY-ONE

Grandfather Jiao

Hunger drove her to wakefulness in the end. Eomen brought her a small bowl of soup, and Bingmei ate it despite knowing what it meant. Word would be sent to Echion that she was recovered, and he was sure to summon her back to the Hall of Memory to revive his queen.

After finishing the soup, she asked Eomen, "Has another princess arrived?"

"How did you know?" Eomen asked. "You've been unconscious most of the day."

"Jidi Majia told me," Bingmei confided in a small voice, glancing toward the doorway where the guard was pacing.

"Ah. Yes, the daughter of King Zhumu has arrived. She has been chosen as another concubine." The spoiled smell of her depression and disappointment grew stronger. "Poor thing. She's very frightened."

"Where are they keeping her?"

"She is being groomed and prepared to meet the master this evening." Her eyebrows sloped down. "If you wish to speak with her, I do not think it will be allowed. There are other concubines assigned to watch her."

Bingmei tilted her head. "How many does he have?"

"The master?"

"Yes."

Eomen's smile looked pained, and a vicious scent of spoiling tubers wafted from her. "We don't know how many he has now. But Jidi Majia said the Iron Rules entitle him to one thousand concubines minus one."

The thought sickened Bingmei to her core. "How could he . . . I don't understand; that is so many."

"It's a symbol of his power," she said with revulsion. "It may take years before he calls all of us. Some will not be called at all."

"I'm sorry, Eomen," Bingmei said, but the woman gave her a scornful look.

"We're all jealous of *you*," she said with a tone of malice. "At least you'll be dead when he's done with you."

The room became stifling, full of raw and terrible emotions. "I need to walk," Bingmei said, desperate to get out.

"Shall I escort you?" asked Eomen, but Bingmei could tell she asked out of duty, not companionship.

"No. I need some air, and I'd like to be alone with my thoughts."

Bingmei rose and lowered her legs off the side of the bed. She was exhausted still, despite all the rest, but the soup had restored some of her strength. The loose white robe she wore had a silver trimming. She tried standing, wobbled a bit, but then found a steady balance. Her skull throbbed where it had struck the floor. All her muscles ached.

As she crossed the room to the exterior door, which was generally open during the daytime, the strength returned to her legs. She walked out without speaking to her guardian, who followed at a distance.

The day was coming to an end, and the sky had layers of orange and pink clouds. It was a dazzling view from the ancient city. She saw people crossing the courtyard below, eunuchs by the look of their uniforms.

Guards patrolled the walls still. She saw smoke drifting from where various fires burned to cook meals, but spied none within the ancient palaces. There was the Hall of Memory, which she walked away from. She also saw the Hall of Unity, which she'd been told was forbidden.

After crossing the way, she took a set of stairs down to the courtyard, gripping a stone railing sculpted to look like twin herons. She twisted her head back and forth, then rotated her shoulders. Her muscles were not only sore but stiff from lack of use, so it felt good to walk. With a surreptitious backward glance, she saw her guardian trailing her down the stairs.

Ahead of her, she saw concubines walking together, about ten in total, each wearing the same type of costume. They walked at an angle away from her. She tried to see if Cuifen was among them, but it was difficult to tell given the similarity of their attire and style.

Everywhere she looked, there were people performing various duties. Some of the eunuchs had brooms and brushed the courtyard from end to end.

A gong rang out, the sound long and ominous, and the people cocked their heads and began walking swiftly in various directions. Confused by its significance, she turned back to look at her guardian.

"Is something wrong?"

"The evening feast," he answered. "For the servants."

Soon the courtyard had emptied, and it was just the two of them, plus the guards lining the walls.

"Are the guards Qiangdao?" she asked him, gesturing toward the walls.

He nodded. "It's a great honor to serve in Fusang. For the obedient."

"You consider it an honor escorting me?" Bingmei said with a teasing tone.

He pursed his lips. "I serve the master," he replied. "Soon he will give me another assignment."

The veiled implication was obvious to her. "Have you spoken to Liekou?"

"Briefly. My charge is to ensure you do not try to escape, not to hold conversation with you." Although her ability to resist Echion had interested him, briefly, he considered her a burdensome task. The feeling smelled of day-old bread.

She missed Marenqo and his sense of humor. Mieshi was occasionally dour, but her moods were preferable to the deep bitterness of Princess Eomen, although Bingmei didn't blame Eomen for her feelings. Everyone who lived in the splendor of Fusang was trapped. Even her nameless guardian was a prisoner to Echion's whims. He thought he was free, but should he fail the master, he was a dead man, and should his ambition rise too high, she had no doubt he'd be replaced by another.

She walked away from him, her heart brimming with anguish for the calamity she'd unwittingly unleashed. But as she walked away from him, toward the forbidden Hall of Unity, a strange feeling came over her. Once again, she had the notion that she'd been here before, that she was part of this place somehow. She eyed the walls, gazing at the light the setting sun cast on them. She'd seen a sunset like this before.

The echoes of some unknown past thrummed inside her, making her pause. She stopped where she stood.

Bingmei closed her eyes, letting the emotions wash over her. And then she started to move, performing the exotic five-birds form that had been unlocked from the cage of memory. It felt so good to be moving, her legs crouching and then rising as her arms swept through the air. Strength filled her. How she wished she could lift herself up and away, fleeing the confines of this beautiful prison.

As she finished the form and opened her eyes, she saw the walls of the Hall of Unity ahead, atop a steep flight of stairs. This place had unsettled her upon her first visit to Fusang—now she felt it beckoning to her.

She started walking toward it with purpose.

"Where are you going?" said her guardian.

She ignored his words and hastened her steps.

He did too—she smelled him approaching before his hand grabbed her wrist to stop her. "That place is for—"

Bingmei twisted around and chopped the edge of her hand into his neck in a stunning blow. Her sudden violence surprised him, giving her the opportunity to wrench her hand free. She ran to the steps and began mounting them.

A warning cry sounded from the soldiers on the walls, who had seen the attack, and the guard she'd injured started chasing her.

The sigils in the meiwood pillars glowed as she approached them. She wasn't sure if they were warning her back or inviting her on. The feelings in her heart propelled her forward.

"You cannot go in there!" said her guardian angrily, huffing for air.

Bingmei reached the top of the steps and rushed to the huge doors. There were nine rows of nine knobs, wreathed in gold, along with two lion-head handles.

In her mind, she saw her hand touching each knob in the first of the rows, one at a time, and she repeated what she saw. As she performed the ritual, she felt her strength increase.

"Stop!" he commanded, coming up behind her.

Bingmei turned to face him, determined still, and when he reached for her, she brought her wrists together and blocked his arm before striking him in the chest with both palms.

A surge of power went through her hands, and he flew backward, knocked off his feet as if by a battering ram, and disappeared over the edge of the steps. She stared in surprise at the power she'd just displayed. Her arms tingled with it.

Bingmei turned around swiftly and pulled on one of the handles. She should have lacked the strength to budge it, but the door swung open enough to let her pass. Excitement burned inside her veins.

The room was thick with shadows from the setting sun. The latticework windows were so high they did not provide much light. A few braziers were lit, but they provided more heat than they did illumination. The room had a polished marble floor inset with gold sigils around the entire border.

She had to lift her foot to cross the threshold, and as she did, she felt the strength vanish. The surge of energy and power she'd experienced siphoned away.

There was a sofa, a table with a plate of half-eaten black rice. A cup. She gazed around and then saw someone walking toward her from the shadows.

Bingmei's heart quickened, and then she noticed another man kneeling on the floor, gray head bowed, facing the wall in a posture of deep meditation. He hadn't stirred, and his position looked very uncomfortable.

Bingmei turned back to the shape approaching her. It seemed to glide instead of walk, and the hairs on her arms rose as a prickle of awareness shot down her spine.

In the dimness of the room, Grandfather Jiao approached her.

Her heart seized with panic and then wonder. She *knew* it was him, although he wasn't gray-haired any longer. His beard was short and trimmed, and he looked so much like her father it made her ache, but she knew it was Grandfather. Some inner instinct screamed that this was what he'd looked like as a younger man.

"Grandfather!" Bingmei whispered in surprise.

He approached her quickly but wearily, as if he'd been walking on a long journey. "Bingmei," he answered. Then he started searching the room, looking behind the couches and scanning the shadows. "Is she here, Bingmei? Have you seen her yet?"

"Who, Grandfather?" she asked in confusion.

"Your grandmother, child, Fupenzi. I'm searching for her still. She came to me, the night before I died, to warn me that I was coming to the Grave Kingdom. When I got there, I could not find her. I've searched for her everywhere. I thought she might be here with you."

Bingmei's emotions roiled within her. "No, Grandfather. I don't even remember her. I was very young when she died of a fever."

"I miss her," said Grandfather Jiao mournfully. "She should be here."

Bingmei pinched her own arm and felt the pain. She was experiencing a waking vision.

"Grandfather," Bingmei said worriedly. "Why are you here?"

He turned and faced her, a strange light glowing in his eyes. "We always come when our posterity is near death," he said. "You will be joining us in the Grave Kingdom soon, Bingmei. If I cannot find you, I am sorry. It is a maze. We are all of us searching for our loved ones."

A stab of pain struck her heart. Her grandfather looked as harried as her mother had in her dream. Although Quion had found comfort in the knowledge the Grave Kingdom existed, she wasn't sure she agreed anymore. There was no calm after death, just more urgency and despair.

"I failed you, Grandfather," Bingmei said. "I was supposed to cross the Death Wall. I didn't do as I was told."

"I know, child. I know. It's too much to put on someone so young. Please find us in the Grave Kingdom, Bingmei. Find your family. Your grandmother loved you so much. I miss her. I miss you all." His pain smelled like spoiled beans. "I found your father, but he left to search for your mother. When you come, find us! That is all I can hope for now. I must go."

"Grandfather!" Bingmei said, tears streaming down her cheeks. She didn't want to be parted from him. There was much she'd left unsaid. Her love for him burned in her chest.

"I must go! Find us!"

He turned and walked hastily back into the shadows. Bingmei charged after him, but when she reached the pillars, she saw he'd already disappeared through the wall. Her heart couldn't bear the pain she felt, the strange longing for the people she'd lost. Her grandfather had been in this room with her. Or maybe her mind had concocted some strange delusion, knowing she was near death. But it had felt so real.

She pressed her hand against the wall. It felt immovable, yet he had passed through it effortlessly. There was a part of his soul that couldn't rest. Bingmei put her face in her hands, crying, and then she heard a sigh behind her and smelled pine-tree sap.

She turned, afraid her guardian had charged in to attack her, but this wasn't his smell. It was the old man she'd seen crouching in meditation.

"Hello," he said in a kindly way. The sap was a pleasant smell. Kindly, absent of any anger or depression. This man was at peace with himself.

He wasn't a ghost. He was real.

"Who are you?" she asked, not feeling threatened, yet still fearful. But as she looked at his face when he came out of the shadows, she saw his resemblance to Juexin. To Rowen. The arch of his forehead, the nose. They were family.

"My name is Shulian."

CHAPTER TWENTY-TWO

Powerless One

Bingmei had guessed he was the exiled king of Sajinau, but her eyes widened in surprise nonetheless. What was he doing in this forbidden palace? "I am Bingmei," she said, stepping closer. How long before her guardian would make it back to her? She suspected she might only have a few moments with the deposed king.

"I don't get visitors," he said with a smile. "Thank you for coming."

"I'm not supposed to be here," she said. "I came following a feeling . . ."

"The phoenix brought you; I know," he said, nodding. He reached out and took her hands in his. His palms were very warm.

"What is this place?" she asked, looking at the shadowy rafters, the light quickly dimming as the sunlight faded.

"This is the Hall of Unity. Such a fancy title, but it's not what it appears. It's a special sort of prison, Bingmei. I must stay here until I waste away."

Strangely, he didn't sound grieved by the thought. If anything, the pine-sap smell grew stronger. He stared at her keenly.

"You are the phoenix-chosen," he said. "I tried so hard to find you." The pressure of his grip increased. "Now, when I depart for the Death Wall, I can leave in peace. I have seen you with my own eyes. At long last."

Her heart beat fast with confusion and desperate emotion. "I failed, Your Majesty," she whispered. "I did not go when I was called. I ran from it. All of this ruin has come about because of me."

"All is not ruined," he said, shaking his head.

Bingmei squeezed his hands, her feelings bleak. "I just saw my grandfather's ghost. In here. Both he and my mother have told me I'll be in the Grave Kingdom soon. Echion is going to kill me."

"You are the one that the phoenix chose," King Shulian said, his voice firm. His eyes locked on hers. "Believe in that. You have a gift of survival, child. You are not as fragile as you fear."

"I am powerless against him," Bingmei said in concern.

He shook his head. "No. *I* am the powerless one. He robbed my kingdom. He slaughtered my army. He murdered my firstborn son and is trying to break my only daughter. In every way, he has sought to rip from me my sense of self, my being, my very souls. But he cannot take from me the last of my freedoms. Whatever else he strips away, he cannot force me to relinquish the one thing that belongs to me and only me." He smiled at her. "He cannot take my taidu."

Bingmei looked at him in confusion.

"My taidu is my attitude, my demeanor, my reaction to adversity. It is the deepest part of our souls, the pearl concealed within the oyster. I have the right to determine how I react to events, good or ill. To choose my own way despite death or pain. Or happiness or prosperity. He cannot pry that pearl from me. Only *I* can give up my taidu."

Bingmei smelled her angry guardian's fury as he charged toward the doors. Her worry intensified. She looked at King Shulian longingly, wanting to preserve this moment. Wanting to learn as much as she could from this wise man.

"But he'll kill me," she said.

He nodded knowingly. "The dead live in the memory of those they leave behind. You were chosen to bring light to those who live in shadow and darkness. I have been communing with the phoenix since Jidi Majia returned with his vision. I, too, have gone to the phoenix shrine. There is a quonsuun beyond the Death Wall, Bingmei, one that is dedicated to the chosen. You will be led there when it is time." He stared at her with eyes full of conviction, as if he were uttering a prophecy in which he deeply believed, and said, "This child is set for the fall and rise of many kingdoms. For a sign of dawn, which shall be spoken again." She felt the emotions writhing within him, and he struggled to speak through tears. "And yes, a sword shall pierce through *your* own soul also. That the thoughts of many *hearts* may be revealed."

Looking past King Shulian, she saw her guardian stride into the chamber. His eyes were full of wrath as he rushed toward them.

"Bingmei," Shulian said, his voice urgent. "Follow the urgings you have had. They come from—"

Her guardian struck Shulian on the back and quickly traced a dianxue sigil with his finger.

This was no mere paralyzing touch. Shulian's breath stopped, and his body contorted in convulsions of pain. He fell limp to the floor, his hands no longer able to grip hers. Bingmei felt tears streaming down her cheeks. She dropped down beside the older man, looking into his panicked eyes. His chest had stopped moving. He couldn't breathe.

She glared at the guardian. "Release him!" she commanded.

He clenched his fist and tried to backhand her as she crouched in front of him. Bingmei anticipated the blow and ducked lower, then jumped at him. Her strength was a fraction of what it had been in the past, but she punched and kicked and tried to injure him in any way she could. He retreated from the onslaught of her attack, blocking or dodging the strikes, before he countered and knocked her to the ground in a stunning blow that cracked one of her ribs.

The jolt of pain made her crumple to the ground in agony, gasping. He stepped over her and walked to Shulian's body. She groaned in pain, struggling to turn around, and saw him squatting over the body, his fist clenched still as if he were about to deliver a death blow.

Hardly breathing through her distress, unable to speak, she pulled herself closer to Shulian. His panic was gone, and she smelled the cool pine-sap scent again.

Kill him.

It was a thought that came as loudly as spoken words, as if the palace walls themselves had uttered the command. She recognized the voice and the horrible stench of Echion that flooded the room, drowning out King Shulian's pleasant smell.

The guardian, teeth bared, struck the defenseless man with a final punch.

Agony and loss tore at Bingmei's heart as she watched the brutal act, unable to prevent it. Despair threatened to choke her as full darkness claimed the room. The sun was gone at last. So was the sweet smell of sap. Bingmei cried quietly, her rib throbbing as her breath came in stuttering sobs.

She watched Shulian's soul rise from his body, as if he were awakening from a nap. He turned to look at her.

I am free. Thank you, Bingmei.

You will never be free from me. Echion's tone was mocking, and the sentiment was one he'd repeated after Prince Juexin's murder. The ancient ruler controlled both the world of the living and the world of the dead.

Overwhelmed by feelings of despair, Bingmei watched as Shulian's soul was yanked away. This was Rowen's father. The two would never be reunited again until the son joined him in death. Perhaps not even then. From what her mother and grandfather had told her, death was a maze where family members searched desperately for each other.

Bingmei bowed her head and wept bitterly.

被埋葬的世界

The guardian brought her back to the concubines' quarters. Bingmei became inconsolable when she saw Eomen and Faguan. How could she tell Shulian's daughter that the king was dead—and that it was her disobedience that had brought it about? The two women stared at her in worry. The guardian ordered them to tend to her injuries before storming away in disgust and rage.

"What happened to you?" Eomen asked with some flickering sympathy.

Bingmei couldn't speak the fateful words, knowing the pain they would cause. She knew the pain of grief, having learned of her parents' deaths the same day she saw Muxidi murder her grandfather.

"What should we do?" Faguan asked Eomen worriedly.

"Maybe they tortured her," Eomen said. They ceased trying to comfort her and began examining her for injuries. Her chest hurt terribly with each breath, and although they eventually discovered the problem and wrapped her ribs in silk to help compress the broken bone, it didn't help. The pain traveled around her side so that both front and back throbbed each time she inhaled.

The darkness of her feelings was unbearable. Smelling them made it worse. She couldn't escape her own stink. She pressed her face into her hands and cried until all the tears were gone. Deadness replaced the pain, and she sat on the edge of the bed, staring at the glowing glyphs in the meiwood pillars through the open doorway.

You have an instinct for survival, the king had told her.

But she'd never felt closer to death. Her mother and grandfather had both warned her she was about to die, and she'd just watched Shulian take his last breath.

After her injuries were tended to, she smelled someone approaching. It took her a moment to identify the person as Liekou, the man who'd hunted her down in Sihui.

She lifted her head, staring sullenly at the door moments before he entered. Eomen noticed this, and her brow wrinkled in confusion. She gasped when Liekou appeared in the threshold of the door.

"Who are you?" she asked.

"Liekou," he said boldly. Bingmei smelled something off about him. A flowery smell that seemed totally out of place. Before, he'd always smelled of self-confidence and power. "I will be guarding her now. The dragon wishes her to be brought to him at midnight to summon the queen. You have been ordered to prepare the queen's chambers. She will determine which concubines are fit to serve her. Go."

Eomen and the other girl bowed and left the room.

She glared at Liekou, but her reaction meant nothing to him. He stalked into the room self-importantly. That strange flowery smell came with him.

"What has happened to Sihui?" Bingmei asked him, still glaring.

"It will fall in the morning," he answered. "The darkness lifts on the third day. When the sun rises, they will see the invasion arriving to attack from the rear of the city, where they are weakest." He smirked at the tale he told. "King Zhumu will be killed. His daughter, Cuifen, I have brought here."

As he said those last words, Bingmei smelled the blooming fragrance again. She suspected she'd identified the source. He had spent two days with the princess on the way to Fusang. He felt something for her, some emotion he wrestled with even now. It was plain as day.

Bingmei hated her gift sometimes.

"Now I will ask you a question. One that has troubled me. When I came for you in Sihui, you ran from me."

"Of course I did," she answered, wincing at a stab of pain from her ribs. "You are my enemy."

He paced to the other side of the bed, his look thoughtful. He turned to face her. "But how did you even know I was there? You were blind. Your feeble attacks against me proved as much. Yet still, you knew

I was coming and warned the others to close the door. And when I came nearer to you, you flinched and backed away." His eyes narrowed coldly. "How did you know I was there?"

She realized, with dread, that she'd unwittingly revealed her power to him. He was an astute and cunning warrior, and he was trying to untangle the knot of the mystery.

"I did . . . sense you," she answered, her throat dry.

"I know. How?"

She stared at him, saw the determination in his eyes. She didn't speak.

He frowned. "If you tell me," he whispered, "I will help you escape Fusang."

The lie was so strong, it made her eyes water. She wrinkled her nose helplessly and looked away. A little chuckle tried to escape her chest, but the pain stifled it.

"You don't want to escape?" he said incredulously.

Her lips formed a little frown. "I don't believe you."

He clasped his hands behind his back and paced the other way. "Budai's steward told me that you have a gift. That you know when someone is lying. That you used it in the service of the king of Wangfujing." He turned sharply, his eyes probing her carefully. "You knew just now that I was lying. I was testing it."

The worry inside her grew, rattling like a pot lid when the cauldron was reaching its heat. She said nothing.

"So . . . you can sense people. Their motives. Even their presence. How does it work?"

"Why should I tell you?" Bingmei answered.

"Because it may save your life," he replied. This time, he wasn't lying. "I have not shared this secret with the master yet. I wanted to understand it myself. It may prove . . . useful to him." There was a hint of dishonesty in his smell at that last comment, but it was subtle. His motives were more complex than that. There was self-interest as well. She suspected she knew why.

She looked away, wondering how she could use this situation to her advantage. An idea struck her. "Will you bring Princess Cuifen to see me?" she asked.

There was that smell again, as soon as the name was mentioned.

"I cannot. She's being transformed into a concubine," Liekou said, the smell tinged with jealousy now.

"You have authority here. See that it's done."

He looked suspicious. "Why her?"

"I have my reasons. Echion is going to kill me tonight after I bring Xisi back. I just wish to speak with her and learn what I can about my friends."

She sensed his distrust, but he was also intrigued, and he *wanted* to see the princess again. Bingmei hoped it was enough.

"I will try," said Liekou.

CHAPTER TWENTY-THREE

Revealed

They came for her at midnight.

Bingmei had paced the chamber, looking for a way out of her situation. The door was guarded by Liekou, who had returned without Cuifen, his smell regretful, and refused to talk to her anymore. Bingmei had tried meditation to see if any new ideas came to her, a way to escape from Fusang. But without the magic of the phoenix to assist her in flying away, she could not see a way out. In her mind, she thought on her encounters with Grandfather Jiao and King Shulian.

The vision of her grandfather made her feel death was inevitable. Yet Shulian had seemed to think not all was lost. He'd believed she could still follow the phoenix's will and cross the Death Wall.

Bingmei regretted that she hadn't attempted it before. If she was going to die anyway, why not perish in an act that saved thousands of lives? Echion ruled beyond the Death Wall too, and her sacrifice might help her parents and her grandfather, Kunmia Suun, Prince Juexin, and countless others.

During her meditation, she poured out her soul to the phoenix, promising to do what she must. Yet her heart achieved no answer. No magic came to relieve her.

The sound of steps came from the exterior corridor.

Liekou stepped outside the chamber to see who was coming. Then he returned and said, "It is time."

Bingmei sighed, disappointed not to have received her answer. Still dressed in the white robes from earlier, she joined Liekou by the door. She smelled a wave of bitter sadness and knew it belonged to Jidi Majia before she saw him. His eyes were swollen, as if he'd been crying.

He must have learned about the king's death. Bingmei pursed her lips and nodded to him.

"The dragon will see you now," Jidi Majia said.

Liekou gestured for her to go first. She smelled wariness about the warrior, a determination to bring her as he'd been commanded. He was expecting her to resist. But what could she do? If she fought him, he would strike a dianxue blow and render her helpless. No, she would face her fate with courage.

She followed Jidi Majia down the corridor. Staring out at the courtyard as she walked, she saw the night sky teeming with stars. The days were much longer now, and night seemed a fleeting thing. She wondered if, at the apex of summer, the sun would set at all in Fusang.

As they turned the corner and headed toward the rampart leading to the hall where Echion awaited them, she said in a low voice, "I'm sorry, Jidi Majia."

He didn't turn to face her, but she smelled a fresh wave of sadness from him. "The dragon consumed his body," came the soft reply. "It was terrible to watch."

A shudder went down her spine. "To what end? He was already dead."

"I believe to assume his essence, his powers. It's how he understands his enemies. They become part of him. Their wisdom, their memories. It made him sick. He's only just recovered."

That last thought was accompanied by a tart scent, a gratified feeling that his old master had at least caused the dragon some discomfort.

"I wish I had listened to you last year," Bingmei said with a sigh. "I'm sorry."

Jidi Majia said, "Maybe in another thousand years the people will have another chance."

The sentiment made her wince with shame and regret, although she could do nothing to change the past.

The moon had just appeared over the wall surrounding the palace, filling the courtyard with silvery light. Dread and apprehension consumed her. After crossing the bulwark, they reached the side door of the palace. Bingmei smelled flowers, but beneath it she picked up the scent of Princess Cuifen, who was hidden in the shadows behind a pillar.

A hand closed around Bingmei's upper arm, stopping her.

"Tell Master we've come," said Liekou.

Jidi Majia turned and looked at the two of them with confusion, but he went to the door ahead of them and opened it.

"This is the best I could do," Liekou whispered. "You sense her?"

"I do," Bingmei replied. They walked together, Liekou's hand still gripping her arm, and went to the pillar.

"Your Majesty," Bingmei said as Cuifen appeared around the pillar, her eyes fearful.

She was almost unrecognizable in the finery of Fusang's court, the same fancy robes that Bingmei had been dressed in upon her arrival, her hair pinned up with tassels and wooden combs.

"Hello, Bingmei," said Cuifen in a tremulous voice. She glanced at Liekou and then looked down. A roselike smell came from her. It was a small smell, barely noticeable through the smell of fear, but Bingmei realized that Cuifen had feelings for Liekou as well. The two of them stared at each other a moment too long.

"You wished to see me?" Cuifen said, her eyes shifting back to Bingmei.

"I wished to tell you that I'm sorry," Bingmei said. "I had sworn to protect you, but I could not even protect myself."

"I bear you no resentment, Bingmei," said Cuifen. "All of us were vulnerable to the darkness." She glanced at Liekou again.

The floral scent coming from the warrior grew stronger, although it was layered with jealousy and resentment. He did not want Echion to have Cuifen, but he still struggled against his feelings. He knew what they could cost him. She felt his grip on her arm tighten.

"Do you know what became of my friends?" Bingmei asked.

The princess shook her head. "I was abducted shortly after you, but we passed huge war ships after leaving the range of the darkness. I fear the dragon is unstoppable now."

The door opened, and Jidi Majia's face appeared in the doorway. "Come," he insisted.

Cuifen slipped back into the shadows behind the meiwood pillar, and Liekou pulled Bingmei toward the door.

"She cares for you," Bingmei whispered to him.

Her words affected him as she'd intended, and he let out a hiss of breath.

"It's not too late," she whispered again as they reached the threshold. "Help me escape."

"Neither of us would make it down those steps alive," he countered, stepping over the threshold. He tugged her with him, and she had only a moment to lift her foot. His feelings were writhing like a basketful of snakes, although his exterior was calm.

The inner sanctum glowed with light from the sigils carved into the meiwood pillars. She saw Echion pacing within, his expression smug and alert. She sensed the Phoenix Blade in the room, and then she saw it. It had been hidden high in the rafters, the blade resting in the jaws of a wooden dragon carved out of meiwood.

Liekou released her arm and then stood by Jidi Majia at the doorway.

"You are dismissed," Echion told the two men, who bowed and then retreated out the door. It shut ominously behind them.

She stood still, her flowing robes settling around her body, and looked upon the two tombs. Once again, she felt the impulse to raise Xisi.

"Did you enjoy your pathetic attempt to thwart my plans?" said Echion. The reek of his smell struck her forcibly again. Part of him smelled like tree sap, but it was such a faint smell compared to his overpowering stench that she wouldn't have noticed it if she hadn't remembered the experience with Shulian so vividly. "He was easily dispatched. Your defiance accomplished nothing."

Although he meant the words, she didn't believe them. Shulian had died revealing to her a great truth. She was in control of how she responded to things. Although Echion might turn into a dragon and consume her as well, she did not have to give in to her fear.

Bingmei started forward, even though she wanted to flee.

"We're all powerless against you," she said. "Does that take the fun out of it?"

He chuckled to himself, though it was a bitter sound. "Of course one with such a limited view of life would conclude that I do this out of a sense of . . . enjoyment. No, it is the challenge that motivates me."

Bingmei cocked her head, still approaching him.

"I understand Shulian's motivation. I've . . . tasted it before. He gave his kingdom to his less ambitious son. I've already forgotten his name. Weak-willed. Devout. Always seeking to please his father's whims. Dutiful." Bingmei could smell how Echion despised those words. "And within a few years, the younger brother would have started a war. I've seen it happen over and over. The brothers would have struggled, locked onto each other's throats in a choking grip, until one or both were dead. They would have destroyed all their father built. Now, if Shulian were truly wise, he would have named the younger son king and poisoned the elder. But he couldn't do that." He had reached her now, his look arrogant.

Bingmei gazed up at him. "Because he loved both of his sons."

"Yes. And love is blindness. It is the greatest lie. I've tested the mettle of men like Shulian for centuries, and the same lessons have emerged again and again. Love doesn't work. Ruthlessness prevails. Cruelty triumphs. Fear is the only thing that wins respect, honor, and obedience. I've tried it all, Bingmei. Benevolence and mercy." He chuffed as if a bitter thing were in his mouth. "Those are the seeds of rebellion. Every civilization breeds its own self-destruction. I have founded my kingdom on the only principles sure to delay the devastation. The Iron Rules. It is my goal to understand and apply all the facets of order so that my kingdom will ultimately create perfection. Every citizen must have a duty. Each duty must be performed with precision."

She wasn't sure why he was telling her all this, but part of her believed that he simply enjoyed the act of boasting. She could sense that he cared nothing at all for the people he ruled.

He spread out his arms. "Do you not see the splendor of what I've created? A palace built to withstand the ravages of time. This place has seen earthquakes. It has withstood glaciers. And, like my empire, it will remain for all seasons and for all eternity. Each time I've been reborn, I've managed to keep my empire running for longer. I've learned to bridle the greed of men like Budai as one would harness a horse. But one immutable law rules all of civilization. The universe itself must remain in balance, or it spins into chaos. And that is why you are here, Bingmei."

He reached out and pointed to the other crypt.

"Bring her back."

He said the words with such loathing that she recoiled.

"Power must be held by *two* or none at all," Echion said, his tone commanding but full of hatred and animosity. It smelled like vomit and made her sick inside.

"But you cannot stand her," Bingmei said in disgust.

His eyebrows arched. "Does that even matter? It is the only way to achieve my full dominion. Raise her from that bier. You will do this."

He turned and walked back to the crypt. Bingmei had opened his tomb with the help of three others, but he grabbed the marble cover of Xisi's tomb with two hands and hoisted it off as if it weighed no more than a plank. His muscles bulged with strength as he set the lid down effortlessly.

Bingmei gaped at him. The action released the same spicy smell that had risen from his tomb. She hadn't smelled his darkness, his depravity, until his corpse was revived.

If she did this, his power would be even stronger. Now that she was here, she balked at the task.

"Come, Bingmei," he said, his arm outstretched to her. "Wake your queen."

In her mind, she thought of the marble plinth outside the hall, the one with the carvings of twin dragons on it. It was a testament of their combined strength and power. They ruled the skies as well as the seas and the land. His command made her shudder.

"Come, Bingmei," he said in a dangerous voice.

"Please, no," she murmured in despair. "Do not make me."

His lips curled back, revealing unnaturally sharp teeth. She could sense his hunger, his rapacious appetite. He wanted to consume her, to sate his hunger if only for a brief moment. Smoke began to ooze from his pores again, the dragon straining to come out.

He reached out with one hand, palm tipped up to the ceiling, and she heard the singing of metal and sensed the Phoenix Blade rushing toward his hand. Her yearning for it melted her heart. She reached out, trying to summon it to her palm as she'd done before, but the blade shot straight into his hand instead, and shoving against his will felt like pushing against solid stone. The Phoenix Blade crackled with energy as its magic was invoked.

The sword tugged at her, the craving for it so strong she felt herself walking toward it. Walking toward *him*. Tears ran down her cheeks.

Echion smiled with victory, gripping the blade.

When she reached the stone tomb, her legs were shaking. The power of the palace radiated around her, pressing in on her.

"Do it!" he commanded.

Bingmei stared down into the crypt at the shrunken figure garbed in colorful silk that had so many different hues it was difficult to pick a dominant one. The corpse was bedecked as royalty. It was clear she had not suffered from the winter sickness. Her skin was darker than Echion's, her hair black as jet. The skin was stretched so tightly across her skeletal face Bingmei was surprised it hadn't ripped with the strain. The bony hands had long, sharp-ended metal covers on the smallest fingers. The hair was braided and held up by a crowning wreath of wooden stays that made it fan out. There was a rune tattoo on the middle of the forehead.

Bingmei, overcome by the weight of the power pressing on her, knelt by the side of the bier, her limbs weak, her willpower wilting. She gazed up at Echion pleadingly, but he stood over her, sword upraised as if he were about to execute her. If only he would!

Sobbing, she knelt by the sarcophagus and pressed her hand against the cool stone to steady herself.

"Draw the rune," Echion said.

Bingmei felt her arm lift, as if a hand—once again—were guiding hers. Strangely, it felt *right*, as if she should not resist the invisible touch. She didn't trust the sensation but was unable to stop herself. Using her tears as water, she traced the rune as she'd done before, her finger moving on its own.

When she was done, she felt relief.

A voice whispered to her the words she'd heard Shulian say.

Yes, a sword shall pierce through your own soul also. That the thoughts of many hearts may be revealed.

Thunder crackled in the sky beyond the palace, and she felt the power of it in her knees. The wind began to howl, and a tingling, deadening sensation shot up her arm and into her heart.

The sound of a delighted sigh came from within the crypt.

CHAPTER TWENTY-FOUR

Power and Posterity

Bingmei fought to stay alive. The pain from invoking the magic was even worse this time, and it felt like needles were jabbing each fingertip. She could sense every clench and release of her heart, and each one was slower than the one before it. Dizziness and excruciating pain washed over her, and she slumped against the side of the sarcophagus. The magic was ripping her souls from her body in a slow, aching release. Part of her longed to accept the soft embrace of death, but her role in this was not done.

A new smell filled the room, and she knew it was Xisi, the queen reborn. It was the smell of jealousy, animosity, spite, malice, vengeance—all these smells roiled into one. But the most prominent of the smells was hatred, a fiery hatred that used all the other emotions as fuel. It stank like charred meat, burnt vegetables, and cinders. It made her gag.

"There," said Echion with triumph. "The empress has returned at long last. Hail, Queen of the Night."

"It took you long enough to bring me back, Echion. Were you even trying?"

Her voice sounded like the smooth strains of a flute, yet it was punctuated by vindictive jabs.

Bingmei lifted her head, and her vision swam as her souls stretched to leave her body. Still, she clung to the mortal fabric of it. The pricks of pain were agonizing, but she accepted the cost and greeted it as a sign she was still alive.

"You thought I would strand you in the Grave Kingdom permanently? If only I could."

"You could and you did, grave lord. And I mean that in its double sense. I've come back to the mortal world at last. How I missed this earthy shell." Bingmei could hear silk ruffling. "And how I loathe *you*."

"You were more silent as a corpse," said Echion. "Here we are, clawing and raking at each other—"

"Like two dragons," she interrupted. "Isn't that what we sold our souls to become? You hate me; and I despise you. That wasn't part of the bargain, yet we should have foreseen it. You were never satisfied by anything."

"How could I be when you never sought to please me? You're a vain, spiteful woman."

"You chose *me*, not the other way," she said with a sly tone.

"If I'd known you didn't have a heart but a fissure of stone, I would not have."

Her laughter sounded like tinkling bells, which belied the venom behind it. The pain started to ebb from Bingmei's heart. The dizziness began to pass. Their snarling and snapping were only amplifying the disgust she smelled in each of them.

"If you'd chosen someone milder, she would not have survived the first transformation. You cannot bear having a rival, an *equal* in power."

"You are *not* my equal in power."

"But I am, and that is what galls you the most. The bridge of immortality was crossed. You alone could not cross it."

"If there were a way to banish you to the deserts of Namibu, I would gladly do so. If there were any pit deep enough to bury your malice, I would order a million men to dig it for you."

"Alas . . . you cannot. We are bound together, you and I. Hate me, despise me, threaten me . . . it avails you nothing. Without us both, your Iron Rules will turn to rust." She sighed. "But it feels so good to be alive again. How long were we dead, and where is the chick who pierced our shells?"

"By my reckoning, it has been nearly eight hundred years," Echion said with disdain. "They've scrabbled hard to survive the harsh cold and the dark winters. If we'd left them alone for much longer, circumstances would have begun to tip against us. I had to intervene."

"Which king prevailed?" Xisi asked.

"The king of Sajinau came the closest. But he has joined the Grave Kingdom and will serve on that side of the Woliu. Shall we open it again, my dear?"

"I am not ready to summon the tianshi," she said dispassionately. "We can go a little longer without their help. My powers are building. It is midnight still?"

"Yes. Perhaps you should rest."

"Perhaps you should swallow poison."

"How many times have you already murdered me?"

"I never grow tired of it, Echion."

Bingmei was appalled by the way they spoke to each other. She was still hunkered down behind the sarcophagus, hoping they would forget about her. The tingling sensations had left her limbs, and she felt anchored inside her body once again. The agony of summoning Xisi had scarred her mind.

"You are hateful."

"You are proud," Xisi quipped in return. "Now where is the hatchling? I felt her hand touch the bier. It's a young one this time? A girl?"

"Stand, Bingmei. Stand so I may slay you with the sword of your ancestors."

"Bingmei? I like her name."

"You should. Because you, too, are an ice rose with plenty of thorns."

"How you like to flatter me," Xisi said.

Bingmei felt her legs pulse from the command, and she slowly rose from behind the bier. When she saw Xisi in her restored form, her jaw hung open in wonder. The woman's beauty exceeded even that of Mieshi. The scintillating colors of her silk robes, jackets, braided work, and headdress were a dazzling contrast to her dark hair and lovely skin. She was young, hardly older than Bingmei herself, yet her voice had revealed a depth of life experience that went far beyond the natural age of her restored body.

"Poor thing," said Xisi upon seeing her. She smelled the woman's disgust for her strange-colored hair and pale skin. According to Echion, the winter sickness was only feared and dreaded because of him—the man who'd crushed the world again and again. Xisi had not been raised on that fear, but Bingmei's appearance likely reminded her of the man she had wed. The man she so clearly hated. And yet, she also smelled the woman's relief. As vain as Xisi was, she was also insecure about her beauty, and Bingmei was too plain and small and pale to be a rival. How could someone so stunning feel so unworthy of admiration? "Look how she trembles! Greetings, Bingmei. You have done a noble deed. 'Tis a pity we must kill you. I should have enjoyed you serving me."

"She is vicious and cunning," Echion said.

"Those are compliments, Husband, coming from you," Xisi said. She stepped forward, her skirts rustling, the jewels adorning her making little noises like glass windchimes. Bingmei's attention shot to those strange pointed cones on her smallest fingers, like dragon claws. They were so sharp at the ends they could rip her skin effortlessly. Fear surged inside her.

Echion still gripped the Phoenix Blade in his hand, the tip pointed down. He brought the weapon up, holding it so that she saw his eyes on each side of the sharp edge. Her fear turned to panic.

Bingmei dropped down on her knees before Xisi. There was no running from the palace as she had before. "Spare me," she said, her voice choking.

"But you are too dangerous to be kept alive," Xisi said with a mocking smile. "It is truly for the best if you die now, when you are so young and fragile."

The lack of compassion that emanated from Xisi's heart was frightening.

An idea struck her mind. Whether it came from her own thoughts or from the phoenix, she didn't know. But the intention was clear. She had to reveal her gift. It was so rare, so unusual, that it might be useful to someone like the Dragon Queen.

"I know I am nothing compared with your greatness," Bingmei said. Echion snorted with disgust. "But I have a gift that would serve your interests." She gave Xisi an imploring look as the queen came to stand in front of her. The queen's jeweled finger pieces glittered at her.

"You have *nothing* that I could want," Echion said. He started forward, sweeping the sword down. She smelled his intention to kill her.

"I can smell people's emotions," she said. Casting a frightened glance at Echion, she said, "Some of the members of your ensign are not loyal to you. They are biding their time, seeking to learn your weaknesses. I can tell who they are." She swallowed, turning back to Xisi. "And the concubines. I know which ones would be rivals. Which ones *he* would care for. I can sense love, anger, and I know when someone lies." Her attention shifted to Echion as he closed the distance between them with growing rage. "That's how I knew you had deceived Budai. How I knew it was you and not Jidi Majia who visited me the other night."

Echion raised the sword again, unmoved.

"Wait," said Xisi, holding up her hand. She smelled intrigued. She smelled *excited.* This was something new.

"She must die!" Echion said. "All else is pointless!"

"Of course," said Xisi. "But I wish to test her words. This could be useful. Very useful in our court."

Echion lunged forward to thrust the sword through her body. Bingmei, on her knees, fell backward to try to dodge the blow, but Echion's reflexes far exceeded hers.

Xisi's nostrils flared, and she lifted her hand. Suddenly Echion was thrown backward, harshly and violently, and crashed against the floor. The blade clanged against the marble tiles and skidded away from him. Xisi turned, her beautiful face twisting with malice as she faced her husband.

"You cannot supersede my power," she scolded. "When I have chosen to protect a child, it is *my* choice!"

Echion's face contorted with wrath, and he climbed back to his feet. He looked haggard, drained by the effects of her power. "She will kill us both if we let her live! Destroy her now!"

"She is a duckling, a chick. She is nothing compared to us. But it is *my* dominion to choose which young ones to protect, to cultivate. The balance, *Husband*, must be maintained. I do not rein in your ambition. And you do not interfere with me either. It is my right to spare her life for now if it pleases me. Even from you."

Echion's cheeks trembled as he clenched his jaw. "How I hate you," he said.

"You don't know the first thing about hatred," she said coldly.

被埋葬的世界

Somehow it had worked. Bingmei had survived. It was a tenuous thing, and she feared the Dragon Queen's protection could easily be lost. After the fateful confrontation in the Hall of Memory, Bingmei had been taken to the queen's private chambers. They were in another palace, one nearly as grand as Echion's . . . but smaller. No doubt that snub was deliberate. The gold plating every piece of furniture glowed in the lights left burning by magic. Velvet cushions and a bed large enough to fit a dragon took up much of the chamber. Along one wall, concubines dressed according to court customs had been assembled in a long row, heads bowed, hands together with fingers splayed. Bingmei saw Cuifen and Eomen among the others.

Xisi walked in front of them, eyeing each of them for signs of imperfection. Her scrutiny smelled of bitter lettuce. Bingmei watched as it happened, fearing to make a sound lest Xisi change her mind. What would she do if Xisi asked her to point out which women were possible rivals? The fear of not knowing nearly paralyzed her.

But she didn't. In the end, she turned to Jidi Majia, who stood at the head of the row, and said, "Send them to bed. It will be dawn soon."

"As you command," Jidi Majia replied, bowing in reverence. The smell of sadness was overpowering. But he was relieved to be dismissed.

All the concubines left, leaving Bingmei alone with the queen. She was frightened but kept her expression vacant.

Xisi turned and beckoned for her to come closer. "I would test your powers," she said. "If you lied back in the Hall of Memory, I will kill you now."

"How will you test me?"

"There is a game the maidens of my court were wont to play. Two truths are spoken. And one lie. Not in that order, of course. One must guess which of the three is the lie. If you can, as you claim, smell it . . . then you will know which thing I tell you is untrue. Do you need to meditate or prepare yourself?"

Bingmei shook her head no, clasping her hands behind her back in a gesture of submission. Although Xisi might look young, she was as ancient and powerful as her husband.

"Very well." She turned her back on Bingmei to conceal her face and any expression that might give away the answer. The patterns on her colorful robes made Bingmei slightly dizzy.

"I am ready," Bingmei said.

"In my earlier life, I was the daughter of a great nobleman and chosen as a maid of the empress. My father was given twelve caskets of gold as my dowry." She paused, letting silence reign.

Bingmei smelled nothing out of the ordinary. She waited.

"Now for the second. My name means the 'west fourth.' When a couple's fourth child was born a daughter back then, that was what she was called. A name of no significance." Again, she paused.

There was no smell of deception, and Bingmei began to worry that her gift might fail her. That Xisi had a way of masking a lie. Or could it be she was saving the lie for the end?

"The final is this. A man once deceived the chieftains into thinking he was a eunuch so he could become my lover. His name was Li Jinxi, and he could comb my hair without leaving a single strand out of place."

That statement was easily the most outlandish, but it no more smelled like a lie than the others had.

Xisi turned around and slightly tilted her head, her mouth in a small pout. "Which was the lie, Bingmei?"

None had smelled wrong. Bingmei, still clasping her hands behind her back, worried that she was being tricked. She could smell no lie coming from Xisi.

"They were all the truth, Your Majesty," Bingmei said.

A glimmer came to Xisi's eyes. "Sometimes the best lie *is* the truth," she said with a cunning smile.

Bingmei's stomach dropped.

"You are right. You *could* prove to be a very valuable servant. You know which of my husband's warriors resent him? You would know which of his concubines secretly love him? Oh, that alone could make this new life very interesting to me. Echion cannot slay you if I forbid it. You know the bronze lions that guard the gates of Fusang?"

Bingmei nodded, restraining a flinch at the memory of how easily they'd killed Zhuyi.

"One has its paw over an orb. The orb symbolizes power and wealth. The other has its paw over a cub. That symbolizes posterity. Both lions are equal in power but different in duty. A dragon always seeks to devour its young—it cannot share power—but rulers cannot succeed in the long term without cultivating those who are loyal to them. I will let you live for now, Bingmei. If you continue to prove useful to me."

"Yes, Your Majesty," Bingmei said, bowing her head, relieved but no less afraid. The woman she'd allied herself to was little better than the man who sought to kill her.

CHAPTER TWENTY-FIVE

Two Souls

The sun rose in the middle of the night, as it always did in summer. Bingmei felt a hand shake her shoulder. She blinked, seeing the Dragon Queen's room sparkling with light. She lay on a couch in a screened-off corner of the room. Too little sleep had left her with the beginnings of a throbbing headache. But she was alive.

"Come, Bingmei," Eomen said, shaking her gently a second time. "She sent for you."

"Who?" Bingmei asked, sitting up and rubbing her eyes.

"The queen. Hurry."

Bingmei left the couch and started walking toward the sound of voices. She recognized the Dragon Queen's voice clearly and heard the mocking edge to it. After Bingmei passed through a partially open screen door, she saw Xisi walking slowly past a row of standing concubines. She was inspecting each and offering little criticisms.

"Who did your hair? It's terrible. Please do not come into my presence like that again. I see the little things. If you don't respect yourself, that is your concern, but your appearance reflects on *me*. Only the best will serve the Dragon Emperor. Now, look at you. Your nails are too long. Let me see your hands. They are too rough."

On and on she went, while Bingmei lingered near the opening of the screen. All the eyes of the concubines were fixed on the queen, and the smells of shame and worry exuded from the room. Xisi reached Cuifen next and said, "My, you *are* beautiful. He will enjoy your company, I should think. What skills do you have? Can you play the harp or sing?"

"I-I can sing. A little," answered Cuifen modestly.

"Then you must practice before me. This afternoon. I will have the head eunuch arrange it. Show me your best work, my dear. My husband will fancy you very much."

As she said this, Bingmei could smell the jealousy like the spray of a citrus peel. Then a darker, angrier emotion bloomed, and Bingmei realized it was Xisi's intent to have Cuifen killed.

"Bingmei. There you are. Come closer."

Xisi had finally noticed her. Bingmei came in with a docile bow.

"Aren't they lovely, Bingmei?" Xisi said. She was wearing a different gown now, more pink than blue, with a different headdress. She still wore the long finger sheathes that ended in sharp points. The smile on her face was as dangerous as it was beautiful.

"They are," Bingmei agreed, bowing again.

Xisi turned to her, a frown on her mouth. "Come. I must give you a gift. Follow me." The queen sauntered away from the consorts, leaving them standing in a row, their emotions still roiling from her criticisms. She took Bingmei to a series of waiting tables upon which sat some small intricately painted porcelain boxes. She examined several before opening one. The porcelain clinked as she lifted the lid off and set it down on the marble tabletop.

Inside was a bracelet of meiwood beads. "This is for you," Xisi said. "Hold out your wrist."

Bingmei obeyed, and Xisi fastened the bead bracelet to her forearm. She noticed glyphs scrawled into the meiwood. The same symbol was written across each of them.

"There," said Xisi in a pretty voice. "Now my husband cannot poison you. He will try, of course. The sigil on the beads is the word for 'rat.' They are highly sensitive to poison. If you lift food or drink that is poisoned, you'll feel the sigils grow warm against your wrist. That's your warning."

"Thank you," Bingmei said, surprised and shocked by the easy manner in which Xisi talked about poison and her husband.

"He will try, anyway. I won't let him succeed. Prove your worth to me, Bingmei, and I may let you serve me in the palace. Right now, you are unfit for service." She smelled the disdain that came from Xisi as she reached up and toyed with strands of Bingmei's hair. "Although it's the beautiful color of phoenix plumage, it is untamed and wild as a yak's hair. And you will never come into my presence again wearing the same robes as the day before. You are not a concubine, so you will not dress like one. Not that anyone would *want* you. But you will garb yourself as befits a warrior. I will even allow you to train with my private guard. Come, Zhuyi."

At the mention of the name, Bingmei turned and looked at the woman who approached them. She wore silk robes with short sleeves, unlike the wider sleeves from Sihui. As soon as Bingmei saw her, she recognized that this was *her* Zhuyi, who had perished on their arrival to Fusang. Her hair was carefully braided, and she had a straight sword slung around her shoulder on a band. A bracelet made of jade adorned her wrist. She had no smell whatsoever, which was why Bingmei hadn't even noticed her enter.

As Zhuyi approached, her face betrayed no recognition of Bingmei. She came and bowed before Xisi. "How may I serve you, Mistress?"

"Take Bingmei to the warrior's hall and see that she is properly attired. No weapons. Not yet. She must still earn my trust. If she wishes to practice her skills, I am content. Though not the phoenix form. *That* is forbidden in the dragon palace. Dragons brook no rivals." Her gaze narrowed on Bingmei. "I heard you did it in the courtyard yesterday. If you try it again, there are orders to shoot you. You've been warned."

The warning sent a jolt of fear through Bingmei's bones. "I-I won't," she said, bowing again. Not smelling Zhuyi felt like a kind of blindness.

"Good. I don't grant many second chances, Bingmei. Seek to please me. Always." She lifted her chin dismissively and turned and walked back to the concubines to continue the ordeal.

Bingmei stared at Zhuyi. "Zhuyi," Bingmei whispered in an urgent undertone.

"Yes?" came the reply.

"You don't remember me?"

"Of course I do. You were part of Kunmia's ensign." The words were flat, devoid of feeling. "Come with me. We must obey."

Bingmei nodded and followed, wondering at her bond sister's transformation. Zhuyi had always been quiet and thoughtful, but something about her lack of reaction and emotions seemed wrong.

"Did Echion bring you back to life?" Bingmei asked.

"Do not use the master's true name," Zhuyi said dispassionately. "You are unworthy to utter it. He is the master. The dark lord. The dragon. Always use their titles. Never their names. They are not like us."

"I'm sorry. This is all very new to me. How did you survive?"

"The dark lord brought part of my soul back from the Grave Kingdom after you escaped. He wished to know more about the ensign, about Kunmia and why she had tried to fight him."

Bingmei stared at her in wonderment. "Only part of your soul is back?"

Zhuyi nodded. "My thinking soul. My feeling soul is still in the Grave Kingdom."

Her words baffled Bingmei. She knew, of course, that every person had two souls—all the legends and stories agreed upon that. But the nature of the souls and what happened after death was a mystery that only Echion and Xisi understood. If the feeling part of her was gone, that explained why she smelled so different.

"We were sorry you died," Bingmei said. "Mieshi is still heartbroken."

Zhuyi shrugged. "I don't remember what that feels like," she said. "And neither will she when she dies and returns. I'm grateful to be rid of emotions. They were always a distraction. We are almost there."

They had wandered outside the palace and down a series of walkways leading to an enclosed courtyard that looked like a quonsuun. A variety of weapons adorned the walls, each with meiwood hilts or poles. The blades had a smoky color and looked very old. Bingmei assessed the height of the stone walls, judging them too high for her to vault over with the meiwood cricket. Not that she possessed it anymore. How she missed it. In the back of her mind, she could sense the Phoenix Blade in the direction of the Hall of Memory.

"This way," Zhuyi said, escorting her through the courtyard to the living quarters within. There were pallets and cots, and the air smelled of perfume. "This is for the female warriors," she said. "In Fusang, men and women are not allowed to train together. The men are kept outside the inner palace. The only men trusted to serve within it are the eunuchs."

"And those who serve the master," Bingmei said.

"Yes. But only a few are given permission. Those most loyal to him. We serve the queen. We are her bodyguards, protectors. Defenders of the palace." Gesturing to a cabinet, she said, "This is where the silk robes are kept. The old garments are put there, in that basket, and they will be washed by the maids and returned. A maid will also style your hair. The mistress likes novelty. She abhors untidy hair. Do not enter her presence as you are now. Do you have any questions?"

"Did you know Kunmia is dead?" Bingmei asked, hoping she could get a reaction out of her.

"Yes," Zhuyi answered flatly. "Do you think I care about things like that now? My past life means nothing to me. It is a great privilege to serve the mistress now that she has returned. When you have finished changing, come practice in the courtyard with me. I will await you there."

Bingmei nodded, saddened by the complacency, the lack of tenderness and feeling. Were the souls truly this separated? Was the other half of Zhuyi's soul wandering the endless streets of the Grave Kingdom, grieving for Kunmia, for Mieshi? Although this version of Zhuyi was as dedicated as the one Bingmei remembered, as much of a rule follower, she'd lost the part of herself that cared who made the rules.

Deep in thought, Bingmei changed her clothes, the movements automatic, then went out to the courtyard to train with Zhuyi. The two of them practiced side by side, repeating the different forms they'd practiced in the quonsuun in the mountains. For a moment, the sweat and the strain of muscles brought Bingmei back in time. She could almost smell the pine needles and the crisp mountain air. Hear the clatter of pans as the cooks prepared meals.

Why had the quonsuuns been built? They were clearly from another era. Had they been a place of refuge for warriors displaced by Echion? Or had he perhaps established them for his warriors to prepare them for service in the palace?

And why had he built the Death Wall? Was there something about it that gave him power over the land of the living and the dead?

They trained together until Bingmei felt her stomach growling for food. She asked Zhuyi where she could get something to eat.

"When you leave, go to the servants' hall just outside the training yard. You can get some bread there all day long. But the mistress will want you eating when she eats. Bathe and then report back to her quickly."

"Where can I bathe?"

"There is a bathing room in the warriors' compound. The water is from the river, and it's terribly cold. But warriors do not need the kind of comforts reserved for concubines. We must be strong as the ice that feeds the river."

Bingmei nodded and went off in search of the bathing chamber. Zhuyi was right, it was terribly cold. After she was done, a maid helped Bingmei comb and style her hair. Bingmei then dressed in a fresh silk robe and pants, cinching it closed with a silk belt.

Suddenly, she thought she smelled warm bread drizzled with honey. The scent was so delectable, she could nearly taste the treat. She stared around the empty changing room, wondering if someone had brought bread into the room.

Only then did she realize it wasn't bread she was smelling, but someone's emotions.

Someone she couldn't see.

Looking across the room, she saw black smoke whipping around like it was caught in the wind. From the core of darkness stepped Rowen. She saw a brooch shaped like a spider on the front of his tunic.

Her jaw dropped in surprise.

The smell was coming from *him*. He stared at her with open admiration, his feelings causing that delicious smell. It made her heart ache with sudden joy. He'd been searching for her.

And he'd come to Fusang to help her escape.

CHAPTER TWENTY-SIX

Impossible

Rowen crossed the room in three quick strides, his smell engulfing her with the proximity. He gazed down into her eyes, his hand lifting to caress her cheek. She was so surprised by his sudden appearance, she didn't know what to say, but that smell he radiated made her knees grow weak. He'd never made a secret of his admiration for her, yet she'd struggled to believe he could feel *this* for her. She was a no one. Short and pale. She hadn't allowed herself to entertain even a whisper of a feeling for him.

"You're still alive," he sighed. His thumb caressed the corner of her mouth.

His touch ignited powerful sensations within her. She wasn't sure whether she should run from them or savor them. Never in her life had she really believed anyone could love her in a deep way. Both the winter sickness and her perverse talent had stood in the way. But her appearance did not repel Rowen—it never had—and he knew her secret too. Still, he had come for her.

The relief at seeing him, a friendly face, finally overwhelmed her resistance, and she wrapped her arms around him, pressing her face against his chest. When his arms encircled her, it felt so natural, so comfortable, so delicious. If this were a dream, she didn't want to awaken from it.

She squeezed him, felt his arms tighten around her in response, and then she looked up into his face. "How did you . . . ?" Words failed her again. Her feelings hopped around like dozens of crickets, growing more agitated by the moment.

"I *knew* he brought you here," Rowen said. "We're connected, remember? After you and Cuifen were abducted, we came up with a gambit to try and rescue you."

"But what about the darkness? And all the Qiangdao guarding Fusang?" she said incredulously. The smell of his love was intoxicating, even more so when she was close to him. She should pull away. She still wasn't sure how she felt about him—the feelings were all so unfamiliar and strange. But every part of her body reacted to his closeness, his sweet smell. Her mouth was so dry it was unbearable.

"Because we had a Qiangdao to guide us," he answered. He traced the tip of his finger down her chin. "Muxidi brought us past the defenses."

Bingmei's eyes widened with astonishment.

"King Zhumu was desperate to rescue his daughter, just as we were desperate to rescue you. We had no choice but to put our trust in him."

Bingmei's relief shriveled.

It must have shown on her face, because Rowen's eyes crinkled. "He's not the same man, Bingmei. Your forgiveness has altered him. I've never seen someone so determined to be helpful. He's had dozens of chances to betray us, ever since we left Sihui. We've encountered Echion's forces again and again, but his knowledge saved us each time. *You* made it possible. If you hadn't done what you did in that ugly dungeon, we would have had no hope whatsoever." He was cupping her cheeks now, staring into her eyes. "I've felt your life has been in grave peril. That it has hung by a silk thread that could snap under the slightest strain. Yet here you are . . ."

In that moment, she wanted him to kiss her, and she feared it at the same time. Two vital forces yanked her souls in opposite directions. Shouldn't she be worrying about escaping? Why couldn't her mind think clearly? The risk he'd taken, that they'd *all* taken, was unimaginable.

"Your sister is here," she told him, and the moment was broken. She smelled his surprise, his sour dread.

"Here?" he said in shock.

Bingmei nodded. "The daughters of all the noble houses have been brought to Fusang. As Echion's concubines." His father had been a prisoner too, but she could not tell him that yet. She knew that he still hoped Shulian would be found. Although he deserved to know the truth, it would break her heart to crush the last flower of hope in his chest. She told herself it wasn't selfish to wait. Telling him now might endanger their escape.

His countenance fell. Bitterness and resentment and loathing mixed, tempering his previous joy. He frowned, trying to master himself and the surge of feelings.

"Jidi Majia is also here."

"And so is Zhuyi," Rowen said, nodding. "I saw her leave. She's changed. She's under some sort of spell."

"She is," Bingmei said. "It will break Mieshi's heart. I don't think Zhuyi will leave willingly. She'll betray us if she finds out. But I would like to try and bring your sister and Cuifen, who just arrived. Are you the only one within the palace grounds? Who else came?"

"Marenqo is here," he said, and Bingmei felt another thrill of hope surge through her. "The fisherman boy." She could tell he was still trying to master his feelings of jealousy. "Damanhur and Mieshi. Jiaohua, of course. We have orders to rescue both you and Cuifen. Muxidi will guide us back to the servants' gate so that we can escape. My job was to find where they were keeping you. Muxidi taught me how to use the meiwood spider so I could slip through the palace unseen. Do you know where my sister is being kept?"

"Yes, I do," Bingmei said. She paused, then added, "She's changed, Rowen. Her spirits are broken."

Rowen nodded. "I can persuade her to come. Do you think Jidi Majia will help or hinder us?"

"He will help us, I think. I will try and talk to him. I'll need time. Go back and tell the others you found me."

"I'll take you right now," he said. "I don't want to let you out of my sight again."

Another voice interrupted them. Rowen's eyes lifted to the doorway, flashing with fear. Bingmei whirled. It was Zhuyi. Her absence of emotion had made her imperceptible.

Bingmei's heart spasmed with worry, fearful that her bond sister would sound the alarm.

"I know you," Zhuyi said, walking into the room instead of leaving. "You're the prince of Sajinau. And it is forbidden for a natural male to be in this part of the palace."

Bingmei pulled away from Rowen's embrace.

"Zhuyi, no," Bingmei said, shaking her head. "I can't let you turn him over to the master."

The other woman continued to advance. "I'm not afraid of you, Bingmei. Or him. I can handle you both."

Rowen touched the spider brooch and was immediately enveloped in black mist. Bingmei felt an icy wind graze the back of her neck as he disappeared into thin air.

Zhuyi's eyes crinkled with wariness. Then she launched herself at Bingmei, her fist coming straight at her nose.

Bingmei dodged to the side and blocked her at the wrist. They traded a series of punches and blocks, and Bingmei felt her reflexes were barely adequate in her weakened state. Zhuyi's skill exceeded hers—it was Zhuyi who had taught her many of the forms. Bingmei dropped to sweep low, but the other warrior leaped back, landing in a low dragon stance, fingers tight in the sword-hand technique.

Bingmei sprang at her, rushing forward to launch a series of snapping kicks, one after the other. Zhuyi dived forward, rolling so that Bingmei was driven toward the door. When Bingmei landed, she turned around just in time to block the attacks coming at her head and chest, ducking and weaving to avoid Zhuyi's arms and legs.

A plume of smoke appeared, and Rowen suddenly materialized behind Zhuyi. Bingmei had thought he'd fled the room, but he'd been positioning himself to help. He punched her in the side and wrapped his other arm around her neck. Zhuyi kicked backward and then flipped him over her back. He landed hard on the marble ground. She followed through with a blow to his face, but Bingmei kicked Zhuyi in the knee. It made the other woman wince with pain.

Upon seeing Zhuyi attack Rowen, Bingmei had felt an overwhelming urge of protectiveness sweep over her. Rowen had not been trained in a quonsuun. Yes, he could fight—she'd seen him do so—but his skills were not comparable to what Kunmia had taught. Those protective urges had fanned something inside of her, and she felt like sobbing in relief as the phoenix power swelled in her breast.

Zhuyi snarled, and she struck at Bingmei with a series of kicks and punches, her movements deft and unpredictable. Yet the power flooding Bingmei made her faster, stronger, and she countered each of them. Grabbing Zhuyi's arm, she dropped to a low bow stance and dragged the other woman off her feet and onto the ground.

Zhuyi struggled against Bingmei's grip, bringing up her knee and trying to pivot away. Bingmei jumped over her and closed her fist in one of the techniques she'd recalled from the phoenix form. Unlike a regular fist punch, the forefinger was leading, allowing all the force to compress in the knuckle of that finger, reinforced by the thumb. She felt the magic swell within her as she struck Zhuyi's forehead with that single knuckle.

The blow stunned Zhuyi. Bingmei watched the woman's eyes roll back as she collapsed and started to quiver from the blow. It wasn't a death strike, but it was enough to have concussed her.

Bingmei rose and backed away, watching as Zhuyi's convulsions grew worse. Her whole body twitched, spittle dribbling from her lips. Bingmei worried that she'd permanently harmed her, but she felt a sense of reassurance that the phoenix magic was safely incapacitating Zhuyi.

Bingmei turned and saw Rowen rising, holding his back as he grimaced in pain. He had a look of admiration on his face. He embraced her again, then looked down at Zhuyi's quivering body.

"She knows about me," he said, his look hardening.

"I won't kill her," Bingmei said, wondering if he was implying that they should.

"I wouldn't expect you to. But this means we need to hasten our escape. Let's hide her at least."

"Grab her legs," Bingmei said and went over and heaved Zhuyi up by the armpits. Together, they carried her to the changing screen. Bingmei used the silk clothes to bind Zhuyi's mouth in a gag and tie her wrists behind her back. She wished she could work knots like Quion.

A thrill ran through her. Quion was close. Her friends were waiting for her.

After they'd hidden Zhuyi and secured her body, Bingmei rose to her feet.

"Come with me," Rowen said firmly. "Getting you out of here is my priority. If we succeed, then we'll go back for Eomen and Cuifen."

"All right," Bingmei agreed. "If we encounter Jidi Majia along the way, then I'll try to persuade him to come. I know the grounds better than you. Follow me."

"Lead, and I'll follow," he said, smiling at her again. She smelled the sweetness again, the scent of honeyed bread.

Bingmei came to him and leaned up on her tiptoes to kiss the corner of his mouth. "Thank you for coming for me."

Her show of affection thrilled him. He smiled again and then disappeared into wreaths of smoke.

被埋葬的世界

Even though Rowen was invisible, Bingmei could still smell him. She'd glanced at the mirror before leaving the training room and knew that her hair was askew from the battle. If Xisi saw her like this, she'd not only be suspicious but angry. That meant she'd have to do her best to avoid the Dragon Queen too. She walked down the corridor alone, feeling that she was being watched surreptitiously. It took some willpower to walk with a purpose, like she'd always done in Wangfujing to avoid attracting unwanted attention to herself.

Yet she couldn't suppress the fear that Echion already knew about Rowen and the others. He was the dragon—his senses were more powerful than hers. Anxiety raced within her. She saw the Hall of Unity and felt pangs of sadness. She would have to tell Rowen that his father was dead. But not yet. His emotions were already strained.

The sky overhead was a brilliant blue, and the sun burned her eyes with its intensity. It was a beautiful crisp summer morning, the air holding on to the morning chill in desperation. As she walked, she was struck anew by the colors of the palace, the beautiful embellishments and intricate woodwork and stone carvings. Again she felt the sensation that she had been in Fusang before the ensign had discovered it. Faded memories teased at her as she walked, smelling Rowen by her side although she could not see him.

"It feels like we've been here before," she heard him whisper.

"Yes," she answered softly, looking ahead and seeing no one on their path. In the memory she'd partially recalled in the concubines' garden, it had felt like someone was with her. Was that person Rowen?

Servants filled the courtyard below them, lining up in rows to perform their palace duties in stately strides. The fear that Zhuyi might recover any moment made Bingmei quicken her stride.

The smell of Xisi struck her strongly, coming from straight ahead.

"Hide," Bingmei whispered and darted to one of the nearest meiwood pillars. As she pressed her back against it, she heard the queen's entourage coming from another building, heading toward the Hall of Memory. Bingmei risked a peek and saw Xisi trailed by a dozen or more concubines.

"It is a pleasant morning," said the queen. "A day that you will always remember, my daughters. At noon we will perform the ceremony to open the Woliu. This will allow many creatures from the Grave Kingdom to pass again into this world. There is nothing to fear, my daughters. All will be made right."

Bingmei could smell the lie as it was spoken. At the noise of their approach, she edged farther behind the pillar. She had to move carefully to stay out of sight. The smell of the Dragon Queen's malice became overpowering. She knew Rowen was still beside her, but even the pleasing scent of his love was suppressed by Xisi's stench.

Bingmei hoped that Eomen and Cuifen were with the entourage. She wanted so much to rescue either or both of them. If there was any way that she could, she would do so. Protective feelings surged inside her again, and the magic of the phoenix tingled in her fingertips. Dizziness began to wash over her.

No, no, no! she thought in panic. Such feelings usually preceded her falling into a deathlike state. She felt herself begin to slump against the pillar, her legs losing strength.

She smelled Rowen's worry for her intensify.

No! Bingmei thought, pressing her prickling palms against the meiwood pillar.

She felt like swooning, fainting, collapsing. The sound of Xisi's footfalls passed her pillar. Her smell of rancor and hatred was so strong it made Bingmei want to choke.

She blacked out and started to fall.

CHAPTER TWENTY-SEVEN

Dying Deeply

Death felt like a sigh. The pangs and worries faded into stillness, and yet she was still there, still aware of Xisi passing with her entourage of concubines, still aware of Rowen and how he had materialized out of smoke to catch her body before it collapsed to the ground. His eyes widened with panic as he held her against the pillar. Bingmei watched her head loll against his shoulder, the open eyes vacant, hollow.

Bingmei felt her incorporeal form ripple against an invisible wind. She saw the frightened look on Rowen's face, his mouth contorting with grief. A gasp of agony left his lips, but he struggled to contain his sorrow while shielding her body with his own.

The entourage passed, Xisi babbling on about the upcoming ceremony and the importance of the virtue of decorum. Bingmei felt that if the breeze became any stronger, she'd float away like a leaf. How strange it was to see herself this way. Although it had happened multiple times now, it still didn't feel normal. It never would.

As the entourage continued down the hall, Rowen slowly lowered Bingmei's lifeless body to the ground. There were tears in his eyes as he stared at her helplessly.

Bingmei saw his compassion, his care, and it pained her even in death, though the sting was not as poignant. It was more the dull ache of a sore tooth.

She looked and saw the end of the column passing, almost out of sight. At the last moment, one of the concubines turned sharply, having heard some noise from their location. It was Eomen. And she caught sight of Rowen crouching behind the pillar.

Rowen, your sister sees you! Bingmei thought to him.

His head snapped up, his eyes wide with shock. He'd heard her, clearly.

His eyes locked with his sister's for a brief second, and then he touched the meiwood spider, and the smoky magic enveloped him.

Bingmei saw him still. He looked a shadow of himself, a half-formed dream, but in her deathlike state he was visible to her.

Eomen was heading back toward them, her brow crinkled in concern, in *recognition*.

Bingmei's gaze followed the rest of the concubines, but they had turned a corner and were now concealed by a wall. A moment longer, and none of the concubines would have seen them. How was it that Eomen had known to look back at that exact moment? She glanced backward once, furtively, before reaching the pillar and coming around.

When she spied Bingmei's body crumpled on the floor, Eomen dropped to one knee, her fancy silk gown fluttering around her as it settled. She touched Bingmei's cheek with the back of her hand and then bent her head closer, listening for the sound of breathing.

Worried emotions flashed across Eomen's face, and then her back straightened, and she looked around. "Rowen?" she whispered.

The magic sloughed off him, and he emerged from the shroud of smoke.

Eomen rose, her expression confused but tender. "I-I thought I'd seen you. I couldn't believe it," she whispered.

"Eomen," Rowen said, coming closer, his hands gripping her shoulders.

"Did you kill her?" Eomen asked in distress. "Or did she faint like she did back in Sajinau?"

"She's dead, yet her soul is still here," Rowen said. "I need to revive her. I was hoping to find you. We're going to escape. Come with us!"

Eomen blinked in surprise and then threw her arms around her brother, half-sobbing. He held her close, cheek to cheek, before pulling away.

"I'll be missed," she said, glancing back. "When are you going?"

"At noon. Where can I meet you?"

"The concubines' garden?" Eomen suggested. "It is not far from here, and the way is not well guarded."

I know where it is, Bingmei thought to him.

"Good. When the disturbance happens, go there. I'll come for you." He gripped her hands and kissed her knuckles. "I'll come for you."

"Thank you, Rowen," she breathed in relief. She touched the side of his face, glanced down at Bingmei's body, then took a deep calming breath and departed from the pillar.

Rowen knelt by Bingmei's body. "You are here but aren't here," he murmured, using the edge of his finger to smooth away some of the fallen strands of her hair.

I'm here, she thought to him. She tried to touch his shoulder, but her hand was insubstantial. His gaze was still on the body lying before him. She saw that her cheeks were turning ashen.

"What do I *do*?" he asked imploringly.

Try shaking me awake. It had worked in the past, but this time felt different for some reason.

Rowen did as she said, gripping her shoulders and gently trying to rouse her. Nothing happened.

"It's not working. What else?"

She didn't have an answer. The visions usually ended of their own accord, not because of anything she did, although Echion had revived her with a spell after killing her.

"Shui, Xue, Po?" Rowen whispered, cocking his head to the side. "Is that what you said?"

Her thoughts had been louder than she'd supposed. *When Echion killed me, he brought me back by drawing the sigils of those three words on my forehead. He used water, blood, and ash when he drew them. But this is different. I just . . . died.*

Nothing had been revealed to her. She hadn't been brought to some other location so she might learn something about Echion.

"Come back to me," he begged.

I don't know how.

His face showed his pain, and it was a strange mixture of bread-like love and bitter grief.

"Just . . . just breathe," he said. "Come back."

I can't, she thought to him sorrowfully.

Rowen continued to stare at her face. His lips pressed firmly together, and he knelt beside her, lowering his head. Was he trying to listen for her breath? It was gone; that was obvious.

Instead, she saw him press his lips against hers.

Something shuddered inside of her, then she felt a strong tugging. The sensation came from her body. Like hooks had snared her spirit, she felt herself snapping back into her body. Immediately, tendrils of stabbing pain shot up her legs and arms as the blood began flowing again. It was pure agony. Her eyes, still open, had not blinked and felt unbearably dry. They immediately began to wet themselves with tears as her eye muscles twitched and blinked uncontrollably.

But despite all of that, her attention was fixed on the feeling of his warm lips on her mouth—on the little puff of breath that went into her as she breathed for the first time since being revived. The act of breathing felt wonderful, and her chest craved more air while her lips craved more of him.

He pulled away suddenly, eyes wide with hopefulness. "Bingmei!" he gasped.

Each new gasp of air felt better than the last, and his smell of love enfolded her in the most delicious fragrance—relief. It made the pain in her hands and feet inconsequential. Blood churned sluggishly within her again, but at least she was alive.

A memory intruded on her, stunning in its clarity. Kunmia Suun had taken her to the shrine on the mountaintop above her quonsuun to practice with the Phoenix Blade, and her mind had flashed to a vision of the past, one she'd believed could not possibly belong to her. It had been a memory of someone kissing her. In that little remembrance, she'd witnessed rows of disciples, all learning together, congregated within a vast courtyard.

A courtyard she now recognized as Fusang.

Bingmei, stunned, sat up quickly and bumped her head against Rowen's chin as he bent down to kiss her again.

"I *have* been here before," she gasped, shaking her head.

His grin was infectious. He gripped her shoulder with one hand. "So you *have* seen it in one of your visions. We were here together." His other hand reached for hers, and his touch made the angry tingles beneath her skin vanish.

"It was only a fleeting glimpse. I think it was of the past, of a past life. What do you remember?" she asked him hopefully. He'd spoken of this before the switching of the seasons. Surely he could explain it to her.

"I . . . remember your smell," he said hesitantly, looking into her eyes. "I couldn't see you, but I knew it was you. We were here . . . together. You . . . loved me." The fresh-baked bread scent was so strong it almost frightened her. But it was only from him, not from her. She'd always been attracted to him, yes, and there was no denying the raw energy that sometimes sprang up when they were together, but she didn't *love* him. Not in the way that he adored her. She wasn't even sure she could feel that way about anyone. The walls of her heart seemed to groan in readiness to slam shut.

"Help me up," she said, wincing.

Still gripping her hand, he pulled her to her feet. She felt him move closer, still holding her hand, trapping her. As he leaned forward, the round meiwood pillar pressed into her back.

"Bingmei," he whispered hoarsely, tipping his head to the side, his lips descending again. A wild feeling filled her, something that threatened to unloose fierce urges within her. Her heart beat furiously, and her mouth went dry, but her mind kept shrieking that they needed to escape. Each moment they spent here was perilous.

"No," she said, turning her head away at the last moment. His lips grazed her ear. She shuddered and then freed her hand and pushed him gently away.

She could smell the sudden hurt. The crushing disappointment. He had risked his life to save her, to rescue her from the clutches of the Dragon of Night. He smelled of burnt sweet rice, the charred part that stuck to the bottom of the skillet.

She saw he was about to say something, and she shook her head, hoping to stop him.

She was too late.

"Can't you see I love you?" he whispered. "Can't you *smell* it?"

She felt tears sting her closed eyes. It was painful hearing the words. They were words that she'd never believed she was worthy to hear from a man because of her winter sickness. There was no illusion, no disguise, no deceit. He'd harbored these feelings for a long time and had struggled to conceal them from her. Even burnt, his emotions smelled delicious. But she did not reciprocate them. At least not to the degree he wanted her to.

She couldn't, not when she knew what she had to do. Somehow the phoenix had sent him and the others to rescue her. And she had sworn to herself that she would obey the call if given the chance.

"Rowen, I can't love you," she said, shaking her head as tears tracked down her cheeks.

He stepped back as if she'd punched him.

"You cannot? Or you won't?" he whispered.

She gazed at him, sensing his emotions, and their closeness choked her. "Don't make this any harder than it already is," she sighed. "I d-don't l—" she stopped, seeing him flinch. "I don't feel the same about you. And I shouldn't."

"Shouldn't?" he asked in astonishment.

"We cannot be like that with each other," she said. "I've seen Echion and his wife for what they really are. It may be too late to stop them." She bit her lip, hating the anguish she felt oozing from him. "But I have to try." She looked into his eyes with determination. "I'm going to cross the Death Wall. And that means we have no future, you and I. Whatever happened to us in the past is enough. I don't remember it . . . or much of it. I'm sorry. I'm so sorry." She wanted to run away, to flee the hurt she was causing him.

He stared at her, raw and grieving and not trying to hide any of it. It struck her viscerally that Rowen, this proud prince, was laying his emotions bare for her. Opening himself to possible rejection. He had not been like this when they first met. He'd always been so controlled.

Part of her wanted to reciprocate. She felt a little bit of her heart begin to crack open, like light peeking in through the clouds.

"You can't go," he whispered. "I can't lose you . . . not again."

"But I'm not *yours*," she said firmly, stifling her feelings again. The knife of her words plunged deep.

CHAPTER TWENTY-EIGHT

Betrayal

Rowen was shrouded by the meiwood spider's magic again, but he couldn't hide his feelings from her, even when he was invisible. He didn't even try. His honesty tormented her. She smelled the tang of bitterness, the regret and longing, the desperation. Experiencing the fullness of his suffering made her sick to her stomach, but there was no way she could alleviate it. They had no hope for a future in this life.

They walked furtively along a side rampart, away from the main halls of the palace. She could sense the Phoenix Blade was still within the Hall of Memory, but that did not mean Echion was with it. Thankfully, she could always smell him before she saw him. She passed servants who came in groups of three or four, some carrying trays, others, vases with flowers. The courtyard below was thronged with servants as usual, but it was eerily quiet, save for the low voices whispering to one another. Some draped garlands of wildflowers along the stone railings. They were preparing for the ceremony, she realized. The dragon and his queen had not finished adding to their fearsome powers.

"Turn this way," she heard Rowen whisper as they approached another covered walkway. Bingmei turned and then caught movement from her peripheral vision. Glancing back, she saw Liekou following them at a distance.

Her stomach twisted. Why hadn't she smelled him?

It struck her that he'd learned from his previous mistakes. He knew what she could do, and so he'd hung far enough back not to be noticed, a hunter stalking his prey.

"We're being followed," she whispered.

She heard a sigh. "It's Liekou. Our luck has turned worse."

"How far away are the others?" she asked.

"We're getting closer. Maybe I should hang back and strike him when he's not expecting it."

Bingmei felt a ripple of warning at his words. "Don't."

"Why not?"

"It's too dangerous. Let's wait until we outnumber him." She also wondered how loyal Liekou was to Echion. His feelings for Cuifen compromised him. She still hoped to use that to her advantage. If he knew they intended to save the princess, he might yet become an ally.

"I don't—"

"Shhh!" Bingmei warned, smelling a familiar waft of sadness.

Jidi Majia turned the corner ahead of them. He held a stack of bamboo sheaves that were bound together with straps of leather, but he fumbled them in surprise at the sight of her. "What are you doing here, Bingmei? Shouldn't you be with the queen?"

She blinked quickly. "Come with me," she said.

"I have to prepare for the ceremony," he said. "I must be there to help with the rites. What are you doing all alone?"

She glanced back and saw Liekou advancing, his brow furrowed with displeasure.

"Come with me," she repeated, touching Jidi Majia's arm. She looked him in the eyes forcefully. "It's time to escape," she whispered.

The steward looked even more perplexed. He glanced over her shoulder at the approaching warrior, then turned abruptly. Together, they walked in the direction he'd come.

"There is no way out of the palace," he warned her. "Every gate is guarded, not just with warriors but by creatures of stone and metal. You can't get past them, Bingmei. Everyone knows who you are and that Echion wants you dead."

"Prince Rowen is walking alongside us," Bingmei said, and she smelled a spurt of surprise, like fresh lime, from Jidi Majia.

"It's true," she heard Rowen whisper.

Jidi Majia shook his head in wonderment. "Your Highness, if you are caught—"

"I will be killed, I know," Rowen said.

"No. Even worse." Bingmei could smell the whiff of revulsion coming from him. "He will *devour* you. Those who betray him, who fail him, are punished sorely and with unimaginable cruelty. The nightmares I've seen since coming here . . ."

Bingmei wondered if his own faith was wavering. Would Jidi Majia betray them to protect himself? But when she smelled him, his scent lacked any duplicitousness. The usual sadness had been accented by a savory note of hope.

"We encountered Eomen not long ago," Rowen said. "She's coming too. You must join us, old friend. We must help Bingmei escape. *You* must help us."

"I will, I assure you," Jidi Majia said. "Even if it costs me my life. Where are we going?"

"There is a garden pavilion in the northwest corner of the grounds."

"Ah, the Garden of Ten Thousand Springs," said Jidi Majia. "The pavilion is in the center, with a round peaked upper roof."

"That's the one," Rowen said.

"We're almost there. It's abandoned still, I think. The work crews are cultivating the imperial gardens on the south side of the palace first."

"Let's go," Bingmei insisted, increasing her speed. She didn't look back at Liekou, but she knew he was there, keeping his distance. She dreaded he'd call out and order her to stop.

He didn't, nor did he stop pursuing them.

When they reached the corner of the palace grounds, the covered walkway opened to a small terraced garden. The trees were still alive, which proved the power of the dragon's magic, but the lawns were brown and decayed, and the smell of peat moss made her furrow her nose. There was no main gate to the garden, and there were no gardeners present either.

In the center of the garden was the pavilion Rowen and Jidi Majia had spoken of. Stone railings set at abrupt angles surrounded it, with four stone staircases leading up to it. The interior of the pavilion was made of meiwood lattices painted red, which concealed anyone taking shelter inside the pavilion. It was an excellent place to hide.

As she crossed the threshold into the garden, she was relieved to smell the sour odor of Jiaohua hiding in the bushes by the entrance. Other members of the Jingcha were also hidden within the bushes by the gate.

She caught the smell of Muxidi just before he emerged from the pavilion. He no longer reeked of murder and death, although there was still blackness in his soul. His lips pursed when he saw her, and she felt guilt and relief battle within him for a moment.

She approached him, Jidi Majia alongside her, and they met at the bottom of the steps.

"It is nearly noon," Muxidi said. "We were getting worried."

Bingmei felt his strong sense of purpose, his willingness to sacrifice himself so that she might escape. His whole bearing had altered. He looked nobler now, more self-assured.

He glanced over her shoulder, his face twisting into a scowl.

Liekou had entered the garden.

Bingmei held up her hand, turning slightly so they were both within her view. "Do not attack him," she said.

Liekou's brow lifted. "How did you get in here?"

"We're going to escape," Bingmei said, turning to face him. "We plan on taking Cuifen, and you may come with us if you'd like. This is your only chance, Liekou. You could not save me, but I can save you."

She smelled his wariness along with the growing anger from her friends and allies. The others wanted to hurt him, to take vengeance on him. They had not forgotten his dogged pursuit. One of the Jingcha had been killed in the river crossing, and he'd slain Mieshi too, only to raise her.

She saw Marenqo step around a stout tree, tapping his staff against his open palm. Mieshi emerged next, her eyes full of vengeance as she stared at Liekou. Damanhur was behind her, and although Bingmei wasn't sure whether they'd reconciled, he was clearly still furious on her behalf. His one hand wielded his sword.

Liekou did not look threatened, but she smelled the sour scent of worry. He dropped into a martial pose, an elegant cat stance, his fingers splayed in the tiger-hands technique.

"Is that your choice?" Bingmei said. "You'd rather stay Echion's slave?"

"I'd rather not be his *eunuch,*" Liekou said. "You think this small band can best him?"

"Yes," Quion said, stepping outside the pavilion. "We do."

Her heart leaped with courage upon hearing his familiar voice and smelling his fishy smell. They were all here. They'd risked their lives to save her. If she got the chance, she'd do the same for them.

Bingmei shook her head slightly as Jiaohua raised his blowgun to his lips.

Liekou looked at Muxidi with open distrust in his eyes. "You turned on the master?"

"I've endured the cost of serving him," Muxidi said. "Fear and death. He blinds men to do his will. My eyes have been opened. *She* is the phoenix-chosen. She's our only hope."

Liekou's lip curled. "She's not much to believe in."

Bingmei took a step closer to him. "I could have told Echion about you and Cuifen," she said. "I sense your heart, Liekou. You're conflicted. You don't want her to be one of his concubines. And Xisi plans to murder her." His face remained impassive, but his heart sprayed out a desperate, worried smell. She came closer. "I could have betrayed you to them, and you'd be one of his eunuchs right now. But I didn't." She gave him a forceful look. "If Cuifen stays here, she will die. Maybe even today after the ceremony. Come . . . with . . . us."

He tilted his head, his eyes full of doubt. "You could be lying."

"You know I'm not."

His resistance faltered. He abandoned the martial stance. "I can't let him have her," he whispered.

"Then go get her."

His brow furrowed even more. "You would *trust* me?"

She took another step. "I know when someone is lying. You cannot conceal it from me. If you swear on your souls that you will get her and come back, that you will not betray us, then yes . . . you can go."

She saw Jiaohua's nostrils flare with disbelief.

But what she smelled was the sweet-cake aroma of possibility. For the first time, Liekou believed he might, just *might*, be able to escape with the woman he loved. He didn't want Cuifen to be enslaved to Echion, and he absolutely didn't want her to be murdered by Xisi. The jealousy and resentment faded from his scent, and hope flamed in his heart like fire.

The sound of a loud gong rumbled from the center of the palace grounds. It repeated a second time, long and still.

Liekou blanched. Fear replaced his other emotions.

"It's the ceremony," Jidi Majia said. "They've started it early."

"No," Liekou replied, shaking his head. "That's the alarm," he said, looking at her. "The whole palace is under alert now. You'll never escape."

But his smell hadn't changed. Jiaohua had lowered the blowgun, but he raised it again abruptly. The warrior turned as the dart shot toward him, his hand thrusting up faster than a bird. He caught the dart midair, just before the point struck the flesh of his neck. He gave Jiaohua a warning look.

"I know another way out of the palace," he said to them. "A place where there are no guards."

It was the truth.

Bingmei cocked her head, the beginnings of a smile on her mouth. "Where?"

"There is a garden on a hill behind thc palacc. It's secret. Only the most trusted members of his ensign know of it." He gave Muxidi a mocking smile. "Is that how you came in?"

Muxidi shook his head no. "We came in through the servant gates."

Liekou nodded. "Those will be guarded. But not the secret gate leading to the hill. Follow the moat along the north wall until you reach the statue of the dragon. Wait there. Stay out of sight from the guards patrolling the wall. If I don't report to Echion immediately, I'll be executed." He looked into Bingmei's eyes. "But I will get Cuifen, and I'll come back. I promise you."

She could smell the distrust all around her. But Liekou wasn't lying.

"Go. We'll wait at the dragon statue."

Liekou bowed and then retreated from the garden. No one attempted to stop him, but Jiaohua looked at her incredulously. Many of them did.

"Rowen," Bingmei said, and he emerged immediately from a haze of smoke.

She turned to Muxidi. "Take the meiwood spider and follow him. See that he honors his word."

Muxidi nodded, and Rowen handed him the meiwood charm.

Turning to Jidi Majia, Bingmei said, "Go to the concubines' garden and get Eomen. Bring her to the dragon sculpture. Hurry, Jidi Majia. We only have this one chance."

"I will," he answered solemnly.

Bingmei sighed as she turned to the others. "We have to trust him."

Damanhur stepped forward, sheathing his sword. He smelled doubtful and worried. "No, Bingmei. We're trusting *you.* With our lives."

She saw Marenqo approaching her, holding the rune staff out to her for the second time. The sight of Kunmia Suun's staff brought Damanhur's words home to her. If she failed, they all did. If she failed, the dragon would win. Again.

CHAPTER TWENTY-NINE

Hunter and Prey

Tension filled the palace grounds following the sounding of the gongs. Worry throbbed inside Bingmei's heart. Even if they did escape Fusang, hunters would be sent out to find them. The dragon and his queen could search the surrounding area from the air. She was weary of always being on the run, but escape was her first thought. One step at a time. She could not worry about tomorrow if it never came.

As they carefully made their way through the abandoned passage north of the Hall of Memory, she sensed the dragons' anger. The walls seemed to exude it. It felt like dozens of eyes were following their progress, and a band of armed warriors might appear around the next bend at any moment, hopelessly outnumbering them. While it was a pleasure to have her old ensign around her again, she felt a keen responsibility for them.

The sun shone down from directly above. This was the time of the ritual, the ceremony that would reopen the Woliu. Would they conduct the ceremony anyway, or would it be put off to search for the intruders?

The sound of rapid footfalls reached her ears—it was a large group, not a single person, and they were behind them. Since they were on a main corridor, there were no hiding places.

Bingmei saw a side alley, heading deeper into the palace. They had to get off the main thoroughfare immediately.

Marenqo looked back, his face turning pale with dread.

"This way," Bingmei said, gesturing to the alley.

There was no time to argue. They darted down the alley as a group, then quickly turned around the edge of the building. There they hunkered down and waited, Bingmei watching the way they'd come.

In a few moments, a stampede of warriors charged down the path. She ducked her head back to avoid being seen. None of the warriors ventured down the alley where they'd gone. She pressed her forehead against the stone, breathing deeply in relief. She'd seen at least two dozen warriors charge past them, and their smell drifted down the alley until it reached her nose. Qiangdao. The air reeked of them.

"Where next?" Damanhur asked, sword in hand again. Mieshi sidled up next to him, her mouth pinched in a frown of worry.

"We'll be safer if we stick to the alleys," Jiaohua said with a look of wariness. "I'll make sure the path is clear."

"Do that," Bingmei said. "But I must warn you. Zhuyi is alive."

Mieshi's face lit up, joy emanating from her in sweet waves, but Bingmei quickly shook her head. "Alive, but only half-alive. She has no feelings. Her loyalty to the dragons is fixed. She cares nothing for us now. If you see her, you must fight or run. She's one of the people hunting us."

"How?" Mieshi whispered. "How did they change her?"

"The dragon only brought back one of her souls," she said.

Her words caused grief and confusion, but they couldn't discuss what had happened or how. Time was a luxury they did not possess. Jiaohua quickly left to scout ahead.

They continued to follow the edge of the building and then took to the alleys, careful to examine both ways to avoid being seen. Bingmei tested the air with her nose at regular intervals, trying to catch the scent of any pursuers.

After crossing several byways, Jiaohua held up his fist. He peeked around the corner again and then gestured rapidly for Bingmei to join him. When she did, he nodded.

"I see the dragon sculpture and the gate," he said. "It's not guarded. But it's out in the open. If we linger there, we could be seen."

Bingmei risked a look and saw the dragon sculpture. Perched atop a pedestal, which made it taller than any of the men in the company, it was tall and long, the body twisted like a snake's. The head was wreathed in iron strips like flames, or did they symbolize smoke? The snout was long and the maw open, revealing stone teeth. Even the hide was delicately carved into scales. The front left paw was raised, and it held a brass sphere that was also wreathed in flames or smoke. It was situated to vigilantly guard the exit gate.

Her experience with the bronze lions at the main gate made her shudder in dread. It would not let them pass without some gesture. Only Liekou knew what needed to be done. They could not escape without him.

"Do you want me to go closer?" Jiaohua asked her.

She thought a moment longer and then shook her head no. Turning to the others, she said, "The gates leading into Fusang were guarded by two lions. Did you pass them?"

"We had to bow before them," Rowen said.

"When we tried to flee the first time we came here," she continued, "the lions tried to stop us. To stop me, specifically. Now that the alarm has been sounded, it may not be so easy getting past this statue."

They waited for a short time, listening for the sounds of guards, waiting for the others to arrive. Once they heard warriors searching the alleys, but none of them ventured closer.

Soon enough, they heard approaching steps. Bingmei smelled a distinctive mix of sadness and hope that told her to expect Jidi Majia. She went back to the edge of the building where they were hiding and peered down the alley toward the dragon sculpture. Jidi Majia and Eomen appeared by the statue. They waited there, searching the streets nervously.

Bingmei gestured to get their attention, but they kept looking along the main thoroughfare.

"I'll get them," Jiaohua chuffed.

But he didn't move quickly enough. The stone dragon leaped off the pedestal and attacked Jidi Majia.

"No!" Rowen shouted in a panic. He cared fiercely about both of them, and she knew he intended to put himself in the path of the rampaging statue. She rushed after him. At least she could help. It was the one thing she could do for him.

Eomen screamed in terror, backing away as the beast sent the steward sprawling. The stone dragon rippled as it moved, as if possessed by some animating spirit. Bingmei gripped the rune staff and charged down the alley, the others following at her heels.

Jidi Majia rolled to the side as the dragon tried to rake its claws down his back.

"Betrayer!" The hissing voice came from the creature's open maw.

Jidi Majia tried to get to his feet, but the dragon buffeted him with its lashing tail, knocking him down again.

Bingmei sprinted harder, passing Rowen, invoking the power of the rune staff. The sigils within it glowed as she rushed up and whacked the dragon's stone hide before it could bite into Jidi Majia's body.

The wood of the staff struck the stone with a loud noise. She felt the magic of the staff draw away some of the dragon's essence. It began to turn, ponderously slow, its snout bared in an evil snarl. When it saw her, its tail came for her head.

She easily blocked it and felt magic drain from it again. The staff grew hot in her hands. She worried it might still summon the killing fog, but their need was too great to be ignored. The staff hadn't summoned the fog the last time they were in Fusang, so she hoped it wouldn't happen now. Marenqo and Rowen pulled Jidi Majia to his feet and ushered him away from the dragon.

"There you are!" mocked the dragon. "You reveal yourself!" He turned sluggishly to face her.

She swung the staff around and hit its snout. A piece of stone broke loose this time, clattering to the path beneath them. Damanhur struck it with his sword, and the metal edge sparked against the creature's flank.

"Open the gate!" Bingmei called to Quion.

He nodded in obedience and rushed to the doorway, his pack heaving against his back. Jiaohua hurried over to help him.

A warning pulse in her mind told her the dragon was coming. Not the stone dragon: *Echion*. The statue had summoned him. He flew over the massive palace, rushing to reach them before they left the gate.

The dragon statue swiped at her with its claws, but she dodged out of the way. Its tail lashed out and struck Damanhur's calf, knocking him down. Mieshi struck at the dragon with her staff. The blow was ineffectual, but it gave Damanhur the opportunity to jump to standing. Her gaze shot to the gate—both Quion and Jiaohua were pulling at the iron handle, but the door wouldn't budge. Like the other doors of the palace, it had nine rows of nine golden knobs. Then she remembered the Hall of Unity where King Shulian had been imprisoned. The memory came as a spark.

"Quion!" she shouted. "Touch a row of knobs first! All of them! Hurry!"

The distraction nearly cost her her life. The dragon shuffled forward, and its jaws snapped shut, nearly clamping around her arm. In the last second, Damanhur managed to shove her aside.

The dragon's teeth bit into his remaining forearm instead. The pain was intense, and she heard him cry out in agony. The dragon jerked its head, pulling him off his feet and slamming him into the ground. But it did not let go of his arm. Blood dripped down its stone fangs.

"Damanhur!" Mieshi shouted in dread. She struck the monster with her staff again and again. Bingmei joined in, trying to use the rune staff to break off the edge of the snout and suck away its remaining power. Damanhur groaned in agony, driven to his knees. His sword fell from his useless fingers and clattered onto the ground.

She felt the dragon coming closer, swooping over the buildings, racing to catch them. They had to flee before it was over. If Echion caught them, they were doomed.

And so was the rest of their world.

"Bingmei!"

It was Quion. She saw him pulling open the gate, his face grimacing with the strain. She felt the palace's magic grasping at them, attempting to prevent them from leaving. He pressed his body against the gate, straining against the painted door, and Jiaohua joined him. They both strained against the painted door.

"Go!" Bingmei shouted at the others. "Get out! He's coming! The dragon is almost here!"

She smelled him now, the dark clotted smell of his murders. Of his malevolence. And then, not to be outdone, she smelled Xisi swooping in, hatred and jealousy emanating from her like poison. Panic made her want to flee, but she also wanted to protect her ensign as Kunmia would have.

Damanhur groaned again. He turned to Mieshi, his eyes desperate. "Leave me!"

"I won't!" she said, tears running down her cheeks. She smashed at the dragon's snout again and again.

Damanhur couldn't free his arm. The one arm he had left. He looked at Micshi, stricken, devastated. "If you love me, go!"

Rowen gaped at his friend. His heart panged with pity and throbbed with respect. He didn't want to leave, and neither did she.

Some of the members of the ensign had already fled out the doorway, but despair held Bingmei still. When she'd fled Fusang before, she'd led the way, sprinting as fast as she could to save her own life. This time, the thought of leaving anyone behind agonized her.

A shadow blotted the noonday sun.

Echion was here.

They were too late.

The beast transformed into man as he landed in the thoroughfare, the impact sending shock ripples through the stone. His jade eyes met hers, and she saw the smile of a man ready to eat her whole. Power radiated from him, nearly blinding her with its intensity.

"Go!" Damanhur sobbed.

Bingmei was sick to her stomach, but she would die fighting as Kunmia had. She began to twirl the rune staff in double circles, advancing on Echion. The look of amusement on his face spoke for itself. He knew that she couldn't beat him—that there was nothing but death awaiting her—and he savored it.

A complicated scent washed over her, one she remembered from Prince Juexin's execution at Sajinau, as a blur of shadows filled the air. Muxidi appeared, shrieking in challenge as he launched himself at Echion and struck at him with Damanhur's fallen sword. The warm fragrance of his self-sacrifice was so powerful, it even eclipsed the stench of the murderous dragon.

Surprise overpowered every other sensation for a moment, but only a moment. His intercession would not buy her much time, so she forced herself to act quickly. Grabbing Mieshi by the arm, she pulled her toward the gate door. Quion still hunched against it, straining to keep it open, his own strength accentuated by the magic of the knobs. Jiaohua beckoned her to run, his face a mask of terror. Rowen held back, watching the scene in horror.

Why did her legs feel like lead in such a moment? She ran, pulling Mieshi away from her lover, and raced to cross the breach before Muxidi fell—the conclusion of the fight inevitable. After they passed it, she couldn't help but look back. She was relieved to see Rowen coming after her with Jidi Majia and Eomen.

Behind them, Echion dodged the former Qiangdao's attack with inhuman speed. The sword was sent flying away, landing far down the alley with a clattering noise. Bingmei saw him transform into the shadowy dragon once more, his slathering fangs biting into Muxidi's middle and hoisting him off his feet. Muxidi's look wasn't one of pain but ecstasy. He arched his back as his soul was literally ripped from his body. It remained suspended in the air like a leaf held aloft by a breeze, before his body was thrown mercilessly into the nearest building, where it struck and then slumped to the stone.

Muxidi's soul hung in the air for a moment before it was sucked away to the north, toward the Death Wall. It struck her that she'd only ever seen one soul rising from a corpse, yet Zhuyi had told her Echion had only brought one of her souls back.

What happened to the other soul?

The dragon's head pivoted, its cruel, reptilian eyes piercing her through the gate.

Outside, they encountered a thin stone path carved through dense vegetation. Trees of every shape crowded around the passageway, which led up a steep hill directly ahead of them. She saw a slanted-roof pagoda atop the hill, high enough that it broke through the trees. When she saw it, it looked as familiar to her as her grandfather's quonsuun. An inner assurance awoke within her that the pagoda would keep them safe.

"To the shrine!" Bingmei called out in warning, her heart in her throat.

She let go of Mieshi and turned to find Quion and Jiaohua rushing from the gate, which slammed shut behind them. Both of their faces dripped with sweat, and they raced from the palace in terror. Bingmei pointed to the pagoda and waved at them to go. As she did so, she caught sight of Rowen, Eomen, and Jidi Majia . . . they were already heading up the hill. In despair, she wondered how many of them would make it.

Come to the pagoda, she heard in her mind. *Come!*

The dragon leaped up onto the wall, its huge wings fanning out, writhing with smoke. It let out a roar of frustrated rage, a roar that split her ears and stabbed her mind with daggers of pain. Bingmei had done everything she could. If they stayed together in a mass, they would all die.

She felt a tingling run down her back as the phoenix magic swept through her. They were not running through a wilderness but a refuge, a park, a place for solemnity and tranquility. Paths crisscrossed up the entire hill, converging at the top. Some had benches for resting. She knew this because she'd been there with Rowen. They'd hiked it hand in hand. The certainty of that struck her like a whip. From the pagoda on top, it was possible to look down and see the entire domain of Fusang. It was the perfect garden, a sanctuary of peacefulness.

The dragon roared again and then launched from the wall, swooping down to snap her up in its jaws. Smoke billowed from its wings, from the maw lined with dagger-tip teeth.

Running wouldn't have saved her. It would have been impossible.

So she flew.

CHAPTER THIRTY

The Smell of Fog

The magic enveloped Bingmei, lifting her into the skies, bringing her above the tree line like a soaring bird. Exhilaration gushed within her, but it was seasoned by fear. She felt the dragon's eyes on her, sensed the blot of its presence at her back. She gripped the rune staff in her hands, the wood warm from the thrum of magic that still pulsed within it.

She flew up toward the pagoda atop the hill, swooping around the taller trees as she gained height. There was no sensation of flapping wings, like a bird, but she felt the rushing ebb and flow, like the tide when it smashed against rocks. She poured her determination into going faster still. But it wasn't fast enough. The rustle of leathery wings filled her ears, and then the shadow of the dragon passed over her.

Her instincts screamed at her to twist her shoulders and dive, which she did, and suddenly she was rushing toward the trees, her stomach lurching up into her throat. She banked away from a tall cedar and came perilously close to its branches, but the sudden move brought her away from the plummeting dragon. She heard its steamy hiss of fury as she continued to bank around the hill, trying to reach the pagoda. The red meiwood poles framing the square pagoda gleamed in the midday sun. Three curved roofs with flaring, pointed tips crowned it. It was built on a base of stone slabs with stairs on two of the four sides. A crooked cypress tree graced the top near the pagoda.

She was almost there. Bingmei fought to ride the wind up to the top, and she quickly began to gain height again. Looking down, she saw members of the ensign scrabbling up through gaps in the trees, struggling to reach the top of the hill.

Suddenly, the dragon was in front of her, wings flapping fiercely, yellow eyes hungry for her death. It came straight at her. She barely had time to swerve to the side, its stench engulfing her, before its jaws snapped at her—and missed. One of its wings buffeted her as she went by, sending her spinning out of control for several perilous moments before she righted herself.

Weariness began to ebb her strength. She felt sweat oozing from her pores. If the magic failed her when she was still higher than the trees, she'd plummet to the ground and die. Unwilling to consider that possibility, she soared up higher, coming around the hill, which tapered the closer she came to the top. She hit a sudden updraft of air and was flung into the sky, rising high above the hill.

The air was cooler at this height, and her insides churned with delight from the incomprehensible view. She could see not only the hill but all Fusang as well. The majestic structures of the Hall of Unity, Hall of Memory, and many other gold-tiled roofs rose above the watchtowers. She also could see the receding glacier and the waterfalls caused by the melting ice. Just to the north, she saw dozens of streams converging into a single valley of pulverized rock, the massive falls smashing into the valley floor.

Echion, who'd been circling the hill beneath her, spotted her at last, and the dragon beat its wings and charged up at her. She banked hard to one side and then twisted to the other. The dragon leaped at where she had feinted and snapped its jaws at her again.

Glancing down at the pagoda, she saw Marenqo reach the top of the hill and run into the shelter it offered. The dragon's long neck wrenched around, and its jaws tried to bite at her again. Bingmei willed herself to move faster, dropping toward the pagoda.

Which was when she saw the white dragon rushing toward her.

You're always so reckless, Husband, Xisi thought with disdain.

The white dragon was leaner but longer, its scales just as hard, and its teeth just as pointed. A ridge of thorny spikes came from its crown down the length of its back. It looked majestic, graceful, deadly.

Xisi feinted toward her, and Bingmei dropped her shoulders and plunged, hoping her smallness and speed would help her escape. Those qualities were her only advantages. With two dragons chasing her, she wouldn't last long.

Her dive helped speed her past Xisi's snout, and she felt a spurt of anger from the white dragon. Bingmei swooped low, spying Quion laboring up the slope of the hill. And that's when she saw the wave of fog coming around the other side. There had never been any fog within Fusang, but they were outside its walls now. Echion had apparently tired of the chase and summoned it in a wave to finish them off. Her friends were racing for their lives, struggling up the incline. She circled around the hill and saw the fog had already encircled the lower slopes. The creeping mist snaked through the woods, sniffing at trees, hungry to unleash the kiss of death on its victims.

It had been so long since she'd seen the killing fog that she'd forgotten the terror it always inspired. The fog curled and sucked away at everything. She saw three stags racing up the hill, only to be snagged by an octopus-like tendril. All three beasts collapsed instantly.

Echion dived down at her, smoking wings billowing like storm clouds.

None of your companions will escape my wrath! came his thoughts at her. *They will all die for trying to aid you.*

Feverishly, Bingmei tried to escape the massive dragon's lunge—and ended up in the trees. She dropped into a stand of cedar, and the trees' massive branches cracked and came smashing down as the dragon collided with them. Black smoke churned in the air as the sound of snapping wood filled the grove. Bingmei glanced down the hill at the fog creeping up toward her and saw Jiaohua struggling to outrun it.

He was looking back as he ran, arms pumping, one hand holding his blowgun. Then he glanced forward, and his eyes found her—she wished to help him, to warn him, to do something, but there was nothing she could do as a snaky coil of the fog wrapped around his ankle. He fell against the earth, his mouth contorted in fear, and the magic snuffed his life away before her eyes. His anguished expression slackened, and he slumped into the posture of repose, as if the weariness of his run had robbed all his strength. But his shoulders didn't move with breath. She knew he was dead, and her heart mourned his loss. His deceitful ways had made her distrust him initially, but they'd been used to support his king and then her. His loyalty had been proven. Her heart ached at the sight of his body.

"You cannot escape me!" Echion said, emerging from the plumes of smoke in human form, the Phoenix Blade in his hand. "Come and die, little bird! You are no phoenix!"

She *would* die if she faced him. She knew that. To her right, she saw Jidi Majia struggling up the hill with Eomen. They both wheezed with the effort.

Was it futile? The fog would climb until it reached the top, until there was nowhere left to hide. The thought of losing all her friends struck her with exquisite dread. Could she save them? She could hardly save herself!

With the fog still creeping up the hill, Bingmei jumped into the air. To her relief, the magic had not abandoned her yet—it lifted her higher. She banked to the left, away from Jidi Majia and Eomen, and Echion leaped too. He swung the Phoenix Blade at her, and she blocked it with the staff. It came again, and again she blocked it as she gained speed. Echion's face twisted with hatred and revenge as he flew after her, transforming before her eyes into the beast.

Xisi swooped down at her from above, gleaming white, a silent menace. Bingmei tried to swerve and felt the daggerlike teeth pierce the meat of her leg. Without thinking, she jammed the end of the rune staff into one of the dragon's eyes. Xisi shrieked in pain and let go, then hissed in outrage.

Bingmei was free again, her wound bleeding freely, and she continued to rise when another updraft caught her, sending her vaulting further into the skies. Both dragons were behind her now, and Echion charged at her, trying to close the distance.

Bingmei saw Mieshi reach the pagoda and dart inside.

Come, my chosen. Come to the pagoda!

This thought was not from her enemies. It felt warm and caring.

The updraft ended, and she once again found herself far above the hill. None of the fog had entered Fusang, but it swarmed the hill and the woods beneath it. Focusing on the pagoda, she swooped down toward it, racing the black dragon. Her leg thrummed with pain, and a quick downward glance revealed her garments were drenched in blood.

Echion's shadow stretched over her. He was going to catch her, she knew, unless she changed her tactic. Bingmei squinted, quelling her fear, and shot straight at Echion as if to attack. The dragon's wings splayed wide, its claws grasping for her. Bingmei broke suddenly, confusing him, and then swept around him toward the pagoda. The dragon screamed in frustration at having missed her again.

Finally, Bingmei reached the top of the pagoda.

The pinnacle of it was a huge golden knob with an iron spike poking from the center. All the stays of the roof sloped up to that point, and the knob was as big as a person. Bingmei hooked her arm around the iron spike and then slid down it to land on the other side. Her leg throbbed with pain as it hit the surface. She pulled the rune staff against her chest and lay back against the rooftop, her pack against one of the meiwood stays. Her lungs burned for air, and she gasped in desperation. She'd made it to the pagoda, but if the dragons flew over her, there would be no hiding.

Looking over the edge of the roof, she saw Jidi Majia and Eomen panting as they tried to reach the building. She heard the clanging of pots, the familiar sound of Quion's pack, and then she heard it thump to the ground in silence. Had the fog caught him? She grieved at the thought. She'd done her best, and it hadn't been good enough.

The flapping of wings filled her ears, and the shadow of the dragon loomed over her. Bingmei was exhausted, her strength spent. She'd tried to escape and failed. Hanging her head in defeat, she pressed her cheek against the roof shingles and quietly cried. It would be over soon. Her struggle had been in vain. The two dragons would rule for another age until the phoenix chose another or sent Bingmei's soul back into the world to be reborn again.

Nothing happened.

As Bingmei waited in suspense for teeth and claws to destroy her, she felt the urge to hold absolutely still, to relax her weary muscles, to release the sadness and let it go. She gave herself over to the tranquil calm that caressed her cheek like the breeze.

As she lay on the rooftop, facedown, she saw the tendrils of fog creep over the edge of the roof. They came swirling up the tiles toward her feet.

Where is she? It was Xisi's voice.

I don't see her in the fog. The reply was from Echion.

A little trickle of hope came from deep inside her. She sensed the dragons above her, could hear their thoughts and feel the wind of their pulsing wings, but they could not see her.

Find her, commanded Xisi. *It could be a trick.*

It is a trick! Where is she? She was on the roof. Now she's gone.

Find her!

Bingmei felt herself lulled to sleep. She smelled a cinnamon-porridge smell that wafted over her.

Mother?

It was Bingmei's last thought before she fell asleep.

被埋葬的世界

When she awoke, she was still on the roof, the sun beating down on her. She sat up, feeling her strength had returned—and was shocked to discover her leg was no longer in pain. It felt perfectly fine, although the torn and bloody leg of her pants attested to the wound Xisi had given her. The rune staff sat next to her.

The killing fog was gone.

Bingmei heard footsteps from below. She rubbed her eyes and tried to understand what had happened.

"Do you see anyone?"

It was Cuifen's musical voice.

"The killing fog must have got them," Liekou replied. "Like it did the Jingcha man we found lower down."

Bingmei heard their steps as the two approached.

Scooting down to the edge of the tile rooftop, she saw Liekou and Cuifen down below, approaching the summit. Walking hand in hand.

Maybe everyone else was dead. Instead of feeling sadness, she felt only peace and comfort. From the edge of the roof, she saw dead animals everywhere. Birds lying in the tall grasses. She saw several more deer had perished and even a fox cub.

"Up here," she said, swinging her feet over the edge. She did not feel the magic of the phoenix anymore. If she wanted to get down, she would have to climb.

"Bingmei!" Cuifen called in surprise.

Liekou looked up at her in amazement. "You survived?"

Bingmei nodded. "I need to climb down. Give me a moment."

"Wait," Liekou said. He approached the bottom of the pagoda. She looked down at him curiously as he pulled something from his pocket.

"I'll throw this up to you," he said. He pitched a tiny object up to her, and she caught it, gazing at it with relief and awe. Her grandfather's meiwood cricket. Tears of joy stung her eyes. She rose from the edge of the roof and then rubbed her thumb along the cricket's back. Its magic sprang to life, and she felt safe to jump down to the ground, which she did.

Cuifen had a sweet smell about her. She still wore the robes of a concubine, but they were disheveled and dirty after the hike up the hill.

"How did you make it?" Bingmei asked them.

Liekou smelled different as well. Solemn, yet floral. "We went to the dragon sculpture as I said and found one of your men, the one-armed fellow, captured by the guards. The dragon was already following you at that point, and so we hid. I drew the sigil on Cuifen's back to protect her from the fog. The fog itself hid us from our pursuers and from the dragons."

Bingmei nodded in understanding. Liekou knew the protections. That made sense.

"Where are the others?" Liekou asked, looking around. "I found the one with the blowgun farther down the hill," he said, nodding the way they'd come. "He's dead."

Bingmei saw Quion's pack lying on the ground at the top of the hill. But there was no sign of the body.

Bingmei's spirits lifted a little more. Could they have escaped after all?

She turned and walked toward the pagoda. That was when she noticed the phoenix carvings on the underside of the roof. She pushed on the door, and it opened, revealing the shadowy darkness within. Bodies were strewn all over the floor. Marenqo, Jidi Majia, Eomen, Mieshi, Rowen, Quion.

Still, her heart didn't hurt. She stared at them in confusion, aware that she could smell each one of them. They weren't dead—they were resting peacefully.

Bingmei hurried to Quion first and shook his shoulder.

His eyes fluttered open in startled surprise.

"Bingmei?" he asked, stifling a yawn.

CHAPTER THIRTY-ONE

Aftermath

Marenqo and Quion returned, carrying Jiaohua's body up to the pagoda on the top of the hill. She had worried about their safety, but the Jingcha captain had served them faithfully, and she wanted to at least attempt to bring him back to life before abandoning the hill. The two men huffed and sweated after carrying the body uphill, and they brought it into the shade of the pagoda and set it at her feet.

There were no benches to sit on within the pagoda, all were outside, but the cool stone floor was a suitable resting place. The mixture of emotions within the confined space overwhelmed Bingmei's senses. While everyone was relieved to be alive, Mieshi was tart with the worry of Damanhur's capture. Liekou and Cuifen, huddling in a corner, smelled of the spring flowers of new love and the saffron of worry about the future. Jidi Majia was sadness and weariness. Rowen couldn't even look at her, his emotions churning with the feelings of a jilted man. The only calm one in the bunch was Quion.

Bingmei realized that their emotions were distracting her. Crouching by Jiaohua's body, she looked up at them, one by one. "Would you all leave, please, while I try this?"

She was their captain, the leader of a broken ensign. And so they obeyed, shuffling out into the late afternoon sky to leave her alone with the corpse.

Quion was the last to go, and before he stepped outside, she asked, "Quion, would you start a little fire? I need some ashes."

He nodded as he stepped away.

After they were gone, and their smells with them, she breathed a little easier. She was still in awe that they hadn't all died. It was the first time, to her knowledge, that *anyone* had survived the killing fog without the mark on their back. She believed it had something to do with the phoenix sigils engraved on the pagoda. When Muxidi had come for her in Sajinau, she'd been roused from sleep in time to escape her bedroom. She'd hidden within an iron urn that had the markings of the phoenix on it. Muxidi had passed the urn, unable to see her. Was that because of the night shadows, or was there a special protection that came with the mark of the phoenix?

There were always more questions than there were answers. She sighed, sad that the knowledge of the past had been lost. Or that Echion had deliberately destroyed it to maintain his power.

There was one more question that needed answering. Could she revive the dead herself? Her power had brought Echion and Xisi back to life. The dragons had brought Zhuyi back to life. Could she do the same with Jiaohua? What if it robbed him of his feelings too?

Before Quion and Marenqo had left to retrieve the body, she had borrowed Quion's water flask to slake her thirst. Now she used it again. Uncorking the stopper, she poured a dash of water into her hand, enjoying the cooling sensation of it. She dabbed her finger in it and then looked down at Jiaohua's body. His two souls were gone. Would she be able to summon them back?

She drew the sigil she'd drawn to raise the dragons. Nothing guided her hand this time. She felt no power flicker through her. The symbol she'd drawn began to evaporate slowly. She stared at it, willing Jiaohua to come back, but it evaporated without doing anything.

Disappointment wriggled within her stomach, but not surprise. It had *felt* different before. And she realized something was missing. Did it have to do with the stone sarcophagi within the Hall of Memory? Both Echion's and Xisi's bodies had been prepared for burial, something she couldn't do for Jiaohua without any supplies.

She had one more idea to try. When she'd upset Echion, and he'd choked her, he had drawn three symbols on her forehead in blood, ash, and water.

Bingmei rose and went outside, shielding her eyes from the sun. She asked after Quion, and Marenqo pointed to some trees on the far side of the hill, the part that faced away from the palaces. She saw him in the trees, crouched over some twigs he'd gathered. She went to him and smiled in appreciation.

He'd managed to make a small fire.

After taking a small burning stick, she said, "Smother the fire. We don't want to reveal ourselves. The longer they think we're dead, the better." No doubt they'd come to retrieve the bodies, but she sensed the two dragons were at war with each other. With any luck, they'd spend enough time fighting for Bingmei and her group to put plenty of distance between themselves and Fusang. Part of her also wondered if the dragons would be allowed to check the phoenix pagoda for bodies. Would the same magic that had protected her and the others keep Echion and Xisi out?

Quion stamped it out with his boot and some dirt.

"Can I borrow your knife?" she asked, and he handed it to her.

Bingmei took the smoldering stick and the knife and brought them back to the pagoda. Once inside, she knelt by the body again. Three words—blood, water, spirit. She had the representations of each now.

After blowing out the embers on the end of the burning stick, she ground the charred part into the stone floor to make ash. She pricked her forearm with the knife to make a little blood well up. The water flask still sat at her feet. She drew the symbols one by one, using the different substances as her ink.

Then she sat back on her haunches and watched, waiting patiently. Again, she felt nothing. Something was missing, and Jiaohua was still dead. He looked peaceful, but so did every victim of the fog. She pursed her lips, shaking her head.

"I'm sorry, Jiaohua," she whispered. "I failed you again. If there was a way . . . if I could bring you back, I would."

As soon as the words left her mouth, she felt something buzz inside her chest. It was a strange feeling of conviction, of rightness. *Certainty*. It began to build inside her, like small sticks catching fire.

I will teach you.

The words came as whispers. She felt a tingle go down her back, a comforting feeling that radiated deep inside her. She blinked, suddenly on the verge of tears. She smelled the cinnamon-porridge scent as love and tenderness swept over her. The same thing had happened, she realized, before she fell asleep on the roof of the pagoda.

"Are you . . . are you the phoenix?" Bingmei gasped.

She felt the little flame of conviction spurt stronger, crackling with life and energy.

Will you come to my quonsuun, Bingmei?

She knew at once what it was asking of her. Jidi Majia had told her of the phoenix's quonsuun beyond the Death Wall. This was her chance to pledge herself to the phoenix. She hadn't missed her chance after all. The old fears began to loom within her mind, but she remembered what she'd promised the phoenix in Fusang. The phoenix had indeed rescued her and released her from bondage. Would she keep her end of the bargain?

When she didn't answer right away, it asked again: *Will you come?*

"Yes," Bingmei said, bowing her head. "I will come."

She felt a surge of joy in her heart, one so powerful it stunned her. The cinnamon smell engulfed her, and she had the sense that if she lifted her head and turned around, she would see her own mother there. The smell was that familiar. She felt an overpowering sense of love and acceptance for the phoenix.

The question came a third time.

Bingmei, will you come?

Why was the phoenix asking her again? Did it doubt her resolve after her previous actions? Of course it did. Bingmei had refused before.

A featherlight touch grazed her shoulders, making her shiver.

"I will," Bingmei said in another choked whisper.

Her answer was accepted the third time. Immediately, her soul was unsheathed from her body, which slumped to the floor. Would her souls be taken there?

Her soul floated up through the roof of the pagoda, passing through it as a shadow. She hovered above the bulb atop the pagoda. Although she'd been even higher before, she'd been focused on her battle with the dragons. Now, she took in the dramatic view of the land to the north. The waterfalls crashing in the valley. The crags of mountains and the Death Wall looming in the distance.

Power pulsed within her, and her vision increased to that of an eagle. She saw *beyond* the Death Wall, saw a forested woodland filled with animals she'd never seen before, including enormous, white-pelted bears. Her vision stretched even farther, and she saw groves of trees covering the land. But what she sought lay beyond that. Farther and farther she saw, and it felt like she was flying.

She saw a series of mountains ahead, crowned with snow even in the summer, but before the mountains, there stretched a series of crags and ravines, with rivers running through the tunnels. It looked like a mountain had shattered, leaving behind tall, jagged columns of stone. Her gaze narrowed on one of the corridors—a vast canyon with steep walls and a river running through it, full of sediment. That was the canyon she needed to enter. Her ghost-self followed the twists and turns that led into the heart of the broken mountains, guided by some internal compass. At the end, she saw a final column, a broken cliff that towered above her. Atop it, fashioned out of stone from the rocky canyon itself, she saw a small shrine through the thick cover of trees. In the middle waited a stone sarcophagus.

On the sarcophagus was the effigy of the phoenix, carved by an expert hand, with plumage and beak and talons.

That was where she must go. And that was where she would die.

The vision closed, and she felt her soul sinking back through the roof, gently nestling back into her body. An overwhelming urge to sleep enveloped her, as it had before, but she heard the whispers again.

Your departure interrupted the ceremony that was supposed to happen at noon. They will open the Woliu at midnight instead. The creatures they summon from the Grave Kingdom will hunt you. Do what you must to escape. I will no longer protect you with the power of flight until you have found the empty tomb. Be vigilant, Bingmei. Their power grows. We will meet at last in the halls beyond the Grave Kingdom.

被埋葬的世界

They gathered around her after she left the pagoda. The vision had sapped her strength, but the phoenix's warning had encouraged her to push through the weakness. She smelled Marenqo's disappointment when Jiaohua didn't come outside with her.

"I could not do it," she announced. "I couldn't bring him back. I can't bring anyone back. But I had a vision." She looked at Jidi Majia and saw his eyes widen with hope. "I know where to find the phoenix shrine beyond the Death Wall. This night, Echion and Xisi will open the Woliu, a rift between our world and the Grave Kingdom. He knows, or at least believes, that I survived. He will send minions to hunt for me."

She sighed and looked at their worried faces. "Where I am going, there will be no return. I do not ask any of you to come with me. In fact, I think I must do this alone." She took a deep breath, struggling to overcome her feelings of dread. "So I absolve you of your loyalty to me. I must go north. Whatever happens after I get there is still a mystery. You may go your separate ways or choose another to lead. But this I know. If we don't leave this hill immediately, we're all going to die. The phoenix won't protect us a second time."

She lifted Kunmia's staff, which she'd brought outside with her. "Thank you for coming after me. I could not have escaped on my own. I will honor your sacrifice with my own. Thank you."

Jidi Majia stepped forward immediately. "I'll go with you, Bingmei. I have no hope of survival otherwise. I'll go."

Quion stuck his hands in his pockets and gave her a determined nod. He'd recovered his pack and looked ready to leave.

Marenqo's lips pressed tightly together. He looked at the others, who were also exchanging glances.

Mieshi had a look of anguish on her face, but her eyes were fierce. "I go with you, Sister," she said. That surprised Bingmei. But then, Kunmia had ingrained loyalty into all of them.

"Thank you," Bingmei said, her voice choking.

Marenqo folded his arms. "If Quion is going, then I am going. At least there will be plenty to eat."

"Do you know how to defeat Echion?" Liekou asked pointedly.

Bingmei shook her head no.

His lips pursed with indecision.

Cuifen gazed at Bingmei. "I think we should go with her," she said to Liekou. "I don't want to go back to Fusang. Ever. She's our only chance."

Liekou nodded, his decision made.

That left Rowen and Eomen. It would be painful if Rowen was there. His heart smelled like the aftermath of a fire, and his presence kept reminding her of what had been—and what could not be. He was broken inside, destroyed. Perhaps it would be better for him if he stayed away from her, but even so, she wanted him to come.

"I'll go with you to the Death Wall," he said. "But I won't watch you die."

It was enough. She gave him a respectful nod. "Let's get as far away from here as we can."

被埋葬的世界

The stars overhead told her it was nearly midnight. This deep into the summer, it seemed as though it never got truly dark, that the sun was only hiding temporarily beneath the cover of jagged mountains. They walked across the hard-packed ice of the glacier. The edges were melting too quickly to be safe. By nightfall they were far enough from Fusang that they couldn't see any of the lights from the palace in the distance.

But that changed at midnight.

"Look," said Marenqo, who had paused to drink from his water flask.

They all turned, and Bingmei's mouth fell open.

The sky was afire with colors. Greens and blues and violets danced across the sky in smoky ribbons. How could broken rainbows be painted in the sky at midnight? This must be the Woliu. The colors rippled and shifted, moving like clouds tousled by the wind. The beautiful display, completely silent, was breathtaking—yet it filled her with dread. The barrier between the world of the living and the world of the dead had been breached. The display filled the entire skyline, and she wondered if the people in Sajinau, Wangfujing, or Sihui could see it, or if they were the lone spectators outside of Fusang.

A wolf began to howl in distress somewhere in the dark mountains surrounding the glacier. Another began to howl moments later. The sounds chilled her heart.

Even the animals dreaded what was coming.

被埋葬的世界

Neither fire nor wind, birth nor death can erase our good deeds. Time itself may forget, but they are still unforgotten.

—Dawanjir proverb

CHAPTER THIRTY-TWO

The New World

Climbing the ice-strewn mountains north of Fusang taxed their strength and endurance. They survived on an endless supply of fish caught by Quion as well as some of the edible plants and flowers found in the desolate but majestic peaks. It was a frequent occurrence to see brooding white-headed eagles soaring overhead.

When night came again for the second time after leaving the lost palace, the sky once again lit up with the eerie rainbow-colored lights, which transfixed their eyes. The haunting display was a signal that something had irrevocably changed. But what that change was, they wouldn't realize until the third day.

They continued to follow the glacier due north, the shortest distance to the Death Wall. Bingmei knew the scenery from the vision the phoenix had granted her. She'd shared most of the details with her ensign, especially about the strange animals she'd seen beyond the wall. Around midday they reached one of the places she'd seen in the vision—a convergence of glacial mountains that fed into a massive river.

They could hear it long before they reached it.

Coming down the icy slope of the mountain range, they found a fertile valley beneath them, carved up by the massive ice. The roar of distant waterfalls they'd heard since midmorning grew into a cacophonous chorus. Waterfalls rushed down the slopes of the mountains on each side of the valley, merging at a crescent-shaped rim of rock that crowned the edges of the valley and thundered into the canyons below. The river it created headed off in a westward direction, joined along the way by other rivulets and waterfalls to create the largest river she'd ever seen.

They paused at the sight of the valley, and as Bingmei looked at her companions' faces, she saw the same awe that she felt. The view was incomprehensibly beautiful, with jagged mountain peaks all around, the colorful gorse and trees on the valley floor adding a delightful contrast.

Marenqo shook his head. "It must be deafening down there. You'd have to shout to be heard."

Jidi Majia wiped a sheen of sweat from his brow. The labors of the walk had been rigorous for him, but he'd surprisingly managed to keep up.

"I've ventured to many distant lands," he said. "But I've seen nothing like this." He held out his hand and gestured to the scene. "Everything has been carved by nature itself. I will never forget this place."

"Should we name it?" Marenqo suggested.

"Could a name capture such a vista?" Rowen asked. "If only others could see this."

Quion smelled of wonder as he stood next to Bingmei, his thumbs hooked in his belt. "It won't be easy getting around it. We'll have to cross some of those rivers. They'll be cold and dangerous."

"You've done it before," Liekou said, giving Bingmei a cunning look. She knew they were both thinking of the way he'd chased them from the mountain caves where they had spent the winter. Not a fortuitous start, but there was no denying he'd made himself useful since joining them. Although she'd distrusted him at first, he never smelled of dishonesty, and his regard for Cuifen had only grown stronger.

"I think Marenqo Valley has a nice sound to it," Marenqo said thoughtfully.

Mieshi gave him a withering look and continued to walk. "We should keep going."

Marenqo sighed with mock humility. "*I* like the sound of it."

They decided Quion was right—trying to cross the rivers leading to the crescent range of waterfalls would be too dangerous—so they went east to try to cross farther upstream. Which was when they discovered the area was heavily populated by bears.

Mieshi stepped in bear scat, and soon after, they noticed tracks crisscrossing the land ahead of them. If they encountered an angry bear, it would be a vicious fight.

Deeper into the afternoon, they found a passable part of the plain, where the water only went up to their knees at the deepest part. And it was there that they discovered dozens of brown-furred beasts roaming the shore to feast on the trout that were as plentiful as the waters.

Mieshi, who'd spotted the bears first from behind a series of boulders, had warned them to approach quietly. Thankfully, the noise from the rushing falls, which nearly surrounded them on all sides, made it so the bears could not hear their approach. But they could be smelled.

"I think that one of them knows something is here," Mieshi said after they joined up. She pointed to a particularly huge one with thick brown fur and a blunt face. It lumbered one way, then another, but kept looking up the slopes where they were concealed.

The smell of fear came strongly from Eomen. "What do we do?" she asked, sidling closer to her brother. He gripped the hilt of one of his blades defensively.

"Stay out of her way," Marenqo said.

"How do you know it's a her?" Mieshi asked.

"No man could be that ugly," he said with a smirk, then waved a hand as if to bat away the remark. "I'm joking. Don't you see the cubs near her? I've seen bears before. Many times. They're protective of their young."

"I've never seen this many," Rowen said, gazing down at the scene. "It's ripe with fish, so it makes sense. If we try crossing here, some of them are bound to notice us."

Bingmei agreed but wasn't sure what to do. "Maybe they're so full of trout they won't bother us?"

"But if we seem like a threat," Jidi Majia opined, "they'll attack."

Bingmei sighed. They watched the scene for a while, trying to see a way out of the dilemma. She was grateful for the nest of boulders that Mieshi had found, which provided some cover. Once they reached the plateau, they'd be exposed to the bears. There were dozens spread out across the plateau in front of them. The bears lumbered from stream to stream. A trout leaped from the water, and in a brilliant display of dexterity, a bear snatched it up midleap.

"They don't sleep in the river," Quion said, rubbing his mouth. "They must have dens nearby. Maybe we wait until nightfall?"

A prickle of dread went down Bingmei's back. It was an awareness, a presence like she'd felt before.

"Hide!" she ordered, and her ensign obeyed rapidly, each person choosing a boulder to crouch behind and beneath, trying to get as low as they could. She joined Mieshi, the two of them barely fitting. From the far side of the boulder, she could see the streams, which would converge farther downstream.

Down below, she saw the massive bear suddenly rise on its hind legs. It was huge, bristling with fur, and seemed to be watching their agitation. Had it heard them? It dropped down on its forepaws and began lumbering toward them.

"What are we hiding from?" Mieshi whispered. "Do you smell someone?"

"No, I feel it. A dragon is coming."

The sensation that went down her back grew so intense she thought she would pass out from fright.

A dragon swooped down from the sky. Mieshi gasped, and she and Bingmei watched as it snatched up a bear in its massive jaws. The beast was too big to be eaten at once, but the dragon killed the monstrous bear in a single thrashing of its swordlike fangs. This dragon wasn't Echion or Xisi. This one had marbled flanks the color of violets with trailers of yellow and orange along its flanks. It didn't blend into the scenery—its scales made it stand out like wildflowers against the rocks. A spine of pointed bones came down its back, and it shook its head savagely before slamming the bear back into the stream. Lifeless, the bear lay still, and while Bingmei and Mieshi watched in horror and fascination, the dragon proceeded to devour it.

The other bears, which had been in the stream seeking their own food, beat a hasty retreat, abandoning the surplus trout to save themselves. The colorful dragon nestled into the waters and picked at the bear with its pointed snout, its long tail lashing in ecstasy as it fed.

Bingmei felt the dragon's presence, that tingling sensation down her back, and quieted her breathing in the hopes it could not sense her. She and Mieshi flattened themselves beneath the boulder, trying hard to remain still.

Over the roar of the falls, Bingmei heard the keening of the bear's cubs as they watched their slain mother be devoured. The dragon could not be bothered away from its meal. The cubs then fled.

The dragon finished its bloody meal, then rose on its haunches and spread its massive blue wings. It lifted into the air, leaving the carcass behind.

They watched it circle the valley awhile before it followed the river to the west.

Bingmei sighed in relief. It hadn't found them. Her own instincts had saved them. Rising to her feet, she bid the others to come. One by one they did, their faces tight with fear, an emotion that they all shared.

"What . . . was . . . that?" Marenqo asked.

"That was a dragon," Bingmei said. "Echion is black. Xisi is white. I didn't know there were others."

Then she remembered the colors they'd seen in the sky each night. The Woliu had been opened. All her life, she had heard the various myths about dragons, but no one she knew had ever seen one before. They were just the carvings left on pottery or sculptures.

Had they all gone into the Grave Kingdom before Echion and Xisi shut the gates? A feeling of dread quivered in her heart. The world was changing, and even the bears had something to fear.

被埋葬的世界

They crossed the icy streams as quickly as they could. Quion gazed longingly at the fish that were so abundant he could have grasped them with his hands. Before they reached the other side, carrion birds had begun to gather around the carcass of the mighty bear. But none of the bears had returned to the river.

They crossed the valley and then started climbing the mountain on the other side. Bingmei realized that without her instinct, without that preternatural warning, the dragon might have spotted them hiding amidst the boulders. Had it been hunting for them, or was the encounter only happenstance? She had to believe it was no coincidence. Echion and Xisi would marshal their forces to find her. And kill her. There was no need for them to drag her back to Fusang. She'd supposed that hunters would be dispatched to try to follow their trail.

She had been wrong to assume they would be human.

The mountains on the other side of the valley were even steeper than the one they'd descended. Their boots crunched in the snow, making an easily traceable trail. But would a dragon from the heights be able to see it? Was that how the dragon had come so close to their location?

They labored up the slope, trying to reach the neck of the mountain before the daylight left. The air became colder as they went, and despite frequent stops to rest, it felt like their strength was failing more rapidly. Eomen and Cuifen were not used to such hardships, and Bingmei watched them both shivering, even though they were wrapped in clothes that were designed for such a journey, clothes shared with them by members of the ensign. Cuifen, especially, suffered from the cold. The climate in Sihui was much warmer.

Building a fire was out of the question, so she pushed the ensign to continue their hike after the sun sank over the peaks late in the day. Each step made her grateful for her martial training, but the pace was agonizing and slow. The afterglow of the sun never truly faded, although stars came winking into view, and the colorful whorl of heavenly lights began to illuminate the sky to the south, indicating the location of Fusang. It was a reminder of the colorful dragon they'd seen earlier in the day.

On they marched, grunting and sweating as they climbed the snowy ridge. Even Bingmei's feet were numb with cold, but stopping to rest could be fatal. If anyone fell asleep, they might not awaken. She smelled their various levels of exhaustion, despair, and morose thoughts. Fear underlaid everything. Would another dragon come for them in the night? Would the violet dragon return? She kept her mind focused on moving forward.

At last they reached the crag they'd aimed for. Eomen sagged to her knees in exhaustion and relief. Liekou put his arm around Cuifen as she buried her face against his chest, weeping softly from the ordeal. Jidi Majia was the last to reach the summit, his wheezes a constant reminder that he was the oldest among them.

Looking up, Bingmei saw the constellations. It was after midnight. She would give them a reprieve, but they wouldn't sleep, no matter how tired.

"Mieshi," Bingmei said, panting. "Don't let anyone fall asleep. It's too dangerous. We'll rest a little while, then we must keep going. We have no cover up here except the darkness. We need to be down the other side when the dawn comes."

"All right," Mieshi said, bobbing her head. Her heart was in pain still from losing Damanhur. But her determination was just as strong, and Bingmei respected her for it. She had no doubt Mieshi would fulfill her duty no matter what.

Just as Bingmei knew she must fulfill hers. She'd been shirking one of her duties, and she felt it keenly as she breathed in Mieshi's grief. Rowen still didn't know about his father, and he deserved to hear the truth from her. Turning to him, she said, "There is something I must tell you. Before we go any farther."

He tilted his head and then followed her away from the others. She smelled a little cinder of hope flare in his chest. She gritted her teeth, determined to do her duty as well.

"We didn't have time earlier," she said softly. "But I wanted to be the one to tell you. You decide when to tell your sister."

"Tell us what?" He looked worried.

She could think of no way to soften the news, so she didn't clothe it in empty platitudes. "Your father is dead, Rowen. I was there . . . when Echion ordered one of his ensign to do it. Your father gave me a little bit of hope that it wasn't too late to heed the summons of the phoenix."

As she spoke, she smelled his grief and regret rise like twin waves ready to drown him. A strong undertow of guilt lurked beneath those waves. He stared at her, his lip twitching with inner pain. Then he looked down at the ground, shocked into silence.

"I'm sorry, Rowen," she said, gently touching his arm. "I know the two of you never resolved things. He was a brave man. A true king."

Rowen gazed at her and then nodded. His emotions roiled through him, his feelings a violent storm washing over her.

"If I tell her, she'll resent me even more," he whispered, glancing at his sister. "But I'm grateful you told me, Bingmei. I'm sorry you have to . . . endure my feelings on this too."

She squeezed his arm and offered a consoling smile.

"I will tell her. Just not now. It's too much after all we've been through." He was about to depart, so she released his hand, but then he caught it and squeezed it. "When you go to the Grave Kingdom. If you see my father . . ."

His voice choked off with grief. Releasing her, he raised his fist to his mouth, trembling. Then he shook his head, unable to speak the words of apology, and walked away. He knelt by Eomen and gave her a comforting hug before shifting to look at Bingmei one more time.

Rowen's feelings for her, although battered by her rejection, hadn't altered. In fact, he cared for her even more. She could still smell his regard, and he still took no effort to conceal it.

She stood alone for a while, and then Marenqo joined her.

He took a long drink from his water flask. "Is that the sun rising already?" he blurted out.

As she squinted, she saw what he meant—a long, thin horizontal line of glowing light that seemed to mimic the sun at the horizon. It was still too early for it. And then she blinked and shook her head.

"No, Marenqo," she said. "Those are torches."

He gave her a baffled look. "Torches?" His eyes widened with understanding. "Oh."

"What is it?" Quion asked, coming up to stand next to her.

"It's the Death Wall," Bingmei said, her stomach clenching with dread and anticipation.

"Bingmei," Liekou said, stepping away from Cuifen and approaching. He pitched his voice low, for her ears only.

"What is it?" she asked him, smelling his worry.

"There are torches in the valley behind us as well," he said. "They're coming for us."

She turned around and looked back down at the valley floor. She'd been so focused on the colorful lights in the sky and the endless climb up the slope that she hadn't bothered looking back until now.

Torches. That was the only explanation for what she saw. Hundreds of torches.

CHAPTER THIRTY-THREE

Yanli

They'd all reached the point of exhaustion before arriving in the valley, long after the sun had risen to reveal them. Bingmei was weary also, but the danger and threat from ahead and behind made her push everyone farther and farther. If they didn't find shelter soon, they risked being trapped on the valley floor. At last, Marenqo and Mieshi returned after scouting out a hiding place where they could obtain some much-needed rest.

Bingmei took the first watch, even though her muscles ached and her sore feet complained. The shelter was a patch of scraggly pine trees studded with boulders and cut through by a stream of cool water. The area had an ample supply of elk scat, and some of the trees looked like they'd been used to toughen antlers. Within moments, the others had fallen asleep, clustered in little groups, despite the coming day. Using the meiwood cricket, she bounded atop one of the largest boulders so she'd have a good view of anyone approaching, either from the Death Wall or the mountain pass they'd crossed in the night.

The boulder was rough against her skin, with sharp angles not quite worn off. It had clearly broken loose from the mountain above and ricocheted off the slope on its way down before shattering into several smaller boulders. What a sight it must have been, tumbling down the mountainside, crushing the trees to splinters. The top of the boulder was so uncomfortable that she didn't fear falling asleep herself. She crouched low, the rune staff before her, watching . . . waiting.

The sun felt warm against her neck, although the breeze still had a touch of winter to it this far north. She slipped some dried meat from her pack and chewed it slowly, savoring the spicy flavor, wondering how long their food stores would last. There were no cities this far north. Only the barracks within the Death Wall itself would have some provisions, but the soldiers who lived there were Echion's minions. And building fires to cook and stay warm would reveal them to their enemies.

Time passed slowly, and the drowsiness of inaction weighed on her. She knew she should wake someone else to take a turn. Her mouth watered at the thought of curling up in the brush and falling asleep. She'd wake Marenqo next . . . or Mieshi. They were both used to the hardships of travel.

Movement.

At first she thought it was an elk, but it was much smaller. She flattened herself against the boulder and cautiously peered in the direction of the movement. After a few tense moments, she spied someone slinking through the woods, holding a hornwood bow with arrow nocked. Bingmei squinted, seeing that he wore a silk jacket and pants decorated with the dragon symbols. His hair was tied back in a queue. This wasn't an ordinary woodsman or hunter. He was part of Echion's ensign.

Bingmei pushed herself slowly away from the edge, ensuring the boulder blocked his sight of her. She hadn't smelled him yet because he wasn't quite close enough. After retrieving the staff, she came over the edge and then triggered the meiwood cricket to leap soundlessly down off the boulder. She went to Liekou, who slept near Cuifen, and shook him awake.

His eyes opened immediately, and he rolled to his feet, smelling of concern. His brow furrowed, but he said nothing.

Bingmei bent close so that she could whisper in his ear. "A hunter is coming with a hornwood bow. He wears silk, like the members of Echion's ensign. He's stalking us in the woods. That way." She pointed in the direction she'd seen him come.

Liekou nodded. "That is Yanli. He can kill a man from atop a tower at a great distance. No doubt he's leading other men to us."

Bingmei breathed out slowly. They had only been sleeping a short while. It would be difficult to flee again so soon.

Liekou put his hand on her shoulder. "I will stop him."

She looked in his eyes. "We both will."

He gave her a doubtful smile. "He knows dianxue. He can shoot an arrow through a boulder."

Bingmei's eyes widened. "How?"

"He can. I've seen it done. It is another lost skill that Echion has brought back, but I know as much as he does, if not more. Wait here." He started to rise, but she caught his arm.

"Be careful," she told him.

Liekou's scent shifted with her concern. He nodded and then quietly went in the direction she'd pointed.

Bingmei shook Mieshi awake, whispered to her what was going on, and told her to awaken the others on her signal. She then crept around the boulder, her back pressed against it. How could a man shoot an arrow through a boulder? But there was no lie in Liekou's words. If he said he'd seen it done, then he had.

She edged closer, trying to get a look.

The twang of a bow traveled through the air, followed by the sound of splintering wood. Bingmei gripped the meiwood staff and peered around the edge of the stone.

She saw the archer now, in a low crouch, half hidden by the brush, the bow held in front of him. He quickly drew another arrow and fit it to the string. Liekou had his back pressed against a dead tree, one whose branches had lost their needles, the trunk gray with black splotches. The archer lifted the bow and aimed at the tree. If what Liekou had told her was true, it would pierce both the tree and the man behind it. Bingmei nearly cried out in warning, but Liekou stepped away from the tree just as Yanli loosed the arrow.

Bingmei watched as the arrow sailed through the tree, shimmering as it did, passing through the blockade as if it were smoke, only to solidify on the other side before clattering off a stone.

Liekou advanced, his face grim with determination. She could smell Yanli now—his sense of vengeance and self-confidence stank like a dumpling hissing in a layer of boiling fat. Another arrow was drawn, and Liekou stepped abruptly to the side, behind another tree. Yanli closed his eyes, focusing his power, but again Liekou moved at the last moment. With each tree he came closer to his target.

Bingmei watched and smelled Liekou's perfect calm.

"You betrayed the master," Yanli said in a dark voice.

Liekou said nothing, dodging behind another tree as the bow was raised yet again. Yanli's lips peeled back into a snarl. He did not like that his quarry hunted him.

Suddenly Liekou ran for him, sprinting to close the remaining distance. Yanli brought up the bow and let loose an arrow. Liekou whipped his arm around, the edge of his hand smashing into the bolt, snapping it in half. The archer's eyes widened with surprise—and so did Bingmei's. She'd never seen the like.

The archer ditched the bow and drew a short sword. The pommel had a gold design that matched the hilt, and the blade immediately began to exude a golden glow.

Liekou rushed the man weaponless and threw a series of kicks at his head. Yanli ducked and rolled to the side, crushing some gorse, and came up, stabbing the blade toward Liekou's heart. Bingmei watched the two warriors fight, both with the skill of a master. A ribbon of red opened on Liekou's arm, but it was traded with a punch to his adversary's throat.

Something from the corner of her eye drew Bingmei's attention—the killing fog creeping through the woods toward the combatants.

Before, the power of the phoenix had saved them from it. But she'd been warned that it would not save them again until after she visited the shrine beyond the Death Wall. Liekou's eyes narrowed as he noticed the reaching tendrils of fog.

Yanli sneered at him. "The sigil has changed, Liekou. The fog will kill you now. It will kill you all!"

Bingmei rushed from the boulder, invoking the magic of the rune staff as she charged toward them. Now that the bow had been discarded, she had a chance to join the fight. Yanli spied her coming, his eyes widening with excitement.

"The sparrow has revealed herself!" he said in triumph. He kicked Liekou in the stomach, and went for the kill with the short blade, only to find his wrist snatched in an iron grip. He kicked at Liekou's knee, but the other man had dropped into a horse stance, holding the blade high overhead.

Bingmei reached them a moment later, raising the magical staff to swing at Yanli's back.

He pivoted, and she had to pull back the strike lest she hit Liekou instead. The tendrils of fog slipped over the gnarled roots of the pine trees, groping through the shrubs to reach for them. Yanli's eyes flashed with victory, but still he couldn't pull the blade down.

Liekou touched the other man's chest, drawing a quick symbol. A paroxysm of pain went through Yanli's face, and his legs crumpled. Liekou pried the blade from his fingers, but it still shone brightly.

"Put it down!" Bingmei said. The magic was attracting the fog.

Liekou dropped it as if it burned him, and as soon as it touched the dirt, Bingmei touched it with the rune staff and started sucking the magic from it.

"Go!" she told Liekou.

His eyes blazed into hers.

"Go!" she repeated.

He fled from the killing fog while Bingmei drained the magic from the sword. Its light winked out, and Bingmei released the power of the rune staff, but it was taking too much time. The fog rippled across Yanli's legs, but it had no effect on him. It was nearly to her boots when she reached into her pocket for the meiwood cricket and used it to leap high into the air. She landed on a pine tree, grabbing one of the larger branches, and then maneuvered her feet onto a lower branch. She feared for a moment she'd fall back down into the fog, but the swaying stopped after a moment. Hanging there, she breathed in the deep fragrance of the pine and felt the sticky sap. She smelled Yanli's fear and panic, could even smell the agony of his heart as it quivered and spasmed from the dianxue touch, which had robbed him of air like it had with King Shulian. Fog shrouded him from her sight, but she smelled him until his life winked out. It wasn't the fog that had killed him.

Looking down, she saw the fog groping blindly, searching for magic and finding none. The staff cooled, and the light faded from the runes. The fog dissipated and then retreated toward the Death Wall once again. It amazed her how quickly it had come, but perhaps it shouldn't be so surprising. Of course it was faster this close to the wall. The magic was tied to the Death Wall, she knew, although she did not understand how.

After it was gone, she jumped back down, and Liekou joined her at the body of Yanli. The man's eyes were open, his mouth slack. She smelled no life from him. Liekou's hand had stopped him from breathing.

She smelled a little hint of sadness coming from him. He'd known Yanli. They'd once been brothers in a way, warriors in the same ensign.

Liekou then retrieved the quiver of arrows from Yanli's body and swung it around his own shoulder. He picked up the discarded hornwood bow, leaving the short blade for her, and marched back to the camp without saying a word.

被埋葬的世界

Bingmei awoke to the awful smell of grief. It was so strong it permeated her dream, reminding her of the day she'd lost her parents and Grandfather Jiao. It was so familiar, so terrible, that it had wrenched her out of sleep. The sun was still in the sky, but it was heading down a westward slope. The mood in the small camp was frigid.

She heard weeping, and as she sat up, she saw Eomen sobbing against Rowen's shoulder. The smell came from both of them, but also from Jidi Majia. So they were all grieving for Shulian at last.

Marenqo saw the look on Bingmei's face and then sidled up to her. "Ah, you're awake. Good."

"What happened?" she asked him after sitting up, the groans of Eomen's sorrow ripping at her heart.

"Rowen told them that he knew Shulian was dead." He cleared his throat. "I'm going to hazard a guess that you are the one who told him last night when you were alone together. Or were you discussing marriage plans?" At the look on her face, his usual smile fell. "Sorry, I don't know when to stop jesting."

"No, you don't," Bingmei said, her anger sparking.

"How did he die?" Eomen asked Rowen, her voice throbbing with emotion. He had never made amends with his father, and she could smell the sour rind of guilt piercing his sorrow.

Bingmei could hardly breathe. She could smell how uncomfortable it made the others to witness such a display of raw grief. It had always made her uncomfortable too. It was one of the reasons she despised her ability.

"Do not make me tell you," Jidi Majia pleaded. "I still have nightmares about it. The wound is too fresh. It did not happen long ago."

"Why didn't I know?" Eomen asked through her tears. "You should have told me!" she said accusingly, shifting her gaze between Jidi Majia and Bingmei.

"It was my fault that your father died," Bingmei said, rising. Their eyes turned to her. She couldn't sit there any longer. "It is *my* fault," she repeated.

Rowen gazed at her in confusion. "How was it your fault?" he asked in a challenging tone. "You said one of the ensign killed him."

"King Shulian was a slave in the Hall of Unity. It's one of the palaces that no one is allowed to enter. He was confined there, able to do nothing. Nothing at all, except live. His helplessness became part of Echion's power. I was led there. I . . . was drawn there. Even though he had nothing left to give, he did have his life. He shared something with me. Some words that I needed to hear. That my taidu is my own, and no one can take it from me. And because he defied Echion with his last breath, he was killed, struck by a dianxue blow and then executed by one of Echion's followers."

She felt sadness herself, joining the heart-wrenching smell of grief. "It's my fault, Eomen. It's my fault your brother died as well. If I had sought to do the phoenix's will sooner . . . if I hadn't put myself before accepting my role as the phoenix-chosen." She was near tears, but she held them back, hating how helpless she felt. Although it was difficult, she forced herself to keep looking at the brother and sister. "He died because of my cowardice. My selfishness. But he did not die in vain. I'm going to the Death Wall. I just hope it is not too late."

Rowen gazed at her, his heart panging with grief and compassion. A tear slid down his cheek. "You watched him die, Bingmei?"

She sniffled. "I did. I saw the soul leave his body and go to the Grave Kingdom. But that is not all. Echion . . . after he was dead . . . devoured him. All of him. His thoughts, his memories, his skills. That's what Jidi Majia didn't want to tell you. Part of your father's soul has made Echion stronger. His honor made the dragon sick, Jidi Majia said. But you should know the truth, as terrible as it is."

They look stunned by the news, their grief even more intense.

"Our enemy is the absence of compassion," Jidi Majia said. "He gloats over his murders. And he will not stop until we are, all of us, devoured. That is the nature of Echion and Xisi. They are pitiless."

Rowen's eyes flared with anger. "I hate him."

She felt the vengeance swirling inside him. Yes, she knew that feeling. She'd shared it once. Bingmei gave him a look of sympathy.

"The Qiangdao murdered my parents as well," she said. "I know what it means to hate like that. But I now believe there is a better way." She sighed. "We must go. If we press hard, we'll be at the Death Wall before midnight. I must try to cross it before daybreak. They're waiting for us."

Mieshi came jogging into the little camp, her hair disheveled. "They've found us."

CHAPTER THIRTY-FOUR

The Color of Dandelions

"How many?" It was a question Bingmei didn't want answered, but she needed to know.

Mieshi's eyes showed courage, but the smell of dread and fear bubbled through it, like a burnt soup. "I lost count after thirty. They're coming in a line, combing through the woods. Some on horse, some afoot. They have the dragon banner."

"Our rest is over, then," Bingmei said, still feeling exhausted. She looked at her beleaguered ensign and felt the urge to protect them from what was to come. Losing any of them was unthinkable. But how many would be able to escape their determined pursuers?

"Maybe we should split ranks?" Rowen suggested. His grief was still fresh, but he resisted giving in to it. She felt his struggle. "Give them two trails to follow instead of one."

"I'll consider it if the situation becomes desperate," Bingmei said. It was a good suggestion, although she didn't know if she should heed it. "Let's move. How far away are they, Mieshi?"

"We don't have long before they reach us. We should go. Now."

They fled through the woods again. In the gaps between the trees, she could see the plains ahead of them leading to the mountains. If they ventured out into the open, there was no hiding. She took them to the edge of the woods so they could better gauge their location. At the edge, she saw the Death Wall looming ahead of them.

It seemed more like stairs than a wall up close. It was the height of three men at its lowest point, studded with square towers at regular intervals. Trees and brush had been cleared away from the foot of the wall, which would make their approach that much more difficult, but off in the distance there were places where the woods dipped in closer to the wall. The wall was too vast for Echion's workers to keep the wildness running along it contained. If the ensign was careful, they could find a place where they could get close without being noticed. Smoke from cookfires wafted near the towers. They were close enough to make out the tiny figures of guards patrolling its vast line. If they went straight toward it, they would be there soon, but she resisted the urge to run. The hunters chasing them had horses. Only under the cover of darkness could they move without being seen, and their window of opportunity would be limited given the season.

After a long period of walking along the edge of the woods, Bingmei ordered them to go deeper into the forest, which was when they stumbled into a search party. Quion's sharp eyes spotted them first, and just as he hissed a warning, a cry of alarm came from the band of hunters. The cry was followed by more cries, deeper in the woods, and Bingmei ordered her ensign to run.

"Do we split up?" Marenqo asked as he jogged up alongside her.

She looked at him and then said, "Marenqo, Mieshi, Liekou—take them out. The sunset is still too far off. When you're done, rejoin us. Everyone else, stay with me, and we'll keep going."

"If you say so," Marenqo said, swallowing his fear. He gripped his staff and nodded to Mieshi. Liekou touched Cuifen's cheek with the edge of his hand before stepping away.

As they hastened away from her best warriors, the sound of clacking staves filled the air, seasoned by shouts of pain. Now that she'd sent the others away, Bingmei knew it would fall to her to protect Jidi Majia, Cuifen, Eomen, Rowen, and Quion. Her insides clenched with dread, and she wished she were fighting with the others.

They'd only gone a few steps when a prickle shot down her back. Dragon. "Scatter!" she shouted and searched for a place to hide. She raced to a tree that had fallen over a gully and slid down into the muck, where a thin rivulet ambled past.

Quion slid in after her, his face flushed with terror. "I saw it," he gasped.

The others had also sought shelter in the gully. Jidi Majia had his back pressed against the gorse, hand on his chest as he wheezed. Rowen and Eomen were crossing the base of the creek to get to the old man.

Bingmei heard a cracking sound, and the tree above them bobbed ominously, shedding branches into the gully. A flash of yellow announced that the dragon had landed on the fallen tree, its claws digging into the bark. Although not as huge as Echion's shadow dragon, it was still the size of a horse. It had yellow scales on its back and sides, with black, green, and red ones along its underbelly. It started clawing its way toward her along the tree trunk, its eyes narrowing. The nostril slats on its snout flared. Had it seen her?

Quion held his breath, sinking into the mud, his mouth open with fear. The beast made a strange clucking sound, almost like a chicken, then the head came up. It had heard something.

Something struck the side of the dragon. A pinecone maybe. And it scrabbled off the log and charged across the top of the gully toward Rowen. She saw his hand pitch back, and he threw something else. The truth struck Bingmei viscerally, he was trying to draw the dragon's attention away from her so she could flee. Eomen screamed involuntarily, and the beast let out an ear-splitting shriek that dwarfed it.

Bingmei's heart went into her throat as she watched the yellow-scaled dragon streak at them. Rowen drew his blades and stepped in front of Jidi Majia and Eomen. The dragon snapped at him, and he dodged its deathly maw, striking at its exposed neck with his blades. She watched as the steel slid off the scales without doing harm. The dragon buffeted him with a wing, knocking him down, and then lifted itself.

He may have sacrificed himself so that Bingmei could get out safely, but she couldn't bear to see him die. She plunged her hand into her pocket and invoked the meiwood cricket. The relic sent her bounding up out of the gully, the rune staff in her hand. The dragon opened its maw, and something came out. Not a fog of blackness but a shimmering mist, like the heat from a frying pan shimmering with oil.

The mist settled over the three huddling in the gully just as Bingmei landed on the dragon's back. She summoned the rune staff's magic and struck the beast hard on the back. She watched Rowen fall, and she hit the beast again, harder. It screeched in pain this time. The sigils on the rune were smoking, she realized—they'd left burns on the dragon's hide.

The dragon jerked and turned on her, but Bingmei leaped clear of its back, rolling in the gorse. When she rose, its snout was rushing forward to bite her, but she managed to swing the staff around just in time to bat the head away. Again the magic burned it, and the beast snarled in pain, flinching back from her. She took one end of the staff with both hands and ran toward the dragon, swinging the weapon around her head in a full circle to build power. It raised a wing to defend itself, but an arrow suddenly pierced it. It tumbled into the gully, thrashing, hissing, squealing in pain.

Then she saw Liekou rushing from the woods, holding the hornwood bow he'd confiscated from the man he'd killed. Bingmei breathed hard and fast, looking for Mieshi and Marenqo but not seeing them. Were they dead? Anguish threatened to overwhelm her.

Liekou jumped atop a boulder, raised another arrow and fired, and she heard the dragon screech a final death cry. The shafts, she realized, were made of meiwood.

She stumbled to the edge of the gully and saw the yellow dragon lying inert at the base, its wings askew, its maw still wide open. Liekou jumped down and wrenched the arrow out of its chest. A syrupy ichor came with it. Liekou gasped in pain and dropped the arrow, holding his hand to his chest. Grunting, he stepped off the dragon and plunged his hand into the gully water. Bingmei saw Quion approaching with a pan gripped tight in one hand. Cuifen walked hesitantly behind him, gazing at the dead dragon with wide eyes.

Bingmei's gaze shot back to Rowen. He sat on his knees, shaking his head, dazed.

It looked like he had mud spatter on his face, and it struck her that he and Eomen and Jidi Majia had taken the brunt of the dragon's hideous breath.

"Are you all right?" she asked, crouching near him, hand on his shoulder.

His head turned at the sound of her voice, but he didn't look at her. "I can't see," he said.

"Neither . . . can . . . I," gasped Jidi Majia. "I am . . . blind."

Pain and regret squeezed around Bingmei like a vise. She should have split the group earlier, as Rowen had suggested. This never would have happened. Eomen sat shivering behind him, in an obvious state of shock.

"Eomen?" Bingmei called.

The princess's chin lifted. Mud and filth were smeared on her face. "I . . . I . . . ," she stuttered and then broke into violent sobs.

"We're all blind," Jidi Majia said.

Voices called from the woods. Men were searching for the source of the screeches they'd heard.

"We must leave. Now!" Liekou said, still wincing with pain. His hand was blistered and bleeding. He washed the arrow in mud and then gripped it in his other hand. "They're coming!" He gestured for Cuifen to come to him.

Bingmei gazed at him, at the others, and realized they wouldn't all make it out.

The fight was over, and they had lost.

"Bingmei, go," Rowen said, struggling to his feet. He groped for her, unable to see her, and she took his hand. "Please. You must go. You're the reason we're all doing this. You have to make it. Not us. Go."

Her heart groaned with pain. Jidi Majia struggled to comfort and quiet Eomen. They looked so desolate . . .

"We can't run like this," Rowen said, shaking his head. He squeezed her hand hard. "Go! You must!"

She knew it was the right thing to do. Just as Bao Damanhur had ordered Mieshi to abandon him when the dragon sculpture had clamped onto his arm. So why did it feel so terrible? She pulled herself up onto her toes and kissed his cheek.

"I'll see you in the Grave Kingdom," she said, choking on her words. She had no doubt they'd all meet there soon enough. The venom on his face sizzled on her lips. She wiped it away quickly.

She smelled his love again, smelled it fiercely and willingly. It exuded from him in glorious waves despite the stink of the dead dragon and the muck of the gully. It overwhelmed her with its intensity.

"Until then," he sighed, reaching out with his other hand to stroke her copper hair.

Leaving him—them—behind was the hardest thing she'd ever done.

被埋葬的世界

They huddled in the wet interior of the gully, covered in slimy leaves and broken boughs. Quion's skills had once again proved perfectly timed, and it was at his suggestion the remaining members of the group—Quion himself, Bingmei, Liekou, and Cuifen—had concealed themselves in the wilderness. They'd followed the gully and chosen a hiding place deeper in the woods, away from where the stream entered the plains. He'd built two little shelters of brush for them to hide in, one for Liekou and Cuifen and the other for himself and Bingmei. The warmth of their bodies helped stave off the chill as they waited.

His plan worked. They heard the crack of limbs and twigs and watched as those hunting them stalked past, unaware their quarry was so near. Echion's minions searched this way and that, heads bent low, but there were no signs to betray them. Quion held his breath as their enemies passed them, and Bingmei did too, fearing that even the sound of breathing might give them away. One group passed, then another, then another. And then the forest fell silent.

Still they waited. They waited until the sun began to go down and the first glimmer of stars winked into view.

Sunset. It had felt like it would never come.

Bingmei leaned her head against Quion's shoulder, grateful for the fishy smell that helped soothe her heartache. She thought on the trail of dead she'd left behind. Kunmia Suun, her parents, her grandfather, Jiaohua, Shulian, Muxidi. For all she knew Rowen was dead too. And Eomen and Jidi Majia and Damanhur. The images of them seemed to pass before her, one by one, an endless procession all marching toward the Death Wall.

At last, when dusk had settled, she rose, and the makeshift shelter collapsed in sticks around her. Upon hearing the sound, Liekou and Cuifen rose too, their faces grave.

"How is your hand?" Bingmei asked.

"It still burns," he said, but there was no complaint in his tone. He had mastered the pain. She saw that the skin was black and blistered, but she couldn't tell whether it was from the burn itself or the mud. Cuifen held on to his arm, her face smudged with dirt and tears, but she looked rested.

"Do you know what happened to Marenqo and Mieshi?" she asked him.

"We were all surrounded. Someone wrestled Mieshi to the ground. Marenqo tried to save her, but I think he was taken too. When I heard the screams of the dragon, I decided to abandon the fight and help you."

Mieshi and Marenqo. They were both probably dead by now too. Or they'd be dragged back to Fusang to be devoured by Echion.

Quion pulled his pack up on his shoulders. It was clotted with rotting leaves, which also clung to his hair.

"We have to cross it tonight," he said, adjusting the straps on his shoulders. He looked resolute. "Best be off."

He was right. Bingmei stared at the woods around them. It struck her suddenly that she hadn't seen his snow leopard since the rescue. She felt terrible she hadn't asked about it.

"Let's go," Bingmei agreed with despair, and the four began walking to the edge of the trees. She took a deep breath, trying to sense any human hiding nearby. No one.

"Whatever happened to your pet leopard?" she asked Quion in a low voice.

"Had to leave her behind," he said, the words calm, but she smelled his sadness.

Everyone had made sacrifices to come with her.

"In the woods outside Sihui?"

He nodded, eyes fixed on the way ahead. "I saw what the dragon did to the people of that city. Darkness hung in the air like a fog. What kind of creature can work such magic, Bingmei? How terrible." His jaw clenched a moment before he said, "He brings nothing but darkness. That's why we have to fight him, Bingmei. We have to."

There was a new smell in him now, one that reminded her of his cooked salmon with spices on it. It was the smell of determination. He had lost so much too, but he would see this through to the end. She felt lucky to have found a friend.

She put her hand in his. "Thank you for being here, Quion," she said, giving him a smile.

He glanced down at their hands. And then he smiled back.

CHAPTER THIRTY-FIVE

The Stairs

Just before midnight, the strange flashing lights appeared over Fusang again. Swathes of violet, pink, and green swirled, along with streamers of yellow and orange. The various colors danced across the sky in hues that were haunting, beautiful, and otherworldly. Bingmei and the others walked across the valley toward the Death Wall, pressing at a fast pace in order to reach the wall before the sun reemerged.

They had evaded their pursuers, but torches wove through the trees behind them, the search for them unrelenting. The uncertainty of her friends' fates tore at her heart, but the only path was forward.

She could sense the phoenix shrine beyond the mountains, as if part of her were already there. Her heart knew the way. If she could get to it, perhaps she could stop Echion before he harmed her friends. It was a frail hope to cling to, but she grasped it anyway.

"The lights are coming closer," Liekou said.

"The torches?" she asked, looking at him in the pale moonlight. Thank goodness there was only a sliver of moon in the sky.

"No, the Woliu, or whatever it is. Look back."

Bingmei and Quion turned at the same time. He was right. The lights had always lingered across the southern horizon, but now the colors were spreading northward, like octopus tentacles reaching after them. It had not done this before.

"They're coming for us," she whispered with dread.

"Then we must go faster," Liekou said.

"My legs hurt," Cuifen complained.

"You must endure it," Liekou told her. "There's no other way."

Gritting her teeth, Bingmei increased her pace. She smelled the worry, like a pot of wilting flowers, coming from the others. She even smelled it on herself. Now she wished they had left the woods earlier and risked being seen by their pursuers.

She wished a lot of things.

She kept glancing back, and each time, the streamers of colorful light seemed closer. When the lights reached the edge of the woods, she could see the treetops swaying in the wind, like a cloud clearing away from the sun and brightening the land beneath it. And then she saw a blotch in the coming lights and a familiar, dangerous prickle shot down her spine.

"It's Echion," she whispered fearfully.

The shadows in the sky multiplied until there were more and more dragons in the sky. A horde of them.

Liekou gazed up at it, his jaw dropping in shock. He looked at her and then said, "Run!"

It was the only thing they could do. They broke into a jog and then a firm run, the meadow grasses whipping against their legs. Torches lit the walls in front of them, revealing the gray stone. They would have to climb a hill up to the foot of the wall, but first they had to cross the plains. Inhuman shrieks heralded the arrival of the dragons.

Bingmei smelled the man just in time. His scent rode on the wind, a greedy, voracious scent drawing her gaze to a silent rider guarding the plains.

"Over there!" Bingmei called, pointing. He was just a smudge in the shadows.

Liekou brought out the bow and fitted an arrow in it just as the man became aware of them. She smelled surprise and victory and then heard the deep, blatting sound of a horn. The tone rang long and deep before the arrow flew from the bow. The sound cut off as the man toppled from the saddle. Frightened, his horse charged away.

They ran past the dying horseman, who gasped and shuddered in the dark. He was no longer a threat to them, but he'd revealed their position and sounded the alarm. The sound of other horns began to bleat in response to the first.

They heard the shriek of a dragon behind them, then the great beast plummeted from the sky and swooped down into the valley.

"Down!" Liekou said, and they all dropped into the grass.

From their position on the soft earth, she sensed the beast behind them, prowling around the dying man. The man yelled in fear, only for his final cries to be silenced by the dragon's jaws. The beast began stalking them in the grass. They could hear its leathery wings, the hiss of the grass against its legs, the clucking noise in its throat.

Bingmei gripped the rune staff in her hands, squeezing it hard, trying to quell her fear. Quion lay next to her, his cheek crushing strands of grass, his eyes wide with fear. She wished she could fly, that she could rise from the grass and soar away, drawing the dragon after her. But the phoenix had warned her that the magic wouldn't come back until she'd completed her goal.

The sound of more horns came in the distance, and the dragon lifted its head and bellowed into the sky. Bingmei squeezed her eyes shut against the noise. She heard a strange sound, a little groan of pleasure, and when she lifted her head, the dragon was gone. In its place stood a man, twisting and contorting, as if transforming into a new and unfamiliar shape.

She gasped as the process ended. This man looked exactly like the one on the horse, the one who'd been consumed, and he smelled like him too. Greedy and voracious. But the scent had a strange reptilian edge to it. He started to search the grass, coming closer to her hiding place. She heard his breathing, the noise of his boots on the grass.

"Come out, little bird," he said in a hoarse voice. "I know you're here, hiding like a thrush."

And then Liekou sprang at him, bringing up the hornwood bow. Cuifen cried out in fear. Light illuminated the stranger's face, his greedy eyes and triumphant grin. He surged forward at a superhuman speed, dodging the arrow, and backfisted Liekou across the face. After knocking him over, he reached down to smash his fingers, which were bent like claws, into Liekou's back, but the warrior spun around and kicked the man's legs. He didn't budge. Bingmei sprang from the grass as the man's fingers struck Liekou's ribs. She whirled the staff and swung it toward the dragon-man's head. He ducked the blow and charged at her, his face savage with hate.

She reversed the attack, summoning the staff's magic. She knew she only had a few moments before the killing fog came to destroy them. It would need to be enough. The dragon-man lunged for her, trying to touch her body so he might trace a dianxue sigil on her. She batted the arm away with the staff and then twirled around, striking him on the backs of the knees. He growled in pain and this time went down, the staff's magic leeching from him.

Then Liekou shot an arrow into his back, and she saw the pointed tip protrude from his chest. His jaws snapped and snarled, his eyes wide with fury, and then he slumped down. Liekou lowered the hornwood bow. He did not try retrieving the arrow.

As they stood over the body, they saw swirling colors begin to ebb from it, leaking into the ground. Then it lay still.

The killing fog groped toward them in the dark. She could see it seeping from the woods just outside the wall, reaching for them with twining arms. She released the magic.

"We have to outrun it," Bingmei said, and they broke into a sprint. Quion and Cuifen rushed after them, running through the grass. The fog reached the dead man and swirled around him, but it was not fooled. It continued to seek them, tendrils weaving around shrubs. Bingmei pressed herself to go faster. Quion huffed for air.

"Cuifen!" Liekou shouted in warning. She smelled the sudden panic in him. She dared to look back, dismayed to see the princess of Sihui dropping to the grass.

But Liekou's shout had invigorated Cuifen. Eyes blazing with fear, she sprang back up, ran faster, and soon outdistanced Quion.

The fog finally became blind to them again and began to seep into the grass, but they didn't stop running.

The hill became steeper, and Bingmei felt the climb in her legs. They ran up the hillock to a stretch of woods. The wall loomed beyond it.

They encountered a stone road at the base of the woods. Wagon ruts were carved into the stone and weeds, and grasses grew in the seams and cracks. The firmness of the stone helped them run faster, and they followed it a short distance before encountering a series of stone stairs cut into the side of the hill, leading up.

Bingmei slowed down as she reached it, gazing up into the gloom of the trees. The lights from the sky had overtaken them, and she looked up, seeing blotches of dark amidst the colors. More dragons.

Liekou looked at her, wiping sweat from his mouth. He hunched over, panting, staring at Cuifen in relief.

"We'll take the stairs," Bingmei said.

"They'll be coming down," Quion said, gasping for breath.

"Then we fight," she said, bringing around the staff.

被埋葬的世界

They darted through the trees leading up the steep mountainside, which helped conceal them from the dragons prowling the skies. The stairs went up the side of the hill at crooked angles, but it was clear they led to the base of the Death Wall. Their knees ached, and the weariness and fatigue became unbearable for Cuifen.

Finally, she collapsed on the stairs and began sobbing.

Bingmei's legs also hurt, but she was more accustomed to such strenuous effort.

Liekou bent down to comfort her. "We must keep going," he said, panting.

"I cannot . . . make . . . another step," she said. "I can't . . . go farther. My knee hurts!"

Bingmei smelled the presence of people and then heard the stamping of boots coming down from the heights above.

"They're coming," she said. "Hide in the trees."

Thankfully, the mountainside was covered in plentiful pine and cypress trees, thick with summer foliage. Bingmei and Quion hid on one side of the stairs, and Liekou carried Cuifen to the other. Nestling into the dark, Bingmei watched as two dozen men ran down the steps, their armor and weapons jangling.

Bingmei lowered her head, listening to the retreating noise as sweat trickled down her back. When she could no longer smell them, she whispered to Quion, "Wait here for a moment." Then she carefully padded over to the other side of the stairs.

Cuifen was half-asleep against a pine tree, her face forlorn. Blinking to try to stay awake, she gazed at Bingmei in a delirious state.

"I don't think she can go any farther," Liekou said in despair.

"You're right. She's spent."

"I . . . I will try," Cuifen sighed, her head lolling.

Bingmei shook her head. "You've done enough, Cuifen." She put her hand on Liekou's arm. "And so have you. I wouldn't have made it this far on my own."

"We're not at the wall yet," he said. "I would see this through."

"I think I can make it," Bingmei said. "If more come down the stairs, I'll hide again. I'll use my cricket to leap over the wall when I get there."

She looked back to where Quion was hiding in the woods. She couldn't see him, but she smelled him.

She pitched her voice lower. "Take Quion with you. He will help you survive in the woods until you can escape. I will do what I promised I would do."

She felt a twinge of guilt. Quion wouldn't want to leave her, but she didn't want him to die. It would ease her mind to know that he had made it out. The rest of the journey she could do herself.

Bingmei cupped Cuifen's face. "Keep her safe," she said to Liekou.

Cuifen smiled in relief, and the flowering smell increased around her. Bingmei slunk into the shadows and started up the hillside, moving from tree to tree. The slope of the hill matched the incline of the stairs, but the trees provided more cover.

The short rest had reinvigorated her, and she climbed at a quicker pace. The night dwindled, the sky overhead illuminated by the strange swirling lights. She'd have only a moment to cross the Death Wall. From the vision, she knew there were beasts on the other side, strange creatures that might attack.

The scent of fish wafted over to her, and she realized Quion had been keeping pace with her on the opposite side of the stairs.

"What are you doing?" she whispered to him, pleased despite herself. He was a clever one, that fisherman's son.

"Keeping up with you," he whispered back.

"Quion," she breathed in exasperation.

"Check your pocket," he said.

Her hand went to it instantly, but she felt only the edge of her leg. The meiwood cricket was gone. Worry bloomed in her stomach.

"Quion!" she accused.

"You promised you wouldn't leave me behind," he said. "I'm holding you to it. Let's keep going. We're almost there. I can see the base of the wall through the trees ahead."

And before she could argue or thank him for his loyalty, he started up the hill again.

CHAPTER THIRTY-SIX

The Wall

As another group of warriors from the Death Wall thundered down the stairs, Bingmei pressed her back against a pine tree, hoping it was wide enough to conceal her. The sky was beginning to brighten as the short summer darkness faded away. Even though she was exhausted from the journey, she could not afford to let her guard down for a moment. She caught a glimpse of Quion across the stairs from her. His elbow stuck out prominently. If she could see it, it meant that their enemies could as well. But there was no way to warn him.

One by one the soldiers charged down, oblivious to their quarry. She could hear shouts and the noise of fighting coming from the lower slopes. Had Cuifen and Liekou been discovered? She hoped not. But what was hope anyway? The beings hunting them defied their understanding. A dragon could be killed with meiwood weapons. But its blood and spit were acidic, and it was capable of breathing darkness. The sky now swarmed with them.

At last the crew was gone, although she heard them thudding down the stairs. She licked her dry lips, knowing that if they didn't cross the

Death Wall while it was still night, they were much more likely to be captured.

She stepped away from the tree and clambered back up the edge of the stairs. She gestured for Quion to come out just as the smell of trouble wafted down to her. One more man charged down, his steps disguised by the commotion of his fellows. He came into view a moment later, hurrying to catch up to the others, and then stopped when he saw her standing in the way.

He turned and started to run back up, shouting for help in a language she didn't understand, but the panicked tone was unmistakable. The meiwood cricket was not in Bingmei's possession, so she raced after him, bounding up the stairs two at a time. Quion charged out from behind the tree and started up the hillside. The guard running from her made it to the next landing and turned up the other slope. His fear of her drove him faster than Bingmei's weary legs could carry her. Her chest burned. He glanced back down at her, babbling in fear, continuing to cry out.

She smelled Quion's fishy smell and realized that he was ahead of her. By running directly up the hillside, he'd managed to reach the stairs at a higher point. She continued to sprint up the steps, trying to get close enough to the man to use her staff. Quion pulled himself up onto the stairs, and the fellow was now trapped between them.

In the dim light, she saw the glint of metal in the soldier's hand as he drew a blade.

She tried to call out in warning, but she was too winded to make a sound. Quion tackled the warrior and they both tumbled down the stairs. They landed, unmoving, in a heap in front of her. Quickly, she grabbed Quion and pulled him off the other man.

Her friend looked dizzied by the tumble and staggered backward. He clutched his side, wincing in pain. Bingmei forced his hand away, afraid to find the hilt of the short blade there, but the fellow still gripped it as he lay groaning on the stone stairs.

"Are you hurt?" she managed to gasp.

Quion shook his head, rising and backing away. The soldier lifted his head, saw the two of them looming over him, and began to whimper in fear.

Bingmei gave his skull a thump with the rune staff, and he slumped into unconsciousness.

"Should we . . . drag the body?" Quion asked, panting.

"Leave it," she said. "Look! The base of the wall is just up ahead. Give me the cricket, Quion."

He shook his head no. "We go together, Bingmei. I'll jump up first, make sure it's safe, and then toss it down to you."

"I could take it from you," she said, stepping forward threateningly.

He didn't back down. "You could. But a friend wouldn't."

She felt like hitting him on the head with the staff, but he was right. She would never harm him deliberately. "If you're going to be stubborn about it . . ."

He nodded. "I am. Come on."

Leaving the soldier where he lay, they hurried up the remainder of the stairs until they reached the edge of the woods where they had been cleared away from the wall. A trail wide enough for wagons had been laid into the ground at the base of the Death Wall. Directly in front of them was an iron door with knobbed rivets in rows across it, nine across, nine tall, like the ones in Fusang. It was a narrow door, and she imagined it opened to stairs leading to the top of the wall.

Soldiers roamed there, holding torches. Their voices echoed down, although they spoke a foreign language. If only Marenqo were still with them. When she thought about her friend, who'd likely been captured or killed, sadness stabbed her heart. She and Quion hunched down in the trees off the side of the path so they'd remain hidden from view.

"Too many guards," Quion said. "Let's go farther down the wall."

She nodded in agreement, and they walked, shadow to shadow, along the edge of the woods, away from the stairs, heading westward.

The eerie lights in the sky were directly overhead now, and she could see the smoke shapes of dragons dancing within them. Echion knew she was here. He'd marshaled his forces to stop her. But he still couldn't see her.

Farther along the trail, they approached one of the square towers that rose higher than the wall itself. She doubted the meiwood cricket could get her to the top of it, but the wall itself seemed within the cricket's reach. It was about two to three times the height of a man and made from interlocking stones. Guards still patrolled it—she saw the moving lights from their torches—but there were fewer in this section than near the iron door.

Looking over her shoulder, she stared at the brightening horizon. People were still abed, but not those guarding the Death Wall.

They waited for a while, watching the guards to look for patterns. Then she heard noises coming from the woods behind her. Sticks snapped and broke. A few guttural voices sounded.

Quion pulled at her arm, nodding for her to keep moving.

They left their hiding place to slink into the shadows closer to the wall. Every step was dogged by enemies. In the growing light, she saw Quion's pallor. He kept looking back, trying to see their enemy. She hadn't smelled them yet.

After traveling a short distance, they approached another square tower. There were fewer torches on it, but she could clearly see the men guarding it. The sun was rising too fast.

"We're out of time. We have to cross now," Bingmei said.

"All right," he answered nervously. "I'll go first. Stand by the side of the wall, and I'll drop the cricket down to you."

"You don't even know how to use it," she challenged. "I'll go first and make sure there aren't any guards to stop us. Give it to me."

He shook his head no. "I don't trust you to drop it down."

"You said I was your friend?"

"You are. But friends know each other's weaknesses too. I chose to come here, Bingmei. And I will see it through. Where else can I go? What else can I do? This is my choice. If I die . . . then I die. But it's *my* decision, not yours." She smelled his determination again, that spicy salmon smell. "Ready?"

She nodded, knowing they didn't have time to argue. It *was* his choice. And she'd made her mind up too. She would do whatever it took to stop Echion and Xisi.

He turned and faced the wall, eyeing the battlement. The noises from the woods behind them grew louder.

"We'll have to chance it," Bingmei said. "Now."

Quion sucked in his breath and marched away from the woods. He adjusted the straps of his bulging pack, which bobbed noiselessly on his back. She felt a little tickle in her nose as he suddenly leaped to the top of the wall.

Bingmei watched him land, and then she raced forward. She watched through the embrasure as he reached his arm out and dropped the meiwood cricket. It landed amidst the dirt and some scrub growing at the base of the battlement. She rushed to it and crouched down, putting her hand on the stone of the Death Wall to steady herself as she picked it up.

As soon as her hand touched the wall, she died.

被埋葬的世界

It happened so fast, so suddenly, that she had no warning at all. Her soul slipped out of her body once again, as if she'd stumbled and tripped and left it behind. She watched as her body slumped to the ground, the meiwood cricket resting in the hollow of her hand.

Panic flooded her. No! This was not supposed to happen. She hadn't reached the shrine yet! A breeze tugged at her, making her float away from her body. Looking up, she saw Quion leaning over the edge of the wall, gazing down at her limp body in a panic. A soldier ran at him from across the slope of the wall, but his gaze was fixed on her.

No! she thought in horror and despair. She wanted to go back inside her body. In vain, she squirmed against the eddies of wind that buffeted her away. And then her senses began to open like peony petals. She lifted higher and higher, until she could see the broad expanse of the Death Wall beneath her. Could see Quion gripping the edge of the stone wall, his mouth widening in shock and despair as he stared down at her, calling to her. Another soldier had seen him, and now two of them were charging at him.

Bingmei floated over their heads, higher and higher, sucked up by the draft.

There you are!

The words boomed through her mind in Echion's angry voice. He was with the dragons in the sky, hunting for her. Her heart wilted with the realization that she was being brought to the Grave Kingdom, a domain that Echion controlled. Trumpeting noises came from the sky as the other dragons reacted to Echion's thoughts.

She gazed down at the wall, and then the blooming sensation in her mind swelled. A vision opened. She heard the rattle of wagon wheels, the groans of slaves heaving stones, the creak of ropes and pulleys, the crack of whips. Dust filled the sky as she watched the construction of the Death Wall. The square towers were there, but the stretches of wall between them were in various stages of completion. The mass of bodies working defied imagination. She'd never seen so many people, stretching as far as she could see in both directions.

In the sky overhead, she saw the shadow of a dragon, looming above them in the dusty haze. Some of the workers cowered in fear, only to receive the lash. The overseers had colored paint on the edges of their eyes, yellow and blue, red and green. And in the way of visions, she knew these were dragon-men, creatures who had transformed and assumed the likenesses of mortals. She watched one man die, collapsing from exhaustion and the inhumanity of the working conditions. As soon as he perished, he was picked up by other slaves and carried away. From her vantage point, she watched them drag the body unceremoniously toward a pit dug within the foundation of the wall. And there she saw other bodies.

The Death Wall was literally built on the bones of the dead slaves.

In the vision state, she felt the dragon's awareness of her, heard the hiss of recognition and anger. Smoke began to puff from the majestic wings as the dragon dived toward her spirit form. It shrieked in anger and fury, its cry splitting the air.

Bingmei was sucked back into her body again, the transition abrupt. Her eyes were hot and dry, and she blinked rapidly. Her fingers and toes tingled with the agony of bloodlessness, but she could not rest. She heard the dragon cry again—not in the vision, but overhead. Echion knew where she was, and he was coming.

Bingmei closed her hand around the meiwood cricket. Her ears felt like she'd been dunked underwater for too long. Strange echoing sounds made it impossible for her to parse what was going on. But she sensed the dragon coming for her, felt its malice and intention to devour her. If it did, would it learn the location of the phoenix shrine? Or did it already know?

Bingmei struggled to her feet, not daring to touch the wall again. Had her sudden death been caused by it or something else? She didn't know. But she wouldn't risk a second death so soon. Looking at the wall, she imagined she could still hear the groans of the slaves and even smell their misery. The extent of Echion's cruelty could be measured from one end of the wall to the other.

Her knees quavering, she grabbed the rune staff and looked skyward. She could no longer see Quion leaning over the wall. The soldiers must have reached him already. Despite the haze of fatigue, she had to press on.

Bingmei clenched her jaw and rubbed her thumb across the cricket.

CHAPTER THIRTY-SEVEN

Rage of Dragons

The magic swept Bingmei up to the crest of the Death Wall, where she landed in a horse stance astride two merlons. She found Quion squirming beneath a mass of guards, who'd pinned his arms and legs. She was proud—despite their superior numbers, they still struggled to hold him down.

To her left, the wall sloped upward with steps leading up to the next guard tower, where she saw shouting guards brandishing spears and bows. Soldiers ran feverishly down the steps, coming to assist Quion's attackers. The wall stretched on, and in the distance, she saw a huge bank of stairs leading to another guard tower. From where she crouched, she could see the trees on the opposite side of the wall, a choking mass of forest and vegetation raw and untamed by man. To her right, the wall stretched the other way, sloping slightly downward, and she saw yet more soldiers charging up toward them.

Bingmei leaped down from the twin merlons and landed near the men who'd tackled Quion. She slid her hands down the rune staff and cracked it hard against the back of the man on top. He arched and yowled in pain, and she grabbed him by the back of his armor and yanked him off.

The soldier beneath him grimaced in anger and hurtled at her, but Bingmei sidestepped, and he missed. She struck the back of his legs and sent him face-first into the stone pavers that spanned the top of the wall. It was wide enough for four men to walk side by side.

The dragon Echion swooped down at them from far above. She felt his malevolence, his lust for her blood, and knew her time to save Quion was perilously short. Another pulse down her back revealed that Xisi was coming as well. She glanced skyward and saw both dragons speeding toward her.

A soldier attempted to grapple her from behind. She brought her head back into his nose, spun free, and then did a double kick to his chest and face, sending his arms pinwheeling back as he fell, knocking down Quion, who had just freed himself. Both sprawled onto the stone floor. Still, attackers came at them from either side, and the sentries from the higher portion of the wall would reach them soon.

Bingmei slipped off her pack and flung it off the edge of the wall on the other side. No going back now.

"Get down the wall!" she yelled at Quion, reaching into her pocket again to hand him the cricket.

He struggled to disentangle himself from the injured guards, blood dribbling from his nose. A bruise was already forming around his eye.

"No," he said, shaking his head as he stepped toward her. "You go down."

"There isn't time to use the cricket twice," she argued. "Go!" Leaving him to be captured and devoured wasn't an option.

Quion, acting quickly, pulled his pack off and quickly dug his arm inside. He fished out a coil of rope and immediately began winding it around one of the merlons. In a trice, he fixed a knot, his hands dexterous and sure, and then pitched his pack over the wall into the mass of trees and wilderness below.

The approaching guards yelled as they came at her with spears. She wove to one side, ducked, and then used the rune staff to deflect a blow aimed at Quion's ribs. Battering the other shafts away, she reversed her grip on the staff and countered, striking one on the head, another in the pit of the stomach, and a third on the chest. A spear glanced her arm, slicing through the layers of her shirts, causing a searing pain.

Bingmei blocked another thrust and pressed forward, whipping the staff around in a long sweeping motion to knock as many skulls as she could. Some of the guards ducked, their martial training evident. She landed once, then flipped around the other way in a reverse tornado kick that caught a man just as he was rising. He smashed backward against the side of the wall, then plummeted over the edge, screaming.

When Bingmei started twirling the staff, the soldiers around her retreated a pace, looking for an opening to jab at her again. She smelled the other soldiers rushing up behind her. The eagerness of their desire to capture her was heightened by the lemony scent of greed. The reward for capturing the phoenix-chosen would no doubt be substantial. She backed up, still spinning the staff, and saw the taut rope jerk as Quion worked his way down the wall. His smell was gone, so she didn't know how far he'd made it. She had to keep fighting a little longer.

One of the men broke the stand-off and rushed at her, jabbing with his spear, his eyes wild with determination. Bingmei dodged the haphazard strikes before slapping the spear down with her staff and kicking him in the throat with the edge of her foot. He dropped his spear, clutching his neck, and turned and ran.

A shadow smothered the light coming from the Woliu, and she heard the flapping of the dragon's leathery wings. From the smell, she knew it to be Echion. If Bingmei jumped with the cricket, she'd be leaping right into its claws, so instead she dropped low and did a forward roll to reach the edge of the embrasure.

The dragon was nearly on top of her when Xisi exploded onto the scene from above. The white dragon struck the black behemoth with her claws, their wings beating madly against each other.

She's mine! Mine to devour!

Bingmei heard Xisi's thoughts ring in her mind like clarion bells. She looked up, seeing the tangle of scaly hides, the wicked teeth snapping and striking at each other.

Begone demoness! Echion roared at her in his mind.

She's mine—my prize! Mine!

The dragons hissed and roiled, lashing at each other, neither able to do the other harm. Bingmei glanced down at Quion's rope as it quivered with the weight of his body. She couldn't act until he was safe, yet she felt so vulnerable atop the wall. The soldiers who had charged them were gaping at the dragons locked in mortal combat, ignoring her.

You let her escape! Fool bride, you had your chance!

She is mine, I say. You have everything and leave me with nothing. I want this. I demand it!

The black smoke wafting from Echion thickened as he raged at her, his fire-coal eyes searing with animosity. *You have palaces, servants, wealth beyond counting!*

You have concubines, generals, and slaves to grovel before you! I want what is mine!

The dragons spun end over end, hovering above the wall as Echion kept trying to get past Xisi.

As she stared at them in fear and awe, an image surfaced in her mind—the carving of the twin dragons in Fusang. The marble slab had depicted them above mountains and sea, enveloped by clouds. Before, she had seen it as a symbol of Echion's power—the emperor and his queen, two dragons united in strength.

The truth struck her as she watched the dragons grapple with each other in the sky above her. The dragons were *fighting* each other in the marble effigy. They always fought, for none of their lusts could ever be sated, not for gold, not for conquest, not for flesh. Power bound them together, but they hated each other. There was no reason for that hatred, only madness. The dragons hissed and clawed at each other, the larger dragon held back by the smaller.

Then the rope went slack.

You are my curse! Begone, wraith wife!

You were nothing before me. I remember your past.

That last accusation caught Bingmei's attention, but not so much so that she would miss her opportunity. She scrambled over to the rope and examined the knot. It was one of Quion's easier knots, and she quickly loosened it. The slack rope slipped away. One less clue to help the others track them.

She heard grunting voices, then saw some of the guards creeping toward her, hunched low with their spears to avoid the battling dragons. Bingmei smelled their fear at the savage display.

She's getting away! Echion shrieked.

Xisi turned to see, revealing her long neck, the black dragon's jaws immediately clamped down on her flesh. The teeth didn't penetrate, but the attack had given him the leverage he needed to yank the smaller dragon out of his path. Xisi screamed in frustration, and clear liquid gushed from her mouth, smoking as if it were on fire. The soldiers crouching directly beneath the dragon fight were all splashed, and their cries of fear turned into wild yells of agony. Bingmei watched in horror as their skin turned gray.

A rivulet of smoking fluid rushed down toward Bingmei. She frantically backed away, reaching in her pocket for the cricket. It was gone.

Shock and disbelief flooded her. Had it fallen out? She looked behind her, trying to spot it amidst the confusion, but it was like looking for a grain of rice. Most of the sentries had turned and fled, but one brave man charged up the slope and jabbed his spear at her. It had a meiwood pole, covered with runes, and the head shimmered with heat as he lunged it at her. Bingmei dodged the blow and spun the staff around to beat him back, summoning the power of her own staff to defend herself.

She was going to lose. Without the cricket, she'd die if she leaped over the wall.

The runes of the staff all ignited at once. She hadn't summoned its power like this before. Some other influence had taken control of it. Terror rocked her senses as streams of green and gold light shot out of the ancient staff. And then it shattered in her hands. The explosion knocked her down as a thousand splinters blasted in all directions, digging into her skin, her hands, her arms, and her face, although she'd turned her head to the side on instinct.

Pain bloomed everywhere. She was on her back, smashed against the embrasure, stunned and shocked. The rune staff was no more. The man with the meiwood spear had been struck by the splinters too, his face a grimace of agony.

The anguish of losing Kunmia's weapon struck her like a hammer. The black dragon lunged for her, jaws open, and the smoky trail of colorless ichor from Xisi's maw reached for her body. She had no way to defeat them anymore—it was only a contest of which of them would get to her first.

Bingmei nearly gave in to death. Fighting was so hard, and she was so very tired, but one thought stopped her.

Death would not bring sleep.

It would only bring slavery.

She would fight until she took her last breath.

Then she saw a little flash of color and movement from the corner of her eye. A small finch with a green breast had landed by her hand, its tiny beak clenched around the meiwood cricket. She watched, stunned, as the wooden charm landed in her palm.

A little bird had saved her life.

Squeezing her hand around the charm, Bingmei gazed up at the vicious dragon, staring into the yellow reptilian eyes that hungered for her soul. She reached for the edge of the embrasure with her other bloodied hand, groaning as she pushed her way back up.

Everything seemed to slow around her, the moment permanently fixed in her mind. Echion's smoke. Xisi's poison. The moans of dying guards. The smell of violence and savagery that hung in the air. And yet she refused to die—she refused to fail.

Bingmei leaped from the wall just as Echion reached her. She plummeted down, seeing the thick trees rushing to meet her in a sharp embrace. The snap of teeth filled her ears as the dragon extended its neck to finish her off.

But she fell faster.

And as she fell, a thousand little birds exploded from the canopy of the trees below, rushing up at her. With high keening whistles, they hurtled up past Bingmei toward the dragons hungering for her blood. They came from everywhere at once. She felt the myriad wings flapping past her as she fell, heard the shrill shrieks of defiance coming from the tiny finches. Their colorful plumage streaked past her, wings flapping, blinding her to everything except their dazzling hues.

The trees rushed toward her. She only had a moment to open her fist and rub the cricket with her thumb.

One moment to trigger the magic that would save her from the fall.

A moment was all she needed. Her thumb grazed the cricket. Her legs tingled with magic as she went crashing into the trees on the other side of the Death Wall.

被埋葬的世界

All of Life is a dream walking. All of Death is a going home.

—Dawanjir proverb

EPILOGUE

The Blind King

Rowen could scarcely believe his idea had worked. They'd hidden beneath the dragon's oily corpse, using one of its wings as shelter. He'd wondered how Bingmei would have felt, smothered by that terrible reptilian stench. He couldn't see, and the pain in his eyes ached, but he had a thirst for survival and listened as the hunting party reached the dragon, searched around it, and then—one by one—left.

The lack of sight heightened his sense of hearing, and he listened until he could no longer discern the snapping of twigs, the slurping of mud on boots, or the distant shout of voices.

"They're gone," Jidi Majia whispered.

"I think you're right," Rowen said.

"And how are we going to escape this wilderness if we cannot see?" Eomen asked, despair thickening her voice.

"One step at a time," Rowen said. "At least we're not dead. Not yet." He pushed against the leathery wing, amazed by how heavy it was. Lifting it brought sounds that had been muffled before, like the hum of insects. He heard a trilling song from a bird nearby, which seemed to be shouting at the hunters to come back and find them.

"Noisy thing," he muttered to himself. "Come on." He groped for his sister in his blindness, found her arm, and helped pull her to her feet.

Jidi Majia rose as well, wrenching himself out from under the dragon's corpse. There hadn't been enough room under the wing for all three of them, so he'd dug his way through the mud at the creek bed to make room.

Once they were all free, Eomen asked, "Where do we go?"

"Let's follow the creek," Rowen suggested. "Hold my hand. I'll go first. If you hear anyone coming, squeeze my hand. Jidi Majia, take her other hand."

"I will, my king," said Jidi Majia.

The title felt like an insult at that moment. But his brother and father were dead. Grief whispered in his ears, but he banished the thoughts. He needed to focus on surviving. He'd mourn his losses later.

Holding his sister's hand, he began to follow the creek. There wasn't much water in the middle of the season, and he felt mostly wet pebbles and mud squishing beneath his boots. He groped in front of him with his free arm to clear away branches or brush that blocked the way. The absence of sight caused fear to wriggle in his stomach. They were in a vast wilderness near the Death Wall. Survival would be nearly impossible.

He refused to give in to the growing despair. For Bingmei, for Eomen, and for all his people, he needed to keep going.

"I hear something," Jidi Majia whispered.

They halted, Rowen's legs trembling. He listened for the telltale sound of cracking limbs or rustling leaves.

He waited and, hearing nothing, asked, "What did you hear?"

"It's a bird," said Jidi Majia. "A siskin. It's been following us."

"What?" Eomen asked. "Like the kind Mother kept in cages?"

"The very same," Jidi Majia said. "This one is wild. I heard it singing when we came out from beneath the dragon. I recognize the sound. It's been following us, chirping loudly."

Rowen took a moment to listen to it. Its birdsong did bring back memories of his mother and her bird cages. She'd kept them in the hanging trees, the palace gardens at Sajinau.

As the memory flowed over him like a river, it struck him that the bird wasn't calling for the hunters to find them. It was trying to get their attention. He didn't know how he knew, but the thought struck him with such certainty, he didn't question it.

"Let's rest a moment," Rowen suggested. Squatting down in the muck, he bowed his head and listened to the trilling of the bird.

The siskin came closer until it was in the trees overhead.

"It's right over us," Eomen said. He could hear the smile in her voice.

Rowen's mind cleared of thought as he listened to the bird. He felt a breeze tickle the back of his neck. He felt the water pass over the edges of his boots. His hands rested in the mud as well.

Draw in the mud.

The strange thought reminded him of being a child again, of playing along the riverbank with his older brother. Sometimes they'd drawn shapes in sand or mud with sticks. That carefree feeling of childhood was a precious thing. He and his brother had been close back then. Juexin had always tried to teach him, to encourage him to follow their father's example. Back then, Rowen had been more interested in copying his brother's example.

Draw in the mud.

The thought came again, unbidden. Was the bird communicating with him? It was a foolish fancy, yet the trilling grew louder, more insistent.

Draw in the mud.

Why? He didn't understand. But the third time the thought came to him, he pressed his finger into the mud and drew a line. It was soft and wet. Power reverberated through him as he drew the line. His finger, of its own accord, began to move. Or maybe some unseen force directed his hand. It was a sigil. A word.

Touch their eyes.

The whisper was more pronounced now. Power flared down his arm.

"Sister," he whispered, his heart quailing.

"Yes?"

With one hand, he gripped her shoulder gently. He felt along her neck and then her cheek. Once he was cupping her cheek with his hand, he lifted a muddy finger.

"Trust me," he said.

She held still, though a shudder rippled through her.

He dabbed the mud against her closed eyes, one by one. Once he was done, he dipped his hand in the mud again, the place where he'd drawn the symbol.

"Jidi Majia, come nearer."

"What is it, young master?" asked his friend, his mentor. Rowen heard him shift and move closer. He reached out and felt Jidi Majia's knee. Then he groped to find his shoulder, his face.

"Hold still," Rowen said. He smeared the mud against Jidi Majia's eyes as well.

As he lowered his hand, he heard the whisper in his mind again.

Have them wash.

He heard the bird trill excitedly. The message was clear, although the source was still a mystery.

"Use the water. Wash your eyes," he told them.

He waited in anticipation, listening as they obeyed his words. He heard their hands splash in the trickling water. He felt something jolt inside his heart, felt the power burst forth from within him.

Then his sister gasped.

"I can see again," she said, her voice throbbing with joy.

A few moments later, Jidi Majia's voice joined hers. "So can I. The mud . . . it cured me!"

It wasn't the mud. It was the word that Rowen had drawn in the mud. He lowered his hand, trying to find the spot where he'd drawn the word, but the flowing water had already eroded it. He reached down and drew a line in the mud, anxious to be rid of the blindness too.

Nothing happened. Worry clogged his throat.

You cannot heal yourself. Only others.

The thought struck him like a slap to the face. The bird began to chirp again, this time in agitation.

"My lord, you healed us!" Jidi Majia said, grasping Rowen's muddy hand with his clean one.

"Rowen?" His sister sounded concerned.

The bird continued to whistle in warning. Then he heard boots sloshing in the creek.

"They're coming," Rowen said.

"What happened?" Jidi Majia said. "You still cannot see?"

"I'm still blind," Rowen said, feeling the bitterness eat away at his heart. Their trail in the mud was being followed. He knew what he had to do. "Go. Both of you."

"We cannot abandon you," Jidi Majia said.

"You must," he answered, reaching out and gripping the older man's arm. "You have to protect Eomen. Get her far away from Echion. What he threatened to do to her . . . you have to save her. I order it, Jidi Majia. As your king."

Eomen flung her arms around Rowen's neck, hugging him.

"We'll go together," she said, squeezing. "We can see now. We'll guide you."

The bird's agitation was frantic.

"We won't. I cannot run. You have to go. Jidi, take her away. Now!"

"Brother!" Eomen said. But Rowen heard Jidi Majia rise to do his bidding. His sister kissed his cheek, a quick press of the lips, and the two of them began to flee. Rowen, kneeling, rose to his haunches and reached for his twin blades. He gripped the hilts, feeling comforted that his sister and friend had escaped.

Why couldn't he heal himself? He didn't understand how the magic of the immortals worked. Nor could he remember the intricacies of the symbol he'd drawn. It had all happened by instinct.

Like what had happened to Bingmei.

He heard a voice shout out a warning. Then, moments later, he sensed he wasn't alone and slowly rose to his feet, drawing both blades. He noticed that the sound of the bird was gone. Had it fallen silent or merely flown away from the commotion of the hunters? Fear trickled from his heart down to his knees. There were so many of them.

He heard a voice snarl in challenge. Without understanding the language, he couldn't respond.

Someone gave him an order. He stared fixedly at the ground, listening to the sounds around him. Another man shouted, and then two of them rushed him at once.

Rowen stabbed the first with his sword and tried to strike the other and missed wildly. He heard a grunt of pain, then felt a body slam into him. He sprawled backward but managed to cut the man on top of him. A hiss of pain, then a release of pressure. Rowen struggled to rise, hearing the noises assaulting him from all sides. Something blunt struck his stomach hard, making him bend at the middle. He lashed out with his weapon, but the warrior overpowered him, wrenching the blades from his hands.

As he knelt in the mud again, his arms were yanked behind his back and secured with ropes. His weapons were either confiscated or left behind. He struggled against his captors until one of them boxed him on the side of the head, stunning him. Soon after, he was hauled to his feet, and they started marching him up the edge of the gully and into the forest. The cracking of wood and rustling of leaves filled his senses.

He'd hoped they would kill him. But no, they were taking him somewhere. The Death Wall? It was probable. Anguish ripped at his feelings. He was afraid and alone, except he heard the trill of the siskin in a nearby tree. Was it following them?

A nightmare he hadn't suffered in years came back to him. As a child, he'd had recurring dreams in which he was a blind boy living at his father's palace. He'd memorized things by touch, just in case the dreams should come true. As a youth, he'd felt it was preferable to die rather than endure losing his sight.

He'd last dreamed of blindness soon before he left the palace of Sajinau with Damanhur. The dream had been impossibly vivid. In it, he was blind again, living in a palace. A woman came to see him, and although he feared she would be repulsed by his blindness, she kissed him. Passionately. He kissed her back, but while he could smell and taste her and feel her hair tickle his check, he could not see her. She didn't speak a word, but she acted as if they were familiar, as if they knew each other. In his dream, she was his wife, although he couldn't, in the fog of it, remember her name.

He'd awakened from the dream gasping, his vision restored. Many times he'd thought about that dream, marveling at how real it had felt. Wondering who the woman had been.

When he'd first met Bingmei, she'd seemed vaguely familiar to him. Her scent had evoked memories of that dream. It had been the first sign of a connection between them. The next indication had been the Phoenix Blade. They had been drawn to it from the first, and he'd recognized the sword from one of his dreams. He hadn't seen it in the dream, of course, but he'd traced the carving of the phoenix until he knew the feel of it by heart.

He had finally realized that the vision was one of the future. That just as two dragons were needed for each to achieve their fullest power, so there were two phoenixes. She had chosen him. She *would* choose him. But how could he tell her that? He couldn't. If he did, he wasn't sure it would happen. And yet, he knew it was important that it should come to pass. She needed to choose him before she died.

It struck him that he'd been blind in his dream. Did this mean he'd always be blind? His heart panged with loss, not just of his sight, but of Bingmei. She had continued to the Death Wall to fulfill her destiny. To die. He could sense her still, to the north. He always knew where to find her.

And then he realized in dread that Echion would want him alive for that reason.

Because he was the only person who could still find her.

CHARACTERS

Batong—八通—member of Damanhur's ensign

Bingmei—冰玫—orphaned main character, has winter sickness

Budai—布达—ruler of Wangfujing

Cuifen—粹芬—princess of Sihui

Damanhur—达曼 回—leader of Gorilla Ensign from Sajinau

Echion—化身—the Dragon of Night, past emperor of the known world

Eomen—幽梦—King Shulian's daughter

Faguan—法官—concubine of Echion

Fuchou—复仇—ruler of Renxing

Fupenzi—覆盆子—Bingmei's grandmother

Guanjia—管家—Budai's steward

Guoduan—果断—captain of the merchant ship the *Raven*

Heise—黑色—captain from Tianrui, leader of mercenaries

Huqu—湖区—member of Damanhur's ensign

Jiao—狡—Bingmei's grandfather

Jiaohua—狡猾—master of Shulian's police force, the Jingcha

Jidi Majia—吉狄马加—Shulian's advisor, also has the winter sickness

Jiukeshu—九棵树—Qiangdao leader

Juexin—决心—crown prince of Sajinau, Rowen's brother

Kexin—可欣—chancellor of King Zhumu of Sihui

Keyi—可以—greedy fisherman

Kunmia Suun—群迷阿苏—owner of an ensign, Bingmei's master

Liekou—埒口—part of Echion's ensign, practitioner of dianxue

Lieren—猎人—part of Kunmia's ensign, the hunter

Li Jinxi—李进喜—Xisi's eunuch lover from the ancient kingdom

Mao Zhang—毛长—businessman in Wangfujing, owner of fishing boats

Marenqo—马任可—translator for Kunmia

Mieshi—蔑视—member of Kunmia's ensign, sharp-tongued

Mingzhi—明智—king of Tuqiao

Muxidi—木樨地—Qiangdao leader who murdered Bingmei's family

Pangxie—螃蟹—an officer in General Tzu's army

Qianxu—谦虚—ruler of Yiwu

Quion—球尼—fisherman's son who joins Kunmia's ensign

Rowen—如闻—prince of Sajinau, younger brother of Juexin

Shulian—熟练—king of Sajinau

Tzu—子—general of all of Sajinau's military

Xisi—西四—Echion's queen, coruler of the Grave Kingdom

Yanli—眼力—part of Echion's ensign, the archer

Zhongshi—重视—Kunmia's nephew, guards her quonsuun during absences

Zhumu—注目—ruler of Sihui

Zhuyi—注意—member of Kunmia's ensign, keen listener

Zizhu—自主—guardian of Bingmei's grandfather's quonsuun

AUTHOR'S NOTE

In this book, I got to begin exploring a world that I've not ventured into before—what happens in the afterlife set in a fantasy novel? One of my favorite scenes in the *Lord of the Rings* is when Gandalf tries to describe to Pippin what lies beyond, that there isn't anything to fear. My daughter loves the Skinjacker Trilogy by Neal Shusterman, which also has an inventive take on existence after death.

I've read many books about near-death experiences and wanted the feelings of these accounts to resonate with readers as well. But interestingly, it was the research of Dr. Christopher Kerr, which he shared in his TED talk, that really gave me many of the ideas here, including the predeath dreams that Bingmei begins to experience. It's a fascinating talk and led to some other examples of people who met ancestors or had dreams of meeting them in the afterlife.

Another major influence has been the TV show *Relative Race*, which my family has been enjoying this year. The series is about four teams who have missing links from their family history, and while it is a competition, they also spend ten days meeting family members and learning about ancestors they didn't know about. The depth of emotion in these true stories is absolutely riveting. And I can only imagine how

Bingmei would react to experiencing the feelings from these contestants as they finally embrace family they've never known.

I have had so much fun writing this story, and I hope you look forward to the final chapter, where answers that have been hidden and lost for thousands of years will finally be revealed. It is a journey I'll enjoy taking with you.

ACKNOWLEDGMENTS

Every book is a team effort. And no matter how well I think I've done crafting an original and unique story, it takes the perspectives of many individuals to see it through to completion. What you have read is the culmination of many points of view, and the final product has experienced a transformation from my imagination to a polished product.

Thanks to Jason Kirk, my editor at 47North, and Angela Polidoro for their enthusiasm in this series as well as their thoughtful and intelligent suggestions. We always try to raise the bar to the next level and make each book the best it can possibly be.

I'm also so indebted to my first readers: my wife, Gina, and my sister Emily. It was Emily's suggestion to end the book where it ended up being. Great call, Sis! To Dan and Wanda, who also help with the editing of my books and keeping them so professional and as free from error as humanly possible. To my street team as always: Shannon, Robin, Sandi, Travis, and Sunil—thank you! You are all critically important to the team.

And I'd also like to take a moment and thank you, my readers. You have enabled this journey as well, and your encouragement, positive comments, and sharing my books with others has truly made all the difference. Wish I could know each of you by name and say thank you.

ABOUT THE AUTHOR

Photo © 2016 Mica Sloan

Jeff Wheeler is the *Wall Street Journal* bestselling author of *The Killing Fog* in the Grave Kingdom series; the Harbinger and Kingfountain series; and the Muirwood, Mirrowen, and Landmoor novels. He left his career at Intel in 2014 to write full-time. Jeff is a husband, father of five, and devout member of his church. He lives in the Rocky Mountains and is the founder of *Deep Magic: The E-Zine of Clean Fantasy and Science Fiction*. Find out more about Deep Magic at www.deepmagic.co, and visit Jeff's many worlds at www.jeff-wheeler.com.